HIS BROTHER'S WIFE

"How did I get in this bed?" she asked.

"You were asleep when I came home. I put you here."

Her dress was tangled high around her legs, and her bare thigh rested intimately against his. She looked at him, and he at her. There was hunger between them, a deep atavistic hunger that went beyond mere passion, beyond reason, beyond propriety.

Tears eased down her cheeks.

"Where's Malone?"

"In Rumangabo reporting the deaths of the gorillas. He left early so he could get there before dark. He asked me to take care of you." Brett shuddered with the tightness of his control. "He'll be back in a few days."

She was free, free from Malone's self-pity, his drinking, his nightly groping.

Free to be with Brett.

"I see." Every nerve ending in her body was tingling, responsive to the man whose body was pressed next to hers. In the bed. In the dark. No one would ever know. . . .

Bantam Books by Peggy Webb:

FROM A DISTANCE
WHERE DOLPHINS GO
WITCH DANCE

From A Distance

Peggy Webb

BANTAM BOOKS
NEW YORK TORONTO LONDON
SYDNEY AUCKLAND

FROM A DISTANCE

A Bantam Fanfare Book / October 1995

ISBN 0-553-56974-0

Published simultaneously in the United States and Canada

Bantam Books are published by Bantam Books, a division of Bantam Doubleday Dell Publishing Group, Inc. Its trademark, consisting of the words "Bantam Books" and the portrayal of a rooster, is Registered in U.S. Patent and Trademark Office and in other countries. Marca Regis-trada. Bantam Books, 1540 Broadway, New York, New York 10036.

PRINTED IN THE UNITED STATES OF AMERICA

OPM   0 9 8 7 6 5 4 3 2 1

For Tom, who gives so freely all the things that matter.

"Earth is crammed with Heaven."

—E. B. Browning.

Acknowledgments

Each time I write a novel, I realize how blessed I am to have so many smart friends. Once again I want to thank my cousin and good friend, Ruth Ann Wilson, R.N., Tupelo, Mississippi, for providing medical information, and my wonderful daughter and mother of my first grandchild, Misty Webb Griffith, Concord, New Hampshire, for advising on legal matters. Also I wish to thank Patricia A. Witt, certified gemologist, A.G.S., Tupelo, for information regarding pearls, and Phyllis Harper, fellow writer and longtime friend, for the anecdote about diamonds as big as golf balls. And for Tom Peacock, mainly of New Hampshire and Maine but sometimes of Mars, a special thanks for sharing delightfully offbeat ideas about Cee Cee as well as for being an enthusiastic supporter and a compassionate and a very dear dear friend.

Author's Note
to the Reader

When I first started writing this novel, Rwanda in the Virungas was a beautiful country at peace. About midway through the book, hell and all its demons descended on Central Africa. Each day as I sat at my computer describing the primeval beauty of the rain forest, I wept for a people without hope and a place that was no more. It is my prayer that by the time you read this, the Virungas in Central Africa will once again be the Virungas in *From a Distance*.

Prologue

NAIROBI, 1995

*H*E REMEMBERED THE SMELL OF THE flame flower wet with dew and the song of birds awakening before the first pink light spread across the east beyond the Virungas. The glowing malevolent eye of the volcanic mountains was with him, and the wispy shade of acacias on smooth stone. Water cascaded through gorges of mythological proportion, its thunder sweeping through his mind and leaving him naked and filled with yearnings that had no name.

The memories were more real to Brett than was his brother, who lay dying. Propped in the doorway of the narrow hospital room in Nairobi, he watched the form on the stark-white bed. Death was close. He could feel it in the stillness that hovered in the room and see it in the faces of his mother and his sister-in-law.

Ruth bent over her husband, one hand holding his in a white-fingered grip and the other tenderly smoothing his blood-matted hair back from his forehead.

"Hang on, Malone," she whispered. "You're going to make it."

"Ruth . . ." The voice coming from the battered lips was a mere croak; the face that the knife had laid open, a grotesque mask. "Don't leave me . . . Ruth."

"Never, my darling. Never!"

The effort of speaking was too much, and Malone closed his eyes. Ruth pressed her chest across his and held herself rigid, as if she could keep him earthbound with the force of her will.

Brett stood apart, his hands balled so tightly, the blunt fingernails cut into his palms. A faint light shaded the windowpane with pink and gold and fell across the white sheets in a muted rainbow. Morning had no business shining on death.

Brett strode to the window to close the shade.

"No. I want the light." Malone opened his eyes and looked at his brother. "Brett . . ."

"Go to him," Eleanor pleaded. Pain and tears had ravaged his mother's face. She left her vigil by the side of the bed and clutched Brett's arm. "For God's sake, Brett, go to your brother."

"I'll race you, Brett. Last one in is a rotten egg."

"If you'll just let me have the car, Brett, I promise I'll pull your kitchen duty for a month."

"Please, Brett . . . No one else can do this but you."

Heavy with memories, Brett approached his brother's bed. Ruth's perfume, sweeter than the ginger that sprang up waxy and white from the jungle floor, stole over him like a forbidden embrace.

"I'm . . . dying."

Brett didn't contradict his brother, didn't dare to add one last lie to the many that separated them.

"Promise . . ." Malone's breath came in labored

spurts now. With a mighty effort he fixed his brother with a fierce blue stare. "Take care of Ruth."

Ruth. The woman Brett hated. The woman he loved.

"I promise."

It was a promise that would plunge him into the very bowels of hell.

Book One

Book One

1.

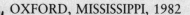

OXFORD, MISSISSIPPI, 1982

MARGARET ANNE BELLAFONTAINE'S carefully created fantasy world was about to come to an end. She sensed it in the stiff posture of the man sitting in the chair, in the narrow line of his lips, and the lowering of his thick black eyebrows.

"Your expenses have run unusually high this month, Margaret Anne."

"You've never complained before, Max."

"I've been too lenient with you."

She poured tea into two china cups in a manner worthy of a highborn Southern lady. Her hand was steady as she passed a cup to him. He accepted with a nod of his head and a slight smile.

Max had always admired her manners.

Maybe things weren't as bad as she thought. She'd managed Max all these years. If she played her cards right, perhaps she could manage him one more time.

"Your generosity has always been a part of your charm," she said.

It was not true, of course. Maxwell Jones was generous only with his dowdy, petulant wife and with the minions who peopled his entertainment empire. They thought of him as some sort of a god.

With his mistress he was a tyrant, demanding full measure for his money.

Margaret Anne thought of him as her security, and she did everything in her power to please him, though it was not easy.

She had dressed painstakingly for his visit, for the one thing he did care about was appearances. She knew she looked perfect, her auburn hair waved loosely around her face, her makeup subtle, her dress demure.

Max liked her that way, a lady in the parlor and a wildcat in the bedroom.

"You always did lie well, Margaret Anne."

"I've had years of practice."

Max set his teacup on the Victorian marble-topped table and got up to stand beside the window.

"How's Ruth?"

"Like any thirteen-year-old. Gawky, stubborn, and headstrong."

"She's growing up."

"Yes."

"She'll be needing many things."

"I'm willing to sacrifice."

"Are you?"

There was more than mere curiosity in his voice: There was something else, a cold calculating tone that made the hairs on the back of Margaret Anne's neck stand on end.

"Of course," she said. "A mother will do anything for her daughter."

"Will a daughter do anything for her mother?"

Too anxious to remain seated, Margaret Anne stood up, smoothed her silk dress over her slim hips, and walked to the piano. She played well. It was one of the many skills she considered necessary for her survival.

She sat on the polished bench and ran her hands lightly over the keys.

"Mozart." Max strode toward the piano and caught her shoulders. "Music won't soothe this savage beast today."

Margaret Anne reached for the top button of her dress. Using the slow, languorous movements he loved so well, she unfastened her dress and let it slide from her shoulders.

"We'll have to make it quick," she said. "Ruth will be home from school soon."

Max never took his eyes off her as he lit his pipe. Margaret Anne stood still for his inspection. She knew she looked good. At forty-four she was almost as firm as a twenty-five-year-old.

He blew a smoke ring in the air, then watched her through the blue haze. Margaret Anne's nerve endings began to scream. They had ten minutes, fifteen at most before Ruth would be home.

What was Max waiting for? She'd have made the first move herself if she hadn't known it would make him angry.

"You never answered my question, Margaret Anne."

"Which question?"

"Will a daughter do anything for her mother?"

Real alarm skittered through her. Forcing herself to smile, she unhooked her bra.

"This is a silly time for twenty questions."

"I'll answer for you." Max stooped to pick up her dress. As he slid it back onto her shoulders, he gave her body the impersonal perusal a butcher might give a side of beef. "I think she will. I think Ruth will do anything you tell her to do."

Margaret Anne clutched the dress to her breasts, and Max walked around behind her and buttoned it. She felt cold all over, but she wouldn't dare show any weakness by shivering.

The smell of Max's pipe tobacco almost overwhelmed her. When he had finished with her dress, Max sat down once more.

"How long have I supported you, Margaret Anne?"

"Nearly eleven years."

"And how long do you expect me to?"

"As long as I can please you . . . and, Max, I plan to please you for the rest of your life."

"That's good to hear. Do you have any idea what it will take to please me today?"

"Name it, Max."

"Your daughter."

Anger flushed her cheeks and burned her body. She wanted to claw the smug, self-satisfied smile off his face. But she understood the art of deceit.

"Max, I'll do anything you ask, sex any way you want it, but my daughter's not for sale."

"Come, Margaret Anne. You do me an injustice. Did I say anything about buying your daughter? This is the twentieth century."

"I'm sorry, Max. I misunderstood."

"Of course you did, my dear." He tamped out his pipe in the ashtray. "I don't plan to buy Ruth, I plan to take her on a little trip."

"She doesn't like to travel."

"Margaret Anne . . . you still don't understand, do you?"

"Perhaps not."

"This is not a request; it's a condition. I'll support you in the lifestyle to which you've become accustomed as well as ensure Ruth's college education in exchange for a two-week holiday with your daughter."

Margaret Anne had never openly defied Maxwell Jones. She picked up her china cup, not because she wanted to drink the cold tea, but because she wanted something to hold on to so he wouldn't see how her hands shook.

"No deal, Max."

"Pardon me?"

It pleased her that she had the power to shock him. She smiled at him over her teacup.

"I said no. I won't let my daughter participate in your 'holiday.' "

The look of disbelief faded from his face, and he reached for his own teacup. They faced each other across the room like two aging gladiators.

"Ruth will be fourteen soon," he said.

Margaret Anne knew perfectly well how old her own daughter was. Max was baiting her, but she refused to bite. Instead, she smoothed down her skirt and sipped her tea—proof positive that in all the ways that counted, she was a *real* Southern lady.

Max waited for her response, his eyes boring into her. She refused to back down, refused to look away. She felt the sweat form between her thighs and trickle down her legs. Thank God it wasn't on her face. Sweating was not only unladylike, it was a sign of fear. She couldn't afford to show Max that she was afraid.

The silence was so thick, it had a smell—the smell of doubt and betrayal. Margaret Anne shut her mind to everything except winning this deadly mind game with Max.

"I'm willing to pay a fortune for what some randy young buck will soon take for free, and you're turning my offer down?"

"You heard me the first time, Max. The answer is no."

He was still for so long that for a moment she dared to hope that she had won. But then he smiled. Chills went down her spine.

"You're not young anymore, Margaret Anne."

She told herself the same thing every morning when she inspected herself in the mirror to see what damage one more day had wrought. Her hand tightened on her teacup.

"I had men before you, Max; I'll have men after you."

"What's the going price for faded whores?"

She felt the sweat on her face, but she refused to give him the satisfaction of seeing her wipe it off.

"How many more years do you think you'll have in your noble profession, Margaret Anne? Two? Three? You'll want a supply of pink lightbulbs. And, of course, you'll have to be careful not to fuck when the sun is shining. Hard to camouflage all those bags and sags in broad daylight."

"You bastard son of a bitch!"

"I thought *real* ladies never cussed. Isn't that what you are, Margaret Anne *Bellafontaine*? A genuine, highborn, blue-blooded, dyed-in-the-wool lady?"

Her hands shook so badly, she had to set down her cup

or risk spilling tea all over her dress. She hadn't meant to lose control. It could be a fatal mistake with Maxwell Jones.

Smiling that demon's smile, he set his teacup on the table.

"You could get lucky, a woman like you with a *wealthy* family. Maybe they'll take you in." She endured his cruel laughter with a straight face. "Or maybe you'll want to run to some of your high-society friends for a little loan to tide you over during the hard times. Rich folks are usually quite magnanimous. Of course, charity does wear thin after a year or two."

He knew her too well. One by one he was tearing down all possible avenues of escape—if there ever had been any in the first place.

Still, she clung to hope, however faint, that she could make him back down.

"Fuck you, Maxwell Jones."

The laughter ceased, and in its place was the flat, deadly calm of a cobra before it strikes. He set his teacup on the table beside his chair and started toward her. With slow deliberation he cupped her face, forcing her to look up at him.

"What do you suppose the job market is like for a woman with no education and no real job skills, Margaret Anne? You think you can learn to be a short-order cook at some greasy spoon? A checkout clerk at Wal-Mart?"

Inch by painful inch he forced her face upward. Any minute she expected to hear the bones in her neck crack. Out of the corner of her eye she could see her Waterford-crystal vase filled with roses, and the jade figurine on her mantelpiece. *Real* jade. Not cheap imitation.

Without Max's support she wouldn't be able to afford a roof over their heads, let alone crystal and jade. She remembered how it had been before Max. A dirty walk-up tenement, hamburger stretched out with flour and oatmeal . . . if she was lucky.

And their clothes. Without Max there would be no more browsing through high-class boutiques for the latest fashions. She and Ruth would be reduced to carport-sale junk and hand-me-downs from the town's high society.

Ruth might as well have the label "poor white trash" tatooed on her forehead.

Forget college. By the time Ruth reached college age, all her spirit and ambition would be gone, beaten down by poverty.

Max eased her neck up another fraction.

"Of course, it's doubtful anybody in the South will hire you after they learn the truth." His voice was silky, soft. "What will you tell your daughter when her friends shun her on the streets, Margaret Anne?"

Any minute her daughter would come through the door, her beautiful daughter with the high cheekbones and olive skin, her spirited daughter with the sparkling dark eyes and the long, free-wheeling stride.

With one word Max could ruin her, ruin them both.

Margaret Anne was a practical woman; she understood what it took to survive. She didn't waste time on regrets; she looked him straight in the eye.

"When shall I tell her you're leaving?"

2.

NEW ORLEANS

*T*HE HOUSE LOOKED LIKE A FAIRY-TALE castle. Maybe it would make up for all the things she was missing back home.

Though she loved Uncle Max practically as much as she would love a father, Ruth hadn't wanted to come. She'd wanted to stay home and hang out with Wanda Kellerman. Wanda's cat was going to have kittens, and she didn't want to miss it.

When she'd argued with her mother about it, Margaret Anne had gently chided her.

"After all he's done for you, Ruth?"

Her mother didn't have to tell her she was being selfish for her to know it. Uncle Max had been there for her when she'd sung in her first recital, when she'd had pneumonia, and even when she'd fallen off her bicycle and had fractured her wrist.

Not to mention that he had given her her one and only beloved dog, and then had flown all the way from Hollywood for the funeral in her backyard when it had died of cancer the previous year.

He'd even gone with her to a father-daughter camp for Brownie Scouts.

She never would forget it. She'd been seven years old and crying her eyes out because all her friends had daddies to go camping with them.

Her mother had said she'd go, and Ruth had wailed even louder.

"You don't have a daddy, and there's nothing I can do about it, Ruth. Now, dry your eyes like a good girl, and I'll help you pack. Wanda's daddy has already said he'd be happy to have two little daughters to watch out for."

"I want my own daddy."

Margaret Anne walked to the phone and dialed.

"Max, Ruth needs a temporary daddy for the Brownie Scout campout this weekend. Can you come?"

Just like that, she'd said it, and Uncle Max had flown out in his private plane.

Ruth studied the man sitting behind the wheel. Her mother had said he was lonely. She guessed he was, not having any children of his own. Maybe that's why he came to Mississippi so much.

She was being selfish as a pig not wanting to come, after all the nice things he'd done for her and her mother. Anyhow, it was only for two weeks. When she got back home, she would tell her mother how sorry she was she'd put up such a fuss. Especially since Margaret Anne didn't get to come.

Leave it to old Aunt Sukie May to get sick. She was always getting sick at the drop of a hat, running Ruth's mother ragged flying off to Michigan or Minnesota or wherever the nursing home was.

When you'd never been to a place, it was hard to remember. It was even harder to be generous-spirited to a person you'd never laid eyes on.

When her mother wasn't looking, Ruth sometimes said "shootfiredamnation" and once nearly broke her toe kicking a piece of furniture at the way Aunt Sukie May was always ruining their plans, but her mother never complained.

Cussing. Another reason Ruth guessed she was going to grow up to be some kind of selfish witch instead of a lady like her mother.

Sighing, she looked out the window at the passing scenery.

The car was as quiet as the school study hall when Mean Green Jeans was in charge. That's what they called Mr. Cogg, who was older than Abraham, meaner than Satan, and always wore jeans that had faded a putrid kind of green.

In the distance Ruth heard dogs barking. She immediately perked up.

"Do you have dogs here?"

Uncle Max smiled at her. He did that a lot. He was nice looking, too . . . for somebody fifty years old. Wanda's daddy wasn't nearly that old, forty-five Wanda said, and he had a bald head and a potbelly. Uncle Max was nice and trim like the tennis players she and Wanda admired on television.

"I have dogs and horses too."

"Do you think I might get to ride?" She was so excited, she nearly forgot her manners. "Please?"

"Ladies always say please and thank you, Ruth. It's a sign of good breeding."

Her mother was a stickler for manners and was always lecturing her about good breeding and showing respect for her elders and being a real lady. The lectures bored Ruth out of her skull. That was just one more difference between her and her mother. Her mother *thrived* on etiquette.

"I'm sure you'll get to ride." Uncle Max's smile got wider. "You'll have the run of the place, Ruth. You can do whatever you like."

"Thanks, Uncle Max."

"You're welcome, sweetheart." He patted her hand. "We're going to have a wonderful time together."

She grinned at Uncle Max, then stared back down the long driveway they'd traveled on. It looked like a ghost tunnel with giant oak trees spreading their branches overhead and Spanish moss hanging down like long, spooky arms. Instead of calling Uncle Max's place a castle, she might refer to it as the House of Horrors. "How I Survived the House of Horrors" or maybe "Nightmare in New Orleans" she'd entitle the essay she'd have to write in English class.

English teachers were so dumb. They made you write things like "What I Did on Spring Break." Why couldn't they think up something interesting, like "How I Learned to Ride Like a Rodeo Cowgirl"?

"Can I ride the horse now? Please?"

"Of course you can, sweetheart. As soon as I stow our bags."

She'd have thought Uncle Max would have servants to put away the bags in a house that big, but, then, she was always fantasizing. Real life was seldom like the movies, her mother told her.

"Come, Ruth. I'll show you to your room."

She followed him up a long flight of marble stairs to *her* room. It was enough to take her breath away. Everything was pure white—the wallpaper, the draperies, the silk curtains that hung around the bed, even the roses that filled the room.

"I had it done just for you, Ruth."

"You really had it done just for me?"

Wanda's daddy had *never* decorated a fancy room for her, even when she'd begged to have her brother's room after he went away to college. Her other brother got the room, while Wanda had to keep sharing with her pesky little sister.

"Yes. Do you like it?"

"It's the prettiest room I've ever seen."

"Good. Give your Uncle Max a little hug."

He leaned down and held on for so long, she got fidgety. Then she felt something soft and wet on her cheek. It was his lips.

When he finally let her go, she stepped back, still smiling in spite of the fact that her cheek felt gooey.

She wouldn't wash her face until he left the room, though. She would never do anything to hurt Uncle Max's feelings. Besides, she didn't want the spring vacation to get off to a bad start.

It wouldn't do to rush her.

Max didn't want an unwilling victim; he wanted a grateful partner.

And he knew just how to make Ruth grateful. She loved the outdoors and had a gift with animals and the natural grace of a born athlete. She also had a hunger for the kind of father-daughter camaraderie he could provide.

He taught her to ride and rope, just as he'd taught her everything else since she was two years old. His life's work was creating beautiful things, and his movies were a testament to his success. But Ruth was his greatest creation.

At thirteen she was astonishing; at eighteen she'd be lethal. She'd need to know how to defend herself—from everybody except him.

When he brought out the gun, she was skeptical.

"Are you sure it's all right? I mean . . . would Mother approve? She's such a lady."

He adored that quality in Ruth, her desire to please. It was going to make what he planned to do much easier. Margaret Anne had done a good job with her daughter. He'd have to remember to thank her properly. A square-cut emerald necklace should be just the right gift to show appreciation and to guarantee gratitude.

"I don't think your mother would mind. Many ladies are too delicate to handle a weapon, but some of the greatest ladies I know handle firearms as easily as they handle their teacups."

Ruth ran her hands lovingly along the mahogany stock. Max got hard just thinking of those hands on his body.

A sense of daring and danger sparkled in her dark eyes. Slowly she wet her lips with the tip of her tongue.

"Teach me, Uncle Max."

He placed the gun in her hand, then stood behind her to steady her aim. Her fresh young smell almost overwhelmed him.

"I'm going to teach you many things, Ruth."

3.

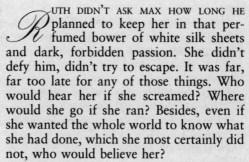

RUTH DIDN'T ASK MAX HOW LONG HE planned to keep her in that perfumed bower of white silk sheets and dark, forbidden passion. She didn't defy him, didn't try to escape. It was far, far too late for any of those things. Who would hear her if she screamed? Where would she go if she ran? Besides, even if she wanted the whole world to know what she had done, which she most certainly did not, who would believe her?

Ruth endured.

And when the two-week nightmare was finally over, she sat in the car beside him without saying a word, without even asking where he was taking her.

It didn't matter anymore.

"You're good, my darling. The best."

With one hand on the wheel, Max slipped his other hand under her dress and slid his fingers inside her cotton panties.

"Remember, my darling, I'm only doing what you wanted me to do," he said.

He'd told her repeatedly how she'd begged for it, and it must be true. She would carry it with her always, that dark, secret shame.

Turning her head, Ruth looked out the window and watched a blue heron swoop down over the bayou looking for fish, watched a flock of egrets settle in a moss-draped tree, watched the sun sparkle on the water.

"Be a good girl," her mother had said before she'd left home, "and mind your Uncle Max."

She thought about the warm, wiggly fuzz ball of a puppy he'd given her after her mother had said they couldn't afford a dog and she'd thought she would never have a pet of her own. He'd even brought a wreath of roses to the doggie funeral.

It had been so easy to do everything Uncle Max had said, even to drink all that champagne the day she'd hit a bull's-eye. That's what had led to all the trouble in the first place.

Her mother would never have picked up a gun, let alone shot one. And she would never, *ever* have got drunk on champagne at the age of thirteen.

Ruth wished she'd tried harder to be more like her mother.

Laughing softly, Max withdrew his fingers. Ruth kept her face turned toward the window.

"Two weeks was not enough," he said. "I should have bargained for six."

Horror coiled inside Ruth. Who had he bargained with?

Not my mother. Not my mother.

"Margaret Anne would have seen that as a fair exchange for her future."

She wanted to scream but couldn't, somehow. She and her mother were a team, two against the world. Margaret Anne Bellafontaine, beautiful and fragile and fair, a true Southern lady—and Ruth, who would never be beautiful but who had enough spirit and guts to fight both their battles.

Her mother had bartered her like a sack of beans.

Her silent screams threatened to become real. Clamping her lips tightly together, she focused on a large waterfowl wading in the shallows of the bayou.

Max smoothed her dress back into place, then patted her knee. The car rolled northward, leaving behind the bayous and the house hidden by oak trees, leaving behind innocent youth and childlike dreams.

"You've learned control, Ruth. That's good. Most women never learn control."

Just over the Mississippi border he pulled into a roadside diner, and they went inside for lunch. At last, other people. But what would she tell them? What would they say?

She ate her meal in silence.

When they reached Jackson, Max stopped, though it wasn't yet dark. For propriety's sake he rented two rooms. Ruth knew he would use only one.

The minute they were inside, he slid the bolt on the door.

"One last night with you, Ruth." She stood as still as a mannequin while he took off her clothes. "I'm going to make every minute count."

She knew things that no child should know, understood what men could do to women as no budding teenager should.

Twice he ordered room service brought to the room without the wrinkled bed, once long after dark, and the second time shortly after sunup.

Finally he bathed her and dressed her, and she slept in the car all the way to Oxford.

"Wake up, sweetheart. We're home."

Ruth slowly opened her eyes. Home was a place she'd known a long time ago. The house that she'd once thought so charming—set among huge oak trees, golden forsythia, and cascading wisteria—was like a foreign land to her. All her points of reference had been wiped out. She needed a map to find her way through this strange new landscape.

"Remember, sweetheart. Smile."

She stretched her lips back and showed all her teeth to him. Max reached for her hand, but she shook him off. As far as she was concerned, he no longer existed. He'd bargained for two weeks. His time was up, and her time in hell was over.

Now she just had to get through the rest of her life.

Sixteen society women sat in Margaret Anne Bellafontaine's front parlor sipping mint tea and eating pecan tassies, a Southern delicacy purchased at a fancy bakery on the Square and served at every social gathering worth mention.

Margaret Anne extracted herself from the group and came forward, smiling.

"Ruth, sweetheart."

Her mother. Her betrayer.

Ruth didn't cringe from the kiss. Max was right: She understood control.

"Max . . ." Margaret Anne kissed his cheek, then took both his hands and drew him toward the circle of women whose upturned faces were plastered with polite smiles.

"Everyone, I want you to meet Ruth's godfather, Maxwell Jones." There was the sound of old money and good breeding and well-concealed lies in her social laugh. "Uncle Max, Ruth calls him."

Ruth felt trapped in the net of smiles that was cast her way. Her face stiff, she returned their smiles. What would their faces look like if they knew the truth, these pampered matrons who gathered at Margaret Anne's house to plan fund-raising events for worthy causes, who thought Margaret Anne was one of them, a fragile Southern belle leading a genteel life on old-family money?

"My, my, Ruth. How you've grown." Nancy McClannahan was the wife of the dean at Ole Miss. "Hasn't she grown, Clara?"

"Yes. Why, she's practically a woman."

What would Clara Bingham, mother of the Baptist minister and wife of a church deacon, do if Ruth told her exactly how much a woman she was, if Ruth explained to her how she could make her uncle Max throw back his head and scream with pleasure?

"What grade are you in, honey?" Clara set aside her tea and concentrated her full attention on Ruth.

"I finish the eighth grade this year."

"A pretty little thing like you. Soon Margaret Anne's goin' to have to beat off the boys with a stick."

A titter of laughter.

Where was the stick when Maxwell Jones had presented his devil's bargain?

Satisfied that she'd carried out her duties of small talk, Clara turned her attention back to the pecan tassies.

Ruth cast around for a means of escape.

Margaret Anne still had one of Max's hands, and he was deep in conversation with the reigning social queen of Oxford, a frail woman with blue hair, and blue veins showing on her bejeweled hands.

Ruth left the room quietly so her mother wouldn't notice. Her suitcases were still in the car. She didn't care. She never wanted to see those clothes again.

The first thing she did when she got upstairs was scrub, until her skin was raw, the cheek her mother had kissed. Then, taking a pillowcase off her bed, she stuffed in pajamas, her toothbrush, two pairs of panties, a pair of jeans, and an old cotton T-shirt that said, "You have to kiss a few frogs before you find your prince." As an afterthought she added her teddy bear.

"What do you think you're doing?"

Margaret Anne was leaning against the doorjamb, her perfume filling the room. Ruth used to love the way her mother smelled, like the gardenias that bloomed along the side of the house in summertime. Now the smell made her sick. It reminded her of the white room in New Orleans, of the things Max had done to her, of the reason he was able to do them to her.

Everything reminded her of that white room.

"I'm leaving."

Margaret Anne came into the room and shut the door. "Max told you. Right?"

Ruth shattered like a dummy blown apart in one of the horror movies she and Wanda went to on Saturday afternoon. Deep inside she'd harbored the hope that Max had been lying, that her mother had known nothing of what he'd planned to do. Even if she *had* known, she could have offered some excuse. Ruth would have forgiven her if she'd said that all her inheritance was gone, that she was desperate and beside herself with fear, that she hadn't known what else to do.

But Margaret Anne Bellafontaine showed no remorse. "You *sold* me!"

"Keep your voice down. I still have company."

"Screw your company."

Without changing expression Margaret Anne tuned the radio to a rock station and turned the volume on high.

"Ladies don't use language like that. I taught you better."

Ruth's control snapped. The shaking started in her legs and moved its way up her body. She had to wrap her arms around herself to keep from falling into little pieces.

"There are a few things you didn't teach me. But Max did. Do you want to know all the things my *uncle* Max taught me?"

"I already know them." Margaret Anne's face and voice never changed. She might have been addressing the socially correct women in her parlor rather than her trembling teenage daughter. "Max taught me first."

Bile rose in Ruth's throat. She ran into the bathroom and vomited. Hanging over the toilet, she heaved until there was nothing left in her except despair.

Her mother was still waiting when she left the bathroom.

"How do you think I've provided for you all these years? Did you think the money just dropped out of the trees? When you were born, I had no education, no job, not even any prospects. I did what I do best in order to survive."

Ruth turned her head away, but Margaret Anne grabbed her shoulders and spoke in a fierce whisper that could still be heard over the music.

"Look at me. I'm forty-four years old. The going rate for faded whores is not very high."

Ruth's shaking stopped, and she stared at the woman she no longer knew, had never known.

"Don't look at me as if I'm some worm. I've been a good mother to you. Everything I've ever done was for you."

"Including selling me as a love slave? I wish I'd never laid eyes on you."

"You selfish little bitch." Margaret Anne swung the flat of her palm against Ruth's cheek. The sting brought tears to the girl's eyes. "Two weeks is all it cost you, two weeks in the company of a gentleman who knows how to initiate a young girl into the joys of womanhood."

"If Max is a gentleman, I'm a virgin. And we both know I'm no longer a virgin, don't we, Mother?"

Two spots of color showed on Margaret Anne's cheeks, but except for those telltale marks, she acted as if she were lecturing a child who'd been tardy for a church picnic.

"Where would all your high-and-mighty moralizing be if you'd ended up in some crummy tenement with no money for food and clothes, let alone an education? Max paid a fortune for your precious virginity. You'll never have to worry about your future the way I've worried about mine."

"Your worries are over. You can have it all. I wouldn't touch Max's money with a ten-foot pole."

Ruth went to her bed and picked up the lumpy pillowcase. She had no idea where she was going or what she would do when she got there. All she knew was that she had to get out of that hateful house.

When she turned around, her mother was at the dressing table inspecting her makeup.

"Use the back stairs. I still have guests." Margaret Anne smoothed her dress over her hips as she faced her daughter. "And don't slam the door on your way out. A slammed door is a sign of a low-class upbringing."

4.

THE VIRUNGAS OF CENTRAL AFRICA, 1982

*M*ALONE KNEW THE MOON AS FEW LOW-landers could, but not the sun, almost never the sun. Nights, the moon was so huge and bright, it turned the elephants' tusks to silver and transformed the moss swaying from the trees to ghostly dancers. But most days the sun could not penetrate the mist. It clung to the mountains like a jealous lover, refusing to budge until late afternoon when the sun finally managed to burn it away.

Malone had lived all his life with cool, damp mists. If there were any justice, the sun would shine on the day he officially became a man.

He tumbled out of bed and walked to the window, dragging the sheet behind him. Mists shrouded Mount Karisimbi, and in the distance the snowcapped peaks of the other volcanic mountains in the Virunga chain were violet in the half light of early morning. Out of the mists came the bark of the duiker calling his mate to the watering hole, and the soft mounting cry of the rabbitlike hyrax protesting the invasion of his territory. The trees were just beginning to take shape, their lacy mosses moving in a languorous, hypnotic dance.

Visitors to the Corday Research Center were always enchanted by the view and mesmerized by the sights and sounds of exotic animals just outside their door.

Malone was neither enchanted nor excited; he was depressed, almost angry.

"All I ask is one sunny day."

He dragged his sheet across the floor and climbed back into bed. If he couldn't have sunshine, at least he could have his sleep.

From high on the slopes of Karisimbi came a hair-raising scream that sent some of the center's visitors racing toward the main house, calling for the police. Hard on the heels of the scream came an avalanche of thunderous, drumlike tattooing.

Malone grinned. Old Doby was at it again. He was the oldest male silverback in the Virungas, and the most prolific. If all the males were as horny as Old Doby, there would be no need to worry about the shrinking population of the mountain gorilla.

The screaming and chest beating continued while Malone drifted back to sleep, dreaming about the sun.

"Malone? Aren't you up yet?" He opened his eyes slowly. His mother was standing in the doorway, her baggy khakis rolled at the leg and her white shirt knotted around her small waist. The cameras that were always slung over her shoulder were missing.

He rubbed his eyes.

"Time 'zit?"

"Past time to get up, sleepyhead. Today is a big day."

Malone grinned broadly. He hadn't been sure his mother would remember.

"Is that ham I smell baking?"

"A ham's baking, potatoes are roasting, and Matuka is planning to make the biggest coconut cake you ever saw."

Eleanor's eyes sparkled as she described the elaborate preparations in the kitchen. "Brett loves coconut cake."

"Brett?"

"Brett's coming home today. How could you forget?"

"I just . . . forgot."

"Hurry and get dressed. I need you to run into Ruhengeri and pick up the coconut. He would be terribly disappointed if I didn't have his favorite cake for his homecoming." When she left, she was in what Malone's father called a dither, running her hands through her curly bob in quick, nervous gestures and striding along as if she were trying to keep up with one of the herds of leaping antelope she photographed.

Malone was glad she left when she did. If she hadn't, she might have seen how close he was to crying.

Crying. On his eighteenth birthday.

He didn't even bother with underwear, just slid into his jeans and the wadded-up T-shirt lying on the floor. Inside the Jeep he floored the accelerator and took the first mountain curve at a daredevil speed, barely keeping control, half hoping he'd wrap himself around a tree on the next one.

It would serve them right. Eleanor and Joseph didn't even know he existed. It was always Brett. No matter what Malone did, he could never hold a candle to the brother who had been born first.

Eighteen stupid years old and nobody cared.

Brett was coming home, flying in from Stanford with degrees running out his ears and honors plastered all over his broad chest, while Malone's scrawny bones were getting sucked on by jungle insects as he did errands for the homecoming feast.

Not the return of the prodigal son, but the return of the favorite son.

"Damnation."

Malone smote the steering wheel with the flat of his hand. Eleanor and Joseph would hang on Brett's every word, as if he'd studied to be God instead of a doctor of anthropology and primatology.

"Sonofabitch."

It had been two years since Brett had last come home.

What would his brother look like? The last picture he'd sent, he had a beard. Did all Ph.D.'s grow beards?

"Big fucking deal."

Suddenly he slammed on the brakes so hard, the tires squealed. A duiker stood in the road looking at him with big brown eyes.

"What you looking at, asshole? Waiting to see a grown man cry?"

The graceful neck turned his way, and the duiker stared as if he could see all the way through to Malone's black heart. Contrite, Malone slumped on the wheel.

"What do I do if some wild Watusi comes up the road, Brett?"

"You get out of the way."

"What if I bang up your car? Shit, man, it's brand-new."

"I guess I'll just have to take it out on your skinny hide." Brett reached over and tousled Malone's hair. Then he crossed his arms behind his head and leaned back in his seat to enjoy the scenery. *"I suggest you concentrate on your driving."*

He'd been only twelve years old when his eighteen-year-old brother had taught him to drive. Not only had Brett taught him to drive, he'd taught him to swim and to throw a fastball and to use the backboard to make baskets. When Malone had been thirteen and Brett had caught him smoking, he hadn't told their parents but had lit up and joined his little brother. Then Brett had quietly told him the many reasons why he had decided not to make smoking a habit.

Only an ungrateful idiot would hate such a brother.

Malone straightened over the wheel and took the Jeep the rest of the way down the mountain at a sedate pace. By the time he'd delivered the coconut, preparations for the homecoming feast were in full swing. Eleanor was so preoccupied, she barely saw him come in.

Maybe she was just being cagey. Maybe the birthday candles were hidden in the cabinets and she was planning an elaborate surprise.

Maybe elephants had wings.

"I'm going to the village for a while," he said. "Is it all right if I take the Jeep?"

"Ummmhummm." His mother nodded absently. He'd lay odds if somebody asked her where he was, she wouldn't remember. Not that anybody would ask.

The village of Kibumba was little more than a group of thatched-roof huts joined by muddy footpaths nestled at the base of Mount Mikenko. The mountain rose straight up, cool and green, the massive trees in its impenetrable rain forest clinging precariously to the steep slopes.

"Damned chilly, fog-dripping jungle." Malone resisted the childish urge to shake his fist at the hated mountains. Today was the day he would put away childish things and become a man.

He wove the Jeep in and out of the villagers, who wouldn't have known a yield sign if they'd seen one and would have cared even less. A few of them called to him in Swahili.

"Hey, Little Gorilla Man."

He answered with a false grin and a wave. How he hated that term. Little Gorilla Man. The man whose father spent all his time up in the mountains studying the habits of the mountain gorillas and whose mother never saw him unless he was at the other end of a lens posing with a primate.

He ducked his head through the doorway, then stood inside the thatched hut, adjusting his eyes to the dimness. A large Watusi named Dinkus waved to him from the bar, but Malone was in no mood for company. He chose a table in the corner, one that afforded a view of the entire room.

A waitress named Sally brought his pombe. He blew the foam off the dark native beer and took a big swig. Sally waited, showing her buck teeth in a huge grin and wiggling her body so her enormous breasts swayed only inches from his eyes. He took another long drink, feeling the alcohol slide through him like liquid fire.

Even Sally was beginning to look good. Malone pulled a ten-dollar bill out of his pocket and stuffed it into the bit of cloth that barely covered her hips.

"Keep the pombe coming, baby," he said in almost perfect native tongue.

She went off giggling.

Villagers drifted in and out, the crowd growing steadily larger as the day wore on. Dinkus left his place at the bar, and two men Malone didn't know took his place. By the time he'd finished his second beer, the hut was filled with the smell of sweat and the sound of Swahili.

Suddenly a hush fell over the crowd, and heads swiveled toward the door.

Malone's mouth fell open. Poised in the doorway was the most astonishing woman he'd ever seen. Imposing, nearly six feet tall, her skin shiny as polished ebony, she surveyed the crowd with slow disdain. Finally, with her jewelry tinkling and her hips swaying in slow, hypnotic rhythm, she made her way to the bar.

When she passed his table, she gave him little more than a glance. If Brett had been with him, she'd have smiled and stopped to flirt. Women always threw themselves at his brother.

Her hips were tight and fine underneath the thin red sarong she wore. By the time she'd propped her elbow on the bamboo bar, Malone knew he had to have her.

Hell, it was his eighteenth birthday. Didn't he deserve a prize?

Filled with alcoholic courage, he made his way to the tall, dark beauty. Forget that his scrawny chest didn't fill out his T-shirt and that his lank hair was dishwater blond instead of thick and black and that he had freckles on his nose. For once in his life he was going to win the prize without Brett's help.

"Hi." He smiled at her, knowing his smile was nice. She didn't say anything, but she didn't tell him to get lost, either.

That was a start.

"My name's Malone Corday." For once he was proud of his Swahili.

"The Little Gorilla Man."

"Yes."

"I'm Lubbie Simbi."

"Any relation to Batubu Simbi?"

"I'm the Watusi warrior's woman."

His insides shook with excitement and fear.

"Is he joining you?"

"No."

If he had any sense, he'd leave now, but it was his birthday and he was hell-bent on becoming a real man.

"I call that a stroke of good luck."

Lubbie set her glass of pombe on the bar and ran her fingers lightly up his arm. She dipped her index finger briefly into her armpit, then flattened her palm on his chest and leaned so close, he could smell the exotic oils she had rubbed in her hair.

"Luck has a way of running out, white man."

She'd called him a man. And it was all because of his boldness.

Smiling, he covered her hand with his. Who needed Brett?

5.

*B*RETT WAS ALMOST BLINDED BY THE beauty of the Virungas. When he was close enough to feel the cool mists that came down from the rich green rain forests, he stopped the Jeep he'd rented at the airport. From a distance came the thunder of waterfalls tumbling down the side of Mount Karisimbi.

He closed his eyes, listening to the music of the waterfalls, inhaling the rich odors of the jungle and the lush fragrance of exotic flowers, absorbing the ever-present mists into his skin.

God, how he'd missed Africa.

Now he understood why the mountain gorillas beat their chests. It was more than a technique to show dominance; it was the manifestation of wonder, a divine exhilaration to be in the midst of an environment of such glorious and brutal beauty.

Raw energy pulsed through Brett. He

felt reborn, a prisoner finally set free from a long and heartbreaking exile.

His years away had been a necessary evil, a wrenching departure from the land that possessed his soul. Nowhere in his beloved Africa could he have prepared himself for a life devoted to the preservation of the mountain gorilla that lived in the deep green jungles of the Virungas. Nowhere but Stanford could he have been as close to the work of experts who had experimented with the development of language in primates.

He was so filled with ideas, so excited by the remarkable possibilities, that he would have gone directly into the jungle and set up camp near the gorillas if he hadn't known how anxiously his family would be waiting for him.

Grinning like a kid expecting his first bike for Christmas, he revved the engine and roared toward home.

Eleanor and Joseph were waiting for him in the front yard, just as he'd known they would be. Except for the wings of gray that fanned into her dark hair from her cheekbones, his mother had not changed.

Laughing, he gave her a bear hug that swung her off her feet.

"You big lug. Put me down." She didn't mean a word of it. He could tell by the way she laughed and the way she clung to his arm, even after he set her back on her feet.

"Big lug, you say?"

"My Lord, you look like a lumberjack. Doesn't he, Joseph?"

"They must have been feeding him well out in California."

Brett and his father clasped each other's shoulders. The man who had always seemed bigger than life was smaller than Brett had remembered, as if he'd stayed out in the jungle so long, the rains had shrunk him. Joseph hadn't been wearing glasses, either, when Brett had last seen him. But behind the lenses his black eyes were as lively as ever.

In the midst of the homecoming revelry Matuka came from the kitchen wiping her eyes with the edge of her apron.

"Mattie, you old reprobate." Brett waltzed her around

the front yard. She giggled like a teenager. Brett was the only person in the family she allowed to call her Mattie, the only Corday who could cut right through her dignity and make her giggle.

"Don't give me that handsome-devil smile." After he'd turned her loose, Mattie huffed around, setting her apron to rights. "You won't get a thing from the kitchen until dinnertime. And that's my final word."

Her bluster fooled no one. Mattie had been letting Brett have his way since he'd been old enough to toddle. She'd been known to sneak forbidden treats to him when he hadn't even asked.

He struck a dramatic pose with his hand over his heart.

"You break my heart, Mattie."

"It's not your heart I'm thinking about breaking. It's your head."

Everybody started laughing and talking at once. Brett grabbed his bags from the Jeep, and they made their way into the house.

"Your room's still the same," Eleanor said. "I haven't changed a thing."

"I won't be staying here long."

"I know. Still, I couldn't bear to change it. I guess I'm just a silly, sentimental woman."

Joseph draped his arm around his wife's shoulders. "You're about as silly as that stubborn old water buffalo who roots up the garden every night, and if you're sentimental, I'm a mountain gorilla."

"You almost are, Joseph."

Brett smiled at the exchange between his parents. They were closer than most couples who had been together a long time, due in part, he thought, to their forced isolation on the slopes of Karisimbi. They had had only each other to depend upon. Any small breach between them would have been magnified a hundred times during nights that were sometimes howlingly lonely, during the desolate rainy season that made getting down the mountain an act of supreme endurance and iron will.

Matuka peeled off from the group and went back into the kitchen, which smelled like heaven to Brett. His parents followed him down the hall.

"I can't tell you how proud and happy I am," Joseph said. "My own son joining me in my life's work. A man couldn't ask for more."

"I can hardly wait to get into the jungle and start field studies."

Brett slung his bags onto his bed, then reached inside and pulled out a package with a crumpled blue foil wrapping tied with a bedraggled bow. He tried to reshape the bow, then gave it up as a lost cause.

"Where's Malone?"

Eleanor and Joseph looked at the package in his hand and then at each other. They didn't have to say anything for Brett to know what had happened: He'd upstaged his little brother again. One of the most important birthdays in Malone's life had been forgotten because Brett was coming home.

He'd hoped that his years away would make a difference, that with him out of the picture his parents would notice Malone's quiet, steady achievements.

Now those hopes were dashed. The old guilt slashed at him, and a muscle ticked in the side of his tight jaw.

"Where's my brother?" he asked again, careful not to show his anger.

"I don't know," Joseph said. "I just came down from the slopes an hour ago." He glanced at his wife once more, then added, "Three of Doby's females are pregnant." As if that explained everything.

"He was here at noon. Let me see, he said something about using the Jeep. He was going . . . I don't know." Eleanor stepped into the hall and called toward the kitchen. "Matuka, do you remember where Malone said he was going?"

Mattie rolled her eyes to the ceiling until nothing was showing except the whites. "That old voodoo village in the Congo." Doom was in her voice and told exactly what she, a civilized Rwandan, thought of such a place. "Kibumba."

She disappeared into the kitchen, and Brett hit the door running.

He heard his mother call his name, but he didn't bother

to answer. There was nothing in Kibumba except trouble. . . .

For once the intense mystical beauty of the jungle failed to move him. All his thoughts were centered on his brother. He remembered Malone at six, his cowlick standing straight up and a fresh crop of freckles blooming across his pale cheeks, coming home with a shy grin on his face and a perfect report card hidden behind his back. It was the day Brett had been named captain of the eighth-grade soccer team. A pale-faced Malone had sat quietly through the victory celebration for his brother. Afterward Brett had found the report card crumpled behind the door of Malone's bedroom.

"Hey. What's this?" he'd said, knowing full well what it was.

"Nothing."

"Nothing! You blow away everybody in the classroom and call it nothing? I call it a reason to ask the old man for a bigger allowance."

Malone had perked up, his freckles shining.

"You think so?"

"I know so. He's in his study now. Why don't you take this down there and ask him?"

Malone had looked down at the shoes he was scuffing on the wooden floor, then back at his older brother.

"Will you go with me?"

"Sure thing."

It had been like that always, Malone cowering in Brett's shadow.

Brett's knuckles showed white on the steering wheel. He'd never meant to cast a big shadow, certainly not one that would hide his brother.

Sometimes he felt as if he were the parent and Joseph and Eleanor the children. It wasn't that they didn't love Malone; it was merely that they were too busy to notice him, too absorbed in their work and in the son they'd planned for and pinned all their hopes on.

Brett had done his best to compensate, but he'd seen how his brother was shaped by their parents' neglect.

The Jeep burst from the jungle and fishtailed as the

road suddenly dropped away. Brett fought the wheel for control and was finally bumping along the plains toward the group of huts that could only loosely be called a village. Another time he'd have been lost in appreciation of the stark, primitive beauty of the village, reveling in the lack of smog and traffic and noise.

Today his focus was the large hut at the edge of the village. The bar. Unless Malone had come into the village to be with a woman, it was the only place he could be.

He heard the shouting before he reached the hut. The voices rose and fell like the beat of war drums, the Swahili words filled with the lust for excitement and the thirst for blood. Out of the cacophony of sound came one name, chanted like a mantra.

"Batubu . . . Batubu . . . Batubu!"

Batubu Simbi. The Watusi warrior. He was revered by a small band of rebels, hated and feared by everyone else.

Though he was suspected of being behind most of the poaching activity in the Virungas, he had never been caught, never even been seen in the vicinity of the crimes. The Corday family referred to him as the Bat, for like that nocturnal creature, he passed unseen through the jungles at night.

Brett had no desire to walk into a brawl involving the Bat on his first day back home. He'd inquire about Malone at one of the huts down the lane. He was turning the Jeep away when he heard a name that froze his blood.

"Little Gorilla Man. Kill the Little Gorilla Man."

Brett was out of the Jeep almost before he'd brought it to a halt. Leaving the motor running, he raced toward the bar.

A storm of sound assaulted him, and a wall of bodies blocked his view.

"Kill . . . kill . . . kill."

The chant grew to epic proportions, and the wall of bodies swayed with the frenzy of warriors sensing victory. Brett was a big man, over six feet of solid muscle, but the Watusis were giants. There was no way he could work his way through that imposing barricade of flesh.

"Malone!"

Brett's bellow startled the onlookers. They parted just

enough to leave a small opening. Using techniques he'd learned on university football fields, Brett lowered his right shoulder and plowed through.

In the flash before he connected with his target, he saw his brother sprawled on the floor with the blade of a bush knife at his throat. Brett went in low, hitting the Bat hard in the solar plexus with the edge of his shoulder.

The blade of the panga flashed, scoring Brett's arm before he could roll out of the way. The smell of his own blood was added to the smell of sweat and fear.

"Run, Malone," he yelled on all fours. "Get out of here."

"Brett!"

"Go." The blade was coming at him again. He twisted sideways, then brought himself upright. "Now!"

Adrenaline pumped through him. The warm blood on his arm was no more than a trickle, but he knew he wouldn't be so lucky next time. He was no match for an angry Watusi with a lethal weapon.

The Bat arced his knife in the air high over Brett's head. Out of the corner of his eye Brett could see Malone hovering on the sidelines.

"Go," he yelled once more, never taking his gaze from his opponent.

Malone bolted.

"The Little Gorilla Man can't fight his own battles." The knife blade whistled as it sliced air over Brett's head, then in front of his chest.

The Bat was toying with Brett. Unarmed and overmatched, knowing his life hung in the balance, Brett decided to try for diplomacy.

"He's just a kid, Batubu. He's no threat to you."

"He touched my woman."

Malone. Malone. What have you done?

"He's full of pombe and arrogance. Today is his eighteenth birthday."

The big Watusi flung back his head and laughed. The sound raised chills on the back of Brett's neck.

"Do you plead for his life or yours, Gorilla Man?"

"His."

"You would sacrifice your own?" The knife whistled

closer. Brett felt its tip score his chest as it ripped the front of his shirt.

"Not without a fight."

The watchers were getting impatient. They'd hoped for a good fight and found all the talk boring. Some of them walked away, but the others began to chant.

"Gorilla Man . . . Gorilla Man . . . Gorilla Man."

"They want your blood." The Bat circled closer.

"Brett!" Malone yelled from the back of the hut. "I've got you a knife!"

"Stay back!"

The bush knife came at him again. Brett ducked low and charged. The impact took them both to the floor. He caught the Bat's powerful arm, grunting with the effort to hold the knife away from his body. Locked together, they rolled across the floor, each trying to gain dominance.

The knife edged closer. Brett felt his strength ebbing. The muscles in his arms and legs began to burn.

The Bat gave a mighty heave and pinned Brett to the floor. In that moment before he knew his life would end, he had no lofty thoughts, no dazzling insights, no flashbacks of his entire life. He wondered if he would ever know the taste of coconut cake again.

The blade sliced downward. Pain seared his face. Blood blinded him. His roar of outrage nearly choked him.

He waited for the end, waited for the final blow that would plunge the knife into his heart.

The weight that was pressing him down lifted. Through a haze of blood he saw the giant Watusi standing over him, the blade of his knife turned red.

"See no evil, Gorilla Man." The Bat grabbed the arm of a beautiful woman in a red sarong, then turned and walked away.

The sound of voices pounded at Brett while his life's blood pumped from him at an alarming rate. He struggled onto his knees, willing the walls to stop closing in on him.

Somewhere through the red haze there was a door. By sheer force of will he brought himself upright, then stood swaying, peering through a curtain of red for a means of escape.

The smell of sweat and blood nearly overpowered him. His knees wanted to buckle, but he refused to let them.

For a moment he heard the roar of waterfalls and the sound of birds calling for the dawn, but he fought the hallucination, fought the weakness that wanted him to lie down on the floor and wait for the blessed peace of unconsciousness to envelop him. Onward he struggled. Finally he felt the fresh air on his face, and he knew he'd made it to the door.

Someone took his arm. He couldn't see through the blood.

"Malone?"

"Oh, my God . . . *your eye.*"

Malone's voice was a piteous wail.

"Get me into the Jeep, Malone."

The effort took the last of Brett's will. He leaned his head against the seat.

"I'm sorry, Brett, I'm sorry, I'm sorry. . . ."

"Drive, Malone."

"Where?"

"The clinic. Ruhengeri." Hot pokers stabbed his left eye. "Hurry."

6.

OXFORD, MISSISSIPPI, 1982

*E*VERYBODY IN HER CLASS WAS NORMAL EX-
cept Ruth. She slouched low in her
chair, wondering if her classmates
could tell what she had done just by looking at her.

Up front the music teacher was talking
about the jazz greats, but she didn't listen.
Music used to be her favorite class, but she
didn't care about anything anymore. Except her kitten. She could tell Miranda everything, and it didn't make a bit of
difference. Miranda loved her anyhow.

She wished she could shut her eyes and
sleep till the end of May, and then school
would be out and she wouldn't have to do
so much pretending.

"Now, listen up, students." Mr. Carr always said that right before he played the
music. It was the best part of the class. Mr.

Carr glanced her way, and she bent over her notebook pretending she'd been taking notes all along.

"This is an artist you won't hear anywhere except on this album. Blue Janeau. He cut only one record, then dropped out of the music scene. Some say he died of a drug overdose. Some say he survived, that members of his band still take care of him in a remote part of the country. Nobody knows. Nobody agrees on anything except that he was one of the jazz greats."

Ruth caught her breath when she heard the first dark, haunting note. It was a trumpet, played with such clarity, the music got inside her skin. She could feel it pulsing in her throat and throbbing through her chest.

She didn't know the song. She didn't even remember the name of the musician. Now she wished she'd listened more closely to Mr. Carr's lecture.

The trumpet ceased, and the musician began to sing. Ruth closed her eyes. The music grew inside her until she *was* the song, clear and beautiful and clean.

"Ruth?"

Mr. Carr was standing over her desk, a frown pinching his face. The rest of her classmates had vanished. There was nothing except an expanse of empty seats and the unforgettable strains of music.

Ruth grabbed her books and clutched them to her chest.

"Is anything wrong, Ruth?"

"No." To her mortification, she realized she'd been crying. She wiped her nose with the back of her hand. "I gotta be going. I'll be late for math."

"I'll write you a note."

She was trapped. When a teacher said he'd write a note, that meant you had to stay. She squeezed her legs together as hard as she could and held on to her books.

"I'm concerned when a straight-A student fails two tests in a row."

"I . . . didn't have time to study."

"Can you tell me why?"

"No. I just . . . got lazy, I guess."

The way he stood there looking at her made Ruth want

to cry all over again. His face was nice, the kind she'd
imagine on Santa Claus if she still believed in fairy tales.

She wished she could still believe.

"Ruth . . ." Mr. Carr sighed, as if he couldn't quite
recall what he'd meant to say and regretted his forgetful-
ness. "You're the only person besides me who has ever
been moved to tears by that music. If you'll drop by after
school, I'll give you a duplicate tape."

"Thank you, Mr. Carr."

"And, Ruth, if you ever want to talk, I'll be glad to
listen. I have three daughters of my own. I understand the
problems of teenage girls."

She wondered whether he would understand why she
had lain naked on silk sheets while scented oils were
rubbed into her skin.

Margaret Anne looked at the closed door. She didn't
have to turn the knob to know it was locked.

"Ruth, dinner is ready."

"I'm not hungry."

Margaret Anne counted to ten. Losing one's temper
was a sign of weakness. Besides that, she would not give
Ruth the satisfaction of causing a scene.

"Do you have that kitten in there?"

No answer.

Margaret Anne had regretted her decision a thousand
times. When she had agreed for Ruth to have one of
Wanda's kittens, it had seemed like a good idea, the only
way to make peace after her daughter had returned home
from her week of rebellion.

She felt herself getting worked up over that week all
over again, as if it had happened only the day before instead of a month before. The worst part hadn't been
Ruth's disappearance, for she was perfectly satisfied that a
resourceful girl like her daughter could take care of herself, especially after Max had trained her. But the furor
that Max had created nearly drove her crazy.

"How could you let her leave?" he'd said after her
guests had departed and they were finally alone the evening he and Ruth had returned from New Orleans.

"She's almost fourteen, Max."

"She's hardly more than a child."

In all their years together she'd never crossed Max, had in fact been afraid to: Her livelihood depended on his good graces. Now old hurts resurfaced—the birthdays he'd forgotten, the Christmas he'd given her a gold charm bracelet while his dowdy wife had got emeralds, the time their trip to Hawaii had been canceled because that stupid bitch he was married to had slit her wrists with a knife used to fillet dead fish and ended up in the hospital surrounded by bouquets. Margaret Anne could have bought groceries for a week with the money Max had spent on flowers.

Now, for the first time in their relationship, she was in the catbird seat. She had a secret weapon, the thing Max wanted most: Ruth.

"Is that what you thought when you were screwing her, Max? That she was only a child?"

She had never seen Max lose his temper. Now a muscle tightened in his jaw, and he closed one fist around the Waterford paperweight on the Victorian table beside his chair.

Margaret Anne stood her ground. Let him hit her. She'd sue his pants off. By the time she'd finished with him, she'd own Hollywood.

Slowly he brought himself under control. His jaw relaxed, and he reached for his pipe.

"Don't even think about toying with me, Margaret Anne."

It wasn't what he said so much as the way he said it that sent chills through her. If she crossed Maxwell Jones, he would ruin her without so much as blinking an eye. If he told the things he knew about her background and Ruth's father, Margaret Anne would never be able to hold her head up in Oxford again. Not only Oxford, but the whole state of Mississippi.

"I'm too smart ever to underestimate you, Max."

She was certain he knew her smile was false, but that didn't matter. Everything about their relationship was false, including the passion. They were so tangled in the intricate web of lies they'd woven that neither of them could ever escape.

She slid onto his lap and ran her hands over his body, just the way he liked her to.

He got up and switched off the lights. She reached for her zipper.

"Keep your clothes on, Margaret Anne."

He took her with a fierceness that recalled their early days together. For a moment Margaret Anne thought they would go on as if nothing had happened between them. But Max's cry shattered her illusions. Buried deep inside her, spewing out his seed, he called out her daughter's name.

That was the last time he'd touched her.

He'd called every day after he got back to Hollywood, not to inquire about Margaret Anne, not to arrange a weekend tryst, but to berate her about Ruth's disappearance.

"She hasn't disappeared, Max. She's just over at Wanda's."

"When is she coming back?"

"How should I know?"

"You're her mother."

"You want me to go over and bodily drag her home?"

There was a weighty silence.

"If she's not back by the end of the week, I'll be forced to change the terms of our agreement, Margaret Anne."

"She'll be back."

Now, standing outside her daughter's locked door, she felt the fury rising inside her again. She wanted to beat on the door and scream, "How dare you? How dare you put me through hell? How dare you be young? How dare you take my place?"

Feeling her brows draw together in a vertical frown, she reached up to smooth away the damaging wrinkles.

"Civilized people don't keep animals in the house, Ruth."

There was movement in the room; then the sound of music drifted through the door.

"Ruth?" She knocked again.

Ruth turned the music up louder. Jazz. A familiar trumpet that made the blood pound in Margaret Anne's temples.

She listened a while longer, just to be sure; then she raced to her room and flung open the closet door. The metal box was at the top of the closet right where it had been for years. She had to drag a chair across the room in order to lift the heavy box from the shelf.

Sitting cross-legged in the middle of the floor, she took a small key from the locket around her throat. Her hands shook when she flung open the lid.

Everything was there—the recordings, the letters, the lock of hair. Ruth couldn't possibly know.

Margaret Anne was just locking the box when the phone rang.

"Mrs. Bellafontaine?"

"Yes?"

"I'm Randy Simpson, the counselor at Ruth's school."

As she listened to him, Margaret Anne felt beleaguered on all sides. It wasn't enough that Ruth didn't speak to her, didn't eat meals with her, didn't so much as acknowledge her presence in the house; now she had to go down to the school and pretend that she was a cross between June Cleaver and Mary Poppins.

"Mrs. Bellafontaine, I'm worried about your daughter. Her teachers say she never participates in class activities anymore."

"I'm sure it's just a phase. You know how teenagers are."

"She was always such a vivacious girl, a real classroom leader. Is anything going on at home that would bother her?"

"Not that I know of. Of course, I have been busier than usual this spring planning the charity ball for the Cancer Society." Margaret Anne looked down at her hands clasped demurely in her lap, then furrowed her brow, just the tiniest bit. "Oh, dear, I do hope I haven't been neglectful. I try to be both mother and father to Ruth. Sometimes it's just . . ." She fumbled in her purse for a delicate lace-edged handkerchief, which she brought to her trembling lips. ". . . so hard to bring up a child alone."

"Now, now." The counselor came around his desk to pat Margaret Anne's hand. He'd let his body go slightly to pot, but that gleam in his eye was a sure sign of sexual interest.

For a moment she let herself speculate on having a little something on the side, something just for herself. Lord knew, she could use it.

If she thought she could get by without Max ever finding out . . .

Margaret Anne brought herself up short. There was no way in heaven or hell she could do anything of the sort and escape Maxwell Jones's wrath.

She simpered a while longer, just to watch Randy Simpson's reaction. He got so red around the ears, she thought he was going to explode. Finally he cleared his throat and went back behind his safe desk.

"Don't worry about a thing, Mrs. Bellafontaine. It's probably just a phase, like you said. We'll keep an eye on her."

"Thank you, Mr. Simpson."

As soon as she got out of the building, Margaret Anne took three deep, calming breaths before she put on her sunglasses and her society smile. In a small town somebody was always watching. You never knew when it might be somebody interesting.

"I will not let this small setback affect me," she said to herself.

Inside her car Margaret Anne took a small jar out of her purse, then pulled down the mirrored visor and smoothed a firming lotion into the tiny vertical creases between her eyebrows.

Ruth played a game with herself. If her mother's car never came back, Ruth's father would return from wherever he was and take her off to a wonderful house with a big garden and a big kitchen and lots of cats and dogs.

"Your mother would never let me see you," he'd say, "but now that she's gone, the two of us will be a family."

Ruth would learn how to bake gingerbread that made the whole house smell good, and her father would help her with her math and teach her things like how to bait a fishhook and how to tell the weather by looking at the sky.

She flung open her bedroom door. The kitten and the

music followed her out into the hall. Ruth played another game with herself: Nothing bad had happened to her in New Orleans. She was the same girl she'd been before she went away, and this was the same happy home.

The sun felt good coming through the upstairs window. She stood in its spotlight and sang along with the tape Mr. Carr had given her, pretending she was a famous jazz singer, all set to do her grand finale and then mysteriously disappear. She knew every word by heart.

The ringing of the phone cut into her live performance. Miranda trailed her down the stairs and curled into a ball at her feet when she stopped to pick up the receiver.

"Hello . . ."

"Ruth? I've been worried about you." It was Max. "Why have you refused to talk to me, sweetheart? You know I would never do or say anything to make you unhappy."

Rage obscured her capacity to think, to move.

"Say something, Ruth. I want to hear the sound of your voice once more."

He spoke in the honeyed tones he'd used when he'd been especially pleased with her. A dark, hateful feeling curled through her like smoke, and a new terror seized her.

I'm just like my mother.

It all came back to Ruth—the things Max had made her do, the awful truth about her mother, the panicked flight from home. She had meant to stay away forever. The first night she'd spent in the alley behind the school, using her clothes for a pillow. Morning had brought rain and reality. She'd had no food, no shelter, and no means of supporting herself.

Unless she became a thirteen-year-old version of her mother.

That horrible thought had driven her to Wanda's. After a week of taking charity and lying about why she had run away, Ruth had gone back home. Not because her mother wanted her to, but because *she* decided to go. She would stay until she was old enough to support herself, and then she'd leave and never look back.

That was her plan.

Most plans had flaws. Hers had two: her mother and Max.

And now he was saying things to her, things she didn't want to hear—dark, wicked things that sickened her.

His voice dropped to a whisper.

"Remember, sweetheart? Remember the things you wanted me to do to you? You remember, don't you, Ruth? Remember how you begged for it?"

She bit down hard on her lower lip, drawing blood. The quick pain jolted her out of the awful spell he was weaving.

"Get lost, Max."

She slammed down the phone, then quickly scooped Miranda into her arms. The kitten's loud purring soothed her. Ruth stood very still while that soft, contented humming wiped out the awful excitement of Max's voice.

"What a good girl you are." Ruth rubbed the kitten's head, then pressed her face into the fur.

"What a good girl I am," she whispered.

With her mother off in the car and Max's voice silent, she could believe in her fantasy.

Almost.

7·

CENTRAL AFRICA, 1982

*T*HE MINUTE LORENA WATSON WOKE up, she knew the buffalo was in her flower garden again. Without even bothering to put on shoes, she grabbed the baseball bat from beside her bed and charged. Sure enough, there he was, front feet planted in her summer annuals, head down, eating as if he owned not only the flowers but the whole damned place.

"Get out of here, you big ugly mutt. Shoo! Scat!"

She raced around the porch wielding her bat, her cotton gown flapping behind her like a bird gone mad. The big animal gave her a mean look as if he couldn't decide whether he wanted to be stubborn and make her fight for the flowers or whether he would just go quietly back where he'd come from and forget the whole thing.

Shouting, she waved the bat at him once more. With a disdainful snort he tossed his head in the air.

If he charged, she was in big trouble. Chances were he'd gain the front porch before she gained the door.

"Don't you mess with me, you ugly lout. I've got twice the balls you do. I'll beat you up and eat you for dinner."

With a final toss of his head, the big buffalo left her garden and sashayed off toward the meadow. She stared at the wreckage. Every night for the last week he'd trampled her flowers, and every morning she marched right down to the nursery and bought some more.

Wanting to survey the damage close-up, she stepped off the porch and right into a pile of buffalo dung. It oozed between her bare toes.

If Lorena hadn't been married to her career, she'd have pulled up stakes and headed home to Georgia then and there; but she was totally devoted, had in fact chosen Africa for that very reason, knowing that nothing less than total devotion would be required to live in a place so far from what she had known as civilization.

Looking down at her feet, she chuckled. "You think a little shit is going to make me give up, mister? Well, you don't know this tough Georgia cracker."

After she'd cleaned up and had breakfast, she drove into town for some more flowers, then spent the rest of the day on her knees in the dirt, replanting, humming, and talking to herself.

"One of these days I'm going to have to get myself a dog."

It took her half an hour to get the dirt from underneath her fingernails, but by late afternoon she was ready for her shift at the Ruhengeri Clinic, so crisp and white she looked as if she'd never seen dirt, let alone spent most of the day digging in it.

She was the dirt-and-dungarees type.

That's what Bubba Wilson had told her when he'd relieved her of the burden of her virginity in the backseat of his Chevrolet.

"You're the dirt-and-dungarees type, Lorena."

"That's not a very romantic thing to say, especially in this situation."

"If you want romance, Lorena, you're gonna have to look somewhere else, but if you want the best lay in Georgia, old Bubba is your boy."

If he was the best, then this whole business was highly overrated, she had decided when it was all over. But she hadn't complained. She'd had fun and Bubba had served his purpose: Now she could get on with her studies instead of mooning around wondering what she was missing.

She'd noted the momentous night in her diary, then had got on with her studies, had in fact graduated with honors —and she'd pit her skills against the very best nurse anywhere in the world.

"You're looking mighty chipper, Lorena," Dr. Tigrett said when she waltzed through the door and stashed her purse behind the desk at the nurses' station. "Any particular reason?"

"Yeah. I was just thinking what a fabulous nurse I am and that you're damned lucky to have me."

"Modesty has always been your greatest charm."

They were still chuckling when the Jeep careened to a stop and a young man rushed into the clinic.

"Help! Somebody has to help my brother."

"Where is he?" Dr. Tigrett asked.

"In the Jeep." The young man suddenly collapsed onto one of the hard chairs in the waiting room as if it had taken all his strength to deliver his message.

Tigrett rushed through the door with Lorena right behind him, but the patient wasn't in the Jeep at all. He was standing by its side, swaying slightly, the left side of his face covered with blood.

Even in his condition, he looked like a warrior-god who might have been worshiped by some ancient culture. He wasn't handsome in a traditional sense; he was merely sensational.

Lorena couldn't have said whether his impact on her was due to the intensity of that single black eye watching every move they made, or the untamed black hair framing well-defined cheekbones usually seen only in statues, or the awesome sense of strength and power in his body.

Whatever it was, she'd been mesmerized by him. She

didn't know how long she would have stood there gaping if Dr. Tigrett hadn't said something.

"Lorena. Take his other arm."

When she touched him, she felt the piercing gaze of that single black eye, and for the first time in her thirty-three years she wished she'd been born pretty instead of plain.

She'd been right about his strength; he didn't lean on them as they walked into the clinic.

"Can you tell us what happened?" the doctor asked.

"Bush knife."

Lorena's heart plummeted. The natives never cleaned their bush knives, and they were used for everything from cutting through the jungle to gutting animals.

His brother rushed them the minute they got into the clinic.

"How bad is it, Doctor?"

"I won't know until I take a look." Knowing the importance of every second, Tigrett never paused in his rush toward the examining room.

"Oh, God . . ." The young man trailed along behind them. "I'll never do anything like this again, Brett. I promise you. . . ."

"Malone!" The patient's voice cut through the babble. "Stand tall."

Malone passed a shaky hand over his face, then turned to the doctor. "Should I fill out papers or something?"

"Later. There are some things I'll need to know."

"Wait outside, Malone." The patient fixed the doctor with a single-black-eyed stare. "I can tell you everything you need to know."

Tigrett had never had his authority challenged by a patient, certainly not one in Brett's condition. Lorena watched the contest of wills as she cleaned away the blood.

"Fine. Let's not waste any more time."

Tigrett adjusted the light to the patient's face. The bush knife had sliced only once, but one slice was all it took. A deep curving line dissected the man's face from eyebrow to cheekbone—no wavering, no jagged edges. But the cut had been made right through the center of the eye.

"Your name?" Tigrett said.

"Brett Corday."

"How long ago did this happen?"

"About two hours."

Lorena put her hand on the patient's arm. She knew what was coming next.

Tigrett bent over the eye once more, being careful, being certain.

"We'll have to do an enucleation."

That he could unflinchingly deliver news that would alter a man's life was a tribute to his professionalism. Lorena was not so tough. Tears stung her eyes and wet her cheeks.

"What does that mean?" Brett asked.

"I'll have to remove your eye."

Brett Corday's stillness was that of the Virungas that surrounded them.

"There must be less drastic measures you can take before you make a decision like that."

"Two hours was too long. You've lost all fluids in the eye, and there is no way they can ever be put back. That means you've already lost your vision. Permanently."

Lorena felt the slight tremor that ran through Brett. But not so much as a single muscle tic in his face betrayed his feelings.

"Why take out my eye?"

"Risk of infection is extremely high with a cut from a bush knife. The eye is too close to the brain. If I don't remove the eye and clean out the wound, you could die."

Brett closed his hand over Lorena's and squeezed twice, reflexively.

"What are you waiting for, Doctor?"

During the next five days the old buffalo came to her flower garden every night and wreaked havoc. Lorena hardly bothered to look, much less to replant.

She lived for her shift at the clinic.

Standing in her slip, she ran her hands down her body. She was solid but not pudgy. Brett Corday was probably used to the very finest—women with flawless faces and slim young bodies.

Lorena Watson was nobody's fool. She knew exactly

how she looked. With her thin, straight brown hair that
defied both curling irons and pins, and the sprinkling of
freckles on her nose, she looked like somebody's homely
cousin who was always being pawned off on unsuspecting
blind dates. Besides that, she was nine years older than
Brett Corday.

What chance could she possibly have with a man like
him, anyway? Lorena got into her nurse's uniform and
was halfway out the door before she went back into her
bedroom.

It took her nearly ten minutes to find the perfume. The
bottle was so old, she couldn't even read the name, but she
remembered it was made by one of those snooty men who
designed tight blue jeans. It probably smelled like horse
piss, buried as it had been for the last three years at the
bottom of her lingerie drawer. Somebody had given it to
her the last Christmas she'd spent in Georgia—probably
one of her aunts, ever hopeful that Lorena would forget
her silly notions of traipsing off to that godforsaken place
she worked, and settle down to marry somebody like
Bubba and have babies.

Being pregnant nine months out of a year had never
been her notion of the good life, but, Lord, sometimes she
did long for the fun that preceded that state of dubious
bliss.

"What the hell."

She turned the bottle up and doused herself. If the rest
of her flowers didn't turn up their roots and die when she
walked by, she guessed the smell wouldn't kill Brett Corday.

He was asleep. A shaft of afternoon light pierced the
shutters and fell across the bandage that swathed the left
side of his face. A lock of thick, untamed hair lay upon the
bandage, so dark, it was blue-black against the stark-white
dressings.

She caught her tongue between her lips and was reaching toward his hair when he spoke.

"What is that fragrance?"

She jerked her hand back and tried to look busy
smoothing the sheet.

"Gardenia, I think. The bottle is so old, the label is worn away."

"It's nice." He fixed her with a riveting gaze as his mouth quirked up at the corners.

His beautiful smile was totally without guile. That, then, was the secret of his impact: Brett Corday had no idea that his mere presence was enough to stun women into stammering silence.

"I'm glad you like it," she said. "Open wide."

She took his temperature, then his blood pressure. Dawdling. Not wanting to leave the room.

"Is anything wrong?" he asked.

"No." *Except that you'll soon be leaving.* "Everything is perfectly normal."

"Good. I'm leaving tomorrow."

Her heart hurt. Now Lorena knew why all her teachers had cautioned not to get personally involved with patients.

"How are you going to get along without my TLC, not to mention my stories?"

"With great difficulty."

"Did I ever tell you the one about Aunt Priscilla?"

"I don't think so."

"One day she showed up at our kitchen door, dressed fit to kill, every hair in place and sprayed so stiff, not even a hurricane could have moved it. She planted her feet together under the table, put her white gloves on top of her purse, and announced, 'Murray's gone. He went away with somebody who would give him oh-ral sex. Please fix me some tea, Lorena.' "

"Did you fix her tea?" Brett asked, laughing.

"No. I asked her what oh-ral sex was. Mother made me wash my mouth out with soap."

"I'll miss your stories, Lorena."

"Hey. My cottage is down on Raintree if you get lonesome for a little tale."

Chuckling, Brett reached out and squeezed her hand. Once. Lightly.

It wasn't much, but it would have to do.

8.

*I*T WAS A DIFFERENT FAMILY GATHERING from the one he'd imagined. Their first meal together since he'd come back from the United States. The first since he'd been released from the hospital.

His mother kept staring at his face, stricken. When Brett caught her at it, she attempted a smile that didn't quite work. His father studiously avoided looking at the bandage that still covered his left eye and the angry red gash down his cheek held together with the doctor's precise stitches. Instead, Joseph talked to the wall behind Brett's head in a voice full of forced joviality.

"Two of Doby's females gave birth today. He let Eleanor get close enough for some great shots. They're both females."

"It's high time," Eleanor said, making a valiant effort to act normal. "We're woefully outnumbered on this mountain."

Though she laughed when she said it,

Brett heard the undertone of discontent. He studied his mother closely. At forty-three she was still a striking woman. She'd been a mere child when Joseph had brought her to the Virungas, an eighteen-year-old bride.

Had she missed the things other women took for granted—concert halls, movie houses, fancy restaurants, shopping malls, next-door neighbors? Until now Brett had never thought about what living so far from civilization would do to a woman like Eleanor.

"I've named them Cee Cee and Dee Dee." If Joseph sensed his wife's disquiet, he gave no sign. "The best studies are those that follow the mountain gorilla from birth. I can't wait for you to get out there in the jungle with me, Brett."

"No!" Eleanor's face turned white as she shoved back her chair and stood up. With her palms flattened on the table, she leaned into her husband's face. "He's barely out of the hospital, and all you can talk about is your damned gorilla studies."

"The decision is mine, Mother."

Eleanor rushed on as if she had not heard Brett's quiet rebuke.

"I won't have it. Do you hear me, Joseph? Isn't it enough that he's lost his eye? Would you have him fall off a cliff and finish the job that drunk bushman's knife started?"

Stunned silence overtook the room. While the Cordays were far from ordinary, they had always managed the semblance of normality within the family circle. In spite of the currents of discontent that flowed deep in the subterranean levels of consciousness, they loved each other, loved in a fierce, protective way that had allowed them to survive twenty-five years of virtual isolation in the beautiful, treacherous Virungas.

"You're overwrought, my dear." Joseph calmly picked up his fork and continued eating. "Dr. Tigrett said Brett will compensate for his loss of depth perception. Besides, he's as familiar with these mountains as he is the back of his hand. The notion that he'd fall off a cliff and kill himself is ridiculous."

Eleanor was not to be placated.

"Don't you dare call me ridiculous, Joseph Corday. You sit there eating as if that's all that matters, while my son . . ." Her lower lip trembled when she looked at Brett's face. "My beautiful son is scarred for life."

Malone bolted from the table. Brett assessed the situation. Eleanor had Joseph, but his brother had no one. Except him.

"Brett, where are you going?" Eleanor asked when he pushed back his chair.

"To find my brother."

He found Malone hunched in the front seat of the Jeep, his knuckles white on the wheel. Brett slid in on the passenger side.

"How about taking me down the mountain, Malone?"

Malone turned a stony face in his direction. Eleanor's words echoed between them. *"My son,"* she'd said, as if Malone didn't even exist. *"My beautiful son."* A stunning reminder that Malone was the plain one, the ordinary one.

"Aren't you afraid I'll run over a cliff and ruin the rest of your pretty face? Why don't you take your own damned self down the mountain?"

Brett caught his brother's arm as Malone slid toward the door.

"Because I don't want the Jeep parked in front of the lady's house all night until I find out how she feels about gossip."

"Hey. All right!" Malone revved the engine and tore out of the driveway; then he grinned at his brother. "Sometimes I'm a jerk."

"You're entitled . . . as long as you don't make a habit of it."

More exhausted than he'd expected to be, Brett leaned his head back against the seat and closed his eye. Perhaps he'd made a mistake in coming back to the Virungas. If he went somewhere else to do his work, maybe Malone's light could shine.

The thought of leaving his beloved Virungas again made him sick at heart. He'd deal with the problem when he was stronger.

"Brett, about your eye . . ."

"I don't want to talk about it."

"You'll look as good as new when the doctors have finished with you." Malone gave him a sideways glance. "Dr. Tigrett says you can hardly tell the glass eyes from the real thing."

"I'm not getting a glass eye."

Malone twisted toward his brother, his face horror-struck. The Jeep swerved perilously close to the edge of a steep embankment. Brett caught the wheel and brought it back under control.

Malone's body was rigid as he turned his full attention toward the road.

Brett understood his brother so well, he could almost hear his thought processes. An eye patch would be a constant reminder of the sacrifice Brett had made. Surgery would wipe away the evidence.

Uncomfortable silences were rare between the brothers, but Brett did nothing to break the one that settled over them. He could have said, "It will be all right." But he didn't.

He was tired. Physically and emotionally exhausted. At the moment, he had nothing left to give.

"Where to?" Malone asked, only because it was necessary.

"A little cottage on Raintree."

"Which one?"

"I'll know it when I see it."

Lorena's cottage was set back from the road, half-hidden behind the moss that swayed like drunken sailors from the limbs of twisted trees. A neat picket fence marked the boundaries of a flower garden that looked as if it had been freshly planted. On the front porch sat two white wicker rockers, and the swing was draped with a colorful patchwork quilt, signs of her Georgia heritage.

"This is it," Brett said.

"You sure?"

"I'm positive." Brett swung from the Jeep. "Pick me up in the morning."

"Sure thing . . . Brett, I owe you my life. I'll do anything in the world for you."

Agony twisted Malone's face. Brett could not remain unmoved in the face of his brother's guilt—and his love.

"Anything?" he asked, keeping his voice light.

"Just name it."

"Come *early*."

"Son of a gun! I'll show you. I'll be here so early, the sun will be ashamed for being a slugabed. Just be sure you're finished with what you're going to start."

His brother drove off, laughing. Relieved, Brett turned toward Lorena Watson's front door. He wasn't sure what he was going to start, didn't even know what he *wanted* to start.

All he knew was that Lorena made him forget.

As he lifted his hand to knock, the enormity of his loss overwhelmed him. Drained of all energy, he pressed his hand over the bandage and leaned his forehead against the rough boarding on the front porch.

No left eye.

No depth perception.

No leaping from mountain crag to mountain crag without second-guessing himself.

No flying his own plane through the bush.

He balled his right hand into a fist and struck the wall. A splinter stung his flesh and drew blood.

Slowly the door swung open, and Lorena's soft hand closed around his arm. Without a word she drew him inside.

Dressed only in a slip, she took his hands and pressed them flat against her breasts. A drop of blood fell on the white satin, leaving a red stain that spread over her nipple. She led him into a small bathroom. He leaned against the door frame while she rummaged in her medicine cabinet. She took out tweezers, iodine, and bandages, then bent over his hand.

The top of her hair was shiny and smelled fresh, as if it had soaked up the scent of flowers that grew in her front yard. He could bury his face in her hair and dream of the softly scented mornings of his youth when he'd been whole and full of dreams and the sun had bathed the Virungas in light that had turned the trees to gold.

His breathing became harsh, filling the room with desire. Lorena looked up, and the box of bandages clattered to the tile. Silently she wrapped herself around him and squeezed. Hard.

He rested his cheek against her hair.

"This is need, Lorena. Nothing more."

"It doesn't matter."

The darkness came upon them without warning, as if the sun had suddenly decided to hide behind the brooding volcanic mountains that guarded the cottage. Lorena reached for the light switch, and in the harsh illumination of an incandescent bulb she cupped his face and kissed the bandage that hid his scars.

"You are so beautiful," she whispered.

He slid her slip from her shoulders.

Bracing her against the wall, he lost himself in her nakedness.

9.

LOS ANGELES, CALIFORNIA, 1984

THE MEMORIES CAME TO MAX AT ODD times. Sitting across the table from his wife, watching the lines in her mouth pucker as she aired yet another lengthy complaint, he remembered another time, another place. He remembered the smell of oil as he'd rubbed it onto Ruth's slender young thighs and the way her tender nipples sat erect in dusky rose aureoles when the fragrant oil touched them.

Not a day, not a moment passed that he didn't think of her. She belonged to him as no one else ever could, had belonged to him from the moment he'd seen her sitting in a pink ruffled sunsuit on the beach pounding the sand with a toy shovel.

It had been one of those hot July days that made wearing clothes an act of stupidity rather than a necessity. He'd just finished a difficult day's shooting on a movie set that had turned into hell. The star had been drunk, the makeup supervisor late, the camera crew mutinous, and the set so hot, the chairs had to be periodically wet down with a hose.

Not wanting to go home and face another of his wife's headaches or bellyaches or whatever kind of aches she'd have that day, Max had ditched his shirt and shoes, rolled up his pants, and gone to the beach with the intention of sticking his feet in the water and forgetting there was ever such a thing as making movies.

He had almost stepped on the little girl. She'd looked up at him with such fierce challenge that he'd laughed aloud. She was an enchantress, all pink ruffles and dark curls and big luminous brown eyes.

He squatted beside her.

"How are you, sweetheart?"

The dimpled chin went up a belligerent inch or two.

"I not a wheat haht. I Roof."

Satisfied that she'd put him in his place, she attacked the mound of sand at her feet with her shovel.

"Where's your mother, Ruth?"

"Gone."

He shaded his eyes and searched the beach. Except for him and the child, it was empty. Had something tragic happened to the mother? She couldn't have been gone long, or surely the child would have been crying.

"What are you building?"

"A dog."

"A doghouse?"

"No!" Ruth poked out her lips and lowered her eyebrows at him. "A dog. *My* dog."

"I see." He laughed again, enchanted by the child's imagination and determination. "What are you going to name your dog?"

"Dange'wus."

"A dog named Dangerous. I like it." His quest for wading in the water completely forgotten, he stretched out beside the child and reached toward her creation in the sand. "May I help?"

"No!" Her lips poked out once more, and she shoved

with a strength amazing in such a tiny person. Her strong will more than made up for her lack of size.

Everything about her delighted him. If he'd had children, he'd have wanted one exactly like Ruth.

"Okay, then. I'll just watch."

She'd left sand on his hand where she'd shoved. As he watched those tiny dimpled hands working on her *"dog,"* Max rubbed the sand back and forth between his fingers, back and forth, back and forth, until the friction became heat, and the heat became an eroticism unlike any he'd ever known.

"Ruth!"

He had forgotten about the mother until he heard her scream. She raced toward them, dark-auburn hair flying in the wind and a large straw bag banging against her tight jeans. Her toe caught in a piece of driftwood buried in the sand, and she lost her hold on the bag. It landed only inches from Max, its contents spilled over the sand—lipstick, suntan oil, hairbrush . . . and a pair of panties.

The bit of black lace had a sassy red bow at the waist and a rip down the side. Max let his eyes roam boldly over the woman whose calling card lay on the beach. She was early thirties, he guessed, stunningly beautiful, her hair disheveled from more than the wind, and her nipples pointed hard as diamonds beneath her thin white shirt. She had the tall, regal body of an aristocrat and the lush mouth and smoky eyes of a courtesan.

He hooked his index finger through the tear in the panties, then slowly stood up.

"Your calling card," he said.

She didn't pretend outrage, didn't protest, didn't even reach for the panties. Instead she treated him to the same bold perusal he'd given her.

"Do you like what you see?" he asked.

"That depends."

"On what?"

"On your generosity."

They studied each other with the possessive looks of predators who understood the quarry was already theirs. The woman wet her lips with her tongue in slow, provocative invitation.

"When I get what I want, I can be very generous." Never taking his eyes from her, Max stuffed the bit of black lace into his pants pocket.

"I can give you *exactly* what you want." The woman smiled. "I'm Margaret Anne Bellafontaine, and this is my daughter, Ruth."

"We've already met." He squatted back beside the child and touched the top of her head. One soft, shiny curl had wrapped itself around his finger. He rubbed the silky strand between his thumb and forefinger. Back and forth. Back and forth. "You shouldn't leave her unattended."

"I could see her from the car."

"I could have snatched her and been gone before you got here."

"It took me a while to get my clothes back on." Margaret Anne bent to retrieve her lipstick, then carefully painted her lips. "I'm a good mother. I do whatever is necessary for my child."

"Pickups on the beach will no longer be necessary."

Sensing her advantage, Margaret Anne smiled. She didn't yet know his name, but the Jaguar on the edge of the beach and the Gucci watch on his arm were all the references she'd needed. He would be her ticket home.

"I'll want a house," she said ". . . in Mississippi."

"Mississippi?"

"Yes. I promised myself I'd go back one day and show them all."

He didn't have to ask what she'd show them. He'd known. A woman picking up men on the beach was hungry for something she didn't have, something he could give her—money and the prestige to go with it. What did it matter where he kept her? In fact, Mississippi would be perfect, about as far removed from Hollywood as he could get. No spying eyes. No scandal.

"Done."

He patted the sand and Margaret Anne sank down beside him. With one hand still in Ruth's hair, he opened his zipper and Margaret Anne's hand slid inside. Without a sound she demonstrated that she was worth the price of a house, and more.

In the single-minded way of children, Ruth ignored

them and pounded the sand with her shovel, intent on making herself a dog.

When Max's release came, it had not been the sensation of sleek wetness that had dominated his mind, but the soft whisper of silky curls between his fingers. With the gut-level instinct that had made him one of the most successful filmmakers in the business, Max understood that he had bargained not for the mother, but for the child.

Ruth. Worth any price.

The high-pitched whine in his wife's voice brought him back to the present.

"I'm going to have to fire her." Betsy's mouth was so pinched with bitterness and petulance that her lipstick bled into the deep groves and made her look as if she'd sprouted pink whiskers.

"Fine." Max didn't know whom she was talking about. And didn't care. "Whatever you want to do."

"She's totally untrustworthy. Yesterday I caught her spraying herself with the perfume I brought from Paris. As if I'd lost my sense of smell along with everything else."

Max shoved back his chair. He had given the woman everything money could buy. He wasn't about to sit still and endure another of Betsy's lengthy monologues on what she had lost.

"I'm leaving town," he said.

"I'll manage on my own." Betsy patted her lips with the white linen napkin, smearing the lipstick even more. "I always have."

She never asked where he was going, never inquired how long he planned to stay. Long ago they'd come to an understanding. When she had caught him in his office with a sixteen-year-old, she had promised silence in return for a guaranteed lifetime of being Mrs. Maxwell Jones with all the privileges of that title, including an unlimited budget. Though the teenager was a known piece of work with acting aspirations, besides, he'd agreed to the terms, promising never again to do anything that might cause his wife public humiliation. Betsy was essential to him—the kind of placid, socially acceptable woman who could provide a safe cover.

The key to keeping his promise was not to get caught.

Get far enough out of town, and anything was possible. That was his motto.

"Have a nice time, darling," she said when he reached the door. It was one of the things he hated most about her, her insistence on pretending the public image of them as a happily married couple was true, even in private.

What would she do if he told her he planned to have a nice time with a girl who was barely fifteen? Would she drop her ridiculous sham if he told her how it had felt to have that sweet, tight young body beneath him?

For two years he'd thought of nothing except having Ruth again. He'd been a fool to agree to only two weeks with her.

It was time to do something about it.

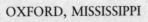

10.

OXFORD, MISSISSIPPI

THE THUNDERBIRD CONVERTIBLE parked in the driveway was sky-blue.

Shifting her books to one hip, Ruth ran her hand over the front fender. The sun coming down through the branches of the oak tree glinted on the polished chrome and reflected off the pristine windows.

A brand-spanking-new sports car. Every teenager's dream.

She set her books on the sidewalk and cupped her face against the glare of the sun so she could see inside. The seats matched the paint job. Sky-blue. The softest-looking leather she'd ever seen.

Who could be visiting her mother in a convertible? It must be somebody old, or they'd be driving with the top down in such pretty spring weather.

It was exactly the kind of car she'd

imagined her father would drive when he returned. For a moment she pictured how he would look: tall and distinguished and handsome, the handsomest man in all of Mississippi, sitting in the living room waiting to take her away.

Setting her books on her hip, she hurried up the sidewalk. Miranda pounced out of the forsythia bushes, tiny yellow flowers caught in her fur like stars. She arched her back and rubbed herself ecstatically against Ruth's legs.

Brought quickly back to the real world, Ruth's silly dreams of her father vanished. She was too old for such childish dreams.

Too old and far too wise.

She scooped up her cat and carried her inside, not because Miranda wanted it, but because Margaret Anne didn't. Ruth slammed the door as loud as she could, then yelled in her most unladylike voice.

"Clear the decks, Margaret Anne! I'm home."

The sight of her quickened Max's pulse.

For two years he'd kept his bargain. He'd stayed away, contenting himself with secondhand news through Margaret Anne and the occasional good fortune of having Ruth answer the phone when he called.

Now he called himself a fool.

Ruth stood in the doorway holding her cat to her breasts. She'd grown tall during his absence, taller than Margaret Anne. Her figure had budded, too, breasts softly rounded and pressing against the T-shirt she wore, her hips flaring slightly, her legs curved and firm beneath her blue jeans. And yet she still had the wholesome, innocent look of a child.

His erection was immediate and intense. He wanted her as he'd never wanted another person in his life. She was child-woman, provocative innocence, chaste seductress, virginal wanton.

"Happy birthday, sweetheart."

"Go screw yourself, Max."

"Ruth! Must you be so sharp-tongued?" Margaret Anne opened the top button of her blouse and patted at the perspiration on the front of her chest with a lace-edged handkerchief.

"Yes. And my claws are even sharper than my tongue. Perhaps you should warn *Uncle* Max."

Max laughed. "You're still as feisty as you were when I first saw you on the beach thirteen years ago, Ruth. I'm glad to see that some things never change."

"Oh, I've changed, all right. *You* saw to that."

"Pay her no attention, Max. She doesn't understand gratitude."

"It's not gratitude he wants from me, Margaret Anne." Spots of anger rouged Ruth's cheeks, and her eyes shot fire as she swung toward him. "Is it, Max?"

"No. I've come to claim what's mine."

He opened a box and spread its contents on the coffee table—an exquisite silk dress. White, befitting a virgin. A shaft of sunlight gleamed on the string of pearls he arranged at the neckline.

"You'll wear it in Paris." His eyes raked Ruth from head to toe. "And when we return, these will be yours."

He took a set of car keys from his pocket and dangled them from his fingers. He didn't have to say more. She'd seen the Thunderbird in the driveway.

In spite of her anger, Ruth could not hide her excitement. He saw it in the widening of her eyes, in the way her tongue flicked out and licked her bottom lip.

Victory was within his grasp. He could see it, feel it, smell it, taste it.

"Three months, Ruth," he said. "That's all I'm asking. Your summer vacation. And when you return, the Thunderbird convertible will be yours."

He swung the keys back and forth, watching her. Without warning Ruth shut down. One minute she was a teenager drooling over a new sports car, and the next she was the child-woman he'd seen in New Orleans, the one whose face told nothing and whose iron control belied her tender years.

With great deliberation she set her cat on the floor and her books on the sofa. Then she picked up the box and left the room, Miranda tagging after her.

Max jiggled the keys in his hands. Nervous. All because of a fifteen-year-old.

"Ruth!" Margaret Anne called after her. "Come back here."

A door somewhere in the back of the house slammed. Margaret Anne shrugged her shoulders.

"She's impossible."

"No. She's just high-spirited." He glanced in the direction Ruth had disappeared. "I wonder what she's doing?"

"Thinking over your offer, I would imagine. What teenager could resist that car?"

He remembered how she'd been at the age of two. Stubborn. Independent. Determined.

"Ruth," he said.

"I have to admire her spunk. Even if she does drive me crazy. Tea, Max?"

"Yes. I might as well do something while I wait." He would have gone after any other woman and enforced his will on her. But with Ruth he was different, had always been different. He wanted more than her body: He wanted her soul.

Silently, Margaret Anne prepared his tea. He diverted himself watching her small ritual, the way she crooked her little finger outward while she poured, the way she pursed her lips while she measured the sugar. She was still an extremely attractive woman.

Her perfume wafted over him as she set his teacup on the coffee table. Her scent, the gardenias that bloomed outside her cottage in the summertime, would always remind him of the Deep South. Something akin to regret passed over him.

"A penny for your thoughts, Max."

"Just remembering."

Her smile was knowing. "I'll go to Paris with you, and it won't cost you a car."

"You used to drive a harder bargain than that, Margaret Anne. What's happened to your spirit?"

"Adversity has a way of wearing the spirit down."

"Don't let it wear you down. I need you to be strong."

"Why? You don't require my presence in your bed anymore."

"To take care of Ruth."

To her credit Margaret Anne didn't show any anger. Max had always admired her ability to handle herself like a lady. He felt a stirring of feelings bordering on respect.

Lifting his teacup, he studied her in silence. Suddenly he stiffened.

"What's that smell?"

Smoke drifted under the door. In the hallway the fire alarm blared.

"Good grief." Margaret Anne started from her chair, covering her heart with her free hand.

"What the hell . . ."

Max's cup clattered against the saucer as Ruth walked through the door carrying a large copper pot. Trails of smoke and the stench of something burning filled the room. Without fanfare she set the pot on the coffee table in front of him.

Her eyes mesmerized him. They were black as the pits of hell and just as full of fire.

This slip of a girl, this mere child, was *challenging* him. Maxwell Jones.

In Hollywood dozens of grown men all but bowed to him when he walked into a room. Scores hung on his every word. A few hated him and plotted his downfall. But *nobody* defied him the way Ruth Bellafontaine did.

She made him feel alive in a way that no other person could.

Smoke curled between them. If he hadn't been a civilized man, he'd have ripped aside her clothes and taken her on the floor.

"Ruth . . . what in the world?" Margaret Anne approached the pot cautiously. Standing on tiptoe, she peered inside. The silk dress lay on the bottom of the pot, charred beyond repair, and the cultured pearls had been reduced to their beginnings, tiny glass beads scattered among the folds of the ruined dress.

"Your dress . . . and the pearls. Oh, my God, the *pearls*." Spots of color burned in Margaret Anne's cheeks. "Those beautiful gifts. How could you? Any woman in the world would be proud to wear them . . . and you *burned* them."

"Why don't you wear them, Mother? Sackcloth and ashes might be a nice change of pace for you."

Max had always been partial to drama. He couldn't have enjoyed a spectacle more if he'd planned it himself.

It almost made up for his disappointment.

He leaned back on the sofa, picked up his cup, and took a sip of cold tea.

"I take it this means you've declined my offer."

"You take it right, Max. I've already fulfilled my bargain with the devil."

Ruth turned on her heel and marched from the room, her head high and her hips swaying in the unconsciously provocative manner of a woman born to love.

Max smiled. He had patience and power, an unbeatable combination. It might be years before Ruth would be his, but she was worth the wait.

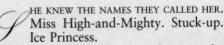

11.

*S*HE KNEW THE NAMES THEY CALLED HER. Miss High-and-Mighty. Stuck-up. Ice Princess.

The last thing Ruth wanted was to be talked about. All she wanted to do was blend in with the crowd, pass through the rest of her school years unnoticed so that she could get out of her mother's house, get out of Oxford, and start a new life.

In the meantime she had the present to deal with. And Wanda was no help at all.

"Charles is nice. So are Bill and Fred. And Jimmy's asked you *twice*. You've got to go to the dance with *somebody*, Ruth."

"Why?"

"Because . . . if you don't go, you'll miss all the fun."

"Going with one of those clowns would be about as much fun as going to the dentist."

"So suffer. But you've *got* to go."

"You keep saying that, Wanda."

"Everybody's *talking* about you, Ruth."

Ruth retreated into silence. Wanda shifted her books from one hip to the other, then kicked a soda can lying on the sidewalk. She had reached her full height at fourteen, while Ruth continued to shoot up like a weed. Now, at fifteen, Ruth was a good head taller than Wanda, with every indication that she would be even more so.

What Wanda lacked in stature, she made up for in grit.

"If you don't go, I won't go."

"Okay."

Wanda heaved a big sigh and tried again.

"You're the prettiest girl in school. You could have any boy you want."

"I don't want any of them."

"You're just being stubborn."

For a moment Ruth considered telling Wanda why she didn't want to go to the dance, why she didn't want to go anywhere with any boy. "Do you remember the week I stayed at your house?" That's how she would start the conversation, and then the rest would come tumbling out and Ruth wouldn't have to carry the guilty secret all by herself anymore.

A robin hopped off the sidewalk and began tugging at a worm in Mrs. Bingham's yard. Spring had come again. The season of promise.

Suddenly Ruth felt lighthearted.

"Do you remember . . ."

"Did you hear . . ."

Stopping in the middle of the sidewalk, they looked at each other and giggled.

"You first," Wanda said.

"No. You."

"Okay, but you're going to just die when you hear this. Absolutely *die*."

"Wanda!"

"Promise you won't tell a soul."

"Cross my heart and hope to die."

Wanda leaned close and dropped her voice to a conspiratorial whisper.

"Mary Love Struthers is *doing it* with a married man.

Meeting him twice a week at a motel in Tupelo. Doesn't that just *gross you out*? Everybody's calling her a slut."

A weight descended on Ruth's chest, and the sun faded. One moment she'd been standing on a sidewalk in the midst of a row of charming antebellum homes, and the next she was plunged into the dark, secret world of Maxwell Jones.

"Ruth . . ." Wanda caught her arm. "Are you all right?"

"I'm just a little dizzy. It's my . . . my period coming on."

"Here." Wanda shoved her books into Ruth's hand. "I'll run in and ask Mrs. Bingham for a glass of water."

"No!" Ruth hadn't meant to scream, but there it was, hanging between them, a scream of guilt and rage and shame, the scream she'd held in for two years.

Max should have been the one she'd screamed at. And Margaret Anne. Not her best friend.

There was only one thing Ruth could do to make up for it.

"I'm sorry, Wanda. Forget about the water. Let's just go to your house so we can plan what we'll wear to the dance."

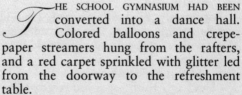

12.

THE SCHOOL GYMNASIUM HAD BEEN converted into a dance hall. Colored balloons and crepe-paper streamers hung from the rafters, and a red carpet sprinkled with glitter led from the doorway to the refreshment table.

Margaret Anne had wanted Ruth to wear white, but Ruth had insisted on red. Now, standing at the edge of the dance floor in the midst of all the pastel gowns, she was glad she had.

"Gosh, Ruth. You're the best-looking girl here."

Her date, Fred Gruber, had a long, earnest face, big ears, and a cowlick that wouldn't stay down. She'd chosen him because he was shy and had seemed the safest pick of the bunch.

"Thanks."

"You look . . . uh . . . exotic." Stretching his long neck, Fred tugged at his tie.

"Thanks." What did boys and girls say to each other?

"You must . . . uh . . . have some . . . uh . . Cherokee blood."

"Yes." Ruth had no idea whose blood ran through her veins. Silently, she damned her mother.

"Do you want to . . . uh . . . dance?"

No. Standing close together. Bodies touching.

Ruth wiped sweat from her face with the back of her hand.

"Ladies don't sweat, Ruth."

Her mother. The lady. The whore.

Fred was staring at her. Had she said something aloud? Oh, help. Just let her dance one dance and get it over with. Then she'd say she had a terrible stomach virus and had to go home.

"Let's dance," she said.

Ruth braced herself, but she wasn't fully prepared when he slid his arm around her waist. Shivers ran through her, and she stiffened.

Fortunately, Fred didn't notice. He pulled her into the middle of the crowd, then stepped back and began to move with a loose-jointed grace that surprised her.

Fast music. No touching. The beat slid under Ruth's skin and thrummed along her veins.

"Hey . . . Ruth . . . you're *great.*"

She could do this. She could survive. Relief made her feel generous.

"Thanks, Fred. So are you."

All the numbers in the first set were fast. Somebody up there must be watching over her, she thought. While they were cooling off with a glass of punch, she promised herself that she'd show her gratitude by saying her prayers every day and going to church even on the Sundays the choir didn't sing.

Now that the dancing was over, she and Fred were back to the awkward stage of not knowing what to say to each other. Wanda and her date rescued Ruth by stopping by to chat.

One by one the muscles along the back of her neck began to relax. Gradually, she found that she could laugh without trying and even put together a witty statement or two that had everybody else laughing.

Wanda dragged her off to the bathroom for girl talk. "Isn't it great?"

"It's kind of fun," Ruth said, and really meant it. Maybe she was normal, after all. Grinning, she laced her arm through her friend's. "Let's go back out there and dazzle them."

Fred was waiting for her by the punch bowl. He had ditched his tie and unfastened the top buttons of his shirt. The grin on his face made him look like a friendly puppy.

"Let's go outside a minute and cool off, Ruth," he said.

Alone with Fred in the dark. She couldn't do it.

The band had started playing again, something slow and bluesy. On the dance floor bodies merged, clung, swayed.

Going outside seemed the lesser of two evils.

"Okay."

Fred offered his hand, but she didn't take it. Outside, the stars were so bright, they looked as if they'd been polished by a host of angels, then spilled across the sky. The beauty caught in Ruth's throat, and she gazed upward, speechless. A stout spring wind stirred the swings nearby, setting the wooden seats asway and causing the chains to creak.

"Hey, you want to swing, Ruth? I'll push."

In the swing she felt like a child again. The wind ruffled her hair and carried her laughter upward while Fred pushed her so high, she could almost touch the stars.

A sense of tranquillity filled her. She could live under the stars forever, a child of nature, innocent and free of the dark chains that bound her. The wind stung her cheeks and blew her tears back into her hair.

Higher and higher the swing carried her. Dreams she'd thought were dead came to life again, dreams of music and beauty and harmony. Someday, somewhere, she'd find the place of her dreams. She'd take Miranda, then get lots and lots more pets, and there would be nothing but joy and kindness and love in her life—*real* love.

When Fred stopped the swing and came to stand in front of her, Ruth looked up at him, exhilarated, laughing.

He moved so fast, she didn't see it coming. Suddenly he was on her, pressing her back against the hard wooden seat, trapping her between the heavy chains.

"Stop it, Fred."

His breathing was heavy against her ear, and his hand was under her skirt.

Max was sliding his fingers into her, saying things she didn't want to hear.

"I'm giving you what you wanted, Ruth. What you begged for."

She covered her ears with her hands. She wouldn't listen.

"Beg for it."

"Please," she whispered. "Pleasepleasepleaseplease."

"Man oh man. You're hot, Ruth. Hotter than a hot tamale."

Plunging his hand down the front of her dress, he groped for her breast.

Who would hear her if she screamed? Where would she go if she ran?

She clenched her hands so tight, the chains bit into her flesh. Flinging her head back, she saw the stars watching her shame.

"Man, I just knew under all that Ice Princess stuff you'd be like this."

"Max taught me first, Ruth, taught me first, taught me first . . ."

"Come on, Ruth. Let go of the swing so we can get it on."

Ruth let go of the chains. A cloud passed over the moon, and the stars hid their faces from her.

Fred closed in on her, panting, his mouth open and his eyes watery.

Ruth aimed for the eyes. She raked with both hands, fingers stiff, nails bared. His howl of outrage was muffled by the fist she slammed into his mouth.

Shoving as hard as she could, she came out of the swing. Freedom was only a few steps away.

He caught her skirt as she raced toward the gym.

"Ruth, what the hell's got into you?"

Max. When I was only thirteen.

She heard her skirt tear as she jerked out of Fred's grasp. Then she was off and running. Not toward the gym. Not toward the crowd. With her skirt in tatters, she couldn't face them.

Her house was two miles away in the dark. Using all her reserves of energy, she sprinted toward home.

"Ruth . . . come back here."

Footsteps behind her. Fred was following. She was a fast sprinter, but what would happen if he caught her?

She stopped and faced him, fists doubled, chin thrust out.

"If you come one step closer, I'm going to scream as loud as I can."

Fred stared at her, hesitant. There was blood on his cheek where she'd scratched him.

"Run away, cock teaser. See if I care."

Suddenly she was sucked into a dark tunnel filled with white silk sheets and the cloying odor of white roses.

"You're good, Ruth. The best."

"No. I'm not." *"You were born for this, Ruth."* She covered her ears with her hands. "I'm not."

"You talk the talk but you won't walk the walk. Cock teaser."

"Beg for it."

"Please . . ."

"Say it like you mean it."

"Please . . ." She held up her hand, warding him off. Darkness swirled just behind her eyelids, and her breath came in ragged spurts. If Max did that to her again, she though she might pass out.

He was laughing. It rang in her ears like the church bell that tolled when somebody died.

Her vision cleared, and she saw that it was not Max laughing, but Fred.

Rage washed over her.

She'd lived every waking moment of the last two years in fear that somebody would discover her dark secret. She'd been so careful. And now all her efforts were in vain. All because of a jerk named Freddie.

She bent over and scooped up the biggest rock she

could find. "If you take one more step, I'm going to hit you right between the eyes."

His steps slowed and his grin faded. She drew back her arm and wound up. Anybody who had seen her pitch on the baseball team in elementary school knew her aim was deadly.

"Now, Ruth . . . don't get your panties in a wad."

She'd won. The trembling started in her legs, but she bit down hard on her lip.

"And if you ever tell, I'm going to beat the living shit out of you."

"Okay . . . okay." He held up his hands if he were already warding off her blows.

She didn't wait to see whether he changed his mind. Filling her lungs with oxygen, she ran as hard as she could. The familiar landscape was a blur to her. She counted on instincts and habit to guide her in the right direction.

The smell of flowers almost overwhelmed her—wisteria cascading down the hillsides, azaleas massed along white-columned front porches, dogwood dripping delicate white blossoms onto newly greening lawns.

Flowers. Always the flowers. Would she never outrun the smell?

"Nothing but white flowers for you, Ruth, the flowers of a virgin."

Max folded back the silk sheet, and she waited. The sweet scent of flowers washed over her, reminding her of the small death that was to come.

A sharp bark brought her to her senses. The brown terrier growled and nipped at her heels. She realized she'd been standing on the sidewalk, lost once more in Max's world.

Run. Run. She filled her lungs with oxygen and raced onward.

The car appeared suddenly out of the night, its horn blaring at her. With a screeching of brakes, it came to a halt in the middle of the street, a dark, hulking menace.

"Hey! Sugar!"

Run! Ruth swerved toward a stand of oak trees. Glancing back over her shoulder, she saw a large man step into the glare of headlights.

"Hey," he called. "Wait."

Panicked, she looked for a means of escape. The car was in front of her, a large fence behind her.

"Hey . . . babe . . ."

Her skirt ripped as she scaled the fence. Ruth raced on, leaving bits of red clinging to the chain links like blood.

A heel broke off one shoe, and she almost lost her balance. Ruth flailed the air, then raced on, lopsided.

Run. Run.

A ditch was coming up. It was deep, filled with water from the spring rains. Could she make it? What if she fell in and broke her leg?

Somewhere behind her was a man who had leered at her and called her *babe*. Taking a deep breath, she jumped. Her landing was solid, but the heel on her good shoe was hopelessly mired in the mud.

She struggled to pull it out. Was that a noise behind her? The bushes on the other side of the ditch were moving. There would be no silk sheets and white roses for her this time. Only the dirty, knowing grin of a stranger, then the awful invasion.

Biting down on the scream that formed in her throat, Ruth jerked her foot out of the shoe, then left it behind in the mud. Behind her a dog barked.

Would she never be able to stop running?

Pleasegodpleasegod.

Her house appeared suddenly, as if a giant hand had dropped it out of the sky. Breathless, she flung herself against the trunk of a massive magnolia tree. Its slick shiny leaves cloaked her.

She stood under the tree three minutes, three hours, three days. Time was meaningless to her. There was nothing except the silent screams and the awful need to vanish from the face of the earth.

Her mother must not see her. That much was paramount. Using a stealth she didn't know she possessed, Ruth somehow managed to get through the back door and up the stairs without being caught.

Inside her room she leaned against the door. A stream of moonlight coming through the windows fell across her, and she saw the pale shadow of herself in the pier mirror across the room. Her skirt was in tatters, and her eyes glowed like coal in skin that was too dark ever to be called peaches and cream, too dark, even, to be called olive.

Ruth put her hands to her cheeks.

"Who am I?"

"Ruth?" It was her mother, knocking at the door. "Is that you?"

Ruth didn't know. Was it she? Or was it a horrible clone of her mother staring back at her from the mirror, a dark, passionate girl-woman made for the pleasures of men?

The knocking was loud and insistent. Ruth could picture her mother's rage, the fair skin flushed a bright rose and her eyes snapping blue fire.

"Ruth? What are you doing home so early? Ruth! Answer me."

Ruth pressed her hands to her ears, but she could still hear the banging. If she didn't answer, it would never stop.

"Fred . . . got sick. And we had to leave."

"I didn't hear his car. Why didn't I hear his car?"

"It . . . ran out of gas. I had to walk the last block home."

Silence. Did Margaret Anne believe her lies?

"Did you have fun?"

Had she? She'd said *pleasepleaseplease*. Had she been begging Fred to stop or begging him to continue?

"Ruth? Why don't you come down and tell me about the dance? I was having a cup of tea. We'll sit in the kitchen together. It will be just like old times."

When she was five, she'd given her mother a homemade valentine, a crooked red-felt heart pasted on a piece of paper bearing the message "I luv U, Ruth." When she was six and had to stand in front of the class at show-and-tell, she'd shown a picture of Margaret Anne. "This is my mother. She plays the piano and sings, and sometimes she lets me help make cookies. I want to grow up to be a beautiful lady just like my mother."

If having a cup of tea in the kitchen would bring back old times, Ruth would be willing to drink a gallon.

But nothing could bring back the old times. Things had

been broken that could never be fixed. A heart. Dreams. Trust.

Didn't her mother know that?

Ruth turned on the television to drown out the sound of knocking.

"The Science Network is proud to bring you tonight's special on the Corday Foundation," the announcer said.

"Ruth!"

She turned up the volume. "The Corday Foundation was established by Dr. Joseph Corday in the late fifties," the disembodied voice screamed at her.

What did she care when it was established? She no longer wanted to be part of a place that established foundations, and sponsored dances where boys could run wild, and tolerated mothers who sold their daughters.

Photographs of a jungle flashed across the screen—and mountains so beautiful, they would have taken her breath away if she'd had any left to take.

"Primarily the work of Dr. Corday and his wife, photo-journalist Eleanor Sims Corday, the foundation now boasts another member of the family, Dr. Brett Corday. Dr. Corday, will you tell us something of your background?"

Ruth turned toward the bathroom. The voice of Dr. Brett Corday followed her there. It was a deep, mesmerizing voice, rather like music.

Ruth didn't want to be mesmerized. She closed the door to shut out the mellifluous voice of Dr. Brett Corday.

There were no windows in the bathroom, and it took her a while to adjust her eyes to the total darkness. But she didn't want the light. She didn't want to see her torn dress and her black eyes that had seen too much.

Faintly, she could make out the outline of the medicine chest. The latch clicked as she reached inside for the bottle of aspirin.

How many would it take? She took out the whole bottle.

Panic seized her, and she felt cold all over. Shivering, she held the bottle to her chest. Was she making a mistake?

Last year everybody had mourned when Brad Howitt

had been found dead in his bed. What a sad and lonely
way to go, they'd said, as if he'd decided to go off on a trip
to some distant and foreign country all by himself. A few
had said how brave.

She hoped they would say nothing about her. If she
knew someplace they'd never find her, she'd go, but she
didn't, so there was no use looking.

She closed her eyes. "Don't think about this. Just do
it."

"Welcome," the announcer of the Science Network said
when she opened her door, as if he were personally delighted to have her back in her own bedroom.

She hurried to the TV to snap it off when the image of a
gorilla filled the screen. The sassy look on its face reminded her of Miranda.

Ruth had forgotten about her cat. Who would feed Miranda after she was gone?

"Welcome to the Science Network, Dr. Brett Corday."

The camera panned back, and Ruth saw that the gorilla
was perched in the arms of a man who looked more like
Heathcliff of *Wuthering Heights* than a scientist.

"And who is this young lady with you?"

"This is Cee Cee." Dr. Brett Corday turned and looked
right at Ruth. She sucked in her breath. The right side of
his face was movie-star handsome, breathtaking. The left
side had a thin curving scar along his cheek and a leather
patch over his eye. It gave him the dark, dangerous look of
a pirate. He stared right at her, his good eye black, bright,
intelligent, accusatory.

Coward.

Her hand trembled on the bottle. "I don't care what
you think," she whispered.

"Two years ago Cee Cee's mother was brutally mur-
dered by poachers." Dr. Corday spoke with an intense
passion of this violent act that had snuffed out life. Ruth
looked down at the aspirin bottle, ashamed.

"I brought her to the Corday Foundation to live with
me. She now considers me her mother." He hugged the
baby gorilla and said, "I love you, Cee Cee."

Ruth's shame tripled. Who would hug Miranda and tell
her how wonderful she was? Who would tell her that she

was the best cat in the whole world and say, "I love you, Miranda?"

Postponing her quest for oblivion, Ruth sank onto the carpet, where she sat cross-legged in front of the television. Dr. Corday sat on a chair facing her, his stare burning a hole through her.

Did he see her dark secret? Her guilt? Her fear?

Mesmerized, she watched him. The gorilla reached up and traced the faint line that curved around his cheek, then touched his eye patch as tenderly as a child touches his mother. Showing her teeth in an enormous gorilla smile, Cee Cee moved her fingers.

"What did she say?" the announcer asked.

"Cee Cee said, 'I love you.'"

The bottle rolled out of Ruth's hand and under the bed. Miranda came out, stretching and yawning. With the grace of her jungle ancestors, she pounced onto Ruth's lap, then curled into a ball, purring.

"Oh, Miranda . . . Miranda." Ruth pressed her face into her cat's soft fur. "I love you. I never meant to leave you. Never!"

Miranda patted Ruth's face as if to say, *I know. I understand. And I love you, anyway.*

"This is it, folks," the announcer said. "The gorilla who talks."

Still hugging her cat, Ruth hitched forward. An animal that could talk! For years she'd known they would have lots to say if only they knew how to say it. Her dog Dangerous had had ways of communicating so that Ruth could understand, and Miranda was so demonstrative, she was practically human.

"For the last two years Dr. Brett Corday has not only been raising the gorilla, he's been teaching her to communicate using American Sign Language. Will you explain how that works, Dr. Corday?"

"Because of prior language studies that had been done with primates, I knew the gorilla was capable of communication. Initially I used the method of repetition. Cee Cee rapidly acquired a basic vocabulary."

"Dr. Corday, there are skeptics who say that these primates are merely imitating what they've seen again and again, that the skills they have can't be termed 'real language.'"

"If you had heard what Cee Cee said to me yesterday about not getting her snack to her on time, you wouldn't have any doubt that she not only knows how to use the language, but she's capable of abstract thought."

"Can you really talk, Cee Cee?" Lights gleamed on the announcer's bald head as he leaned close to the gorilla.

Cee Cee stuck out her tongue at him, then proceeded to make rapid-fire movements with her fingers.

Dr. Corday's hearty laughter filled Ruth's bedroom, and with it came the first hope she'd felt in two years.

"What did she say?"

"Cee Cee said, 'Egg man dumb.' She insulted you not once but twice, first by referring to your baldness and then by denigrating your intelligence."

"Well, I'll be . . . ." The announcer broke into a sheepish grin.

Wild horses couldn't have dragged Ruth from the TV set after that. She leaned forward and hung on Dr. Corday's every word.

Project Cee Cee was his life. He spent every waking moment with her deep in the jungles of Central Africa teaching her to communicate. When he spoke of the Virungas, it was with the passion of a lover. Chills went through Ruth.

"Think of the possibilities," he said. "We're training her in the wild. Someday we'll reintroduce her into her natural habitat. Her first desire will be to communicate with the other gorillas. Will she teach them to use sign language, or will she adopt their ways and forget hers? But most important, can and will she tell us what they know?"

Dr. Corday's voice drew Ruth deep into possibilities she'd never dreamed of. When the program was over, she turned off the television, then sat in front of the blank screen, still seeing a dark, craggy face with a leather eye patch.

She owed her life to him. He had come in her time of greatest need. For two years she'd been a shell, a shadow. Now a tiny glimmer of light shone in the dark places of her soul, and dreams she'd thought dead began to stir to life.

She stretched her hand toward the television and traced the line where his scar had been, upward toward his leather eye patch. As her hand rested flat on the blank screen, she tasted the salt of her own tears.

"Thank you, Dr. Corday," she whispered.

A strange energy pulsed through her palm as if she had miraculously connected with the dark, mesmerizing man who had touched her from a distance and given her hope.

Book Two

13.

OAHU, HAWAII, 1994

MALONE WAS SICK OF GORILLAS. EVERY-
where he went, it was Cee Cee
this and Cee Cee that. Endless
questions. Microphones thrust into his
face. Spotlights making him sweat.

"Does Cee Cee really paint pictures?"

"Does she understand what she's saying?"

"Does she really *cuss*?"

That last question always made him
laugh. Just a week before, she'd called him
a dirty stinkpot, all because he'd said she
looked ridiculous in her pink hair bow.
Brett encouraged her by laughing at everything she did.

That gorilla was getting too big for her
britches. So was his brother, for that matter.

What right did Brett have to send him
off on these stupid fund-raising tours?

Brett was far better suited for public appearances. And Malone had told him so. But Brett had been adamant.

"You're the best man for the job, Malone. One look at that sincere, innocent face, and donors can't wait to write out big checks."

"Cut the bull, Brett. What they really want is you."

"I don't care what they want. I'm not going to leave Cee Cee. Every day in her development is crucial. Besides, I don't like to leave the Virungas."

"Screw the Virungas."

"See. You need a change of scenery. It will do you good to get away."

What he wanted was to get away permanently. He longed for a simple life in a simple town where he could practice his veterinary medicine and raise lots of dogs and children. Hawaii wasn't bad, but it was too exotic, and in that respect too much like the Virungas.

Someday he'd go somewhere and have a life of his own, maybe Texas or Alabama or Virginia. In the meantime Brett needed him—Brett, who had sacrificed his eye for his brother.

He glanced up from his notes at the crowd filling the hall. The woman in the back of the room stood out like a rose in an onion patch. It wasn't her clothes that set her apart, the simple white dress that skimmed her curves, nor even her face and body, awesome as they were. It was her presence. Walking down the center aisle, she commanded the auditorium as if it were her kingdom. Heads turned as she passed by. Women whispered behind their hands. Men wolf-whistled.

Malone turned to the young man sitting on the stage with him, Rick O'Callaghan, president of the Society of Anthropology.

"Who is she?"

Rick didn't have to ask who he was talking about.

"The Polynesian princess?"

"Really? She's a princess?"

"Who knows? Some call her a voodoo witch."

"I believe it. I'm already under her spell."

"Well, good luck, pal. Ruth Bellafontaine is unapproachable. She can freeze a man at twenty paces with that icy stare of hers."

It wasn't frostbite that Malone was getting, but something at the other end of the temperature zone. Caught up in his own private inferno, he stared at her, couldn't take his eyes off her, even after his name was called and he was deep into his lecture. Fortunately, it was a spiel he'd made so many times, he could have delivered it with a pack of wild dogs snarling at his heels.

Dark, exotic, mysterious, Ruth stared back at him. He didn't know half of what he said, but he guessed he'd made sense, for when his lecture was over, his audience applauded, then pressed toward him for further questions.

He craned his neck, trying to see over their heads. He couldn't see the white dress. He'd lost her.

"Dr. Corday?"

Suddenly she was there, standing in front of him, perfectly beautiful, perfectly poised. He tried to smooth down his cowlick and straighten his tie at the same time. She was going to think he was a complete idiot.

"Yes?" He tried to sound wise and generous.

"I'm Ruth Bellafontaine, a graduate student here at the university. Your lecture was tremendous."

"Thank you." The way he sounded, he might as well have scuffed his feet and said, "Aw shucks, ma'am."

"No. Thank *you*. For more than the lecture, actually. I owe my being here to Dr. Brett Corday."

Always Brett.

"My brother."

"He's your brother?" Her smile was glorious. All because of Brett. "I was only fifteen when I saw him on television. I'll never forget it."

So what if she wants to talk about Brett? Seize the opportunity, fool.

"Why don't we go somewhere quiet so we can talk about it?" They'd said she was unapproachable. He was careful not to take her arm. "I think there's a coffee shop around the corner."

"Maybe . . . just a quick cup. I'm . . . not working tonight."

They sat on opposite sides of the booth. He wished he

had the boldness to reach for her hand—at *least* her hand —but he still had a cowlick and the awkwardness that went with it, especially around beautiful women, and she was the most exquisite woman he'd ever known.

Tongue-tied, he stared at her.

"I could hardly believe my eyes when I saw that you'd be lecturing here," she said.

He couldn't believe his eyes, either. Or his good fortune. She smelled like something good to eat. The waitress took their order, coffee for her, coffee and a sweet roll for him, when actually he'd wanted to order Ruth Bellafontaine, sprinkled with sugar, wrapped in cellophane, and delivered in a take-out bag. He'd take her back to his hotel room and . . . His mind boggled at the thought of what he would do. Trapped as he was between the steamy jungles of Africa and an endless parade of hotel rooms in strange cities, he had had very few occasions to test his limited appeal to the opposite sex.

"I owe my being here to your brother," Ruth said.

"Yeah?" Scintillating conversation, certain to inspire awe in his listener. "He's quite a guy, my brother. You know him?" *Idiot. She said she'd seen him on television.* "I mean . . . you said you were fifteen . . ." *Great.* He pulled on his tie, loosening, then tightening, the knot. "He's such a celebrity . . . not like that Hollywood mess, but . . ." He grabbed his tie and nearly choked himself to death with the knot.

She laughed, but he could tell it was not *at* him. It was a beautiful laugh. Full-bodied, sexy as hell.

He took a huge bite of sweet roll, then licked his fingers, watching her. He could have watched her for the next three days and never tired of the view.

"I feel as if I know him because of his work. What anthropology student doesn't? And in an indirect way he's responsible for my being here. I'd love to thank him in person, but thanking you is the next-best thing."

"That's me," he said, grinning. "Malone Corday. The next-best thing."

"Oh. I didn't mean that." She touched his hand, then drew back as if she'd been stung and stared down at her coffee cup.

Why, she's shy. The discovery gave him such courage that he almost laughed aloud.

"Of course you didn't," he said. "I knew the minute I saw you that you wouldn't hurt a flea. That pretty smile and soft accent. Southern, isn't it?"

"Yes. Oxford, Mississippi."

She flashed her sweet smile at him once more. He felt like a king.

"Mississippi. What brings you so far from home?"

"Scholarships."

"That's it? Scholarships?"

Scholarships and rage, Ruth thought, remembering the last confrontation she'd had with Margaret Anne.

"It's all settled," her mother had said. "Max has already paid your tuition. You'll go to the university right here in Oxford."

So her mother could keep track of her. So Max could retain his hateful hold on her.

"No. I'm going to Hawaii."

"How? Who's going to pay for it?"

"I am."

"With those dinky scholarships? Do you think that will be enough?"

"I know they won't be enough. I'll find a job."

"Doing what?"

"Anything but what *you* do."

They'd fought that bitter battle so many times that Margaret Anne no longer rose to the bait. Only the heightened color in her cheeks betrayed her.

"You'll never make it without Max's money."

"I'll show you."

And she had.

Times when she'd had nothing to eat except soup and crackers, she'd remembered a man who had transferred his courage and passion and vision to her from a distant and mysterious place.

And now she was sitting opposite his brother, a sweet, funny, charming man who made her wish for things she couldn't have: an ordinary home, an ordinary life. Even a husband and children.

But she knew better than to hope, knew better than to

reach out. She had once, during her sophomore year. Her past had been very far behind her, and she had been such a long way from home. It had seemed reasonable that, after all that time, she'd done her penance, she'd earned the right to have things normal people had.

And so she had reached out.

Eddie Lester had been his name. She'd met him at the nightclub where she sang. A nice man with a sweet smile and perfect manners, an accountant who stopped by every Thursday night for two drinks and the early show.

First he'd invited her for coffee between sets, then a picnic on the beach. In broad daylight, what harm could come? she'd asked herself. His manners had remained impeccable, even in the back of the darkened movie theater after she had finally accepted a real date.

Going out on Thursday night after her last set had become routine for them. By the end of their second month together, she had learned to trust. By the end of the fourth, she had learned to feel.

When he'd kissed her good night on the small stoop at her apartment, she'd been surprised at the quiet pleasure she'd felt.

"Eddie," she'd whispered. "Do you ever think about . . . our future?"

"Our future?"

"Yes. You know . . . a little house of our own, kids, that sort of thing."

"You're talking marriage here?"

"Yes."

"I'm already married, kid."

She'd sunk onto the top step and covered her face with her hands. Eddie had squeezed her shoulder.

"I'm sorry, Ruth. I've been meaning to tell you."

"Why? Why did you do this?"

"My wife, Ella, is . . . drab, you know, kid, the kind of good woman a man feels like a chump for saying anything bad about. And it's not that I don't love her. It's just that my life is so colorless. The first time I ever saw you sing, I thought to myself, now there's a woman who could make a man feel like somebody. And so every Thursday, when Ella goes off to her girlfriend's house to play bridge, I take you out and feel like *somebody.*"

Ruth hadn't felt like *somebody:* she'd felt soiled all over again, as if Max had suddenly come back into her life and snatched her soul.

Now she lifted her coffee cup and studied the man sitting opposite her. He didn't look like the kind of man who would snatch anybody's *spoon,* let alone soul.

And yet she'd be foolish to hope. Besides, he'd offered her nothing more than a cup of coffee.

"I thought you were going to say you were a Polynesian princess returning to claim your kingdom," Malone said.

"You've been listening to rumors."

"Yep. That's me. All ears. Are you going to mete out some appropriate punishment? Like chaining me to your ankles and dragging me across the sand?" His lopsided grin made him look like a naughty little boy.

"No," she said.

"Why not? I think I'd like that."

The conversation was getting too personal. Ruth looked at her watch.

"Look at the time. I've kept you far too long."

"Not long enough." He smoothed his cowlick. "Ruth, I'm . . . hmmm . . . staying a few days."

"How nice. There are lots of things to see here."

"I wasn't thinking of seeing the sights, I was thinking I'd like to . . ." *Fall into your arms and kiss you blind, then waltz you down the aisle and carry you back to the Virungas.* Malone Corday. Winner. ". . . see you again."

"I don't think so."

He took off his glasses, polished them slowly, then put them back on his nose.

"I know I'm no prize, but I have a big . . . heart—and all my own teeth." He stretched his mouth in a big grin. "The hair is mine, too, every stubborn straw-colored inch."

"You're such a nice, funny man." When Ruth laughed, her eyes crinkled at the corners.

"Cee Cee taught me everything I know."

"I know a few people who could benefit from her training." Suddenly her eyes were troubled. "What's it like in the Virungas?"

"Beautiful. Brutal. Lonely . . . Ruth, I want to see you again."

"Please don't take this personally, but I really don't have time for social activities. Working on my dissertation is about all I do these days."

He had so little courage . . . and so little time.

"Ruth, I have only three days."

He reached for her hand, but she snatched it away and scrambled across the seat.

He knew he was no prize, but he hadn't thought the idea of touching him would cause such panic. Under ordinary circumstances he'd have let her go, then consoled himself with beer. Lots of it.

But these were no ordinary circumstances. It wasn't every day a man found a woman like Ruth. Fate had gift wrapped her, then handed her to him on a silver platter. He'd be a fool to let her go.

"Please." He caught her wrist. "Please."

The panic left her eyes. Was that pity he saw? God, how he hated pity. *Poor Malone. So homely. So ordinary. Not at all like his brother.*

He knew the things people said about him.

He would rather be dead than have Ruth pity him.

And yet . . . he'd rather have her pity than nothing at all.

"Don't leave," he said.

Ruth sank back against the plastic seat. He picked up the napkin she'd left beside her coffee cup and folded it so the coffee stain was on the underside. Then refolded it so the stain was on top.

"I didn't mean to be rude," Ruth said. "I would never do that."

"I know. You're not like that. You're beautiful and wonderful. . . ."

"No. I'm not wonderful."

He recreased the napkin, then placed it carefully on top of his own.

"I'm not either," he said.

Her smile was so gentle, so appealing, it made his heart swell.

"Think about it," he said, plunging headlong before he could lose his courage. "We can have three lovely days together, and if at the end of that time you think I'm worse than chicken pox, you can tell me so and go about your business."

"And what will you do?" The laughter was back in her eyes.

"I'll go off to darkest Africa and lick my wounds."

"Malone, you're a perfectly charming man, and I know you're going to find some lucky woman who is perfectly willing to spend more than three days with you." She stood up and offered her hand. He'd lost. "Thank you for a lovely evening."

He squeezed her hand, holding on long enough to imagine he felt her quickened pulse.

"If you change your mind, this is where I'm staying." He wrote the number of his hotel on a fresh napkin he snatched from the holder. "Call me. For a cup of coffee. For a chat. For a lecture on the dietary habits of primates. *Anything*."

She took the napkin and walked out the door, out of his life.

Malone Corday. Loser.

He ordered another cup of coffee. Under the glare of the streetlamps, he could see her white dress pulled tightly against her hips as she walked away.

Please call.

The words on the page blurred, then faded altogether. She was too tired to study. Ruth leaned her forehead against her palm and felt the dampness. Tears. How long had it been since she'd cried? She couldn't remember.

Taking a folded tissue from her purse, she dabbed at her eyes. Crying in a public place because of Malone Corday.

No. Not Malone. That wasn't fair. He was a dear, sweet, funny man. And that was the problem. He made her hope again. Hadn't she learned not to keep hoping for things she couldn't have? Homes with roses blooming along a picket fence and a fire crackling in the grate were for the unsoiled.

She scrubbed furiously at her cheeks, then tried to concentrate on the article about Brett Corday's language studies with Cee Cee, but the tears wouldn't stop. Malone Corday had somehow unplugged a dam that was threatening to drown her, or at least embarrass her. People were beginning to stare.

Ruth put on her dark glasses, returned the magazine to the stacks, then grabbed her books and headed out the door. Bright sunshine gave the campus the picture-perfect look of a slick magazine ad touting the beauty of the islands. Hibiscus hung, red and yellow, like huge bells waiting for some naughty child to set them aringing. Scarlet poinsettias banked along the sidewalks made Ruth remember a Christmas when she was five years old and Max had given her dog, Dangerous, a blue sweater to wear when the temperature dropped low and the humidity in Mississippi made thirty degrees feel like ten. She'd wrapped her arms around him and told him she'd love him forever.

"And I'll love you forever, too, sweetheart," Max had said.

Sinking to a bench under a banyan tree, Ruth wrapped her arms around herself and shivered.

"What's a pretty lady like you doing out here all by yourself?"

The squeaky voice belonged to a fuzzy puppet, a monkey with long arms that tapped her on the shoulder. Startled, she looked over her shoulder directly into the face of a man whose glasses were steamed from the earnest sweat on his face, and whose cowlick stuck straight up like an obstinate weed.

"What in the world . . . Malone?"

"Nope. Not Malone. Hector." Malone slid onto the bench beside her, crossed his legs, and perched the puppet on the makeshift horse. "Whee! Yeah!" He used a squeaky little puppet voice as he swung his leg back and forth. "This is great, Ruth. Wanna try it. I bet old sourpuss Malone wouldn't mind."

"I think I'll pass." She could feel a smile form somewhere deep inside her and push its way upward.

"You'll miss all the fun."

"I usually do," she said.

Malone's leg stopped swinging. Turning to her, he slowly removed his glasses, wiped the steamy lenses, then put them back on his nose and studied her.

"That's what I thought," he said in his normal voice. "That both of us usually miss all the fun."

That he was perceptive shouldn't have surprised her. The Corday family couldn't have achieved what they had by mere luck.

She'd made it a practice not to look men in the eye. The eyes revealed too much. But today she made an exception. They stared at each other, she shifting her load of books, and he transferring the puppet from one leg to the other.

"Yeah," he said finally. "I've got brains . . . brains enough not to slink off to my hotel in defeat without trying one more time to convince you to go out with me."

He'd said he would be in Hawaii only three days. Two, now. What would it hurt to pretend for two days that she was innocent, to try to recapture some of the dreams?

"Where to?"

His grin was that of a small schoolboy who had just won the spelling bee.

"You mean that? You want to go somewhere with *me*?"

"I think they're selling fresh coconut on the beach, and it occurred to me that since . . . What's his name?"

"Hector."

". . . Hector has done all the work, he should get a reward."

"Hey, I'm jealous."

"You don't look jealous. You're grinning."

"That's because . . ." Malone reached for his tie, then realized he wasn't wearing one and actually blushed. "Ruth . . . do you mind if I . . . if Hector holds your hand?"

She'd stake her life that he didn't have an insincere bone in his body. And yet . . .

"You're not married, are you?"

"Nope."

"Engaged?"

"Nope."

"Have another woman waiting for you in your hotel room?"

"Actually, I had six pawing at my door this morning trying to get in, but I borrowed the commode plunger from the maid and chased them all away. Told them there was a woman I was going to see who was better than all eight of them put together."

"You said six."

"Well, it was six without my glasses. Eight with."

Ruth laughed with sheer joy.

"Both of you may take my hand."

She felt the little fuzzy puppet paw in her palm, then the solid grip of Malone's hand. Not even for a moment did she consider shrinking from his touch.

14.

LOS ANGELES, 1994

IT RAINED THE DAY OF THE FUNERAL. Everybody thought Max's cheeks were wet with tears.

One of the illnesses his wife had imagined over the years had finally killed her. The ropes groaned under the weight, and Max saw not a casket but a giant millstone being lowered into the ground, a millstone named Betsy, taking her whining ways and extravagant spending, her thin, puckered mouth and her skinny hipbones, with her.

He stood over the grave, determined to watch until all the dirt was put back in. She'd come back from the brink of death so many times, he wanted to be sure she was really dead this time.

"So sorry, Max." A hand clasped his shoulder. It belonged to Caldwell Summers, a cameraman who frequently worked on Max's movies. "We'll all miss her."

"Thanks. So will I." Lies came more easily to him than the truth.

Dirt thumped against the casket. Winter rains had made the earth clump together in waxy clods. Betsy would have hated the way it stuck to the sides of her expensive vault.

"I can't believe she's really gone." Prissy Luther appeared at his side, dressed from head to toe in fur, although it was a mild fifty degrees. Betsy would have approved. She always got her fur out in November and wore it through March, no matter what the temperature was.

"Hard to believe," Max said.

"Sixty-two. So young." Prissy dabbed at her eyes. "You never know who will go next. It could be me." She shared her dear departed best friend's habit of hypochondria.

The last clod fell on top of the casket.

"It could be," he said, leaving Prissy with her mouth open and her high heels sunk in the mud. When he got inside his car with the black-tinted windows, he laughed until tears rolled down his cheeks.

At long last Betsy was dead. Now nothing stood between him and his prize.

15.

OAHU, 1994

TWO DAYS OF ROMPING LIKE CHILDREN. Of holding hands while the surf pounded at their feet and the sun streaked their bare shoulders with gold. There were no walls for them, no smoky dives, no sleazy motels where the blinking neon signs shone through the window and turned naked thighs orange and blue. Without asking questions Malone sensed that she needed to stay close to nature, where everything was fresh and clean.

Sitting on the sand with Hector perched between them, they watched the sun turn the water the color of a strawberry ice. Malone touched her hand, then laced their fingers together and squeezed.

"I'm leaving tomorrow," he said.

"I know."

"Will you miss me, Ruth?"

"Yes."

"Honestly?"

"You're good company, Malone. Smart, and very sweet."

Sweet. He could settle for that. At least for now.

"Tonight we'll go somewhere special, Ruth. Anywhere you want to go. You name it."

"I can't."

"You can't?"

"I have to work."

"Maybe I can pick you up after work."

Ruth thought of the nightclub where she sang and the dress she wore, red-sequined, neckline slit to the waist, hemline to the thigh on one side, the kind of sleazy, come-on dress Margaret Anne might have worn to entice men to her bed before she'd found Max to pay all the bills.

When she'd first gone to work for Bernie at the club, she'd balked about the dress, but he had insisted.

"You're paying me to sing, not to put my body on display," she'd said.

"This is not about displaying your body, Ruth. It's showmanship. My clientele likes the whole package—great songs, great voice, great body."

"No. I won't wear them. I'll go somewhere else."

"Fine. Go somewhere else. You'll be back."

She'd tried the clubs all around the island, but everywhere she'd gone, it had been the same.

"Sorry, we don't need a singer."

She'd tried other jobs, waiting tables, working as a maid in hotels, even selling hot dogs at a little stand on the beach, but nowhere else could she earn enough money to supplement her small scholarship and make ends meet.

So she had returned to Bernie's club and put her body on display.

So much like her mother. Doing what it took to please a certain kind of man. Her only consolation was that the clientele could look but not touch.

She untangled her fingers from Malone's and walked to the edge of the water. The sun had sunk so low, it looked as if it were falling into the ocean. Everything came to an end sooner or later.

Malone touched her shoulder, his grip light, his fingers

gentle. He was sweet. So sweet. She covered his hand with hers.

"This is nothing personal, Malone. I sing two sets at the Blue Moon, and it will be very late when I finish. You're flying out tomorrow; you need your sleep."

"I don't need to sleep, Ruth. Not when I can be with you."

"Let's say good-bye now, Malone. No complications, just thanks for a lovely interlude."

"I can't. Ruth . . ." His fingers tightened on her shoulders. "I've never even kissed you. May I?"

Kisses were for people with dreams. But Malone looked so forlorn, she couldn't refuse. Steeling herself for the hateful invasion of her mouth, she tipped her face up and closed her eyes. He pressed his lips to her cheek.

Astonished, Ruth felt the sting of tears. She blinked rapidly so he wouldn't see her crying.

"You sing?" he said, releasing her and squatting to toss shells into the water.

"Yes. I learned at church. When I was barely walking, I found out they had music in the sanctuary and refused to go to the nursery."

"Stubborn little kid. Will you sing for me, Ruth?"

Why not? There was something so pure about his request, and the sun setting over the ocean looked almost sacred.

"Amazing grace," she sang. "How sweet the sound." Her voice was rich, deep, full of pathos and passion. Gifts from a father she didn't even know. "That saved a witch like me . . ."

"The word is 'wretch,' darling."

Her mother stood on the front porch, a spring wind blowing her lilac-colored dress against her legs, and tears streaking the mascara down her cheeks.

Ruth leaned far out of the swing so she could reach the floor with one foot and set it back into motion. In the face of her mother's tears, the swaying comforted her.

"Mommy, why are you crying?"

"Because you sound like your daddy."

"Who is my daddy?"

"Somebody wonderful who had to go away."

At four it hadn't seemed important to know where he was and why he had gone.

Now, at twenty-six, it merely seemed too late.

The words of the song hung in the air between them. Had Malone noticed her slip of the tongue? Would he say anything?

"That's beautiful," he said. "Everything about you is absolutely beautiful."

He need never know about the room in New Orleans, about the white satin sheets and the white roses.

"Please leave now while you still think I'm beautiful."

She looked away from him, out over the ocean, and laced her fingers tightly together behind her back. Malone reached up and gently pried them apart. Then he kissed her fingertips, all ten of them, and walked away down the beach.

When he was almost out of sight, she noticed Hector sitting crumpled in the sand.

"You forgot . . ."

The wind caught her words and carried them out to sea. She picked up the puppet and hugged him to her chest. The heat of the sun, caught in his fur, warmed her.

He sat in the shadows so she wouldn't see him. The red dress she wore might have been a warning to him. Stop. Walk away. But it was too late for warnings—far, far too late.

He was desperately in love with Ruth, "desperate" being the operative word. Going back to Africa without her was unthinkable. What would she say when he proposed? What would they all say?

He pictured it, his family gathered around the telegram. "I'M MARRIED STOP BRINGING WIFE HOME ON NEXT PLANE STOP SIGNED, MALONE."

Eleanor and Joseph would wonder how he could possibly marry somebody he'd known only three days. They would certainly question his judgment, probably even his sanity.

Brett would understand, as he always did. He would know that love didn't care whether you knew someone three days or three years. It either happened or it didn't. Time was of no importance.

Smoke filled the room, fogging blue and mysterious around Ruth as she leaned close to the microphone and crooned. It was a love song, a love song for a lovesick man.

What if she said no?

He gave his cowlick a quick swipe, then took a sip of his beer for courage.

Of course she'd say no. A man she'd known only three days. A homely one, at that.

He should leave. Shove the beer aside and stay deep in the shadows so she'd never know he'd been there, never know he'd already changed his plane reservations, never know what a fool he was.

Her head was bowed over the microphone, the spotlight caught in her shining hair. "Someone to watch over me," she crooned, as if she really meant it, as if her heart were aching with loneliness . . . and hope.

He gripped the cold handle of the beer mug. For Ruth he could be that man. For Ruth he could be anything.

The crowd applauded, some standing on their feet, cheering and whistling. Catcalling.

"More! More!"

"Show us some tit, baby."

If Malone could have picked the man out in the swirling smoke, he'd have smashed his dirty mouth.

Ruth left the stage quickly, not even bothering with a bow, her red sequins sparkling in the glow of the footlights. Where was she going in such a hurry? Her car? If he didn't get a move on, he'd miss her.

Malone Corday. Second best.

He knocked the chair over in his haste and tripped over a pair of big feet.

"Excuse me," he said.

"Take it easy, buddy. There's no fire around here that I know of." The man took a deep draw on his Havana cigar and blew smoke in Malone's direction.

"Sorry."

The smoke nearly choked him. He could no longer see her red dress. Where was she?

• • •

Every night at the Blue Moon it was the same. She slid
into the music, lost herself in its rhythm and beauty, and
then the catcalls brought her back to reality. Standing in
the narrow hallway, she leaned her head against her dress-
ing-room door, trying to forget all the things they said.

"Ruth!"

Malone's big feet pounded on the dingy linoleum. His
shirt was bright yellow, new from the looks of it, with
creases where it had been folded, in two straight lines
down his chest. His pale hair flapped around his ears as he
ran, and the wire frames of his glasses glinted in the glare
of the naked bulbs spaced along the water-stained ceiling.

Seeing him was like discovering a fresh lemon drop in
the midst of a compost heap, a pure bit of sweetness all
wrapped in shiny yellow cellophane, untouched by the rotting vegetation around it. For a moment Ruth's heart
lifted. Then she remembered what she was wearing. A har-
lot's dress. Designed to entice.

Look. See my body.

"You're made for love, Ruth," Max said.

Malone stood before her, out of breath, his glasses halfway down his nose and sweat making circles on his new
yellow shirt.

"I couldn't let you go," he said.

"We said good-bye this afternoon."

"Not good-bye, Ruth. Never good-bye." He reached
for her hand, and she felt how he trembled. No man had
ever trembled for her. "I couldn't . . . I came to
say . . ." He shoved his glasses back into their proper
place. "I want to marry you, Ruth."

The wonder of his proposal bloomed inside her as
bright as the forsythia that burst golden upon the hills of
northeast Mississippi every spring. She pictured herself as
the wife of Malone Corday, loved, cherished, respected,
cleansed.

"I know I'm not much," he said, hurrying on, taking
her silence for refusal. "But think about it . . . you can
finish your dissertation at the feet of the man whose name
is synonymous with gorilla research. Gorilla Man, they

call Brett in Africa. All the while you're being worshiped and adored by a man with his own hair and teeth."

This man she'd known only three days, this virtual stranger, was offering her something she'd longed for without even knowing it. Suddenly she realized how hungry she was, *starved* for his goodness, for the kind of steady contentment he would give her.

And yet, what could she give him in return?

"Malone, you don't know how honored I am by your proposal. . . ."

"Ruth . . . before you say any more, let me say this. I know you don't love me. I've seen myself in the mirror, and I have sense enough to know that I'm not much to love. . . ."

"Oh, but you are! Some woman is going to adore you."

"I don't want *some* woman, Ruth. I want you. Only you." Tenderly he lifted her hands and skimmed his lips across her knuckles. "Just give it a try. That's all I ask. Go to Africa with me as my wife, and if at the end of six months you're not happy, you can come home. Free and clear."

"You'd do that for me?"

"They say if you love something enough, you can let it go and it will come back to you." His hand tightened on hers. "Maybe I'm lying to you. Maybe I could never let you go. All I know is this, Ruth: I love you and want you to be my wife."

The sound of the saxophone drifted down the hallway toward them, a smoky, mournful sound, wailing about broken hearts and lonely lives. At the end of the hallway the night watchman banged open the outside door and reached for the light switch, then, seeing Ruth, called, "Sorry, didn't know you were still here."

"Yes, I'm still here."

"'Bout closing time," he said.

"Thanks, Ralph. I'll be leaving soon."

Looking at Malone, at the eagerness and hope shining in his face, Ruth was filled with a kind of yearning that went beyond hope: She was filled with possibilities. Making coffee for two in a small kitchen with a sunny window big enough for Miranda and a potted red geranium. Sitting side by side in front of a glowing hearth with blues softly filling the room. Sharing private jokes. Having a shoulder to lean on when she cried. Her yearning was so great, it almost spilled over into words. "Malone," she nearly said, "will there be laughter? Kindness? Hugs? Can you love me just as I am?"

There was the crux of the problem. Malone had no idea who or what she was. And she didn't dare tell him.

She twisted her hands behind her back so she wouldn't be tempted to reach out for him. It would be cruel to give him mixed signals.

"Please don't think I'm not tempted, Malone. I am."

"Ruth, don't say no. At least say you'll think about what I've said a while longer. You can call me at my hotel. Any time of the night. Whatever your answer is—yes or no —you can tell me on the phone. I'll be awake waiting for you."

"Malone, I don't want to give you false hope. I can't marry you."

"I don't want your answer, Ruth—not yet." He shoved back a limp, sweat-dampened lock of hair that had fallen across his forehead. "Just call me."

When she started to protest, he placed a finger over her lips.

"Later . . . please."

He was so dear, so kind. How could she refuse him?

"I will," she said.

"Promise?"

"I promise."

He smiled as if he'd won a million-dollar lottery. She hated that she was going to be the one to wipe that look of wild, delirious anticipation from his face.

"Can I walk you to your car, Ruth?"

She had meant to change clothes before she left the club. She didn't like wearing the sequined dress any longer than she had to. But it was already very late, and she didn't want to be with Malone any longer. Every moment she spent with him weakened her resolve. His enthusiasm was contagious. How easy it would be to get caught up in his dreams, to forget everything except the rosy future he painted for them.

At the car he kissed her on the cheek, then opened her door and handed her inside as if she were special. She hadn't felt special since she was thirteen.

"I'll be waiting, Ruth."

She said good-bye, then drove away without looking back. She didn't have to look back to see him standing under the streetlamp, his new yellow shirt awash with nervous sweat and his face shining with hope. The memory would haunt her forever.

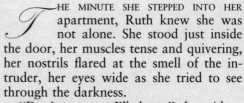

16.

THE MINUTE SHE STEPPED INTO HER apartment, Ruth knew she was not alone. She stood just inside the door, her muscles tense and quivering, her nostrils flared at the smell of the intruder, her eyes wide as she tried to see through the darkness.

"Don't move or I'll shoot," she said.

Her Beretta was in the purse hanging around her shoulder. The room was pitch-black, all the curtains drawn against the moon that spilled over the Pacific, bleaching it silver.

What should she reach for first? Her gun or the light switch?

"There's no need to use your gun . . . though I've absolutely no doubt that you can, since I'm the one who taught you." The lights came on. Max stood indolently, so sure of his power, so certain of his charm.

"I taught you many things, Ruth. Remember?"

The quivering started deep inside, and a chill spread until she felt as if she'd never be warm again.

She felt the heavy weight of her gun. What would happen if she pulled it out and shot him?

"I taught you well. You could hit me dead center, right in the heart." Max had always been able to read her thoughts. "But then how would we celebrate the bull's-eye?"

With champagne and silk sheets and the hot, hard invasion that she hated.

"Get out." The shaking increased until it vibrated in her very bones.

His easy laughter mocked her rage.

"I'm glad to see your spirit is still intact." Slowly he moved toward her. "If you'd really wanted me out, you'd have used the gun."

She stood before him as powerless as a mongoose before a cobra.

"We both know what you want, don't we, Ruth?"

Age had not marred his looks nor diminished his power. All the old feelings swept over her—naked fear, shame. When he was close, she smelled his aftershave and the lingering aroma of white roses.

White roses. Always white roses.

But she was no longer thirteen.

"If you take another step, I'll start screaming."

"I always did know how to make you scream, Ruth."

"I'm not that scared little teenager anymore."

"No. You're all woman."

Like a predatory lion, he circled her, pausing every now and then with his head tilted as if he needed a different angle to study the changes in her. When he was behind her, he slid his fingertips along her bare skin. Her hand tightened on the gun. Why couldn't she pull the trigger?

She felt his hands on her zipper, heard the metallic whisper as it glided downward. She was in New Orleans, and the tub he'd prepared for her was waiting. He would join her there, rubbing his hands over her body, soapy slick, saying wicked words her mother would make her wash her mouth out with soap for saying.

Her dress fell to her waist, and Max was in front of her, his eyes boring into her, seeing beyond her skin and past her bones, penetrating all the way to her dark, secret shame.

"You make me sick," she whispered. The person who really made her sick was herself. She caught her dress and held the bodice tightly to her chest.

"Let the dress fall, Ruth."

The gun was tangled under the red sequins. If she pulled the trigger, who would die? Max or she? Did it matter?

"Let it go. I want to see your body."

"No."

"You belong to me, Ruth. I've finally come to claim what's mine."

He was as still as a lion cornering its prey, every muscle in his body tensed, poised for action. Why didn't he move? Why couldn't she?

"I don't belong to you. I've made my own way in the world with no help from you or Margaret Anne."

"Do you sing for your supper, sweetheart?"

"Yes! I sing. It pays the bills."

"No. *I* pay the bills." His smile was slow and danger-ous. "Who do you think owns the club?"

"You're lying." She couldn't bear to look at him, couldn't bear to see the truth in his eyes.

"Why do you think you were paid six times what you're worth all these years? Because of your *singing?* You're not that good, sweetheart."

"Damn you to hell."

"I've just come out of hell, and now I've come to get my reward."

In one smooth motion he came to her and stripped away her dress. Powerless, she watched him wet his fingers with his tongue, then trace her nipples.

"No," she whispered. She was like her mother, after all. The discovery was cruel, almost too cruel to bear. The years of penny-pinching and sacrifice melted away under Max's touch. Ruth felt herself falling, falling victim to his dark power.

"Do you still get wet when I touch you, Ruth? Do you still get slick when I look at you?"

"No! You own my mother, but you don't own me."

She jerked out of his grasp and ran to the phone. Her hands were trembling so hard, she dropped the receiver. Max replaced it on the cradle.

"What are you going to say, Ruth? That you've caught a prowler in your house?"

Covering her mouth to hold back her screams, she sank onto the sofa.

His laughter was soft, mocking, as he pulled a key from his pocket and tossed it toward her. It clanked against the coffee table, then lay between them like a covenant.

"Did you think I'd let you get away, Ruth? Did you think you could escape me by refusing my money, by coming to Hawaii?"

She couldn't tell whether the glitter in his eyes was madness or passion. All she knew was that she was sucked into him, stripped of her soul, robbed of her will.

"When I found out where you were living, I bought the apartments. I've known every move you've made since you came here. I bought and paid for you when you were two years old, and I've been buying and paying for you ever since."

He closed in on her swiftly. His arms were still hard and muscular, his body fit and trim. He caught her face between his hands. She was trapped.

"You're mine, Ruth, and I've come to claim you."

"Noooo . . ."

His kiss was expert, persuasive, everything she remembered and everything she'd tried to forget.

"Tell me what you want, sweetheart. Say it out loud. 'I want you in me, Max.' Beg for it the way you used to."

She shoved him hard. Laughing softly, he pulled his pipe from his pocket, slowly tamped in tobacco, then stood watching her through the blue haze of smoke.

"I'm the only man you'll ever respond to, Ruth."

"No . . ."

"I created you, Ruth. I know what you want, what you need. Nobody else will ever be able to satisfy you. And that's a truth you can never escape."

She had a vision of herself ten years from now, fifteen, twenty, running around the globe always looking over her shoulder, always feeling the hot breath of Maxwell Jones at her back. Running until at last there was no place left to run, and finally suffocating on the smell of white roses.

Max sat down on the sofa and propped his feet on the coffee table. Reaching for her hand, he laced her limp fingers between his.

"We can stay here until you finish your dissertation. This apartment is not much—but, then, we've never required space for what we like to do."

Cold sweat beaded her brow and popped up along the upper rim of her lip.

"Afterward we'll return to L.A. Betsy's dead. I've sold the house and bought us another one. You can work or not. Whatever you choose. As long as you're there to satisfy my needs." He took a long draw on his pipe, watching her through the smoke. "You still know how to satisfy my needs, don't you, sweetheart?"

Ruth's eyes searched the room until she saw Miranda, cowering under the wing chair. She sprang from the sofa and scooped up her cat, holding that familiar, comforting warmth against her chest.

She could think of only one way out . . . and she was going to take it.

"You'll have to get someone else to satisfy your needs, Max. I'll be in the jungles of the Virungas."

"I've always wanted to visit Central Africa."

"Three's a crowd, Max." Ruth stroked her cat. "I'll be there with my husband."

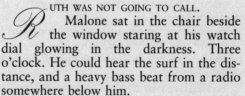

17.

RUTH WAS NOT GOING TO CALL. Malone sat in the chair beside the window staring at his watch dial glowing in the darkness. Three o'clock. He could hear the surf in the distance, and a heavy bass beat from a radio somewhere below him.

The hotel was old, not very well constructed, but like most hotels on the islands, it boasted a beach and a view of the water.

Malone took off his glasses and laid them on the wicker table beside his chair. His shirt was so wet with nervous sweat, it was sticking to him. He smelled like a pig. Might as well take a shower. She'd turned him down, but at least he could make himself presentable. He still had his pride.

Most times he'd sing in the shower, but not tonight. Tonight was not a time of celebration. The water beat his hair down around his ears. Below him somebody turned the volume up so loud, the heavy bass reverberated over the noise of the shower.

Or was it the phone?

What in the hell was he doing in the shower? What if she decided to call?

He nearly slipped on the bar of soap as he bolted from the stall and grabbed a towel. It *was* the phone.

"Coming," he yelled, knotting the towel around his waist as he ran into the bedroom.

The phone was silent. He stared at it. Enraged. The silence cut through him as brutally as the panga had laid open Brett's face. Ruth had called, and he'd missed her. She would never call again. He was doomed to loneliness, bachelorhood in the damned dripping Virungas with nothing but old buffalo cows giving him the eye.

It was so quiet, he could hear his own blood in his ears. Even the radio downstairs was still.

There. They'd started it up again. That bass beat.

Malone snapped on his bedside light. The beat reverberated through his room. But it wasn't a radio at all. It was the door.

A chair got in the way of his shin, and the rug tried to snag his feet. He was panting like an out-of-shape jogger trying to do the Boston Marathon by the time he flung open his door.

Ruth stood in the hallway in her red-sequined gown, clutching her purse and a cat.

"Ruth . . . darling!"

"Can I come in?"

Her face was white and set as wax. Had she come to tell him no?

"Of course."

The doorway across the hall opened, and an old lady in pink foam curlers stifled a scream. Malone crossed his hands in front of his towel, and Ruth giggled nervously as they both dashed into his room and shut the door. He leaned against it.

"Whew. Close call. I thought she was going to wrestle me to the floor and have her wicked way with me."

Fool. Jabbering like a jaybird when he wanted to grab Ruth and squeeze an answer from her.

Say yes, Ruth. Say yes.

She stood in the center of the room, holding her cat protectively against her chest. It was a very old feline with soft gray fur and wicked green eyes that watched his every move.

"Malone, I have to say this fast or I might not say it at all."

"Go ahead. I'm listening."

"If your proposal still stands, I want to marry you."

"Yes! Ruth, you can't know how happy this makes me. This is the best thing that's ever happened to me. I can't believe it. You're going to marry me!"

There he was, babbling on like an idiot again while she stood quietly, her eyes bright with . . . tears. God, she had tears in her eyes. He didn't know whether to offer her comfort or to keep his distance. He hated the towel around his waist. Maybe if he had a chest like Brett's, he'd have looked enticing. Instead he felt ridiculous.

No, he wouldn't hug her. She might change her mind and leave. Or throw up.

"I don't love you, Malone." One tear slid down her cheek.

"That's all right." He'd known that, so why did it hurt to hear her say it?

"No, it isn't. It's not right. You deserve someone who loves you."

"Look, I want you. That's all that matters right now. The rest will come in time."

Another tear slid down her cheek, then another. He didn't know what to do except get her a glass of water.

"I'll be right back." He bolted toward the bathroom. There was no ice in the bucket. He had nothing to offer her except tap water. He let the faucet run awhile, hoping it would get cold, but it remained as tepid as piss, and just as palatable.

Turning toward the door, he glimpsed himself in the mirror. He hadn't combed his hair after he'd left the shower. It had dried in spikes that stuck up all over his head. He looked like something dreamed up by special effects for an outer-space movie. The creature from beyond. He tried smoothing it down, but it popped right back up. The comb made it worse.

To hell with his hair. Ruth was going to marry him.

She smiled at him when he handed her the water.

"You're so sweet." Tipping her head back, she took a long drink of water. He was fascinated by the play of muscles in her slim throat. Someday he'd lick her throat, starting at the top and going all the way to the little indentation where her pulse beat.

Shoot. Not someday. Soon. Maybe even tonight. Suddenly he wished he'd taken the time to remove his towel and put on his pants.

"Tomorrow we'll get blood tests, and while we're waiting, we can make plans. We'll call anybody you want to. Do you have parents in Mississippi?"

"No!" She took another long drink of water, then set the glass on the wicker table. "My mother is there, but I'd rather not call her. . . . You know how mothers are."

"Don't I? She'd probably be heartbroken that you were getting married without her." Ruth didn't say anything, and he couldn't think of what to say next. He glanced at the bed, then back at Ruth. She hadn't brought her bags with her.

"Well . . . ," he said, yawning and thinking about the bed.

"I came in such a hurry . . . it really was a last-minute decision. Malone, I'd rather not go home tonight if you don't mind."

They both looked at the bed once more.

"May I . . . ?" she said.

"You can . . . ," he said at the same time. Then, "Ladies first."

"I don't want you to get the wrong idea," she said.

"Certainly not. I'll sleep in the chair. I think it folds out into a lounger."

"I wouldn't want to deprive you of your bed. I'll take the chair."

"I wouldn't hear of it."

"You're a very considerate man, Malone."

She sat on the edge of the bed and bounced once, testing the springs. He turned sideways to hide his arousal behind the skimpy towel.

"You don't mind the cat? Her name is Miranda."

"Not at all. I love animals." To show his sincerity, he rubbed the cat's head. His hand accidentally made contact with Ruth's breast. Or was it an accident?

She scooted away from him.

"Sorry," he said.

"Certainly." A bit of color began to creep back into her face. But the track of tears was still on her cheeks. "Can I borrow something from you to sleep in? A T-shirt or something?"

"I'll get it."

In the closet he did a slow count to ten. He'd be a fool to press her now and blow it.

She took the shirt and went into the bathroom. By the time she came out, he had laid a blanket on the chair and had pulled on boxer shorts and a T-shirt, though he always slept naked.

"Good night, Malone."

Her legs were long and beautiful. She climbed into bed quickly and covered herself to the chin.

"Good night," he said.

Knowing she wore nothing under the shirt was enough to keep him awake for several hours. Soon, though, it would all be his.

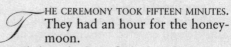

18.

THE CEREMONY TOOK FIFTEEN MINUTES. They had an hour for the honeymoon.

And then the long flight to Africa.

As Malone removed his tie in his hotel room, he looked like a little boy about to discover Christmas. She turned her back so she wouldn't be blinded by his eagerness.

"Till death us do part," she'd said, and now was the beginning. She had to make it a good one. Drawing a deep breath, she slid out of her white dress.

He had his shirt off now. And his shoes. She watched his bare feet as he crossed the carpet. They were long and narrow, with a sprinkling of dark hair on the top. She'd expected pale blond. His chest was smooth, hairless. But what about his other body hair? Would it be dark?

He ran his hands up her arms and cupped her breasts through her silk slip.

She shivered. From the glint in his eye, she could tell that he thought it was from pleasure.

"I'll be gentle with you," he said.

Max had been gentle at first. She caught her lower lip between her teeth and squeezed her eyes shut. A wave of nausea swept over her.

"Malone . . ."

"I guess you're a little scared that we won't be good together at first. But don't worry about that, Ruth. We have the rest of our lives."

The rest of her life with a husband she didn't know in a land she'd never seen. And she couldn't bear for him to touch her.

What had she done? Her future stretched before her as endless and frightening as the foreign land where she was going.

With his thumbs circling her nipples, Malone bent to nuzzle her neck. The sound she made was like the cry of a small, wounded animal.

"Ruth?" His head snapped up. "Are you all right?"

"Yes . . . no." Her knees buckled, and she sat suddenly on the bed. "I'm sorry, Malone. I can't do this right now."

"I understand." He would never understand, but she didn't tell him so. The bed squeaked under his weight as he sat down beside her and took her hand. "You're cold." He reached for her other hand, then chafed them both between his.

"When I was in the second grade, I won the part of the pumpkin in the school play. I remember I had only one line: 'Behold, I'm the biggest pumpkin in the pumpkin patch.' I practiced and practiced. I'd stand in front of the mirror every day and say my line." His hands were warm as he rubbed hers . . . warm and extremely comforting.

"The night of the play I dressed in my little stuffed orange suit and my little hat with the green stem on top, but when I got out on stage, I completely froze. 'Behold,' the teacher whispered from the wings, but all I could do was stare at the sea of faces in the darkened auditorium. 'Behold,' she kept saying. Finally somebody behind me said my line. I was so scared, I just stood there and wet my pants." He kissed her hand. "It's all right to be scared, Ruth, just don't wet your pants."

At that moment she almost loved him.

"Malone Corday, you really are a wonderful man." Squeezing his hands, she smiled at him.

"God, you're beautiful. Brett's going to love you."

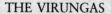

19.

THE VIRUNGAS

"Do you think she'll like us?"

"What's not to like, Eleanor?"

She wished she'd never asked the question. Sometimes Joseph reminded her of a lump of oatmeal: He was just *there*. He never took anything seriously except his gorillas.

Another woman on the mountain.

Eleanor's misgivings about Malone's sudden wedding were almost outweighed by her joy at the thought of female companionship. She left her vigil at the window and rearranged the flowers she'd picked, enormous trumpet-shaped blossoms, bright red, drooping gracefully on their stems.

"What about the flowers? Do you think they look all right?"

"Ask Brett. He knows more about that stuff than I do."

"You'd think this was just an ordinary day instead of the day you're going to meet your daughter-in-law. Aren't you the least bit excited, Joseph?"

"What's to get excited about? Malone is the one who should be excited."

Malone. Not Brett. It didn't seem right, somehow.

"Do you think Brett will ever marry?"

"Not unless some woman accidentally falls out of a plane and lands on top of his mountain." Joseph laughed at his own joke.

"I don't think that's very funny. You'd think by now some woman would have snatched him up. He's so . . . magnificent."

"I'm surprised women aren't storming his mountain in platoons."

"I don't know why I ever bother to try to carry on a sane conversation with you."

"Because I'm all you have, my darling."

She turned away so he wouldn't see her face. All these years, and Joseph had never even been suspicious. As she studied his face, crinkled with laughter, she was sorry for thinking of him as a lump of oatmeal. He was a brilliant, somewhat absentminded man, totally devoted to her. And she really did love him in all the ways that mattered.

Fate had been kind to her. She hoped that same kind fate sent her a daughter-in-law she could love.

The door banged open, and Brett came inside, bringing the smells and the feel of the mountains with him. Pure. Clean. Enduring.

"Sorry I'm late. Are they here yet?"

"No. And you're forgiven. What do you think of the flowers? Do you think she'll like them?"

"Malone wouldn't dare marry a girl who wouldn't like your flowers."

"You always say the right thing."

Brett squeezed her waist, then roamed around the room eating from all the snack trays Matuka had filled.

"Relax, Mother. She's going to love you."

"Did Malone call and tell you anything about her?"

After so many years of having no one except Matuka to talk to, Eleanor was hungry for this new daughter-in-law.

One reason she'd never gone anywhere was that she didn't have anybody to go with her. She and her new daughter-in-law would take motor trips together, sometimes to buy supplies, but sometimes for no reason at all except to talk girl talk and giggle.

Ruth. A strong, steadfast name. She hoped her daughter-in-law matched her name; otherwise, the Virungas would wear her away to nothing.

Suddenly Eleanor realized her son had not answered her question. He was standing at the window, his hands gripping the windowsill, his back as stiff as cardboard packing.

"Brett . . . what's wrong?"

"They're here."

Joseph looked up from his magazine and absently patted the top of his hair, but Eleanor flew to the window to stand beside Brett. The woman Malone helped from the Jeep was exquisite, hair and eyes as black as a panther and skin the color of warm, dark honey. In cream-colored linen and pearls, she was elegant, stunning. She would have expected Brett to bring home such a woman. But Malone? It boggled her mind.

"Good Lord," she said. "Beautiful, isn't she?"

There was a long silence before Brett answered her.

"Yes. She's beautiful."

"Maybe you should go outside and show Juma where to put their bags."

"Mother, Juma's been with us nearly twenty years. If he can't find the guest cottage by now, we should fire him."

Her son had never been so pricklish with her. Curious, Eleanor watched as he stalked to the other side of the room. When he was beside the fireplace, he propped one arm on the mantel, leaning sideways so his eye patch was turned away from the door.

Sharp pain sliced through her, as if the panga were still carving away at her heart. If Ruth cringed from the sight of her son's eye patch, she'd . . . She got so worked up at the idea that she didn't know what she'd do.

"Joseph." He sat in his chair as if a fog had suddenly descended over him and he was trying to figure his way out. Her voice was sharper than necessary, but, Lord, it did look as if Joseph might not be so distant, today of all days. "Let's greet our daughter-in-law together. Come and stand beside me."

Joseph ambled over. Even the way he walked irritated her today. She hoped her irritation didn't show.

She could hear Malone laughing just outside the door. Any minute it would burst open, and the Corday family would never be the same. Five instead of four. And one of them a stranger.

Eleanor smoothed her denim shirt. Should she have worn her blue silk dress? It was too late to worry now, for the door swung open.

And her daughter-in-law took her breath away.

"My dear." She took Ruth's hands. "Welcome to the Virungas." She'd meant to kiss her cheek, but there was a deep reserve in Ruth that didn't invite instant familiarity.

"Thank you." Ruth's voice was soft, full of the cadences of the South.

Joseph clapped both hands on Ruth's shoulders and kissed her cheek.

"Welcome to the family, Ruth."

Eleanor was astonished—and a bit jealous—that Joseph, for all his earlier nonchalance, had managed to do and say exactly the right thing. Her own greeting echoed in her ears. *Welcome to the Virungas.* Indeed. As if she were a travel agent and Ruth a tourist on a three-day jaunt.

"I hope you're hungry, Ruth. I think Eleanor has managed to cook everything on the mountain."

"Pay Joseph no attention. He loves to tease." Eleanor glanced at Brett. Why was he standing on the other side of the room without so much as a word? "This, of course, is Brett. I'm sure Malone has told you about his brother."

As if she had to have someone tell her about Brett Corday, Ruth thought. As if he hadn't been the first person she'd spotted when she'd walked into the room. Even now, after she'd given herself time to adjust to the idea of seeing the man who had exercised such a powerful pull over her for so many years, Ruth had a hard time keeping her excitement from showing. They mustn't see, this new family of hers, how he made her face feel hot. They must not know how her breath rushed up and tried to clog her throat. They might get the wrong idea, and she wasn't going to let anybody get the wrong idea about her, ever again.

Ruth hoped she looked perfectly normal as she moved toward Brett Corday. How could anyone be normal moving toward an icon?

"He didn't have to tell me," Ruth said. "I became a student of anthropology because of Dr. Brett Corday."

He'd held himself in profile to her since she'd entered the room, showing only that side of himself that was unmarked. When he turned full face, the full impact of him took her breath away. She couldn't speak, couldn't move. She saw the fierce challenge in his eye, the look that said *Don't you dare pity me*. She wished it was pity she was feeling. She wished it was sympathy. She even wished it was sadness. Anything except the frantic, pounding rush of blood that threatened to drown her.

"I'm so happy to meet you . . . at last." Did she dare touch him? Did she dare not?

Eleanor watched as the beautiful woman who belonged to her youngest son presented herself to Brett. Something was not right. They stood opposite each other as stiff as new shoes that wouldn't give an inch, no matter what you did to them, and for a while it looked as if Brett were not even going to acknowledge her presence, let alone take the hand she offered.

Eleanor breathed a sigh of relief when he finally nodded, though the nod was neither friendly nor welcoming, but the kind of curt acknowledgment he would give to somebody he wished would simply vanish from his beloved Virungas.

Ruth stood, uncertain, her hand wavering between them. Suddenly it seemed that her hand was the only object in the room. Even Malone, who had to have a guide to find his way through a dinner-table conversation, noticed that his brother was ignoring his wife's outstretched hand.

"Shit, Brett. I know she's beautiful, but I didn't think she'd render you speechless."

"My apologies, Ruth. You *have* rendered me speechless."

Brett touched her hand, and Ruth felt the tingle all the way to her toes. It was more wonderful than she'd imagined, and more terrible. She couldn't get her hand away fast enough. But he didn't seem to notice. When he pulled back to the mantel, she felt as if she were in Mississippi and he in Africa.

"You're a lovely and welcome addition to the family," he said.

Eleanor saw right through him. Brett was probably the worst liar on the face of the earth. Did he know something she didn't know? Had Malone sent him a separate cable? Was this girl pregnant with somebody else's child? It would be just like Malone to fall for a pretty wrapping without checking out the whole package.

"Why don't you tell us all about yourself, Ruth." Eleanor made a mental note that the pearls weren't real, which didn't necessarily tell her a single thing.

"Mother . . . why don't you feed us before you get into twenty questions? It's been a long flight. I don't know about my wife, but I'm starving."

Malone started toward her with his love and intentions clearly visible on his face, and Ruth fixed her face in a welcoming smile, forced herself to watch him with the fond anticipation of a new bride. When he slid his arm around her, she glanced sideways at his brother. It was only a fleeting glance, but that was all it took. In that one moment she saw what she had done, saw the enormity of it, the horror. By taking the easy way out, by fleeing instead of staying to fight, she'd consigned herself to a life of fiction. Exactly like her mother.

"Why don't I show you where to freshen up?" Eleanor said.

Ruth could have kissed her feet. Escape. At last she could escape the room where expectations far exceeded reality, where the reality was so twisted that only fantasy would make it possible for all of them to survive.

"That sounds good." Ruth was careful not to look at Brett, careful to focus all her attention on her mother-in-law.

"Let *me* show her. She's *my* wife. She belongs to me now."

Belongs to me. Like a chair or a favorite suit or a new bird-dog puppy. Ruth's heart was so heavy, she was surprised her feet could move. Their laughter followed her, Joseph's genuine and Brett's merely polite. Would they be laughing if they knew?

As soon as Malone and Ruth disappeared down the hallway, Eleanor took Brett to task.

"Is there something about this woman that you're not telling me?"

"Mother, she'll hear you."

"You can't hear a stampede of elephants in that bathroom. Besides, the way Malone looks at her, he probably won't be able to keep his hands off her."

"Eleanor's right," Joseph said. "We might not see them again for hours."

Brett stalked toward the door, grabbing a handful of pretzels on his way.

"Where in the world are you going?" Eleanor asked.

"I don't have time to stay for dinner. Cee Cee needs me."

"I need you. Brett, I'm counting on you."

"I've met Malone's wife. She looks okay to me."

"That's it? You're just going to leave?"

"She seems to be a nice lady. Isn't that all you want? My opinion?"

Eleanor was astonished. Brett had been practically rude to Ruth, and now he was acting like a rebellious teen with her. It wasn't at all like him. Eleanor guarded her family unit with the ferocity of a lioness, but family was practically sacred to Brett. The loyalty and love that burned in him was of almost saintly proportions.

Eleanor was both proud of and awed by that quality in her son.

What was wrong with him? She'd rarely had occasion to find fault with her firstborn, but she was in no mood to tolerate anything except the best from him today.

"If you walk out that door, don't you expect anything else from me, Brett Corday. Ever again."

"What? No coconut cake?"

The smile he gave her was more like the old Brett.

"Absolutely none."

"You know this is blackmail."

"When it comes to family, I'm not above anything."
Including living a lie. The thought spilled through her
mind from nowhere, like a carton of cream in the back of
the refrigerator that had been forgotten until it was suddenly overturned.

It was the wedding that had set her mind askew, the
sudden marriage and the dreadful premonition that it was
not a union of love but one of convenience. Whose?
Ruth's or Malone's?

Suddenly Eleanor was too tired to move. Feeling her
age, she sat down in a chair. Furthermore, she planned to
sit there until she had to get up, and she dared Joseph to
say anything to her. Brett, either, for that matter.

In the bathroom Ruth kept soaping her hands as if
she'd never get them clean. Maybe she wouldn't. Maybe
she was like Lady Macbeth, with the blood of the entire
Corday family on her hands.

"Honey, you're going to wash the skin right off." Malone wrapped his arms around her from behind. "Not that
I mind being in such close quarters with you."

She minded. She wanted to bow her back up and cast
him away like a coat that had suddenly grown too hot and
too tight. The reason was standing down the hallway leaning against the mantel.

Ruth looked down at the water running over her hands.
She couldn't stay in the bathroom forever. She had to face
him. Them, she corrected herself. There would be no him.
There *could* be no him. Only Malone.

Her husband nudged closer, and even if she hadn't
known what a man's hard organ pressed against her hips
meant, she'd have felt the heat of his desire. If it had been
possible, she'd have crawled into the drain and hoped the
water washed her all the way back to Hawaii.

But it was never possible to go back, only forward. And
she'd be damned if she'd cower in the bathroom like some
timid, cornered animal. She'd chosen her path, and she
was determined to make it a *good* one, no matter who
stood at the mantel filling her with a wonderful, horrible
confusion.

She pulled the towel off the rack and briskly dried her hands.

"Let's go, Malone. I want to get to know your family."

"You've already wowed them. Especially Brett."

"I don't want to wow your family . . . just to be a part of it."

"You already are, sweetheart. You became a Corday the minute I slipped my ring on your finger."

"Ruth Corday. I like the sound of that." And she *did*. A new name. A new life. And she was going to fill it with respect and kindness and genuine affection in the hopes that love would come. She'd make it come.

Lifting her chin, she took her husband's arm and marched back into the bosom of her new family.

"Atta girl," Malone said.

When she heard them coming back, Eleanor popped out of her chair like a piece of toast from a toaster.

"Oh, good, you're back." She sounded like an anxious debutante, hoping to be selected for the lead at a coming-out party. *Help.* "Brett . . ."

She turned to her son, then froze. His eyes were fixed on his brother's wife . . . and hers on him. The hair on the back of Eleanor's neck stood on end. Had the serpent finally entered their Garden of Eden? Was this woman to be Eleanor's punishment for her sins . . . after all these years?

This new fear gave her tongue wings.

"I was just thinking . . . since you've eaten everything in this room except the mantel clock, perhaps you'd better escort your new sister-in-law to the dining room."

For a heartbeat Brett held his stiff posture, and then he offered his arm.

"Gladly. May I?"

"Of course. I'm so anxious to hear about your work with Cee Cee . . . and to meet her."

"I think that can be arranged, though I'll have to warn you that she doesn't take kindly to strangers."

"Then I'll try not to be a stranger."

Ruth was astonished that she could sound perfectly normal, that she could let her hand rest in Brett Corday's arm as if her whole insides weren't ringing like a buoy bell gone wild in a heavy wind. If she thought about her reaction to him, considered *why*, she might possibly lose her mind on her very first day in Africa. And so she wouldn't let herself think. She'd concentrate on making each minute a building block for her marriage so that eventually, when she added them all up, she'd have something solid and reliable, something that couldn't be shaken by a simple glance from a single black eye.

Just ahead lay the dining room with red flowers on the table, lace curtains drawn back to catch a pale light that had found its ways through the mists, and oak chairs substantial enough for big men, arranged and waiting for this family she'd become a part of. Joseph moved to the head of the table, and already Eleanor was sitting between him and Malone. That left her to sit beside Brett. The two empty places yawned ahead like jaws waiting to suck her in and devour her. Suddenly she saw her marriage for what it was, a sham, the rash act of a foolish woman. If she was going to survive, she'd have to stop being foolish and start being smart.

"What a perfectly lovely room," she said, smiling. "Every bit as warm and inviting as my new family." She intended to do more than survive; she intended to triumph.

Malone smiled at her as if she'd invented happiness. Feeling like a hypocrite, she sat in the chair Brett pulled out for her.

"Have you had any hands-on studies with primates, Ruth?" he asked.

Hands-on. His hands were still on her chair, barely brushing her skin, raising goose bumps at the back of her neck. Ruth carefully unfolded her napkin and placed it in her lap. It was a good place to hide her hands so no one would see their trembling.

"I've had very limited experience with primates. We had two chimpanzees in our lab, Quantum and Do Re. As you can guess, one of the people who named them loved math and the other music."

Everybody laughed as if she'd said something extremely clever. The laughter washed over her like balm. Malone reached for her hand. She squeezed it and held on. Tight.

Ever so tight. She was going to make everything work. She *had* to.

"Brett will spend the next four hours talking about primates if we let him," Malone said. "Don't give him too much of an opening."

"Thanks for the warning. I don't plan to give him any opening at all." Everybody laughed once more, not having any earthly idea that Ruth was not talking about gorillas.

"Why don't you tell us how the two of you met," Eleanor said.

"At Malone's lecture."

"I was bold." Malone wagged his ears at Ruth.

"You were shy . . . but very sweet."

"I swept her off her feet."

"I always keep my feet planted firmly on the ground."

The easy banter between Ruth and Malone somewhat eased Eleanor's mind. Even Brett had loosened up enough so that his smile didn't look as if it had been pasted on.

In her years on the lonely mountaintop at the mercy of a capricious and sometimes cruel fate, there were few givens she could count on. Two of them were Brett's unfailing kindness and good manners. She was glad to see that he had them back. At least partially.

Eleanor had let her imagination run wild, fed as it was by her overwrought state. She patted her younger son's arm.

"One of you tell us the *real* story," she said.

Over roast pork and dumplings Malone told the story of his courtship of Ruth, making them all laugh with the story of Hector, the puppet.

"I think Ruth fell in love with Hector, instead of me."

Ruth smiled at her husband, but rich color suffused her cheeks. At first glance it might have seemed to be love, but long years of peering at the world through a lens had taught Eleanor to search for and find the truth. What she saw was a shining sort of hope coupled with an elusive sadness. She studied Ruth, hoping to be wrong.

"Why don't you tell us about yourself, Ruth—your family. I can tell you're Southern by your accent. I grew up in Alabama, myself. Joseph says he can still hear the grits and molasses in my voice." There she was, sounding like a nervous debutante again, but Eleanor couldn't seem to help herself. She'd so hoped to feel an instant affection for her new daughter-in-law, when all she felt was a vague fear mixed with awe.

Maybe love would come in time.

Ruth spoke of her life in Mississippi with detachment, as if she viewed it from afar, perhaps on a film that had blurred over the years. The only time her voice was alive with passion was when she spoke of her studies.

"Bellafontaine? I knew a girl once by that name, from New Orleans, I think. They had a sugar plantation down there. Could she perhaps have been a relative of yours, Ruth?"

"No."

This was dangerous ground her mother-in-law was forcing her to tread upon. Smiling and silent, Ruth refused to step into treacherous territory.

"It's not a common name," Eleanor persisted.

"Mother . . ."

The subtle warning in Brett's voice was unmistakable. Ruth felt as if he'd suddenly drawn a sword, thrown a cloak about her, and pulled her from the jaws of a dragon. She wanted to curl up in his lap like a little girl and bury her face against his chest, his very broad and delicious chest that showed just a glimpse of dark hair in the neckline of his white shirt.

She concentrated on keeping her hands perfectly still, on keeping her eyes and her mind focused on Eleanor.

"I just thought perhaps your father's people were from there," Eleanor said, persistent. "Mobile, perhaps? Bellafontaine is a prominent name in south Alabama."

"My father's dead."

Ruth hated the ease with which she lied. But, then, she'd had long years of practice, of being Ruth the Ice Princess instead of Ruth the rich man's whore.

A heavy silence fell over them, as if the death had been recent and they were all still in mourning.

"Well . . . ," Malone said.

"So . . . ," Joseph said at the same time.

They all looked at each other, strangely uncomfortable. Everybody except Brett. He looked determined.

"Malone and Ruth have had a long flight, and I'm sure they could use some privacy right now."

"You got that right, big brother." Malone pulled out his wife's chair, then bent to kiss her cheek and whisper in her ear.

"Thank you for the lovely meal, and for making me feel a part of this family." Now that Brett had rescued her once again, Ruth could be gracious and charming. So very much like her mother.

She wouldn't let herself think of Margaret Anne. Mississippi was thousands of miles and thousands of years away.

Eleanor and Joseph walked them to the door, but Brett hung back, one foot propped on the andirons, both hands gripping the mantel.

Ruth wouldn't let herself glance back at him, afraid of what she might see, afraid that if she did, she might not be able to go through the door and shut it behind her.

Outside, Malone kissed her cheek. "Let's go home, honey."

"Yes," she said. "Let's go home."

Eleanor stood at the window watching until they were down the path.

"After all that time, that entire meal, we know nothing about her." She knew she sounded petty and nitpicking, but she was past caring. A ghost was walking on her grave, and she felt the chill.

"Now, Eleanor." Joseph patted her arm. "She's a perfectly lovely young woman."

Brett was so rigid, his back looked as if it had been carved in stone. When he turned around, she could see a muscle working in his clenched jaw.

"We know that Malone loves her," he said. "And that's enough."

Abruptly, he wheeled away from the fireplace.

"Brett . . . ," she called.

But he was already out the door.

20.

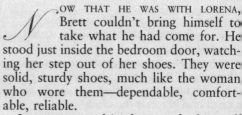

NOW THAT HE WAS WITH LORENA, Brett couldn't bring himself to take what he had come for. He stood just inside the bedroom door, watching her step out of her shoes. They were solid, sturdy shoes, much like the woman who wore them—dependable, comfortable, reliable.

Lorena stopped in the act of taking off her stockings.

"Brett, what's wrong?"

"You know me too well, Lorena."

"Nobody will ever know you well. You're full of mystery." She padded toward him in stocking feet, buttoning up the front of her dress as she came. "But I do know you well enough to know that a little tea and sympathy are in order."

He sat in a straight-backed chair while she brewed the tea. She hummed while she worked, glancing over her shoulder every now and then to smile at him.

If he had any sense, he'd marry Lorena. Forget about the age difference. Forget about children. She was a good woman, an honest, hardworking, plainspoken woman who always knew exactly what he wanted.

But he would never marry Lorena. Especially not now. Guilt consumed him. He didn't like to think of himself as a person who used others, and yet that was exactly his purpose in coming there.

"I'm not complaining, mind you." Lorena handed him a cup and sat down on the chair facing him.

"How did you know what I was thinking?"

"Because I was thinking it too. I was thinking that I'm getting tired of dealing with that damned buffalo in my flower garden and too old to satisfy a man like Brett Corday."

"You'll never grow old, Lorena. Your spirit is too young."

"It's not my spirit that's sagging and wrinkled." She laughed heartily and took a big drink of tea. Lorena did everything with relish. Of all her good qualities, Brett found that one the most endearing. "What you need is a lovely young woman with enough grit and gumption to stand by your side come apes or high water."

As Ruth would stand by the side of his brother.

China clattered as Lorena set her cup down and squatted beside his chair. She put both hands on his knees and leaned toward him.

"I've hit the nail on the head, haven't I? Tell me about her."

"There is no woman, Lorena. At least not for me."

"But there *is* one, right?"

He'd never lied to Lorena and never would. "My brother's wife."

"Malone is married? My Lord, I didn't even know he was dating."

"Ruth is not the kind of woman men *date*. She's the kind men *capture,* the kind they beat their chests over, then throw over their shoulders and carry into the jungle."

Lorena said nothing, but her dark eyes moved over his face, alive with interest and sympathy. That she knew exactly when he needed sympathy was another reason he should marry her. He caressed her work-roughened knuckles.

"I acted a fool over her, Lorena. For the first time in my life, I tried to hide my eye patch."

"Your eye patch is beautiful. *You're* beautiful."

"I'm scarred. And I didn't want Ruth to see . . . and so I was rude to her."

"You could never be rude to anybody."

"I got over it, finally, and managed to act like a civilized human being. But I was *jealous,* Lorena, jealous of my own brother."

"Don't be so hard on yourself. You just found out you're human, after all. The *hard* way, right?" Her grin was knowing and bawdy. "Am I right?"

"Well, maybe. Just a little."

"A *little.*" Lorena snorted, measuring out the size she had in mind with her hands. " 'Bout like this, right?"

"Maybe a little bigger."

"Braggart."

They chuckled together as she bent over the cabinets, taking full advantage of the situation to wag her butt at him.

"Tell you what I'm going to do. I'll stir us up a big pot of soup, and you can talk about anything that suits your fancy, anything except why I don't take that job back in the States. Shoot, if I went back to Georgia, folks would drop dead at the sight of me. 'My Lord, Lorena,' they'd say, 'you're wrinkled up like a prune. How will you ever catch a husband looking like that?' "

The sound of her voice soothed him, made him forget.

"What would you tell them, Lorena?"

"I'd say if I caught one, I'd have to throw him back."

"Why?"

"Compared to the big ole catfish I've had, they're all fingerlings."

Lorena always made him laugh, and that, more than anything, was the reason he kept coming back. All these years.

"Are you expecting flattery to get you somewhere, Lorena?"

She set her pots down and put her hands on his shoulders.

"Just having you for a friend is enough."

"For me, too, Lorena."

As long as he had her, he knew he could survive.

21.

"THIS IS IT, RUTH. OUR HOME."

Her home. Deep in the Virungas. A hundred miles from the nearest village, but only two miles from the main house. Close enough to Eleanor and Joseph not to feel totally isolated from humanity, but far enough away to give the sense that she and her husband were alone. A married couple. Starting to build a life together.

And she'd started out with a pack of lies. The one she'd told Eleanor about her father still burned in her throat, but it had seemed the best thing to say at the moment, a way to stop the questions of her parentage once and for all.

She looked around her new home. It was a small cottage with wooden floors polished to a high sheen, braided rag rugs the colors of a sunset scattered about, simple furniture made to endure rather than to look pretty. Plantation shutters on the windows were open, letting in the smells and sounds of Africa. Ruth loved the simplicity of the cottage, loved its look of courage and endurance and warmth. There was even a potted plant in the window, not a red geranium as she had imagined, but an exotic-looking plant whose name she didn't know.

But she would find out. She'd find out everything about this land to which she'd come.

"It's not much," Malone said, taking her silence for disappointment.

"It's absolutely charming." She walked to the window and bent over the potted plant. The fragrance wasn't sweet like the gardenia outside her bedroom window in Mississippi, but something wild and mysterious. She was glad. She wanted everything about her life to be new and different. "Your mother must have put this here."

"I'm sure she did. Eleanor likes to manage things. Throw it out if you don't like it."

"Oh, but I love it. I'll have to remember to thank her."

She loved everything about her new home—the endless sweep of sky, the mountains that shrouded their secrets in mists, the strange, haunting cries of animals she didn't yet know—everything except her husband. The knowledge that she didn't love him saddened her beyond imagining. She felt like a thief. And worse. In her panicked haste to make herself safe from the black magic Maxwell Jones wove around her, she'd robbed Malone of the right to find a woman who would give him the love he deserved.

But she would try. With every bit of strength and breath in her body, she would try to love this man she'd followed to Africa. She would be good to him, as thoughtful and gentle and kind as he was to her. And if there was any redemption for her, if somewhere in the uncaring universe there was a Being who cared, perhaps real love would come. One fine morning she might awaken and look at Malone sleeping on the pillow beside hers and realize that she'd loved him all along, that it just took a while to understand what real love was.

"Please, God," she whispered. "Let this be so."

"Did you say something, darling?"

"No . . . I was just wondering . . . which side of the bed do you sleep on?"

The glow on his face made her ashamed.

"You mean you're going to sleep with me? I mean really . . ."

"I'm your wife, Malone, and this is our home."

He started toward her and tripped on the rug. "Shit, I'm as nervous as a bridegroom."

"I believe that's what you are."

"I'll be good to you, Ruth."

"I know you will."

"That's a promise."

The bed was covered with a patchwork quilt in shades of purple, the colors of the shadows that descended on the mountain looming just beyond their window. Already the fates were kind to her. She couldn't have endured a white bed.

Malone stood beside the bed, so shaken with love, he was powerless to move.

"I've never done this with a bride before." His grin was sheepish. "I don't know whether to go into the bathroom and change into pajamas. . . . Heck, I don't even have any pajamas."

"That's all right."

"I guess I won't be needing them anyhow."

His humor eased her own embarrassment and fear. Malone's belt buckle clattered as it hit the wooden floor. No man had ever touched her except Maxwell Jones. She shivered.

"I'll be gentle with you, Ruth."

She expected to feel revulsion and fear when he touched her, but his kisses were tender and sweet, given not out of great need, but out of great love. She genuinely tried for a response, but all she felt was a deep sadness that she couldn't return the love he so freely gave. If he noticed that she didn't reciprocate, he didn't say so.

Drawing back the covers, he pulled her down beside him onto the soft mattress.

"Touch me, Ruth."

It was a command she understood. All the old horror

came back to her as Malone placed her hand around his erection. She flinched from that hateful contact.

"Honey? Is something wrong?"

"No. Just nervous." Lying to him, she felt tarnished, unworthy. Would the lies ever cease to hurt?

Malone kissed the side of her neck. "It will be all right, honey. Trust me."

"I trusted you from the very beginning, Malone, trusted you enough to follow you all the way to the Dark Continent."

"They're going to have to change the name now that you're here, darling. The Magnificent Continent or maybe something more passionate. How about the Erogenous Zone?"

How he made her laugh. Wasn't laughter the first step toward loving? Oh, she hoped so. Opening her arms, she embraced him. Already he was rigid, the tip of his shaft pushing against her pubic hair. From a distance came the call of a strange bird, deeply mournful as if he had some secret sorrow he wanted to share with the world.

Her mind swung backward to a steamy hot afternoon in New Orleans when Max had ravaged her in the backyard while the loons called ceaselessly from the lake. Sometimes she still heard the loons.

Revulsion filled her—revulsion and something close to panic.

"Oh, please." Her broken whisper was more than a plea for freedom from fear; it was a supplication for mercy and grace.

If there was any justice in the world, the bird would cease its calling, and Malone, in one pure, clean stroke, would forever wipe Max from her mind.

"Please," she whispered once more, expecting a miracle.

"That's what I love to hear," Malone said, his breath hot against her throat. "Eagerness. A wife who can't wait to feel me inside her. It's going to be wonderful, darling. I promise."

She braced herself, waiting. In one smooth stroke he was in her, but where was the purity? Where was the redemption? Instead she felt the familiar jolt of shock and outrage, and the certain knowledge that she had brought everything upon herself.

"Ruth . . . Ruth." Malone moved in ever-increasing rhythm.

She knew how to endure. Closing her eyes, she thought of all the things she loved best—sitting beside a warm fire with Miranda in her lap, taking long walks in the woods, singing along with the jazz greats.

The woman on the bed had nothing to do with her. As she had with Max, she floated out of her body, taking her heart and soul and spirit with her. No one could ever touch that part of her.

Unexpectedly she thought of the dark, brooding man beside the fireplace. Brett Corday. Malone's brother. Her body quickened, and her husband, thinking the response was due to him, rewarded her with whispered encouragements.

Deep shame filled her, and a fear unlike any she'd ever known. What terrible monster had she become? Someone even worse than her mother, a woman who couldn't satisfy the husband pumping and heaving above her unless she thought of his brother.

Even animals wouldn't stoop that low.

Making her mind a careful blank, Ruth lay in her quiet cocoon of deep-purple mountains shrouded with mists. But one memory would not go away: the gleam of a single black eye. As she had at the age of fifteen, she focused on it, taking courage, taking strength, determined not merely to endure, but to triumph.

Finally it was over.

When Malone rolled off, he pulled her into his arms and caressed her hair.

"It was great for me, Ruth."

"I'm glad."

"We'll be better together after we get used to each other." He settled her head on his shoulder. "You're probably just a little tired."

"Yes," she said, knowing that she lied.

He ran his hand down the length of her thigh. "You're good, Ruth. The best."

Shame fell upon her like a damp, gray fog. She hadn't

openly swapped her body for money, the way her mother had, but perhaps what she had done was even worse. She'd exchanged her body for freedom, and Malone had no idea of the price he was paying.

If she rolled away, he would be hurt. And if she cried, even quietly, he'd feel the dampness on his bare chest. Thinking how she would roam this new continent she now called home, how she would make it her own, she lay quietly in her husband's arms and swallowed her tears.

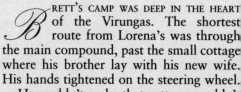

22.

BRETT'S CAMP WAS DEEP IN THE HEART of the Virungas. The shortest route from Lorena's was through the main compound, past the small cottage where his brother lay with his new wife. His hands tightened on the steering wheel.

He couldn't go by that cottage, couldn't bear to think that Ruth might be looking out the window and see his eye patch gleaming in the moonlight. Worse yet, she might think he had driven by to spy on them, as if he cared that they were tangled as close as the vines that intertwined the enormous trees of the rain forest.

The Jeep jarred his teeth together as he left the main trail and bounced over the rutted path that wound upward. The blackness of the dense rain forest soothed him. Tonight he didn't even want the moon shining on him.

He came into the light suddenly, into

the compound that sprawled at angles on the contours of the mountain slopes.

When he'd first come back to Africa, he'd set up a simple tent close enough to the mountain gorillas that he could monitor their lives around the clock. After Cee Cee had been orphaned, the camp had grown. Knowing how quickly she would outgrow the tent and need facilities that would contain her, he'd built a multipurpose compound. The west side was designed to house a grown gorilla, the center portion served as his living quarters, and the east wing housed Bantain, his twice-weekly housekeeper, who served as security guard while Brett was away, as well as an occasional visiting professor who came to observe Brett's work.

Cee Cee was waiting for him inside her fenced-in recreation area. Bantain had left the outdoor lights glowing, for Cee Cee hated the dark. The gorilla's face was pressed against the fence, and when she saw him, she beat her rag doll against the chain links and jumped up and down so hard, she almost lost her hair bow.

Brett was immediately drawn into the artificial world he'd created. If he hadn't known himself so well, he might have believed that the sight of a three-hundred-pound gorilla in a pink hair bow could make him forget everything.

"Hello, Cee Cee," he called. "How are you?"

She immediately turned her back and pretended not to notice him, a behavior pattern she'd started using when she'd entered gorilla puberty.

"How was dinner?" he asked.

She kept her back staunchly toward him. The cold shoulder. Punishment for being gone so long.

He let himself through the gate, then moved so that he was in her line of vision. Adopting a typical gorilla stance, he hunkered in front of her and began a conversation, speaking and signing at the same time.

"I had a good trip in the wheels move. What did you do?"

Cee Cee turned her back, then glanced over her shoulder and signed.

"Brett no-good stinkpot."

"Why?"

She pouted a while before she decided to turn back around and converse with him. Brett let her take her time, knowing that these conversations evolved Cee Cee's way or not at all.

Finally she placed her doll between her haunches and signed, *"Cee Cee sad, no like Brett go, dirty stinkpot."*

Brett was absolutely delighted with Cee Cee's responses. Over and over she proved that she was not only capable of abstract thought, but she was capable of the emotions generally considered distinctive to the human race—jealousy, hatred, and love.

Until the 1960's man was the only creature thought capable of speech. In an age when everything that had been accepted as true was called into question, the singularity of man's language was considered inviolate.

When Dr. Francine Patterson and others had started doing language studies with primates, the world at large had scoffed, and even the scientific community had been skeptical. "Signing is no proof of language. The animals are merely imitating," they'd said—until a gorilla named KoKo had proved them wrong.

She had shaken the entire world out of its smug complacency. Once the barrier of speech was removed between man and the lower animals, what other astonishing revelations were in store?

Brett wanted to go beyond the studies done with KoKo. His vision was so sweeping that he was awed by the possibilities, awed and sometimes frightened.

More and more his studies with Cee Cee concentrated on delving into her thought processes, in getting her to express her feelings rather than merely to learn new words. Long ago her vocabulary had surpassed his expectations, and daily she added to it, both with words he taught her and words she coined to meet her needs.

"Stinkpot" and "dirty stink" were her terms for people who displeased her. Only the week before she'd delighted him by asking to ride in the "wheels move," her term for Jeep.

Since she would never have need of a vehicle, he had not bothered to point out that particular object and teach her the word. But she had stood at her fence and seen him drive away too often not to have some curiosity about the Jeep.

"*Cee Cee go wheels move,*" she'd demanded when he'd returned from a quick overnight trip to Ruhengeri to see Lorena. At first he hadn't known what she was talking about. But she had been adamant. "*Brett go wheels move. Leave Cee Cee sad, go 'bye, wheels move.*"

"*Cee Cee want to go with Brett?*" he'd signed.

"*Yes. Go wheels move.*"

It was then he'd understood she was talking about the Jeep. Since then he'd started explaining his absences.

"*Brett go see Malone,*" he signed to explain his latest absence.

"*Malone stinkpot.*"

"*No. Malone is good.*"

"*Not good. Take Brett. Cee Cee sad.*"

She made such an exaggeratedly sad face that Brett had a hard time keeping from laughing. But he knew better. Above all things, Cee Cee liked to be taken seriously.

"*Food will make Cee Cee happy. Does Cee Cee want a banana?*"

"*No. Stink fruit. Not make happy.*"

"*What will make Cee Cee happy?*"

She looked at him with such a doleful expression that he got tickled all over again.

"*What will make Cee Cee happy?*" he asked once more. Repetition was often necessary to emphasize the importance of a question.

"*Brett,*" she signed.

"*Brett what?*"

"*Brett make happy. Cee Cee love Brett.*" She covered her eyes with her hands, then peered between her fingers with a coy expression on her face.

Instantly Brett was alert. This was new behavior for Cee Cee. Always when she'd expressed her love, she'd done it openly, like a child, coming to him with tight hugs and big gorilla kisses.

"*Brett loves Cee Cee too. Cee Cee fine animal gorilla.*"

"*No!*" She bared her teeth to show emphatic disagreement.

"*Yes. Cee Cee fine animal gorilla.*"

This time she stuck out her tongue, then huffed to the corner of her outdoor enclosure. On the way she lost her hair bow. With a yelp of rage she snatched it up, then tried to fasten it back onto her head. It kept slipping off, for she had no skill with mechanical things such as barrettes.

Eleanor had given the pink bow to Cee Cee on her eighth birthday. It was now bedraggled beyond repair, but it was one of Cee Cee's favorite possessions. The mere suggestion that it be replaced with a new bow brought howls of rage from her.

Brett picked up the ribbon and fastened it back in Cee Cee's fur. Looking deep into his eyes, she solemnly pronounced, *"Cee Cee not gorilla. Cee Cee fine female woman."*

Fine female woman. Terms she always applied to Eleanor.

The look Cee Cee gave him was filled with such conviction that he dared not argue. Instead he took her hand and led her into the compound to prepare for bed. As she curled her blankets into a nest, she regarded him with the same intense scrutiny she'd used outside.

The look was intelligent, almost human. How much did she understand about what he was trying to do with her? She'd been removed from her habitat when she was merely an orphaned infant, but on some deep primeval level did she long for the old ways?

"Good night, Cee Cee," he signed after she'd settled on her blankets.

She gave her head a sad shake and refused to talk to him.

"Is Cee Cee sick?"

Again, the head shake.

"Sad?"

Slowly she lifted her eyes to his and began to sign.

"Want Brett stay."

"I'm not leaving, Cee Cee. I'll be down the hall in my bed."

"No." She emphasized her sign with an adamant shake of her head. *"Brett stay."* She patted the blanket beside her. *"Sleep Cee Cee here."*

Sometimes he could tease her out of her moods with humor.

"No. Cee Cee snore."

"*Cee Cee fine female woman not snore.*" She lowered her eyes in the same coy manner she had earlier. "*Lonely sad lonely, heart bad.*" Looking mournful, she pounded her chest for emphasis.

Man was not meant to be alone. Male and female He had created them. Two by two they went into the ark. Even a gorilla knew that.

Cee Cee's longings touched some deep, empty core within him, and suddenly he saw his entire life's work in a different light. In taking her out of her habitat, had he taken away the very essence that made her a gorilla? Was he on a mountain playing God?

After the unsettling encounter, he didn't have the heart to reduce Cee Cee to an entry in the daily record book. Instead he went outside and stood in the deep-blue twilight, trying to recapture the sense of euphoria he always felt when he was alone with nature in the country he loved.

Tonight, though, he felt nothing but uncertainty and gut-wrenching loneliness.

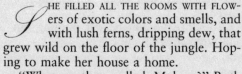

23.

*S*HE FILLED ALL THE ROOMS WITH FLOW-
ers of exotic colors and smells, and
with lush ferns, dripping dew, that
grew wild on the floor of the jungle. Hoping to make her house a home.

"What are these called, Malone?" Ruth
bent over a particularly lovely flower, neither vermilion nor pink but some shade in
between.

"I don't have any idea."

"You don't *know*?"

"To tell you the truth, I don't care. I've
always hated the jungle."

She propped her elbows on the windowsill and leaned out the open window.

"I love it. I want to explore every inch
of it." She turned back to her husband.
"Do you have any guidebooks I can use,
something to help me identify the trees and
flowers and birds?"

"You don't need a guidebook. Brett will

take you. He's crazy about all that shit. Knows the jungle like the back of his hand."

At the mention of his brother's name, Ruth's heart gave a little lurch. Thinking of Brett somewhere in the jungle filled her with an excitement she hadn't felt in years.

"I should be up there with him," she said before she thought.

"What?"

"Working, I mean. My dissertation is still at the bottom of my suitcase. Professor Hicks is going to retire this year, and if I don't finish my dissertation, I'll have to be assigned to somebody else."

"I know how much you admire him, honey, but what would it hurt if you had to have somebody else? Relax and enjoy being a bride."

Enjoy that nightly pawing? She suppressed a shiver.

"Professor Hicks is the best, Malone. And if I'm going to work with the Corday family, I want to be well-grounded in my field. Besides, he's the only one who knows both primatology and anthropology." He had his back up. It hadn't taken her more than three days with Malone to learn that when things didn't go his way, he could get as stubborn and puffed up as a toad. As much as she hated resorting to feminine wiles, she'd learned that they worked with him. Turning from the window, she smiled. "Besides, you're the one who lured me here with the promise that I could study with your brother."

He melted.

"Look at you, all flushed. You need to get used to this climate before you go traipsing all over the jungle. And that's what will happen when you go to Brett's camp. He'll drag you all over the jungle looking for gorillas."

"I'm okay. It's just excitement over . . . studying at the feet of the master." She wanted desperately to believe that what she'd said was the truth, but she'd become such a liar that it was hard to know whether she could even tell the truth to herself anymore.

"Honey, what's the rush? We've only been here two weeks."

She'd spent two weeks in the white room with Max. Trapped, with no way out. Her pulse beat hard against her temples, and her breath came in short spurts. Smothering. She was smothering. Leaning far out the window, she sucked in air.

"What's wrong, sweetheart?"

What *was* wrong? Malone was a wonderful, dear man who did everything he could to please her. He brought her breakfast in bed, massaged her feet, told her funny stories that made her laugh. He even loved her cat. Still, she felt not the faintest stirrings of love. Maybe there was no such thing. At least not for damaged people like her.

"Is anything wrong?" he asked once more, coming up behind her and putting his hand on her shoulder.

She was what was wrong.

"Nothing. Just breathing all this good fresh air."

She wrapped her arms around Malone's waist and leaned her head on his shoulder.

"You are such a good man," she said, meaning it.

He kissed the top of her head, then the side of her neck.

"Why don't you give yourself a little more time before thinking about work, sweetheart? After all, we're still on our honeymoon."

How could she tell him it felt more like a prison to her?

"I know. But I really must get started." His hands were on her buttons. And all she felt was a sense of dread. She caught one of his hands and brought it to her lips, hoping to distract him, but his breathing was already labored, his eyes hooded.

"I was thinking an afternoon walk would be nice . . . Malone."

He didn't even hear her.

He'd promised to be patient with her, and gentle. But there was no gentleness in him now. Her thin white cotton blouse ripped as he shoved it aside. She shivered as he closed his mouth over her nipple.

But they were not shivers of anticipation.

"I can't get enough of you."

She wished he could. She wished she could wave a magic wand and satisfy his sexual appetites so that she never again had to do this with him, this terrible pretense, this damnable lie that further blackened her soul.

"Ruth!"

She stood like something that had taken root in the rug, but he didn't seem to notice. Her breath left her as he jerked her onto her back and shoved her skirt over her legs. His breathing was labored as he ripped her panties aside.

Maybe he had noticed, after all. Maybe this was her punishment for not responding.

He drove into her so hard, she scooted across the rug. She felt a sharp sting as the nap burned her shoulders.

She clenched her jaw to hold back her scream. Outrage? Revulsion? Surely not with her husband. Not dear, sweet Malone.

But this time he was neither dear nor sweet: He was a wild man, sweat dripping off his forehead and nose as he pounded her into the thick rug. She felt like a piece of meat. Was he trying to tenderize her? Hysterical laughter bubbled in her throat, but she bit down hard on her lips, so hard, she could taste her own blood.

It was over quickly. Malone adjusted his clothes. She lay against the rug with her eyes closed.

"Ruth?"

She wanted to shrink away when he touched her shoulder. To scream. To run and never stop.

"Are you okay, honey?" There was concern in his voice.

"Yes."

"I . . . don't know what got into me."

"That's all right." She made herself look at him, forced her mouth into a smile. "I guess these things happen."

"Yeah. I looked at you there at the window, the sun on your skin, that thin blouse . . . God, I could see the shape and color of your nipples. Then, when I touched you, it was like taking that first bite of ice cream. I just couldn't stop."

"I'm a married woman now. I'll get used to it."

The minute the words were out of her mouth, she knew she'd said the wrong thing, but it was too late to take them back. Malone got a funny look on his face, then turned his back on her and walked away.

She could hear ice tinkling against glass, then the slosh of liquid.

"Can I fix you a drink, Ruth?"

At two in the afternoon?

"No, thank you."

"You're sure? It might help you relax."

Relax? Sprawled on the rug with her legs spread and her panties lying torn beside her? Slowly she gathered her clothes about her and got off the rug. She felt a hundred years old.

Malone was watching her. There was a puzzled look on his face, like a child who'd broken the cookie jar when all he ever intended was to take one cookie. She stood on tiptoe and kissed his cheek.

"It's all right, Malone. Really it is."

He set his drink on the bar and squeezed her tightly against his chest.

"God, Ruth. You're my life. I don't know what I'd do if I ever lost you."

"You'll never lose me."

"Promise?"

He looked so innocent with his limp hair hanging over his forehead and the hangdog expression on his face that it was impossible to be upset with him.

"Promise?" he asked once more, as if he couldn't bear to trust a silence between them.

She brushed his hair back and kissed his damp forehead.

"I already did. 'Till death do us part.' Remember?"

"Yeah. I sure do." When he grinned, he was the old Malone, the sweet man she trusted. "Look, I'm going to make this up to you. I'll go walking with you. Heck, I'll even explore the whole damned jungle."

"That's sweet of you."

"Sweet, heck. It's selfish. I can't bear to have you out of my sight."

Prickles stood up on the back of her neck. She wanted her marriage to work. Wanted it desperately. But not at the cost of her independence.

"I think I'll go by myself. I would really like to do some exploring on my own."

"It's a jungle out there."

This time she wouldn't be cajoled by his humor.

"I'll take a map. How hard can it be to get around? I've seen the trails."

He wasn't convinced. "You might get lost."

"I learned survival skills as a Girl Scout. Besides, I never get lost."

"I'd never forgive myself if something happened to you."

"Malone, I really need to do this by myself."

"I understand."

He didn't look understanding; he looked crestfallen. Ordinarily she would have relented, but at the moment she had nothing left of herself to give.

"This is my home now, Malone. I can't be dependent on you to show me every little thing."

"I guess you're right. . . . Look, I think there is a book or two around here that will help you." He began to rummage in the bookshelves. "We used to have visitors staying here all the time when the foundation was young. They were always wanting to know the name of everything they saw. Thought it made them sound smart, as if they'd lived here for years. . . . Ah, here it is."

The book was a fat, slick volume complete with color photographs. Malone whipped a sheet of paper out of the desk and drew a map of the compound.

"You can take the Jeep. Follow any of these trails. They all lead back to the compound here. And this one goes to Brett's camp."

She tucked the map into her skirt pocket.

"I'll miss you every minute you're gone, honey."

She squeezed his hand and patted his cheek, wishing she could tell him the same thing. In the bathroom she ripped off her clothes and scrubbed until her skin squeaked. If she could invent a way to make her insides as squeaky clean, she'd make a million dollars and retire to some mountaintop retreat with her own gorilla group. Living a dream. Just like Brett. *With* Brett?

The thought coming out of nowhere took her aback. If her mind was going to be her betrayer, then she'd have to become a refuge from thought.

Outside, Malone waited on the front porch with Miranda.

"'Bye, darling." He reached for her. "Be back before dark."

She squeezed him extra tight, waiting for a sign, a small stirring of warmth, a little tug at her heart, *anything* . . . waiting and waiting. Finally she let go.

"I promise," she said.

With a little wave of her hand, she was off.

It was quiet in the jungle—no traffic, no people, no pollution, just Ruth and the giant trees that dipped and swayed in the soft winds that blew down from the mountains. When she was out of sight of the cabin, she stopped at a bend in the road and sat at the wheel, soaking up the peace. The smells of the earth were good, rich and full of promise; the land itself was wild, exotic, different from anything she'd ever known, the kind of place that would begin to grow inside her, filling her up until there was no room left for the steamy nights in the white bedroom filled with white roses.

A carefree exuberance overtook her, and she shook her fist in the general direction of New Orleans.

"Damn you, Max. I won't let you win."

She set the Jeep back in motion, and it seemed natural, somehow, to gravitate up the mountain toward the man who had exerted such a mysterious magnetism on her since she was fifteen years old.

Besides, Malone himself had suggested it. Hadn't he said Brett knew everything there was to know about the jungle?

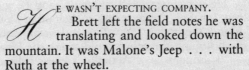

24.

HE WASN'T EXPECTING COMPANY.
Brett left the field notes he was translating and looked down the mountain. It was Malone's Jeep . . . with Ruth at the wheel.

He'd known she would come sooner or later. Hadn't she said she wanted to meet Cee Cee? But somehow he wasn't prepared for this invasion, either physically or mentally. In the two weeks since she'd come to Africa, he'd buried himself so deep in his work that it was almost as if she didn't exist.

Foolish pretense. She existed not only as vibrant matter that took up space on his mountain but as undaunted spirit in the subterranean levels of his mind.

And now she was coming to him.

He had been out all day with Doby's group and probably smelled like a gorilla. Would he have time to change clothes?

No, the Jeep was too close. She'd be at his door any minute now. At least he would comb his hair.

In the bathroom he splashed water on his face and grabbed a comb. Leaves and bits of bamboo clung to his hair. He looked like a battered one-eyed bug.

"Hello! Anybody home?"

The notion of slicking himself up for Ruth was a silly vanity. She was family now. What did it matter how he looked, after all? He set the comb down and adjusted his eye patch.

"Coming."

Ruth was standing in his doorway smiling and slightly apologetic, a guidebook of Central Africa clutched under her arm.

"I hope I'm not disturbing you."

"No." Not in ways he could explain. "I guess you've come to see Cee Cee."

"No. Not Cee Cee."

"I see," he said, not seeing at all.

He got sidetracked suddenly, and he guessed she did, too, for they stood staring at each other like strangers who found themselves traveling a foreign country together, each hoping the other could speak the language.

"I thought . . . Actually, I guess I didn't think. I was out exploring, and suddenly I found myself on the trail that leads here."

It was the most flattering thing he'd ever heard, that she'd found herself coming to him without even knowing why.

"I was going exploring, you see . . . ," she added. "Oh, I've already said that."

"Africa is a wonderful and magical place."

"Malone said you know the jungle like the back of your hand."

So Malone had sent her. He was crazy to feel deflated, as if he were a balloon and somebody had let out all the air.

"I probably shouldn't have come without any warning. I apologize for interrupting you. I'll just go quietly so you can get back to your work."

She couldn't leave. Not yet.

"Stay . . . please." He reached toward her, almost touching her. Almost. Ruth. His brother's wife. Quickly he rammed his hands into his pockets. "I mean . . . it's all right."

He was making a complete fool of himself. Very few women came to his camp except Eleanor and an occasional reporter, and he had no idea what to do. An unusual state of affairs for him—he *always* knew what to do. On his mountain among the gorillas, he was king. Now, facing Ruth, he was a knave.

"You must be very busy," she said. "I apologize for interrupting your work." Sudden color bloomed on her cheeks. "Oh . . . I've already said that too."

Her cheeks were turning the color of very fine wine. He watched, fascinated. Ruth shifted her book from one hand to the other. Body language. A subtle signal that he'd been staring too long.

"No. I'm the one who should apologize. Standing in the door like a fool. Forgive me, Ruth. I'm not used to company."

"You're forgiven."

"I've been at it since five o'clock this morning. It's time for a break. Come in and I'll tell you exactly where to find everything in that guidebook."

"Thank you, no. Actually, I wondered whether you might go with me."

The idea of going in the Jeep with her made him feel like a teenager. It had been a long, long time since he'd felt that vaulting sense of freedom and invincibility.

"Why not? I'll drive so you can look."

Ordinarily it was a chore he hated, playing tour guide to greenhorns who desecrated the sacred tranquillity of the rain forest with their restless fidgeting and their endless chatter. But Ruth was different. Serene.

He soon forgot she was there. Because she didn't intrude, he lost himself in the wonder of the land and discovered that translating that wonder for her was the same as praying.

"Once there were seas of exotic animals here," he said, "wildebeest and oryx, and mighty herds of elephants." He could see them roaming the plains as they once had, masses of them, sleek and wild and free, as much a part of the land as the mountains that cast their shadows over it.

"But man encroached on Africa, raped and pillaged its resources in the name of civilization. The animals know how to hide from us now."

Ruth gazed into the distance, across the slopes and gorges, her eyes misty, her hair lifting softly off her neck in the breeze that drifted down from the mountaintops.

High on a ridge above them, a large cat showed itself.

"Look, Ruth. Up there."

"A panther?"

"Yes. You've just seen a rare sight."

She crossed her hands over her heart, and there were tears in her eyes. Now he understood why Malone had married her without knowing anything at all about her background. In one small gesture she had revealed her soul, and it was pure and lovely.

Somewhere deep inside, Brett exulted. He drove the Jeep up a steep trail that overlooked a waterfall tumbling into a gorge so green that the color spread outward and upward, suffusing the air with a clean, fresh smell and even lending an emerald tint to the sky.

"It looks newly created," she whispered.

"Yes," he said, pleased and touched. "It's my favorite spot."

They sat side by side, not speaking, not touching, simply sharing the miracle of creation in awed silence. A small herd of duiker stole silently out of the shade. Two of them made their way to the edge of the water to drink while the others grazed and lolled about on the thick carpet of grass. One of them, a baby on spindly, uncertain legs, capered between two adults, occasionally sprawling on his hindquarters, sometimes losing the balance in his forelegs so that his wet black nose pressed into the grass. Finally he got the feel of movement, and his loose capering became a lovely fluid movement, a dance of joy.

The sun dropped suddenly behind the mountain, turning the sky to a brilliant palette of gold and red and purple. A single shaft of light caught in the small duiker's fur so that he was transformed, ethereal, golden.

"Look!" Ruth clutched Brett's arm. Her gaze was riv-

eted on the baby duiker, and there was such a glow of
pleasure on her face that her skin looked as if it had been
lit from within.

"That's so beautiful I could cry."

She already was. Totally unaware. Tears shimmered on
her eyelashes, rolled down her cheeks. He couldn't take his
eyes off them. Off *her*. Off her cheeks, soft and beautifully
defined. Off her hand, resting lightly on his arm. Her nails
had pale half-moons, perfectly shaped. They made her
look fragile, vulnerable.

He stared at those cream-colored half-moons, and such
a sense of loss came over him that he could have wept. If
he'd been Malone instead of himself, he would have had
the right to hold a pair of fragile hands, to watch them do
simple tasks—lift a teacup, smooth a collar, caress a
baby's cheek. If he hadn't chosen to hide on a mountaintop, he would have been the one to sit in the lamplight and
watch as those pale half-moons were slowly buffed to a
fine sheen.

He dared not move lest Ruth notice him watching her
hand and take it away, embarrassed at what she saw in his
eyes.

Naked longing.

Not for her. Not for his brother's wife. But for all the
things she represented. For all the things that had been
denied him—or that he had denied himself.

She must not see. He pulled his gaze away, turned it
upon the sunset that was painting the Virungas. No one
who had seen it had ever failed to be awed, though most
visitors tried to hide their awe, as if it would mark them as
children rather than adults. Ruth was not afraid to let her
wonder show.

Side by side, not moving, not speaking, they watched
while the sky changed from gold and red to deep rose
streaked with violet, and finally to gold-veined purple that
faded to blackness so thick, it was impenetrable.

Only when darkness descended around them did Ruth
stir. Like a woman waking from a trance, she flexed her
shoulders and shifted her legs. Then, suddenly aware, she
glanced sideways at Brett.

One single star bloomed out of the blackness, and its

light fell across her hand with the same bright force of a
missile seeking its target. Both of them looked at her hand
resting there on his arm, so easy, so natural . . . and
then, suddenly, at each other. Such a look—as if they had
just discovered how the eyes could see past skin and bone,
past cloth and buttons, past lies and pretensions, straight
to the heart.

Ruth's fingers tightened, her fingernails sinking slightly
into his skin. Brett felt the prick of pleasure-pain, even felt
the half-moon shape of her nails.

Their eyes wouldn't let go. Finally, desperately, Ruth
dragged her hand away.

Brett ran his finger lightly over the grooves her nails
had made in his skin. The movement vibrated through her
so hard, she hugged herself to stop her shaking.

"Malone!" she said, as if he had materialized out of the
darkness. "I promised him I'd be home before dark."

Brett was suddenly angry with his brother, furious that
he sat at home in the safety of his cottage while his wife
was in a pitch-black rain forest she didn't even know.

"Don't worry. I'll take you home."

"I'm not worried about getting home. I just don't want
Malone to be worried about me."

"Malone's a big boy. You're not responsible for his
moods."

Ruth seemed to shrink from him, though actually she
didn't move at all.

"I didn't mean that he's moody," she said.

Brett felt a vague sense of disloyalty, as if he'd stabbed
Malone in the back.

"No . . . I didn't either. It's just that night comes so
suddenly to Africa, you had no way of knowing when to
start back home."

"I guess I have a lot to learn."

There was a forlorn quality in her voice, a little-girl-lost
tone that made Brett want to pick a fight with somebody
for causing it. Just about anybody would do.

"Give youself time, Ruth."

"That's what Malone says . . . about everything."

About everything? What things?

He had no right to know.

He turned the Jeep around and headed down the mountain. Neither of them spoke until they were almost to his camp.

"I can go the rest of the way by myself," Ruth said.

"No."

"I'm not some hothouse flower, you know."

"I know. Still, I'm taking you home."

"It's nice of you, and I don't want to seem ungrateful, but how will you get back?"

"Malone will bring me."

"Yes . . . I forgot."

Forgot what? Malone? The questions burned in him, but he didn't dare ask.

They rode along with the sounds of the jungle echoing around them, the calls of the night birds, the bark of the duiker, the trumpeting of a lone elephant, and far in the distance, the muted drumming of a male silverback gorilla.

"You don't think he'll be mad?" she said.

"Malone?" he asked, as if he himself had forgotten his own brother. "He won't be mad . . . or upset, either. He knows you're with me."

"Not exactly."

"He doesn't know you're with me?"

"I'm not sure. He said you'd show me the jungle, then I said I thought I'd explore by myself, and I started out that way, but before I knew it . . ." She stared out the window in silence, then turned to him, ethereal in the pale lights from the dashboard, like someone he'd imagined. "I don't think he knows."

"I'll explain . . ." Explain? As if he and Ruth had done something wrong. ". . . that I wanted to show you the sunset over the gorge. There's no way you can get home before dark if you see the sunset over the gorge."

"Thank you."

"You're welcome."

He could see the lights in the cottage and the shape of Malone as he stood at the window. Looking for his wife.

"Ruth . . ." Brett slowed the Jeep.

"Yes?"

Her face was a pale oval, her eyes so dark, he could see nothing except a pinpoint of brightness in their centers.

What had he been about to say? Crazy, to be so absent-minded.

"Come to see me anytime you need me." Would she get the wrong idea? "You're family now, and I'll do anything for my family." Unconsciously, he touched his eye patch. "I just want you to know that."

"Thank you, Brett."

She touched his arm, the fragile half-moons on her fingernails silvery and shining in the moonlight.

"Malone's waiting," he said.

Her hand was warm on his arm, and when she withdrew it, he felt a chill.

"Yes," she said. "Malone's waiting."

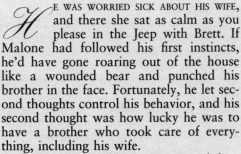

25.

H E WAS WORRIED SICK ABOUT HIS WIFE, and there she sat as calm as you please in the Jeep with Brett. If Malone had followed his first instincts, he'd have gone roaring out of the house like a wounded bear and punched his brother in the face. Fortunately, he let second thoughts control his behavior, and his second thought was how lucky he was to have a brother who took care of everything, including his wife.

"Ruth!" He couldn't wait to touch her, to feel her against him. His wife. Sometimes the wonder that she'd said yes to him caught him high up under the ribs in such a gut punch, he nearly lost his breath. "Darling!" He flung open the door of the Jeep and pulled her into his arms. "I've been so worried about you. What took you so long?"

"The sunset," Brett said. "Over the gorge. I took her there. It's my fault that she's late."

Malone thought of himself sitting alone staring anx
iously out the window while Brett watched a sunset with
his wife. Always second-best. Old feelings stole over him
threatened to destroy his reason.

"We didn't mean to worry you, darling."

"We," she'd said, as if the two of them had planned it
He looked at his brother, tall and handsome, sure of him
self in ways that Malone never could be. Why had Ruth
gone to Brett after telling him that she wanted to explore
alone?

But he could forgive her anything because she'd called
him darling. A first. Did that mean that she was beginning
to love him? Just a fraction as much as he loved her?

"What can I say? You're a woman worth waiting for
sweetheart." Did she actually snuggle into him? Usually he
felt a slight resistance, as if she were made of some kind of
material that would bend only so far without breaking.

"Thanks for taking care of her, bro."

"Anytime."

Anytime? Malone was immediately ashamed of his jeal
ous thought. Brett would do anything for the family, and
that now included Ruth.

Malone leaned into the Jeep.

"Scoot over, bro, and I'll take you back up the moun
tain."

"No need. I'll walk."

"Walk! Shit, there's a rainstorm brewing. You'll get
soaking wet before you get halfway."

"Good. I need a bath."

"I noticed."

Ruth apparently didn't see the humor in Malone's re
mark. Her face full of concern, she was leaning into the
Jeep toward his brother.

"I'll feel terrible if you have to walk back home because
of me," she said.

"Actually, I need to walk so I can check on poaching
activity. They do their dirty deeds at night."

"Will you be safe?"

"Yes. I'll be safe."

Malone felt shut out. And petty. He should be proud of
his wife's compassion.

"Ruth, darling, let's say good night to Brett and go inside."

"Thanks for the tour, Brett."

"Anytime, Ruth."

Why was she still leaning into the Jeep? And why was Brett still sitting there?

The rains came upon them suddenly, not in drops the way an ordinary rain should begin, but in a great deluge, as if a river had burst high in the mountains, its waters flung upward and downward at the same time. The earth turned instantly to mud.

Brett barreled out of the Jeep and struggled to get the top up. Malone slogged toward the Jeep to help him.

"I'll do it," Brett yelled over the rain. "Take care of Ruth!"

As if he needed to be told what to do with his own wife.

"Screw the poachers!" Malone yelled. "Take the damned Jeep. I'll have Bantu bring me up tomorrow to get it."

Brett waved him off. Malone wrapped his arm around Ruth's waist and sprinted toward the cottage. Inside, they shook the rain off themselves, but it did no good. They were already soaked.

"Will he be all right?" Ruth stared out the window, trying to see through the driving rain.

"He's stayed out in worse rains than this just to study his damned gorillas. Your worry is wasted on him."

"Wasted! How can you say that? He was very kind to me."

"And what does that make me? Chump of the year?"

Ruth looked at him as if he'd socked her in the face, but he didn't budge from the window. Ordinarily he would have said something funny to ease them out of their first major battle, but he wasn't feeling funny. He was feeling left out.

"I didn't say that." Ruth turned her back to the window, but she still held on to the windowsill. What did she think he was going to do? Wrench her away?

What he wanted to do was not be on opposite sides of the room fighting with his wife, but he didn't have sense enough to end it. Not yet.

"I would have gone with you to see that damned sun set."

"Is that what this is about? That I watched a sunse with your brother?"

"What else did you do?"

If looks could burn, he'd have been black from head t toe. She looked at least six feet tall as she stalked from th room.

"Ruth . . . wait." He caught up with her at the door "Honey . . . I didn't mean that. I don't know what go into me."

Ruth looked at the liquor bottle he'd left sitting on th bar, judging the level of liquor, studying it the way Bret had studied him out by the Jeep.

"Can't a man have a little drink to keep from bein worried crazy over his wife, who's gone into the jungl with nothing but a guidebook?"

Ruth put her hands on his cheeks, and Malone knev that everything was going to be all right. He felt like cryin with relief.

"I'm sorry I worried you."

"I'm sorry I acted like such a pissant. Forgive me?"

"All's forgiven."

"Why don't I build a little fire, and we can pop som corn and rub each other's feet and plan how we'll mak our first fight into a funny story to tell our grandchil dren?"

"I think I'll change out of these wet clothes first," sh said.

"Need any help?"

He wagged his ears at her, a real talent, guaranteed t make her laugh. It didn't work this time. She walked to th window and stood looking out, though there was nothing she could possibly see in the pitch-blackness, not even th rain. Suddenly he was afraid, as if some wild animal wer waiting just outside the window to snatch his wife away He wanted to call her back, to beg her to turn around and face him, but the set of her shoulders held him powerless

When she finally turned around, the look on her face reminded him of one of the statues he'd seen in wax muse ums—Joan of Arc, maybe, or one of the generals of Worl

War II. Fearless. Determined. Not somebody you'd want
to mess with.

"I'll be right back," she said.

As he watched her disappear, he poured himself a
vodka and tonic. To take the edge off.

26.

RUTH PULLED THE SHEET AROUND HER and leaned over Malone's back so she could see his face. He was sleeping soundly, his mouth slightly open, his hair hanging over his eyes. Gently she brushed his hair back from his forehead.

"Poor baby," she whispered. The night before, he'd had too much to drink because he'd been worried about her. She'd make sure that never happened again.

Easing out of bed so she wouldn't wake him, she tiptoed to the window. The torrential rains had stopped, but the jungle looked like a sauna, steam rising everywhere, thicker in some places than others, so thick, she couldn't see the trees.

Could she see to drive?

She set the coffee to perking, then hurried with her bath. Anxious to get started.

Miranda wrapped herself around Ruth's legs while she sat at the kitchen table, nibbling a piece of toast and composing a note to her husband.

"Sweetheart, thank you for a lovely evening. . . ."

It *had* been lovely. Sitting on the rug beside him, eating popcorn before a cozy fire. Only two things had marred it: worry over Brett walking through the downpour, and the three vodka and tonics Malone had consumed.

He'd gone to sleep the minute his head had hit the pillow. Ruth had been grateful for the respite, and then had felt guilty because she was grateful.

Miranda climbed into her lap, purring, and Ruth finished her note.

"I'll be at Brett's compound most of the day, working on my dissertation."

She hoped Malone would remember that she'd told him time was running out, that if she didn't get to work, she'd miss the opportunity of finishing her dissertation with one of the most respected professors of anthropology in the country.

"Please don't worry if I'm not home by dark. You know how it is to get so involved in a project that you forget the time."

She toyed with the idea of merely signing her name, then decided that would seem cold and distant.

"Love, Ruth," she wrote, feeling hypocritical.

But she *did* love him, in the same way she would love a wayward child.

Ruth propped the note on the kitchen table where Malone would be sure to see it. Squatting, she hugged her cat.

" 'Bye, Miranda. Be a good girl and take care of Malone."

Miranda sounded like a miniature freight train as she wound herself around Ruth's legs.

"Sorry I can't take you, old girl. But I'm going to meet somebody who might not love cats the way I do."

Just thinking about meeting Cee Cee gave her shivers. Or was that the real reason she was shivering?

She wasn't going to dwell on it. Wanda used to say that if you thought about something enough, it would come true. At thirteen Ruth had believed it. At twenty-six she did not. Still, it seemed logical that the most important things in your life would consume your thoughts.

She made herself think of her husband.

She filled Miranda's dishes, then made one last check on Malone. He was on his back now, his snores filling the room. He probably wouldn't even know she was gone until noon.

She took the map he'd drawn, just in case, but her sense of direction had always been good. In Girl Scouts she'd always been the first to earn her outdoor medals—camping, hiking, trailblazing. After Max, she'd been the only girl in her troop to win in archery—all that practice with the gun having paid off.

Suddenly the steam over the jungle seemed denser, threatening. She put Max from her mind. He belonged to another world, another life. She was a Corday now, under the full protection of the Corday name.

"Come to see me anytime you need me," Brett had said.

Wrapping the thought around her mind like a warm blanket, she felt comforted. Her grip on the wheel loosened; even her toes, curled tightly against the soles of her sandals, relaxed.

For the first time in years she sang for the sheer pleasure of making music, an old tune she remembered from Sunday school, "Heavenly Sunshine." If she'd thought about it, it might have struck her as strange that she was singing about sunshine when the sun was nowhere to be seen, but she wasn't thinking; she was merely *being* and *enjoying*.

As she topped the last ridge, she saw Brett in the front yard waiting for her, rising out of the mists like a mythical god. Without warning, her heart lurched, as if something else had been lying in wait for her in the mists.

Not wanting to think about what it might be, she beeped the horn and waved.

"You came out to meet me," she said, inordinately pleased.

"I heard the Jeep coming up the mountain. I knew it would be you."

In spite of the mists, the song about sunshine still soared through her mind, and she smiled at Brett.

"I can tell the sound of Malone's Jeep," he added.

"For a minute there, I thought you might be psychic."

"No. Just an ordinary guy."

"Not ordinary," she said, meaning it, then hoping he wouldn't take it the wrong way.

"Thank you, Ruth." He leaned into the Jeep, and she suddenly felt the total impact of him. Like being face-to-face with a rare and beautiful animal.

She held on to the steering wheel as if she were headed somewhere instead of having just arrived.

"I'm glad you made it through the rain last night," she said. "It was so dark."

"I'm not afraid of the dark."

"Sometimes I am."

Her quick confession took them both by surprise. She'd learned the hard way how to dam up her fears. Now, suddenly, a tiny crack had sprung in the wall. If she didn't shore it up, the dam was likely to burst. She gathered up her material.

"I brought all my notes. For my dissertation. I hope you don't mind that I came without warning."

"Do I need to be warned?"

There was laughter in his face. She loved that quality in the Corday men, the ability to ease a painful situation with laughter.

"You and Malone. Always kidding around."

As Brett opened the door, she pictured her husband lying tangled in their bedcovers, still sleeping. The contrast between brothers was enormous—one dynamic, enthusiastic; the other soft, unfocused. That she should be so happy in the company of the one who was not her husband made her feel disloyal to the one who was.

It was too late to turn back now, even if she'd wanted to.

"I can't wait to get started," she said.

"Here. Let me carry that."

Brett relieved her of her notes as if they were an enormous burden instead of a small stack of papers. The old-fashioned courtliness of the gesture touched her more than she would have dreamed possible. She thought of other things he did, little things—opening doors, offering his arm, telling her to come anytime she needed him.

As she walked beside him with the mists swirling at their feet, she stole a glance upward. Because of his eye patch she was on his blind side and had no need at all for stealth. And yet the force of her feelings made her shy and somehow bold at the same time.

"I want to brief you thoroughly before I introduce you to Cee Cee," he said. "She is far more complex than most people imagine, and I don't want to do anything in haste that might turn her against you."

He even wanted to ensure her a cordial welcome from a gorilla. Another small kindness.

Whatever she felt for him, whatever had risen unexpectedly out of the mists to take control of her, could be tamed, could be turned into nothing more than gratitude, admiration, and genuine affection.

"I'm so glad I have you," she said.

Ruth reached out. Softly he intertwined their fingers, then closed his hand around hers. Connected to him, she felt anchored and secure.

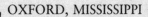

27.

OXFORD, MISSISSIPPI

*I*T WAS ALMOST LIKE OLD TIMES.
A ray of sun coming in through the window glinted on the silver teapot. She'd bought pecan tassies for the occasion because they were his favorite pastry.

"You're looking good, Max."

"Thank you, Margaret Anne."

Her feelings were hurt that he didn't return the compliment, but she hid them well. He didn't like pouting women.

Nor did she berate him that she'd had to learn of his wife's death from the six o'clock news on television. It was enough that he finally was back.

Like fine wine, he'd improved with age. Margaret Anne felt a stab of resentment . . . and fear. Then she remembered her trump card, her ace in the hole, which was as good a way as any of describing where her daughter was. She'd read that in the newspapers too: "Malone Corday of the famous Corday family weds Ruth Bellafontaine."

Wedded her and bedded her, then took her off to the Virungas. The only thing Margaret Anne knew or cared to know about Africa was that she'd seen some of the finest male bodies in the world in a color layout of the Congo in *National Geographic.*

Max prowled the room, pausing in front of the mantel to pick up the photograph in a filigreed silver frame.

"I see you have his picture out again."

"I no longer have to hide it. Ruth will never be home again."

"Do you still love him, Margaret Anne?"

She remembered him at sixteen, his beautiful body gleaming with sweat from the fields. She remembered the long, tapered fingers as they held a dipper of ice water for her to drink, and years later as they'd moved over her with the mastery of a virtuoso.

"Does it matter?" Her hands trembled as she picked up the teapot, then reached for a china cup.

"No." Max caught her hand and pulled her from the chair. "There's only one thing that matters."

She didn't dare risk spoiling the moment by asking him to spell out what it was that mattered. It had been so long since she'd died the small death, so very long, but she waited, knowing how he liked to take the lead.

Much to her joy, he led her upstairs to the bedroom where the sheets were cool and the air perfumed with summer flowers. Then he drew the shades so the room would be dark.

That suited her to a tee. No matter how hard she tried, her body had given in to the effects of age and gravity. Feeling flushed as a schoolgirl, she undressed and lay down on top of the clean sheets. Her breasts had always been her best asset, and by holding her elbows tightly at her sides she could still keep them perky, even lying down.

"Beg for it," he said after he'd undressed.

"Please."

"Say it like you mean it."

If she wanted him any more, she'd be on her knees

begging, and Max had always known it. What new game was this?

"Please," she whispered. "I've wanted you for so long that I'm dying. Please, Max. Make me live again."

He turned his back to her. Was he going to leave? What had she done wrong? Choking back her protests, she forced herself to wait, making no sound, no move that would call attention to herself.

He pulled a small bottle from his coat pocket, then stood at the window looking out. His naked thighs were still strong and sturdy, his naked back beautiful. Had he had other women while she'd waited alone in Mississippi? Young women with taut butts and firm breasts and flat bellies? Women who could be on top without worrying that their faces would sag when they bent over to kiss him?

Just looking at him put her so close to the edge that she had to cross her knees and squeeze. He hated for her to have any satisfaction that he was not directly responsible for.

"It's been so long," he whispered, still gazing out the window. "So long."

Suddenly he was beside her, bending over the bed.

"You're going to love this, sweetheart." He'd never called her sweetheart before. Smiling, he poured oil into his palms and began to massage her breasts, heating the oil, releasing the fragrance. Her nipples jutted hard as diamonds against his slick palms, and the whole room smelled of white roses.

"Hmmmm. Max . . ."

"Don't talk."

"Can I moan?"

"No. No sounds."

His hands were skilled, and with each caress her confidence returned.

"Nobody can satisfy you the way Margaret Anne Bellafontaine can," she said, gloating.

He jerked back, then sat on the edge of the bed, his head between his hands.

"Max? What's wrong?"

"You're not Ruth."

Cold sweat broke out on her forehead, and suddenly she was afraid as she had never been. But she wouldn't let him see her fear, for a display of any weakness would mean certain defeat. She left the bed and got her pink silk robe from the closet. The oil he'd rubbed on her would stain, but that didn't matter. Nothing mattered except playing out this new and dangerous game . . . and winning.

She snapped on the lamps, then came around the side of the bed where he sat hunkered. When he looked up at her, there was a spark of the old interest in his face, a fleeting twinkle in his eye. She was glad she'd changed the bulbs to pink. Pink was flattering to women of a certain age.

"She's not coming back, Max."

"I trained her so that no one else can ever satisfy her. She's like you; she'll be back."

Genteel Southern women knew how to laugh through their pain. It was a lesson Margaret Anne had learned well when she was young.

The sound of her laughter was as brittle as the yellowed pages in her diary.

"She's not like me, Max. She's stronger. She's beat us both." She propped both hands on his shoulders, then parted his knees so she could stand close. "She'll never be back. I'm all you have of Ruth."

He wrapped his arms around her waist and buried his face in the front of her pink silk robe. Margaret Anne closed her eyes, thinking she'd won.

Suddenly he pushed her from him so hard, she had to catch the bedpost for balance.

"Do you think I'm going to let her go?"

28.

THE VIRUNGAS

ELEANOR WAS GLAD TO BE OUT WITH HER cameras. She'd been cooped up in the compound too long. It gave her too much time to think, and she didn't like the direction her thoughts had taken lately.

Squatted beside a scrubby acacia tree, she took aim at the sunrise coming up over the gorge. After the night's rains it was spectacular, as if angels had spilled colors across the sky, then polished it to a high gloss. Mud squished under her feet and spattered the legs of her trousers, but she didn't notice. When you'd lived in Africa as long as she had, you got used to the mud.

And the flies. And the animals. And the mists.

Lucky for her, the mists had come down in patches this morning, covering the compounds, the roads, and the jungle, but leaving the gorge as bright and clear as freshly washed Waterford crystal. As the sun climbed over the peaks of the Virungas, the vivid rose in the sky faded to pink.

"Come on, come on." She swiveled to get all angles, her shutters clicking furiously. "Give me just a few more minutes."

She was already past deadline with the photographs, and there was only so much patience she could expect of the long-suffering editor of *Exotic People and Places*.

"One more good shot. That's all I ask."

Still focusing through her lens, she moved down the gorge so she could get closer to the waterfall. Suddenly her feet slipped.

"Damned mud!"

Holding her camera out of harm's way, she landed hard on her bottom. Her teeth jarred together, and she lost her wind, but she'd saved her camera. Reaching back with her left hand, she braced to push herself off the ground. Mud oozed between her fingers and soaked the seat of her pants.

"Damn."

She balanced her camera on her knees and fumbled for the handkerchief in her pants pocket. By the time she got her hand clean enough to shoot, the sunrise would be over. She found her handkerchief, eased her left hand out of the ooze . . . and screamed.

Her hand was red with blood. The camera toppled to the ground as she scrambled onto all fours. Blood was everywhere, on her pants, on the grass, soaked into the ground where it had mixed with the rain and become a small river of vermilion. The smell nauseated her.

Like a cornered animal at bay, she swung her head around. A tiny duiker lay like a broken Tinkertoy, his spindly legs at odd angles from his body, his black eyes open and staring, and his throat slit.

Another scream rose in her throat, and she crammed her clean hand in her mouth to stop it. She hated blood. It seemed impossible that one small animal should have so much.

Eleanor leaned over and retched. Then she gathered her camera and went to the base of the waterfall to wash her hands. No need to bother about her pants. They would never come clean.

Joseph was somewhere beyond the ridge observing the giant male silverback Petey, and his wives and offspring, but it was not to her husband that Eleanor turned.

With the blood still coloring her mind, Eleanor drove like a madwoman, out of the gorge, through the rain forest, and into the clearing. She had to find her son.

Suddenly Brett was there, standing beside his front door. And with him was Ruth.

Eleanor braked hard, her tires spewing mud as she came to a stop.

They turned and saw her. And she saw them, saw their faces, shiny as newly minted dimes, and their hands, fingers intertwined, joined, connected. Brett and Malone's wife.

She didn't stop to think. She only knew what she saw. And that she hated it. Hated what it would do to her sons. Hated what it would do to her family.

"Mother. We didn't expect you," Brett said.

"Obviously."

Ruth's smile vanished. She released Brett's hand and stepped apart from him. Guilty. If Eleanor hadn't been a moderately civilized woman, she'd have slapped her new daughter-in-law's face.

"Ruth drove up this morning to observe my work."

"Is that what they call it now?"

"Brett . . . I'll leave."

"No, Ruth. Stay."

He caught her hand to stop her. Eleanor didn't think she'd ever seen him so mad. Especially not at her. But she was his mother, and not about to back down. She knew exactly where his backbone had come from.

Certainly not from Joseph.

"Eleanor, you owe Ruth an apology."

Her sons called her Eleanor mostly when they were displeased with her.

"I would say *she's* the one who should be apologizing."

"Whatever you're thinking is wrong."

"How can you possibly know what I'm thinking?"

"It doesn't take a Philadelphia lawyer."

"Please." Ruth said. "I don't want to cause trouble."

"You haven't caused any trouble, Ruth." Her son kept a firm grip on Ruth's hand. Eleanor felt as if she'd been drummed out of her homeland and set adrift in a leaky boat. "Mother, it's not like you to judge without knowing the circumstances."

Eleanor passed her hand through her hair. She was as shaky as an old woman. Maybe that was her problem. Age. Menopause.

"You're right. It's not like me. I do owe some apologies, to both of you. I jumped the gun and I'm sorry. Can you forgive me, Ruth?"

"Certainly. No harm done."

Eleanor knew it was a gracious lie. She'd done enormous harm. She'd derailed a relationship that had never got on track in the first place. And now probably never would.

"Brett?" Her son's face softened, and he reached out and pulled her into a bear hug. "Thanks. I needed that."

"Any particular reason?"

"I guess you didn't notice my pants?"

"Mud?"

"Blood. There's a young duiker down by the waterfall with his throat slit."

"Poachers."

Eleanor knew what the word meant. Another long and frustrating battle to ensure the safety of the mountain gorilla.

Brett gazed toward the jungle as if he were seeing the slain duiker in its small pool of red . . . and all the blood that would follow.

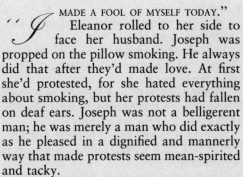

29.

"I MADE A FOOL OF MYSELF TODAY."

Eleanor rolled to her side to face her husband. Joseph was propped on the pillow smoking. He always did that after they'd made love. At first she'd protested, for she hated everything about smoking, but her protests had fallen on deaf ears. Joseph was not a belligerent man; he was merely a man who did exactly as he pleased in a dignified and mannerly way that made protests seem mean-spirited and tacky.

He had many rituals. Smoking after sex was one of them. Though the sex didn't satisfy, over the years Eleanor had learned to take comfort from the rituals.

"I doubt that you could ever do that."

"Well. I did. And with my new daughter-in-law."

"I'm sure she'll forgive you. She seems like a nice young woman."

"Maybe she'll forgive me, but I doubt she'll ever forget what I did."

"What did you do?"

"I practically accused her of trying to seduce my son."

"Malone!"

"Not Malone." She wanted to call Joseph an idiot, but she'd already done enough damage for one day. "Brett."

"Brett would never do anything like that."

"I know that. But I let my imagination run away with my temper, and as usual it landed me in more hot water than I needed."

"A little hot water is good for you every now and then. Cleans out the cobwebs."

She leaned on his shoulder and played with the hairs on his chest. It saddened her that they had turned gray.

"Do I have cobwebs?"

"Not that I've noticed. But, then, maybe I haven't been looking in the right places."

Joseph could always make her laugh. At least they still had that.

"Do you think she loves Malone?" she asked.

"She married him."

"Why? We'd never heard of her until he went to Hawaii. He was gone only a few days, for petesake. What was all the rush?"

"Why not? I fell in love with you the first time I ever kissed you. The three months we waited didn't make a bit of difference in the way I felt."

Sighing, Eleanor rolled back to her side of the bed and turned her back to her husband. Joseph put his hand on her shoulder.

"You worry too much, Eleanor. Why don't you take a few days off? Go to Nairobi. Do a little shopping. You've always enjoyed that flight."

"With the poaching starting up again?"

"Brett and I organized patrols. We've got that under control."

"Besides, I hate shopping."

"Take a nice day trip. Go visit Luke." Eleanor stiffened. "I saw him in the village last week and he asked about you."

"What did you tell him, Joseph?"

"That you're as busy as ever . . . and just as beauti-ful."

Joseph squeezed her shoulder. Totally unaware. She'd move heaven and earth to keep it that way. "Don't you think it's time to put an end to this rift between you?"

"There's no rift between us. I just don't have time to waste on social calls, that's all."

Eleanor was glad her husband couldn't see her face.

30.

HEN MALONE WAS A KID, HE'D learned how to turn disappointments into surprises. Did his parents ignore his good grades because Brett had won a debate trophy? Well, think how surprised they'd be when he finished at the top of his class.

Now that the honeymoon was over and it was time to get back to work, why not turn the work into pleasure? Besides, he'd acted an ass and needed to apologize. This seemed a good way to begin.

Malone decided to wait until Ruth was out of the tub before he told her about the surprise. He tamed his cowlick with styling gel, then went out onto the porch swing to wait for her in the cool night air. She loved it outside. It seemed the appropriate place to make amends for all his sins, which were legion.

He didn't like to think about them, but while he waited for her, he made himself.

Remembering was like trying on a hair shirt so he'd know it wasn't really what he wanted to wear.

It had been nearly eleven o'clock that morning before Malone had woken up. He'd found Ruth in the kitchen, bent over a note on the kitchen table, weeping.

He'd thought he was the cause, and his heart had stopped for the merest fraction of a second. The note was to him. He was certain of that. She was telling him good-bye in a letter because she didn't want to see him face-to-face.

Who could blame her?

"Ruth. Ruth." He'd stood in the doorway, forlorn, saying her name twice before he could stop himself, and because he didn't know what else to say.

She'd turned her back to him and wiped her eyes with a dish towel that had lain crumpled on the kitchen counter, the one he'd used instead of a pot holder the night before, when he'd been popping corn on the stove. His throat had gone tight thinking how he'd never share popcorn with her again.

"I'm sorry," he'd said. "I know I was a jackass last night, and I won't ever be again. Cross my heart and hope to die."

"This is not about you, Malone."

When she'd turned around, she'd been perfectly composed. That had scared him more than her tears.

"Look, I understand that you need to be independent, and that's all right with me. Fact is, I wouldn't want a wishy-washy woman."

"It's not that, either."

"What, then?"

She'd crumpled the note and crammed it into her pocket.

"This morning I went to Brett . . ."

While he'd been sleeping off his liquor, his wife had left him and gone to his brother. And why not? Brett was always the one who fixed everybody's problems. It was only natural he'd step in and console Ruth.

What else had Brett done besides console Ruth?

"What were you doing up there?"

The minute the words were out of his mouth, he'd

wished he could have taken them back. But he couldn't. All he could do was hope she wouldn't walk out on him. It would serve him right. What had ever made him think he could keep a woman like Ruth?

When the set look on her face had vanished, he'd nearly cried with relief.

"I was working on my dissertation, Malone."

He had vowed to himself then and there never to take another drink of liquor. It caused him nothing but problems.

"I'm sorry, honey. I didn't mean that the way it sounded. Forgive me?"

How could she not forgive him when he looked at her with that little-boy's smile? Besides, it was easier to forgive him a couple of drinks too many than to forgive herself for being too happy in the company of his brother.

"I guess I should have awakened you to tell you I was going," she had said. "I really didn't mean to do anything behind your back, Malone."

The tears were in Ruth's eyes again. Malone couldn't stand that he was the reason his wife was crying.

"Oh, hey, now." He'd held out his arms, and she'd leaned her head on his shoulder. "I didn't mean to sound like a grumpy old bear. You're free to come and go as you please around here, and don't you ever let anybody tell you any different."

"Not even you?"

He'd been glad to see her smile.

"Not even me," he'd said.

"Something terrible happened today."

"Not to you, I hope."

"Eleanor thought . . ." Ruth had paused to clear the catch from her throat. Eleanor's accusations had hit too close to home. Not that Ruth would ever be unfaithful to her husband with his brother, but perhaps the secret longing was a sin just as great. She made herself put her emotions behind her and focus on an immediate problem: "Eleanor saw a small slain duiker in the gorge."

"Damned poachers."

"That's what Brett said, only he didn't say 'damned.' "

"Brett never says damned. He's damned near perfect."

"You're the one I married."

"That's because I was the one you met."

The truth had socked her in the gut like a football thrown too hard, knocking the wind out of her. If she let the truth get a foothold on her marriage, she might as well pack her bags and head back to Mississippi. Taking a deep breath, she had kissed Malone's cheek.

"That's because Hector swept me off my feet." Could anything good be built on lies? "You, too, of course."

"I married an angel. A damned genu-ine solid-gold angel. Not only does she put up with my shit, but she cries over small dead animals. . . . That was why you were crying, wasn't it, sweetheart?"

For a moment Ruth had been so quiet, he'd thought she might be crying again, but then she'd tipped her face up to him and smiled.

"Yes, Malone." How many more lies would she have to tell? "That's why I was crying."

Relieved that the crisis was finally behind him, he'd carried her to bed to kiss and make up. As always, he was the one who'd done most of the kissing—but he wouldn't think about that now, not while he was waiting for her on the porch swing with a big surprise in his pocket. When the screen door popped open, he patted the seat of the swing.

"Come sit beside me, sweetheart."

She came to him softly, her skirts brushing against his legs, and he set the swing in motion.

"It's beautiful out here, isn't it?" she said.

He tried to see the beauty through her eyes, but he saw nothing except the same stifling jungle and hostile mountains that he'd hated for years.

"Yes." He'd agree to anything tonight.

"Malone . . ."

"Hmmm . . ."

"I've been thinking a lot today . . . about us."

So this morning's truce in the kitchen had been only temporary. He should have known he wasn't going to get off so easily.

"Well, I don't know about you, but I think we make a damned fine topic for thought."

"Not about us, actually, but about our future. I really do want this marriage to work, Malone. I want it to be wonderful."

"I thought it already was."

"Well . . . I didn't mean that it wasn't." How could her husband be so clueless? Didn't he feel the tension? Feel how she shrank from his touch? And yet the very thing that made him unaware was going to work in her favor—in *their* favor. If he believed they had a great marriage, her chances of making it work were that much greater. "Certainly not that, at all. I mean . . . it's going to take me a while to adjust . . . to Africa."

Ruth went as still as the dead, and Malone didn't have the courage to say anything to fill the void. From the distance came the sounds of restless jungle creatures, each as distinct as a fingerprint.

He guessed she'd mistake his silence for stupidity, but she probably already thought he was stupid anyhow, compared to Brett. Everybody else did. But there were some things a man had to keep to himself. Like worry over money. Hell, yes, he thought about their future. But how could a man say to his wife, *Look, honey, I want us to have a big house in the valley, and not this little shack within spitting distance of my family, but the fact is, I don't have the money, and at the rate I'm going I probably never will.*

No, there were some things a man had to keep from a woman in order to protect her, if he was any kind of a man at all.

Sweat broke out on his forehead—the sweat of fear. The swing died down, and he didn't have the heart to start it moving again. It was so quiet on the porch, he thought he could hear insects growing wings.

When he was near screaming, Ruth reached for his hand and squeezed.

"Malone . . ."

"Yes."

"I want you to know that I think you're one of the sweetest men I've ever met, and I'm deeply grateful to be your wife."

"Ruth, you make me the envy of every other man in the

universe. Do you have any idea how absolutely fabulous you are?"

"I'm *not* . . . I'm . . ."

She left the swing—just got up and left him sitting all by himself, feeling like an idiot. She didn't huff off, didn't even stand all stiff and proper like somebody mad, but there was something determined about the set of her shoulders and the tilt of her chin, something brave—noble, even. He felt worse than a worm.

What had he said wrong now? And how in the world would he ever know how to fix it? Shit, if he were Brett, he wouldn't be making these god-awful mistakes with his very own wife. He'd know exactly what to do and say.

While he was floundering in the unknown waters of matrimony, his wife turned to him again. But she didn't come back to the swing: She leaned against the porch post as if she needed all the support she could get.

"We never talk about some really important things." Ruth had no experience with good marriages and great families. Certainly Margaret Anne Bellafontaine had not set a good example. And yet Ruth had seen how marriage could work, seen how families could be. Seen it from afar. Seen it with Wanda's parents, seen it with her sixth-grade baseball coach, seen it with her ninth-grade music teacher. True, great family dynamics were rare, but just as she'd been determined to create a dog out of sand, she was now determined to create a good family for herself . . . and for Malone.

"We never talked about children," she said.

"I like the little boogers. Used to be one, myself."

"Be serious."

"Okay. I'm serious." He made a doleful expression that caused her to laugh. That's what he did best—played the clown, made people laugh. It was a talent that had got him out of more tight places than he'd ever thought possible.

But *children*. Good Lord. He'd always imagined himself with children, but in an abstract sort of way, kind of like imagining himself with a hairy chest and biceps bigger than grapefruits. Besides that, he was too selfish to want to share the pleasures of Ruth right away with little snot-nosed brats. And what if they looked like him?

"I was just thinking that the Virungas are a sort of paradise," she said. "A really beautiful place for making a fresh start."

"A fresh start?"

"I mean a *good* start, a good start on a marriage . . . and a family. Don't you think children sort of make a marriage complete?"

"I think that's what Eleanor and Joseph thought about Brett."

Ruth's heart ached for the little boy he'd been, always outclassed by an older brother who was obviously the family favorite. She'd never let that kind of favoritism mar her family.

She sat down beside him and eased her arm through his.

"And you," she whispered, smiling.

"Of course. And me."

"You *do* want children, don't you, Malone?"

"Right this very minute?"

"I love your sense of humor. I really do. But we can't go through the rest of our lives making light of everything. We're not puppets. I didn't marry Hector: I married *you*, and right now I'd like to know what you think."

It was time for more than a clown's smile. It was time for a miracle.

He eased his arms around her waist and was rewarded by her softness pressing against his side. What more could a man want?

"We'll have a family, sweetheart," he said. "We'll have as many children as you want. But first I have a little surprise for you."

"A surprise?"

"Yes. You like pretty places, don't you?"

"I like being anyplace that's different."

"Different?"

"From Oxford, Mississippi."

"How about London?"

"I've never been there."

"Would you like to go?"

"Perhaps . . . someday."

"What about tomorrow?"

"You're kidding."

"No. I'm not kidding. It's time for me to get back to work. Brett's the Gorilla Man, but I'm the money man. Without me this outfit doesn't run."

"You're a great money man, Malone. Very convincing."

He kissed the top of her head. How was it that he could feel like shit and like a million dollars all at the same time?

"Tomorrow I fly to London for one of those god-awful fund-raisers, and I thought you might like to go with me."

"What a lovely thought."

"The fund-raising will only take a little of my time, and the rest we can spend together, doing whatever you want to do."

"I know it will be lovely, Malone, and I'd like to go with you. Really I would. But I must finish my dissertation first. Time's running out."

"I see." He didn't see at all. But he wasn't about to make the mistake of fighting with her again.

"Tomorrow Brett is going to introduce me to Cee Cee."

Malone counted to ten before he answered her.

"She'll love you."

"Oh, I do hope so."

Later that evening, long after she was asleep, he eased out of bed and took the tickets out of his pocket. Mr. and Mrs. Malone Corday, seats 9A and 9B, destination Heathrow Airport, London. He locked Ruth's ticket in the top drawer of his desk, then climbed back in beside her.

"Malone . . ." Sleepy-voiced, she turned to him.

He slid his hands under her gown and spread her thighs apart. She rolled onto her back, compliant. Grunting and swaying above her, he thought how he'd meant to take her to see Buckingham Palace.

Things in his life never turned out the way he meant them to.

31.

SHE WORE A HAT WITH RED RIBBONS. It made her look sophisticated and exotic, as if she'd dressed for some special occasion, though there was no occasion at all, merely a short trip up the mountain to see him.

It pleased Brett that Ruth might have worn the hat just for him. It pleased him too much. And he didn't even like to think how he'd changed his eye patch three times and watched out the window for her.

"Hi," he said. "I like that hat."

"You do?" She touched the end of the red ribbon, smiling.

"Yes. Women don't wear hats much nowadays."

"I love hats. I guess that makes me old-fashioned."

That pleased Brett, too, the notion that she was old-fashioned with old-fashioned virtues such as honesty and pride and honor.

A breeze stirred the red ribbons, and the ends brushed softly against her cheeks. Such a pretty sight, that red ribbon against her skin, moving in the wind like a caress.

For no reason at all Brett suddenly felt afraid, as if something wild were trying to take control of him, something he would know how to defeat if only he knew its name. It stole his voice, this nameless fear, and he found himself staring at the bit of red ribbon without any notion of what he ought to say or do.

Ruth brushed at the ribbons on her cheek, flinging them over her back. The fact that he could no longer see them resting scarlet against her dark-golden skin gave him some relief, though not enough to discover his voice again.

"I suppose Malone's in London by now," Ruth said.

Somehow that was the key to Brett's recovery. Malone.

"How long will he be gone?" he asked.

"Three days."

"That should give us plenty of time to establish some great rapport."

It wasn't so much what he'd said as how he reacted to the words, once spoken, that gnawed at Brett like a fierce animal. Suddenly it seemed as if all noise had ceased, and there was nothing left except the sound of their breathing.

"With Cee Cee, you mean?" Ruth said finally.

"Of course. With Cee Cee."

This time when they went inside, Ruth didn't reach for him. After what had just happened in hidden places deep inside him, he didn't know whether or not he would have taken her hand even if she'd reached for his.

He guessed he'd never know.

3₂.

*S*HE'D LAIN UNDER HIM COMPLIANT . . . and as responsive as a wax manne-quin. His wife.

"That was a brilliant lecture, Malone." The sound of a colleague's voice brought him back to the present.

"Thanks." Travel weary and homesick, he found the praise balm for his soul. What he would like to do that minute was leave and fly home to Ruth, but what he *had* to do was make the big push for money. The coffers of the Corday Foundation had never been overflowing, but within the last few months they'd been dangerously low. Almost daily a new animal-preservation group sprang up, and the available charita-ble contributions were spread thin. Not that Joseph and Brett complained. Like the gorillas they loved, they could live off the jungle. But now more than ever Malone wanted to put the foundation on solid fi-nancial ground.

He looked at the people seated around the dinner table
—wealthy, pampered people with nothing more to do
than figure out which charity they would choose as their
big tax write-off.

It was time to go in for the kill.

"The Corday Foundation is doing a great job in preserving the habitat of the mountain gorilla," he said, "but
as you know, that takes funding. I've prepared a report
that shows the increase in the gorilla population since the
establishment of our . . ."

"All in due time, Malone, my boy. What we really want
to know about is your brother's work with Cee Cee. Tell
us more about Dr. Corday."

Always Brett. As if Malone hadn't worked his tail off
earning a degree in veterinary medicine. As if he hadn't
earned the right to be called Doctor.

"Brilliant man, your brother."

"Absolutely," Malone said. "The best in his field."

Would Ruth have been more active in bed if Brett had
been the one holding her? Suddenly he had a vision of
them on top of the mountain: Ruth, lying in his brother's
arms; Ruth, twisting herself around Brett, panting, eager,
hungry.

"You want to know what my brother is doing while I'm
sitting in expensive restaurants drinking expensive wine?"
What *was* his brother doing? He jerked up the carafe, and
as he poured, wine spilled over the side and pooled on the
tablecloth. Immediately ashamed for his jealous thoughts,
Malone smiled at his guests, hoping to charm, hoping to
make them forget the white linen napkin he'd laid over the
red spill.

"I hope you have all day," he said.

Malone always knew how to draw a laugh from an
audience. As he launched into a recital of Brett's accom-
plishments, he took mental note of the level of wine in the
bottle.

It was low. When it ran out, he could order more.

That was his only consolation.

33.

CEE CEE HATED THE STINK FEMALE ON
sight. Facing the corner, she drew
her arms tightly across her chest and
poked out her lips.

"She's sulking," Brett said.

"Does she react this way to all strangers?"

The stink female had a nice voice. It reminded Cee Cee of the songs Brett used to sing at night before she fell asleep. She covered her ears with her hands. She didn't want to like the nice voice.

If she ignored them, they would go away. She could smell the stink female behind her. Peeping over her shoulder, she saw Brett's mouth moving.

"She's never done this before," Brett said.

"Was it something I said? Something I did?"

"No. You behaved correctly, Ruth. It's Cee Cee whose behavior needs adjusting."

Cee Cee's fingers worked swiftly and silently.

"Dirty stink female. Cee Cee hate."

"Is she signing?"

"Go away, stink woman."

"Yes," Brett said. "But I can't see her fingers well enough to know what she's saying." *"Cee Cee, you have a visitor. Her name is Ruth,"* he signed.

Cee Cee twisted her head and bared her teeth at Ruth. *"That's not nice, Cee Cee. Where are your manners?"* Brett was not happy with her.

Cee Cee checked the top of her head to see if her pink hair ribbon was still in place, then turned around and grinned at Brett. Her grin froze when she saw Ruth's hat.

Slyly she bent over her hands and signed, *"Cee Cee want hat."*

"She's shy," Ruth said.

"Cee Cee's many things. Shy is not one of them."

Peeping between her fingers, Cee Cee grinned up at them. Ruth squatted beside Brett. Cee Cee's hand was a blur as she snatched the hat and rammed it on her own head.

"Ruth, leave the area," Brett said. "Now. Move slowly. Don't do anything to upset her more than she already is."

Cee Cee had her own swings. She leaped for the highest one, holding on to the hat with one hand and catching the steel bar with the other. Grinning, she set the bar in motion.

She was happy now. She had Brett all to herself.

"Cee Cee, why did you do that?"

"Want hat."

"It doesn't belong to you. It's Ruth's hat."

"No. Belong Cee Cee."

"Give it back."

"No. Belong Cee Cee." She punched her chest emphatically to emphasize her point. Then she leaned down and punched his chest. *"Hat belong Cee Cee. Brett belong Cee Cee."*

"It's all right, Brett. She can have the hat," Ruth said from outside the bars.

"Ruth, I can't allow her to get by with this kind of insurrection."

Agitated, Cee Cee hung on to the hat and made her swing go higher.

"Cee Cee, give me the hat." Brett signed emphatically and used his mad voice.

Cee Cee smiled at him. He didn't smile back. She tried to engage him in a game of peekaboo. He held out his hand for the hat.

Putting on her saddest face, Cee Cee took the hat off her head. She offered it to Brett, but before he could take it, she snatched off one of the red ribbons.

"Cee Cee," he said.

"Let it go, Brett. It's all right."

Cee Cee placed the red ribbon on top of her head and signed, *"Cee Cee fine female woman."*

But Brett didn't see. He was already outside the gate.

Her fingers moved rapidly, making the same sign over and over: *"Cee Cee sad."*

But there was nobody in her cage to see her, nobody to care.

Ruth's hat dangled from Brett's left hand as he led Ruth away from Cee Cee's enclosure. He rubbed the soft, woven fabric between his fingers.

"Thanks for rescuing my hat," Ruth said. "Though it wasn't necessary."

"Yes, it was. If I let Cee Cee get out of control, my entire project is lost."

"Of course. I should have known that."

She pushed her heavy hair back from her forehead. The underside of her arm was as delicate as the wings of butterflies. And just as vulnerable.

Staring at skin that looked as soft as velvet, he circled the pad of his thumb on her hat. A fine sheen of sweat broke out on Ruth's upper lip. His thumb moved on the straw brim, round and round. Her pink tongue darted out, licked her bottom lip.

"Ruth . . ." Funny how the underside of a woman's arm could make a grown man forget what he was going to say. "Here's your hat."

As he placed the hat on her head, her hair curled around his fingers, dark, shiny, silky—and he knew, without a shadow of a doubt, that when he went to bed that night, he'd still feel her soft hair clinging to his skin.

"I'm sorry about the torn ribbon," he said.

It fell across her cheek and dangled under her chin.

"Just pull it off. It doesn't matter."

Ruth turned her face up to his, and angels stole his breath away.

"I think it will come off if you just give it a yank," she added.

"I don't want to hurt you."

"You won't."

She looked up at him, bright and expectant. His hand trembled. Her cheek was close, so very close.

"I trust you," she whispered.

So did his brother.

Brett gave one quick jerk, and the torn ribbon came off in his hand, but not before he'd felt the texture of her skin, like velvet, as he'd imagined, underneath his fingertips. He stepped back quickly, stuffing the ribbon into his pocket.

"There, now," he said. "It's over."

Her tongue bathed her bottom lip, and he wondered how such an innocent gesture could make him want to explode with yearning.

"Yes. It's over," she said.

And he knew it was, knew it had to be. Before she suspected. Before he committed some irrevocable act of dishonor that would destroy them all.

34.

SOMEBODY WAS SENDING HIS WIFE FLOW-
ers. He'd been gone only three
days and already she had admirers.
Probably somebody who knew Malone,
somebody who was certain it would take a
better man than he to satisfy a woman like
Ruth.

The white florist's box lay on the hall
table, a note from Eleanor propped beside
it. "These came this morning. I knew you'd
be home today and could take them up to
Ruth."

He considered ripping the box apart and
tossing it into the garbage can. But that
would be childish.

His wife was a beautiful woman. Before
he came along, she'd probably had suitors
lined up for miles trying to win her favors.
Why shouldn't one of them still be trying
to win her?

In the kitchen he poured himself a glass
of liquor for courage. Just one.

Why hadn't he thought of flowers?

For a moment he thought about tossing the card and substituting a note from himself. The bile of self-disgust rose in his throat.

What kind of man was he becoming?

Next time he'd bring flowers. Jewels, too, if he could afford them.

He tossed down the drink, then poured a second glass. For luck.

If he left now, he'd get to Brett's compound in time to bring Ruth back to their cabin before dark. If absence really did make the heart grow fonder, she'd be so grateful to see him that she'd fall into his arms before they could even get the door shut.

He popped a breath mint into his mouth and slicked his hair back. Then he picked up the florist's box and headed up the mountain to get his wife.

They were not in the compound.

"Ruth! Brett!" The sound of his voice echoed off the walls. Clutching the florist's box, he hurried through the compound, searching the rooms.

They were nowhere to be found.

Malone clutched the box so hard, the sides caved in. For three days his wife had been with his brother.

Brett . . . always Brett . . .

"Mother! Daddy!"

Malone had tied his shoes all by himself. His parents would be very proud of him. He raced down the hallway. They were standing in Brett's room, hovering over the desk.

"Come see what I can do."

They didn't even turn around.

"Not now," his father said.

"In a minute," his mother said.

He peered around them to see what they were looking at. It was his brother's science project.

"Someday our son is going to win a Nobel prize," Eleanor said.

It didn't take a genius to figure out which son she was talking about. Brett, who was the brightest and the best.

The leather patch on Brett's desk accused him. A man who had sacrificed an eye for his brother would never make a play for his brother's wife.

Malone smoothed the sides of the florist box, then followed a path into the jungle. In the distance he could hear their voices blending with the distinctive sounds of Ol Doby bossing his gorilla group around. When Brett was not working with Cee Cee, he was outside studying the behavior of one of the gorilla groups. Why hadn't Malone thought of it sooner?

He could hear his wife's laughter and the soft cadence of the South in her voice. Sweat popped out on his brow. God, how was he going to keep from making love to her right there on the spot with his brother watching?

Giant ferns whispered beneath his feet, and he caught a glimpse of bright plumage as a bird took flight through the dense, dripping rain forest. For a moment it was suspended, wings beating the sultry air, as if the power of its song held it aloft. By now he guessed Brett had taught Ruth the names of every bird, every flower, every tree.

The sound of her laughter drifted down to him. He hadn't heard her laugh like that since he'd brought her to Africa.

What else had his brother taught her?

Impatiently, he pushed aside the ropes of greenery dripping into his pathway.

"Damned nuisance." He couldn't comprehend how Brett could stand it day in and day out. Malone would go crazy up here.

The path curved sharply into a lush green clearing, and suddenly there she was. Ruth. His wife. Her face radiant and her hand resting in the curve of his brother's arm.

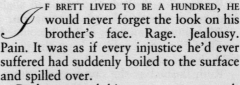

35.

*I*F BRETT LIVED TO BE A HUNDRED, HE would never forget the look on his brother's face. Rage. Jealousy. Pain. It was as if every injustice he'd ever suffered had suddenly boiled to the surface and spilled over.

Ruth squeezed his arm once, convulsively, then let go.

"Malone, I didn't hear you," she said.

"That's obvious."

She stepped apart from Brett. Guilty.

Guilty of what? Of being so incredibly lovely that she made his heart ache?

Brett wanted to hold her close and protect her from the unjust accusations he saw in his brother's eyes. But were they unjust?

Did it count that he'd spent the last three nights sleepless, battling thoughts he had no right to be thinking about his brother's wife? Did it count that he'd wanted to do everything he knew his brother must be thinking?

But he'd done nothing. He'd been Ruth's teacher, and she'd been a vivacious, charming, remarkable student. Didn't he deserve the small, secret pleasure of her hand touching his arm? Of her face turned up to his, radiant with laughter?

He wouldn't dignify his brother's silent accusations with an explanation.

"I'm glad you're back, Malone," he said. "How did it go?"

For a heartbeat he thought Malone was going to press the issue, but suddenly his face relaxed into the easygoing, charming smile Brett knew so well. Knew and loved.

"Great. I brought in big bucks for the foundation. I expect everybody to be properly grateful."

"Are you hinting for a raise?"

"Hinting, hell. I'm outright demanding it. A man with a wife has certain needs, you know." Malone put his arm around Ruth's waist, then bent down to nuzzle her neck. "You can take that both ways, honey."

Ruth's face flushed. Did she pull slightly away from Malone, or was that Brett's imagination?

What kind of monster had he become? Hoping Malone would fail so he could pick up the pieces . . . the way he'd always done.

Ruth flushed as she saw him watching her. He *hadn't* imagined her discomfort. His emotions seesawed wildly between hope and fear, between the absolute conviction that fate would not be so cruel as to set Ruth in his path, then make her unattainable—and the dark premonition that some new despair awaited his beloved brother.

Immobilized, Brett watched Ruth's flush spread under his intense scrutiny, saw her cast desperately around for a way out of the uncomfortable situation.

"Oh . . . you brought flowers," she said.

Brett hadn't noticed the florist's box. He would have given his other eye for the right to bring Ruth flowers. But even that small gesture was forbidden to him.

"I wish I'd thought of them," Malone said. "Actually, these are from somebody else. They arrived this morning."

"Someone else sent them?"

Malone chuckled. "Hey, honey, don't look so belligerent. I'm the one who's supposed to get fighting mad over these things." He handed her the slightly crumpled florist's box. "Why don't you open them and see who they're from? If it's somebody you don't like, I'll send Brett to beat the shit out of them. He's good at that."

It was the first time Malone had ever referred, even obliquely, to the fight in the Congo. Though he said it as a joke, Brett felt the full thrust of his brother's resentment.

"I'd better get back to the compound to check on Cee Cee," Brett said. "She pouts when she's left alone for too long."

The sooner he was out of their sight, the better off everybody would be. He set his face toward the rain forest, toward the massive trees that arched over him, cathedral-like, and a silence so deep, so mysterious, it was almost holy.

"Brett!"

Ruth's cry ripped through him, tearing a jagged edge out of his heart. Her eyes were enormous and her face had gone pale. He rushed toward her, anxious to console, eager to protect.

"What is it, honey?" Malone slid his arm around her shoulders.

Brett froze, helpless, watching Malone do what any good husband should. But it was *his* name she'd called. At night when the sound of the male gorillas filled the jungle and the moon shone silver on the tusks of elephants, Brett would remember. Funny how one moment could change the entire tenor of a man's life. He used to measure the quality of his life by his great leaps of scientific achievement, and now he measured it by the small attentions of a woman who could never be his.

White roses lay scattered at her feet.

"It's roses," she whispered. "White roses."

"Holy shit! There must be five dozen of the suckers." Malone bent to pick up the fallen flowers. "Does the card say who they're from, honey?"

"There's no card."

"No card! What kind of fool sends an expensive bouquet like this with no card? I'll bet the florist forgot to put it in. We'll call and find out." Malone gave Ruth a handful of flowers, then bent to pick up the rest.

She stared at the roses in her hand, tears trembling on the ends of her eyelashes. Then, slowly, her chin came up, and she ripped the petals apart, flinging them as far from her as she could. As she raced past Brett, a capricious breeze caught the crushed petals and swirled them around her like snow out of season.

"What the devil?" Malone hopped to his feet. "Ruth . . . wait. You forgot the flowers."

There was no reply except the sound of her feet running on the pathway.

"Leave them," Brett said.

"What the fuck? Don't you tell me what to do."

"Didn't you see her face? She doesn't want the flowers. *Leave them*."

"Since when did you become an authority on *my* wife?" Hands balled into fists, face mottled red, Malone squared off against his brother. "Just what kind of *research* went on in this compound while I was gone?"

It took all Brett's willpower to keep from smashing his fist into his brother's face. Instead he grabbed the front of his shirt and hauled him up short.

"Don't you *dare* besmirch her with your filthy accusations. She's pure gold, and if you don't understand that about her, then you don't deserve to be her husband."

Malone sagged, the fight draining slowly out of him.

"Hellfire . . . shit." He put his hand on Brett's shoulder. "I'm sorry, bro. I don't think anything happened between the two of you, it's just that she's so damned beautiful and you're so damned . . ." He shrugged his shoulders. "You know what I mean."

Brett knew exactly what he meant. They were victims of their upbringing, Brett suffering from too much attention, too many expectations, and Malone from too little. He put his arm around his brother's shoulder.

"Go to her, Malone. She needs you."

"Thanks, Brett. Anything I can do for you . . . you need anything, anytime, just call me. I mean that."

"Just go."

He couldn't bear to watch Malone comfort his wife.

After his eye had been ripped out, he'd learned that the best antidote to pain was work.

Assuming the gorilla posture, Brett hunkered in the edge of the clearing to watch Doby and his clan. Ignoring him, the giant male silverback leaned against a tree trunk while three of the young females groomed him. When two of his adolescent sons came too close, feeling the need to challenge the leader, Old Doby bared his teeth and grunted. They swung onto the nearest branch and pretended they'd been playing a game of tag all along.

Doby's group was the most stable in the Virungas. Because of his age he was wiser than most of the male silverbacks, and because of his size most predators left him alone. Brett studied him the way any doting father would a prospective son-in-law.

In order for Project Cee Cee to succeed, she must mate, and she would soon be in estrus.

As Doby glanced his way, Brett's thoughts swung wildly toward Ruth and Malone. What were they doing now? Was he comforting her with soft words against soft pillows? Was he being tender with her? Understanding?

Involuntarily his hand closed over a rose at his feet. He smoothed the bruised petals, his hands as gentle as they had been when he'd touched Ruth's cheek. Over and over he caressed the crushed petals, remolding them until they became a perfect rose.

Touching the rose to his lips, he cried out like a wounded lion. There was the sound of heavy footsteps, and the sudden loss of light as a shadow fell over him. The giant male silverback stood only inches away, his face filled with such concern and his eyes so wise that Brett felt as if he were confronting his best friend.

In their studies with the mountain gorilla, the Cordays had been careful to remain at a distance, merely to be observers. Their main concern was the protection of the species, and in order to survive, the gorilla had to retain his natural suspicion of man, the most lethal predator. Too, human contact brought diseases to the great apes, diseases their bodies were unable to counteract.

Brett barely breathed as Doby continued his kindly observation. Though the gorilla outweighed him many times over, he felt no sense of danger, no threat, only an elation that he was experiencing something so magical, so mystical, it might never happen again.

The need to explain his situation to his unexpected comforter overwhelmed him. But how could he tell Doby that having his eye ripped out was nothing compared to having his heart torn from his body?

"I don't know if I can bear this terrible burden, Doby," he whispered.

Slowly the great dark hand reached out and touched his shoulder. Brett felt the comfort and the sting of his own tears.

36.

$\mathcal{S}$HE WAS AT BRETT'S COMPOUND BEFORE Malone caught up with her.

"Ruth!"

What would happen if she kept running? If she climbed into his Jeep and never looked back?

"Ruth. Wait a minute, honey."

She huddled in front of the compound, her arms wrapped around herself. She didn't think she could bear it if Malone touched her, not after the white roses.

"What was that all about?" he asked.

"Nothing."

"Nothing? You throw six dozen roses in the dirt and tell me it's nothing?"

He was her husband; he deserved some sort of explanation. But how could she ever explain Max and what he had done?

"I'm sorry, Malone. It has nothing to do with you."

He looked as if he might be going to argue with her, but to her great relief he grinned.

"Hell, I don't want to talk about flowers somebody else sent you, anyhow, not after being away from you for so long. Come here, woman."

She shrank back when he reached for her, but he didn't notice. When he nuzzled her neck, she thought she might scream.

"Malone . . . please. Brett might come back."

"He's up there with the gorillas. He won't be back for hours."

His hand was already under her skirt, clawing at her panties. The fragrance of white roses almost smothered her. Ruth thought she was going to faint.

"Oh, honey . . . sweetmercifulheavens . . . baby . . ."

Malone picked her up, kicked open the door, and headed to the nearest bed.

No, God. Please. No.

Muted golden lights, the last of the day, spilled through the enormous bank of windows in the large room. Bookshelves lined one wall, neatly filled with volumes on primate language and behavior, on anthropology and biology, on astrology and psychology. In one corner was a CD player, and propped against it was a battered guitar. An open copy of *Cyrano de Bergerac* lay on the seat of a slatted rocking chair.

"Please, Malone. Not now. Not *here*."

But Malone was past hearing. Or caring. Already he was in her, pumping so hard, the bed moved, setting into gentle motion the two objects intertwined on the headboard . . . a leather eye patch and a length of red ribbon.

Ruth closed her eyes and endured. When it was over, she'd leave and never come back.

37.

HOLLYWOOD

HE HAD THE COMPLETE SCHEDULE IN front of him: dates, times, places. He couldn't have been more pleased if somebody had presented him with a blueprint of their lives. But the thing that pleased him most was not the schedule; it was the balance sheet.

The Corday Foundation was in deep financial doo-doo. And Max was the only one wearing wading boots.

Too excited to sit still, he prowled his new house, going first to the white bedroom. It was an exact duplicate of the upstairs bedroom in his house in New Orleans. The white roses on the bedside tables were turning brown around the edges. He made a mental note to order some more.

Everything had to be perfect for Ruth. With one last look at her room, he returned to his study, punched the intercom, and buzzed the man who made his household run like a well-oiled machine, who would cut off his finely boned, snobbish British nose before he'd reveal any of Max's private affairs.

"Clifford, get me San Francisco."

38.

THE VIRUNGAS

THEY HAD MADE LOVE ON HIS BED.
Rutted like two animals in
heat, too eager for each other to
go the length of the hallway to the guest
room. The pain that hit Brett nearly drove
him to his knees.

Her scent was on his sheets.

Hanging on to the door frame, he
swayed at the edge of his bedroom, riveted
by the fragrance and the images of Ruth
that crowded his mind—naked upon his
bed, glowing as if the sun were caught beneath her skin, breasts rising and falling
with passion too hot to be denied.

Like a sleepwalker he approached the
bed, then lay upon it, fully clothed. One of
her dark hairs lay upon the pillow. He
clutched at it the way a drowning man will
grasp a lifeboat. Her scent wrapped itself
around him, soaked through his shirt and

into his skin, invading him, filling him until he had the
sensation of holding her, of sinking into her sweet flesh
and possessing her.

But his brother had been the one to possess her—not
he. There were two scents upon the bed.

"No!"

He jerked upright, sweat dripping down his face and
wetting the front of his shirt. Filled with disgust, he jerked
the sheets off the bed and threw them onto the floor. Then
he ripped his shirt off and flung it toward the rocking
chair. It hung for a moment on the back of the chair,
swaying crazily before it fell into a heap on the floor.

Brett had always defined his life with order. He lived on
a rigid schedule, keeping a tight control over his records
and over his emotions.

The sight of his shirt on the floor released something
primitive in him. He stripped all his clothes off and stalked
from the room. When he came back, he was armed with
mop and bucket, with dust cloth and lemon wax, with
fresh sheets and air freshener. Buck naked, he cleaned the
room until there was not a single sign of them left, not a
wrinkle, not a hair, not a whiff.

Dripping with sweat, he stood in the middle of his bare
and shining room. Alone. Leaving his cleaning supplies, he
approached the bed once more. With its crisp white sheets
tucked in with sharp corners, it was as stark and bare as
his hospital room in Ruhengeri.

He stretched full-length on the bed, naked, arms and
legs spread-eagled, reclaiming his territory, marking it
with his scent like an animal. The fresh smell of lemon
wax and the sharp pungency of the air freshener soothed
him. He took deep breaths, and gradually a new fragrance
invaded his senses, a fragrance that belonged only to her.

His hand closed over the red ribbon hanging on his
bedpost, and as he pulled the bit of satin to him, he
thought about passion, about how it could lie inside you
for years without ever showing itself. And then unexpectedly it could grab you right around the heart for no other
reason than that a soft and lovely woman calls your name.
Now, with the ribbon against his cheek and the fragrance
of her so evocative, he imagined she lay beside him on the

bed—he heard her voice once more, a soft, shattered cry, calling out to him. Not to Malone, but to him.

Pain sharper than the panga that had sliced his eye caught him deep in the gut and wouldn't let go. Ruth's plea was one he could never answer, because he had always loved his brother first and best . . . because he would always love his brother.

"Ruth!"

His voice sounded like the cry of a wounded animal. Still clutching the ribbon, he crossed his hands over his chest, holding her there against his heart.

39.

NEW YORK

WHITE ROSE PETALS DRIFTED AROUND her like snow, landing at her feet and piling up around her legs, falling so thick and fast it was like being buried alive.

"Brett . . . Brett . . ."

Ruth woke up drenched with sweat, her heart pounding so hard, she had to put her hand over her chest to keep it from jumping out. Beside her, Malone lay flat on his back, mouth slightly open, his breathing slow and even. And then she realized what had awakened her: the sound of her own voice, calling Brett's name, over and over, just as she had done every night since she'd taken flight off his mountain.

Three weeks without seeing Brett, without hearing the sound of his voice, without feeling his touch upon her hand, briefly, fleetingly. Three weeks. An eternity.

She leaned close to check that Malone hadn't heard. No one must ever hear. No one must ever know. And eventually, if she tried hard enough and lived long enough, she'd forget how Brett had looked on that mountain, and how much she'd wanted him to answer her, how much she wanted him to answer her still.

She went to the window and drew back the curtain. There wasn't much sky to see. Not that it mattered. There were so many lights in New York, it was hard to tell daylight from dark, anyhow.

"Honey." Malone lifted himself on his elbow. "Are you all refreshed from your nap and ready to party?"

Slowly she lowered the curtain. When she faced her husband, she was smiling.

"Let the good times roll," she said.

Later, in a darkened theater on Broadway, Malone reached for her hand.

"You're great. The best wife a man could ever have."

She saw herself with a Best Wife sign around her neck, scarlet, the color of shame. She imagined herself going through the rest of her life, the sign getting heavier and heavier, until she was so weighted down, she fell to the ground and prayed to be trampled.

"You're not so bad yourself, Malone Corday."

"You know how to turn a man on, Mrs. Corday. I don't know if I can last through this show."

In the darkened theater he nuzzled her neck. He hadn't shaved since morning, and she knew she'd have a beard burn the next day, the kind teenagers got from necking in dark cars on back country roads.

If beard burn was what it took to save her marriage, she'd gladly sacrifice her tender skin. Wasn't that the point of coming with Malone on this whirlwind fund-raising tour of the U.S.?

After the show she and Malone went to the Essex House to meet supporters of the Corday Foundation. They'd come from all over the United States to hear him speak—from Texas and Alabama and Mississippi and North Carolina, from Colorado and Idaho and Utah and Montana. She knew she should be trying to remember their names, but it took too much effort. All the energy she had was gone, used up in the flight off the top of Brett's mountain.

"Quite a little wife you have there, Corday."

"I think so." Malone wrapped his arm around her waist. "Darling, you remember Newton Ellis, don't you?"

"Of course. Mr. Ellis, how lovely to see you again."

How smoothly she lied now. She could leave Africa and make her living that way. Ruth Corday. Liar.

"I was just telling Sue Evelyn here, there's some great jazz in this city if a country boy like me can only find it. You like jazz, Miz Corday?"

"Call me Ruth. And, yes, I do." As long as she wasn't the one singing it in a tight whore's dress.

"Why don't the four of us skip on out of here after this here shindig and cozy up in a corner somewhere? We might even get down to real bidness. That's spelled D-O-N-A-T-I-O-N-S, if you want to know." Mr. Ellis winked at her.

"Actually, this is sort of a delayed honeymoon for us, but if my wife doesn't mind . . . Is that all right with you, sweetheart?"

Did he ever listen when it *wasn't* all right with her?

She thought of the red ribbon swaying on the bed, spinning round and round, irrevocably tangling itself with the leather eye patch.

"Honey?" Malone's brow puckered the way it often did these days. The badge of concern. The dubious honor she'd bestowed on the husband she had pledged to love and cherish till they were parted by death.

Death had already parted them. The death of hope. It had died on that mountaintop in the Virungas when she'd called out his brother's name.

All the king's horses and all the king's men couldn't put Humpty Dumpty together again. But Ruth was going to try. With every ounce of strength she possessed, she was going to *make* her marriage work.

"It sounds like fun." She smiled at her husband, and he leaned over and kissed her cheek.

That was the way Sue Evelyn captured them, looking for all the world like a man and a woman in love.

"Something to remember the honeymoon by," she said as she snapped their picture.

While the camera whirred and spit out the lie, tears the size of tennis balls clogged Ruth's throat. If one of them spilled over, she'd say she had developed allergies.

"Newlyweds," Mr. Ellis said, laughing. "You'd better enjoy it while it lasts. This is the happiest time of your life."

"Yes," Ruth said. "The happiest time of my life."

BOSTON

As Malone left the lectern, Ruth smiled at him. But not the way she'd smiled at Brett. For a moment a black despair obscured his vision; then, shaking it off, he went down the aisle and took her hand.

"Let's get out of this crowd before we get cornered. I want to show my wife how happy I am she came with me on this fund-raiser."

"I'm glad you're happy, darling."

If she was so damned glad, why did her face make him think of an underprivileged poster child?

When they got up to the room, he didn't bother with preliminaries, but braced her against the wall and rutted into her like a male gorilla with an overdose of testosterone. She received him with pale endurance.

He felt himself building to a climax too quickly, as he always seemed to do lately. He wondered if it mattered to her whether it was fast or slow. It was a question he didn't dare ask. There were lots of questions between them lately that he didn't dare ask.

She sighed when he withdrew. Relief or regret?

He didn't want to know.

"Why don't you freshen up, sweetheart, and we'll go to the bar downstairs and have a little nightcap?"

"You go ahead, Malone. I'm a little tired."

From doing what? Certainly not from her exertions in the lovemaking department.

She went into the bathroom, and he could hear her preparations to wash all evidence of him away.

He followed her, intending to apologize for not taking the time to get a condom. She was bent over the wastebasket, taking the wrappings off a disposable douche. Something strong and angry rose in him.

"Don't!" She looked up at him, startled. "Don't wash it out." Hadn't he read somewhere that once a woman bore a man's child she was a tiger in bed? "I want children."

"Malone . . . I don't think this is the time. . . ."

"When is the time? Tell me, Ruth. When is the right time?"

"You're upset. This is not the time to talk."

"I'm not upset. I'm damned mad." He gripped her shoulders. "I fuck you, but you don't fuck me. Why is that, Ruth?"

Her chin shot up, and she got that look that said he'd gone too far. Hell, that was the story of his life. He was always doing and saying the wrong thing.

"I have no intention of getting into a shouting match with you, Malone. Let go of me."

He didn't want to let go of her.

"What would it take to make you moan with pleasure? Huh, Ruth?" He saw fury in every line of her body. *Good.* At least he had a reaction. "What would it take? . . . Brett?"

She slapped him so hard, he actually spun around. He'd be lucky if he didn't have a shiner.

He could hear her getting her suitcase out of the closet. Panicked, he followed her into the bedroom.

"Sometimes I'm such an asshole," he said.

"Sometimes you are."

She paused in the act of throwing a white silk gown into the suitcase. He knew the exact moment she changed her mind about leaving him. Her shoulders sagged; then she straightened them back up and began taking her clothes out of the suitcase.

"Does this mean you're not going to leave me?"

"I'm not about to give up on a good man like you, Malone Corday."

She shoved her suitcase back in the closet, then sat on the bed and patted a space beside her. He sat down, careful not to touch her.

"The problem with us is that we don't do much talking," she said.

"I didn't know there was a problem with us. Let's don't talk about it tonight."

The really sad thing about it all, Ruth decided, was that Malone was telling the truth.

"Let's kiss and make up," he added.

"Kiss and cover up is more like it. And everything will still be there tomorrow. The jealousy, the drinking . . ."

She figured she was the biggest hypocrite on earth, focusing on his problems. But how could she talk about her own? She knew why she cringed from him; she just didn't know when she'd get over it.

He squeezed her hand. Hard. There was such a look of sincerity in his face, she wanted to pull his head down to her breast and soothe him as if he were a child.

He really was a fine man—loyal, loving. Maybe a child was all they needed. . . .

"I promise I'm going to do better," he said.

"Me too," she said. "I'm sorry I slapped you."

"I deserved it."

They sat that way for a while, holding on to each other, afraid to let go, afraid their future would vanish before their very eyes. She wasn't going to let it vanish. She was going to fight for them, for their marriage, for their future.

"Malone . . ."

"Hmm . . ."

"I think you will make a very good father."

"Ruth? Does this mean . . . ?"

"Yes, Malone. I want to have your child."

"I've always pictured myself teaching my son all the things Brett taught me."

"Brett?"

Was she glowing because she'd spoken Brett's name, or at the prospect of having a child? He was insane to be jealous every time she glowed. She was a beautiful woman, prone to dewy looks. Malone firmly squashed the green-eyed monster. Hadn't he promised to do better?

"Joseph never had time. He was always off with his gorillas. But I promise you that I'll be there for our kid. I'll even take the midnight dirty-diaper shift."

They sat side by side, wrapped in their separate fantasies, contemplating the child they might have.

"You might already be pregnant," he said.

"That's always a possibility." She leaned her head on his shoulder. "I want us to get this marriage on very firm ground."

"If that's where you want it, that's where I'm going to put it. . . . Ruth?"

"Yes?"

"I'll do anything in the world to keep you. Anything."

Shivers ran through her. As if someone had just walked on her grave. She pushed the thought aside.

As if he'd read her thoughts, he held her close.

"By the time this honeymoon is over, it'll be on such firm ground, you'll be bouncing when you walk, Mrs. Corday. You and the little one." Lamplight shone on his blond hair as he bent over and kissed her stomach.

Did she dare hope again?

"Malone, where will we be tomorrow?"

"Philadelphia."

"And after that?" Perhaps by the time she got home, she'd be pregnant and happy, and they'd both be laughing about the rocky early days of their marriage.

"Paradise, my darling. Pure paradise."

40.

THE VIRUNGAS

*S*OMETIMES BRETT FELT LIKE A COWARD, hiding away on his mountaintop with his gorillas and his memories. Usually, though, he just felt like an ordinary man, doing what it took to survive. And surviving meant never seeing anything that would remind him of Ruth—particularly of Ruth and his brother together.

As he rounded the curve in the road, their cabin came into view. Empty now, for they were in the States. Doing what? He didn't like to think about it. Thinking put him in a place that felt like hell.

He turned his face quickly away from their cabin and toward the main house. Joseph and Eleanor would be waiting.

He parked his Jeep and went inside. The house smelled like lemon wax and coconut cake. He stood in the doorway, inhaling deeply and smiling his appreciation.

"What's the occasion?" he asked.

"Your visit," Eleanor said. "It's so rare."

"Sorry. I've been busy." He could tell his mother didn't believe him. He'd never been a good liar. "Where's Joseph?"

"Late, as usual. Don't worry. He'll be along when he remembers that we were going to talk about which group would be the best for Cee Cee. *If* he remembers."

Brett prowled the room, grabbed a handful of peanuts near Joseph's easy chair, picked up the latest copy of *Time* magazine that lay on the coffee table, walked toward the fireplace . . . and stopped dead still. The picture was in a silver frame on the mantel.

"Do you like it?" Eleanor asked.

Ruth smiled at him from the photograph. He lifted it and ran his fingers gently over the lines of her cheeks, her eyes, her mouth.

"It came in yesterday's mail. From Boston. Since I don't have a wedding picture of them, I thought it would be a good one to frame. What do you think, Brett?"

His fingers moved over her face once more. He could actually feel the texture of her skin.

"In his letter Malone said they're enjoying their honeymoon. I think this trip will be good for them, give them some time alone without all of us breathing down their necks."

Eleanor's voice sounded very far away. He had no thought except the beautiful image in his hand. Ruth. His brother's wife.

"Brett?"

As if a fog had lifted from his brain, Brett saw his brother, arms wrapped around Ruth, kissing her cheek. Her smile was for Malone. Carefully, he set the picture on the mantel and turned his back on it.

"What time do you think Joseph will be here?" he asked. "I need to get back up the mountain."

"It's not Cee Cee that has a fire under your tail. It's her." Eleanor stalked to the mantel and jerked down the picture.

"Leave Ruth out of this."

"Leave her out? Gladly. I'd gladly leave her out if I

could. I wish to hell I could. I wish to hell she'd never come to Africa."

"Don't say that."

She ran her fingers through her short bob, then sank to the sofa as if all the steam had suddenly gone out of her.

"I don't know what's happening in my own family. What's happening in my family, Brett?"

"Nothing. Nothing is happening."

"That wasn't 'nothing' I saw at your camp. And it wasn't 'nothing' I saw when you picked up her picture. I know that look. What I don't know is what kind of hold this woman has on you."

"Her name is Ruth. She's not 'this woman'—she's a part of our family, your daughter-in-law and my sister-in-law."

He stalked toward the door, unable to bear the dissension that had come into the house.

"Swear to me," she called after him. "Swear that nothing is happening."

Holding fast to the doorknob, he turned to face his mother.

"I swear to you nothing is happening. Nothing will ever happen."

Eleanor didn't believe him. Not that her son would lie. Brett would never deliberately lie to her. What she was afraid of was that he was lying to himself. Somehow Ruth had tangled them up in a web that was pulling tighter and tighter until it would strangle them all. Brett. Malone. Joseph. Even Eleanor herself.

"Not while I have breath in my body," she said to herself.

There had to be something she could do to save her family. Without thinking, she grabbed her hat and headed to the Jeep. There was one man who could help her, one man she needed to see.

As she drove up the long, winding driveway of the sprawling plantation, Eleanor put everything from her mind except the favor she'd come to ask of Luke Fisher. Through the vaulted archway she could see him in the barn with his thoroughbreds.

He turned at the sound of her Jeep, then stood with one slim hip propped against a stable door and a wide-brimmed leather hat pushed back from his forehead.

"Eleanor . . . it's been a long time."

"Yes. Almost two years."

"Eighteen months, two weeks, and six days."

She hadn't expected him to count the days. The sharp jolt the knowledge brought her was not sadness, but something much more poignant—a wild, almost forgotten tenderness. She steeled herself against the feeling, made herself assume a brisk walk and a no-nonsense manner.

"I suppose you could call me a fair-weather friend," she said.

"I call you many things, Eleanor, but never that." He took a step toward her, arms outstretched.

It was a simple hug that had kept her away for so long, a hug that had almost got out of hand.

"No. Please." Holding up her hand, she stepped back.

"Sorry. There will be no repeat performances of what happened in this barn the last time." The brightness in his eyes told her that his memories were just as vivid as hers. "Let's go inside out of the heat."

The scent of hay and leather and horseflesh clung to him . . . as always. Eleanor inhaled deeply, allowing herself that one small pleasure.

But nothing else. Not even the satisfaction of letting her hip brush against his.

He didn't engage in idle chatter, didn't attempt to fill in the two-year gap that separated them. She sat in a bent-willow swing on his screen-covered porch and watched him make tall, cool drinks, ice tinkling against crystal, silver spoons stirring the pale-gold liquid, linen napkins holding moisture that dripped from the sides of the glasses. Ceiling fans stirred the humid air.

Suddenly she realized she'd missed more than Luke; she'd missed the small niceties of civilization.

His hand touched hers when he handed her the glass. It was no accident. Luke Fisher never did things by accident. She was careful not to react.

"I have a new daughter-in-law."

"Brett?"

He lingered beside the swing, studying her while he set it in gentle motion.

"No. Malone. He barely knew her." Unable to contain her unrest, Eleanor sprang from the swing and set her drink on the patio table. Glass clattered against glass. Liquid spilled on her hand.

Luke wiped away the moisture with a linen napkin, then wrapped his large, sunburned hand around hers.

"Sometimes miracles happen, Eleanor."

The trembling started in her knees. *Miracles.* She could hardly bear to think of them.

So long ago.

She'd been young, secure in her marriage, smug in the knowledge that she was a strong woman who could handle anything, particularly two small children and several groups of mountain gorillas while her husband was abroad raising money for the foundation.

Suddenly her secure world had been torn apart. A small band of Watusis, long discontent with the French government, had massacred a French diplomat and his staff, then set off on a warpath that left blood and carnage in their wake. Trapped in her remote mountain compound, Eleanor had barricaded the doors and armed herself with Joseph's .38 Luger.

One day, at the sound of hoofbeats she'd pointed her gun out the window.

"Eleanor! Don't shoot. It's me, Luke Fisher."

Luke Fisher, the man who had been a good neighbor and a staunch supporter of the Corday Foundation since their arrival in Africa.

"I've come to take you and the children down the mountain."

He'd risked his own life and the health of his fine thoroughbreds in order to rescue them. The roads had been blocked. The villages had been a bloodbath. They had waited in the compound until night; then, under cover of darkness, they had taken the steep trails down the mountains.

Brett had ridden behind her, his arms clinging tightly around her waist, and Luke had ridden with baby Malone cradled securely in his arms.

They'd reached his plantation after a grueling six-hour ride.

"You'll be safe with me," he'd said.

During the next twenty-four hours she'd felt safer and more pampered than she'd ever been. On her second morning at the plantation, a sound had awakened her. The baby crying? Brett having a bad dream? The Watusis at the door?

She'd stolen out of her bedroom, her thin gown clinging to her with the sweat of fear, her bare toes curling against the cool, polished wooden floors. Rounding the corner, she'd bumped into a broad, bare chest. Luke had put his hand over her mouth and dragged her close to keep her from screaming.

"Shhh. It's me, Luke. Everything is all right."

From the moment he'd pulled her into his arms, she'd known that nothing in her life would ever be all right again. Whether it was need, a sense of danger, or mere proximity, she would never know. But she and Luke had come together with the explosiveness of mating thorough-breds. They'd made love in the hallway, standing up. It had been over in less than ten minutes.

Afterward she'd adjusted her gown, trembling. She'd closed her eyes, and tears had squeezed from under her eyelids.

"This will never happen again," she'd whispered.

"No," he'd agreed. "Never."

They'd looked at each other, both seeing the lie.

"Eleanor . . ."

She'd reached for him, and he'd carried her into his bedroom. There they'd made lingering, miraculous love until the sun had painted the plantation the polished gold of morning and the children had stirred.

They couldn't get enough of each other. Once when they'd thought the children were asleep, they'd made passionate love on the kitchen floor. Brett had almost caught them. By the time he'd got to the kitchen for his drink of water, Eleanor had been sitting at the table holding her robe together and Luke had had his pants on.

At the end of four days, when the threat of war was

over and the path toward home clear, he'd begged her to
stay.

"I love you, Eleanor. I've loved you since the day you
came here with Joseph. Stay. Please."

"I can't. I can't leave Joseph."

"Is it because you love him or because you're afraid to
love me?"

"Both."

Luke had not begged, had not tried to change her mind.
He'd merely carried her and the children back up the
mountain and delivered them into the hands of a tearful,
grateful Joseph.

She'd never lain with Luke again, never even allowed
herself to touch him in a casual manner . . . except that
once—two years earlier when she'd been photographing
his champion horse for a magazine layout. A simple hug
had turned to deep kissing and frenzied fondling. In one
desperate moment she'd almost negated all her years of
sacrifice.

To make up for her betrayal of her husband, she'd
sworn to devote herself to him and his life's work, to do
everything in her power to make the Corday Foundation
one of the most respected ventures in the history of science, and the Corday family unshakable.

Nothing would stand in the way of her goal . . . except perhaps her own weakness. Even after more than
twenty years her passion for Luke was as fierce as it had
been the night they'd first come together. What she had
with Joseph was an enduring respect and tender regard.
What she'd had with Luke was a miracle.

Remembering, Eleanor wrapped her arms around herself to contain the trembling. Luke caught her shoulders,
not to pull her close, but merely to comfort.

"Regrets, Eleanor?" he whispered.

Sometimes, lying beside a husband who waded the shallows of the deep pool of passion that lay hidden inside her,
she had many regrets. But neither Joseph nor Luke would
ever know.

"Never," she said.

Luke released her abruptly, then drew a pipe from his
pocket and took his time tamping in tobacco. Watching

his slim, sun-browned fingers holding the fragile pipe bowl, Eleanor almost lost her resolve. How would it feel to have those hands on her once again?

More and more Joseph camped on the slopes of the Virungas with his beloved mountain gorillas. More and more Eleanor spent the long nights in an empty bed.

Luke had never married. She didn't have to ask why. Every time he looked at her, she saw the reason in his eyes.

To save herself, she didn't look at his eyes, but instead sat in the swing so she could see the vast expanse of pasture, so rich that it looked as if it had been freshly painted green and left out in the sun to dry.

"Do you want to tell me why you came, Eleanor?" Luke said finally, breaking the long silence between them.

Such loneliness overtook her that she thought she might die.

"Yes. I want you to rescue me once again."

"Eleanor . . ."

"I'm sorry. I shouldn't have said that. I don't know what got into me."

"I do. And so do you."

She did know. Of course, she did. She was a selfish witch. She wasn't about to start anything with him, but she had to know that he still wanted her, had to see it in his face.

Abruptly, she left the swing and perched on the porch railing, but putting that space between them didn't help at all.

"I came to see you because you're the only person I know who can throw the kind of party I have in mind."

"And what kind is that?"

"The kind that will heal a lot of wounds, answer a few questions, and make the Cordays a family again."

"You've got it, Eleanor . . . anything you want."

She knew it was time to go. Before she made a fool of herself—something she seemed to be very good at lately.

41.

OXFORD, MISSISSIPPI

*T*HE INVITATION LAY OPEN ON THE dressing table. Margaret Anne read it a second time to see if she dared believe her eyes.

Why now? After so long? Was it a peace offering?

Oh, surely it was. She had to go looking her very best.

She raced to her closet to see what she had that would suit the occasion. At her touch the soft dresses with full skirts swayed on their hangers like a garden of pastel flowers. She'd take the yellow voile and the pink, and most definitely the lilac. It had a matching straw hat with a long lilac chiffon scarf that would hang down her back and blow in the breeze. So old-fashioned. So ladylike. So perfect.

Flushed with excitement, she rummaged to the back of her closet, searching for the hat. The red dress was hidden behind her winter coats. She came upon it unexpectedly, like stumbling over treasure. Even though it was covered with plastic, she could still smell the smoke caught in its satin folds. From pipe tobacco. A special blend that had to be shipped from some exotic island. She didn't remember which one.

All she remembered was the way she'd felt when she'd worn that dress, the way he'd made her feel. The pain and beauty of the memories almost brought her to her knees. Rocked by her emotions, she held on to the dress until she could let go without falling. Then, smoothing the skirt where her fingers had crushed the satin, she rushed to the attic to be with him.

A thick layer of dust coated the old trunk and the cracked mirror that hung above it. Heedless of her clothes, Margaret Anne lifted the lid and pulled out the packet bound with pink ribbon.

On top was a dog-eared photograph of the two of them when they were children, holding hands, their snaggle-toothed grins wide in their dirty faces. The sacks slung over their shoulders were almost as big as they were, and behind them, row upon row of cotton gleamed like yards of white ribbon.

Margaret Anne was wearing a pair of shorts and a halter top made from feed sacks, but it was so hot that even that brief garment was soaked with sweat and sticking to her skin. Though the heat had made his face as slick and shiny as the polished mahogany table at the Big House, he offered her the first drink of ice water from the tin bucket.

"Whatcha gonna do when you grow up, Maggie?"

"I'm gonna marry me a rich man and be a fine lady so I can live in a Big House, and ain't nobody gonna call me Maggie no more. How 'bout you?"

"I ain't stayin' no place hot and pickin' cotton the rest of my life like our daddies. Nosiree, I'm gettin' me a job somewhere cool."

"Doin' what?"

"I don' know. Some'in."

They filled the dipper once more and poured the ice water over their heads. Then, slick as otters, they raced through the cotton fields and beyond the shabby tenant houses where the smell of mustard greens with fatback was a permanent part of the air. On the banks of a narrow creek a stand of oak and sweet-gum trees grew so thick, the ground underneath was cool even when the temperature was pushing a hundred.

They flopped down and leaned against each other, giggling. From the distance came the sound of a lonesome trumpet played with all the passion and pathos of a man beaten by life, but too old and too tired to do anything about it.

"Someday I'm gonna get me a trumpet, and it's gonna be as silver and shiny as the evening star. Lissen, Maggie. Ain't that the sweetest sound on God's green earth?"

Propped against his skinny shoulder, she'd thought it was, and years later, lying in his bed, she'd believed that that sweet sound would always be a part of her life.

Each photograph in the packet brought a new memory, a fresh pain. By the time she came to the last one, tears were rolling down her face, streaking her mascara and dripping off her chin. In the last photograph they were naked on the bed, his head on her full breasts and his hands covering the enormous mound of her stomach. He'd set the timer on the camera so they could pose that way.

"When the baby's born, we'll set the timer and take a family portrait," he said.

But there had never been a family portrait, would *never* be a family portrait. All their dreams had turned to dust the night she'd worn the red dress.

That day, their last day together, he'd cut his first record. Riding high with power and success, he'd spent every penny he had on the red satin dress.

"Tonight we're gonna celebrate, baby."

"It's beautiful." She held the red dress to her. "I've never had anything so beautiful in all my life."

"Stick with me and there's gonna be diamonds as big as golf balls."

"And we'll go home and parade through those cotton fields like Mr. and Mrs. Astorbutt. We'll show them all, won't we?"

"That's right, baby. They won't never call you nigger lover no more."

She had a front-row table at the club where he and his band played, the Purple People Eater, a little hole-in-the-wall dive on a back street in L.A. He dedicated all his songs that night to her and the baby. Between every number he blew her kisses.

"Diamonds as big as golf balls, baby," he mouthed.

She laughed, was still laughing when they went up the narrow back stairs to the small loft for the celebration party that Slick Williams, the drummer, was throwing. Booze flowed like manna from heaven. He'd had his share, but he'd turned down the drugs.

"None of that shit, man. I'm gonna be a daddy."

Somebody had slipped angel dust in his beer. It sent him on a bad trip from which he'd never returned. And never would.

Blue Janeau. Billed by the critics as the greatest natural jazz performer since W. C. Handy.

"Blue . . . Blue . . ."

The pictures slid from her hands as she bent over, sobbing and calling his name. Dust she'd disturbed swirled around her and settled into the folds of her skin. After a while she had no more tears to shed. She scrubbed her face with the back of her hand, then carefully rearranged her treasures and tied them with the pink ribbon.

Never again would she hear him play the sweet, sad blues while the sweat from their lovemaking dried on their skin.

As she placed the packet back inside the trunk, Margaret Anne caught a glimpse of herself in the mirror. She was as cracked and musty as it was.

She pulled an old cloth from the trunk and draped it over the mirror, then closed the lid and hurried downstairs. In the bathroom she showered, and although no one was coming to call, she completely redid her face, then put on her prettiest voile dress that showed off her legs.

There was always the possibility that some nice young delivery man would come to the door looking for directions. She would invite him in for something cool while she looked in the phone book to be sure of the right address, and he would see how shapely her legs were, and she would take his hand . . .

Silly dreams of a silly old woman. Somehow Max would find out, and he'd cut her off without a cent. Worse yet, he might decide to tell that Margaret Anne Bellafontaine was no more descended from Southern aristocracy than a cat could fly to the moon, that in fact she'd been disowned from a dirt-poor, sharecropping Delta family named Gilmore because she'd run off with a mulatto. And then where would she be? The laughingstock of the town. A disgrace.

Margaret Anne pulled back the neck of her dress and patted her skin with a scented handkerchief. The heat was as oppressive as her life.

Was there no way out?

Suddenly her gaze fell on the invitation, still lying open on her dressing table. Another chance.

She'd wear nothing but shades of purple and pink on her trip. They made her look at least ten years younger.

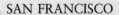

42.

SAN FRANCISCO

*C*HU LING HAD NO TROUBLE GETTING A private audience with Malone Corday. The twenty-five-thousand-dollar check he'd written to the Corday Foundation did the trick.

The boy had a weakness for vodka and tonic, he'd been told. Ply him with enough of them, and he'd agree to practically anything. His other weakness was the woman, his wife. An exquisite creature. Chu Ling could see how a man could lose his head over such a woman.

"Your generosity is greatly appreciated." Malone Corday's voice was slurred. He was already feeling the effects of too much drink.

Chu Ling didn't have to motion for the waiter to refill Corday's glass. He owned the club. The waiter had already been told what to do; he waited in the shadows like a yellow cat, his eyes missing nothing. He gave good measure for the exorbitant salary Chu Ling paid him. It was a good deal for both of them.

Chu Ling loved a good deal. Underneath the snowy white tablecloth he rubbed his palms together in anticipation of the one he was about to make.

"Your foundation does excellent work," he said. "I think excellence should always have its reward. Don't you?"

"Damned right."

"You have many large contributors, I suppose?"

"Not nearly enough. And no one as generous as you."

"I can be an exceedingly generous man."

"Your check speaks louder than words."

"There's more where that came from."

Chu Ling smiled. The boy was practically salivating at the idea of more money. Swiftly, he changed the topic, catching him off guard. Best always to have your opponent off guard.

"Your wife is a very beautiful woman."

"Yes, she is."

"A woman worthy of beautiful things. You give her beautiful things, don't you?"

"Only this sensational body." Corday's laughter was bitter. "Sometimes you have to settle for what you can get."

"On the contrary. The wise never have to settle."

"Maybe in your world. Where I come from, you have to settle."

"Why?"

"Hell . . . how should I know? I'm just a mere errand boy."

"You're far more than that. You're a resourceful, brilliant man with an extraordinary wife. You deserve wealth, success, and power."

"Yeah, well, from your mouth to God's ears."

"You're the one who does all the traveling in the Corday family?"

"That's me, Malone Corday, gypsy errand boy, always on the go."

"Travel gives you many opportunities."

"Yeah, to bore everybody to tears with my lectures and to answer umpteen million questions about my brother and the talking gorilla."

Silently, the waiter appeared to refill Corday's drink. Already he was reeling. If Chu Ling didn't close the deal soon, Corday wouldn't be sober enough to stand up, let alone talk business.

"Opportunities beyond your imagining," Chu Ling added as he pulled a velvet case from his inside pocket and laid it on the table. He waited until he had Corday's full attention before he unsnapped the lid. The rubies glittered against the dark velvet.

"For your beautiful wife," he said.

"I can't possibly afford something like that."

"It's a gift."

"A gift?"

"The first of many."

Corday picked up the necklace and studied it under the lamplight.

"Are these things real?"

"The best money can buy."

Corday studied the necklace a while longer before laying it back in the velvet box.

"But it has a price, right?"

Chu Ling was delighted. The plan would not work if Corday didn't have brains, and he'd just proved he had.

"Everything has its price." He held the box so the rubies would catch the light. "A woman like your wife . . . most men would find her worth any price."

Corday studied the rubies in silence. When the waiter came to refill his glass, Corday waved him away.

"Name it."

"I want baby gorillas."

"No!" But the initial horror on Corday's face faded as he gazed at the ruby necklace. "You don't know what you're asking."

"I know exactly what I'm asking. And I'm willing to pay top dollar."

"I shouldn't even be listening to this."

Chu Ling understood that the art of the deal was subtlety.

"I hear talk of a theme park in the Virungas on the slopes where the Corday Foundation does its work," he said.

"The talk is merely a whisper. You must have big ears."

"My ears are sharp. So is my perception. Such a park will bring in many rich tourists, will it not?"

"Why don't you tell me? You seem to have all the answers."

Chu Ling smiled. The fact that Corday was still at the table was more than a good sign; it was capitulation. Chu Ling had already won. Still, he played out his hand. Knowledge was power. Best that Corday know the full extent of Chu Ling's power.

"They'll come in tour buses to the mountains, bringing disease to the mountain gorilla. Everything will change. The gorillas will gradually die."

Chu Ling watched his opponent over the careful steeple he'd made of his fingers. Corday already knew everything he was being told. Chu Ling could tell by the grim set of his face.

"Very few gorillas will survive," Chu Ling continued. "The few that do will move deeper into the jungles, away from the tourists. There will be no need for the Corday Foundation because nobody in power will be interested in preservation of the mountain gorilla. The only thing of interest to anybody will be tourist dollars."

"You've done your research well."

Chu Ling merely smiled. He never conceded the obvious.

"You paint a grim picture," Corday added.

"You have the power to change it."

"If I do what you want."

"My money will allow the Corday Foundation to continue its work and continue to bring the gorilla's plight to the attention of the world. Without me it's only a matter of time before you fold, the gorillas are forgotten, and the theme park is built."

Corday lifted the necklace, held it under the lamplight. Fire from the multifaceted stones spilled across the tablecloth.

"You're asking me to destroy the very thing I've worked for all my life."

"Think of it as sacrificing a few for the good of many. I'm not a greedy man."

"How do you propose to do this?"

"You're smart. You can figure out how to get them out of the country, a few at a time so no one is suspicious."

"It would take a long time to set up."

"I'm a patient man."

"It would be very expensive."

"Ahhh. Money." Chu Ling smiled.

"Yes. Money."

"I think we can come to some terms that will be very much to your liking."

When Ruth woke up, there was a ruby necklace on her pillow. The light she'd left on for Malone was caught in the stones that gleamed fiercely up at her like the fire of a dragon. At first she thought she was dreaming. Reaching out, she touched the necklace, and when she discovered it was real, she knew she wasn't in the midst of a dream but in the thick of a nightmare.

"Malone?"

She sat up and covered herself completely with the sheet, as if a thin bit of percale could protect her from what she might see. Malone sat in a maroon brocaded wing chair near the foot of the bed. His tie was askew and his hair stood up in spikes, as if he'd just come through a high wind.

"What time is it?" she asked, as if the dials of the bed-side clock weren't clearly pointing to three.

"Time to do something for my beautiful wife, that's what time it is."

He came around the bed, ripped aside the sheet, and held the necklace against her throat. Her skin felt hot and cold at the same time, as if a jagged chunk of ice had been held there too long.

"The necklace makes you look like a queen."

"Where in the world did it come from, Malone?"

The drugstore on the corner, she hoped he'd say. Or a cheap costume-jewelry shop in Chinatown.

"A gift, from an admirer of the Cordays."

"It's not real, is it?"

"Damned right it's real." He fumbled with the catch. "Shit! Fucking thing won't fasten." He leaned closer, and the smell of liquor almost overpowered her.

"Let's not fool with it tonight, darling. Why don't you come to bed?"

"I want to see you wear it." He lost his balance and fell into her. Propping himself on his elbows, he grinned at her. "Did you save the last dance for me, sweetheart?"

"I've saved all my dances for you, Malone."

Her smile felt as stiff as plaster of paris. Gently she untangled herself, then walked to the mirror and fastened the rubies around her neck. She didn't know a thing about jewelry, but it didn't take a gemologist to know that this piece would easily see a family of four through a year of crop failures.

Propped against the pillows on her side of the bed, Malone grinned at her.

"You know what you look like? A genuine Polynesian princess. Rubies are made for you, sweetheart."

"They do look good against my skin. Lucky for you, I'm not the diamonds-and-rubies type." She reached back to unfasten the necklace. "They should bring a pretty penny for the Corday Foundation."

"Leave them on, Ruth." She caught his eye in the mirror, and what she saw turned her blood to ice. She saw the deadly look of a cornered tiger. "Those jewels are not for the Corday Foundation. They are for you."

"But, Malone . . ."

"I earned them, and you are going to wear them."

Where? Gorillas didn't care what she wore. As if he'd read her mind, he answered her question.

"Eleanor's planned a wedding reception for us. When my wife walks in, every head in that place will turn. And they'll all know that Malone Corday is finally a winner."

Until that moment Ruth hadn't realized how heavy rubies were. Almost as heavy as guilt.

43.

THE VIRUNGAS

THE MINUTE RUTH ENTERED THE ROOM, Brett knew why he had come, why he had finally rejected all the reasons he'd come up with for staying away from the wedding reception at Luke Fisher's ranch. Reason had nothing to do with why he came. It was desire—desire so raw, it melted his insides and burned holes in his retina.

If she looked, she'd be terrified of what she saw.

"My God, she's stunning. Don't you think she's stunning?" he heard someone say.

He had forgotten Lorena was with him until she spoke.

"You don't need to answer that. Your face says it all."

He didn't comment on that, either. The great thing about Lorena was that she dropped time bombs in the middle of silences and was content to let them sit there and tick.

"Look at that necklace she's wearing. Is it real?"

He hadn't even noticed the necklace. It was the face that held him spellbound.

"It looks it," he said. "Must be a family heirloom."

Malone could certainly not afford such jewelry.

She was holding Malone's arm, smiling up at him the way she had in the photograph, smiling in a way that looked like love.

"Why don't I get us something to eat and drink?" he said. "Then we can sneak out of here."

"If I thought you had something on your mind besides escape, I'd be only too happy to skip the whole damned party. I'm out of my league here. Shit, most of these people have more money than the whole state of Texas. There are enough private planes on Luke Fisher's landing strip to outfit a small air force. And look at the jewels on that woman over there. Hell, I could live three years on what those diamond earrings cost. Besides, these shoes are making sausage out of my feet." Lorena made a rueful face at her two-inch heels, modest by anybody's standards. "That's what I get for being vain. I don't know what made me decide to try to be beautiful instead of comfortable. I couldn't hold a candle to your sister-in-law if I had a figure to die for and solid-gold titties."

Even while he laughed, he was thinking what it would be like to press his lips against Ruth's throat and feel her skin heat up the way it had when she'd left her scent on his bed.

His hands curved into fists, and he rammed them into his pockets just in time to hide them from his brother.

"My God, they're coming this way, and I'm standing here beside the world's most desirable man looking like a dish mop. I think I'll head to the kitchen and blend in with the cleanup crew."

Feeling selfish at his blatant neglect of a woman as fine as Lorena, Brett took one hand out of his pocket and placed it on her upper arm.

"You'll stay right where you are. I'm proud to be seen in your company. Always have been and always will be."

"I think you really mean that, don't you?"

"Yes. I really do."

Suddenly they were standing in front of him, his brother and his brother's wife.

"Well, hell, stay gone nearly a month and my own brother can't come across the room to say hello." Malone clapped him on the shoulder.

Brett returned the shoulder clasp, careful to keep his eyes off Ruth, who was standing so close, he could smell her perfume. He believed it might just be possible to die of too much desire.

"Hello, Malone." He made introductions without looking at Ruth. "How was the trip?"

"How was the *trip,* he says." Malone didn't have to answer the question. His full-bodied laughter and his good humor said it all. "My wife's wearing a king's ransom in jewels, and my brother asks how was the trip. How about something like, 'Congratulations, Malone.'"

Malone had bought the rubies, then, to celebrate. He'd gone to the bank and taken out a loan because of the best news a man could have. His wife was pregnant.

From a strictly scientific viewpoint Brett knew that it was possible for someone who had turned into a lump of salt to still have movement. His eyes swept over Ruth, noting her high color, her radiance.

"Congratulations," he said, but he wasn't looking at his brother when he said it.

Ruth touched the rubies at her throat.

"These were a gift." Her voice was low, throaty, like music sung on a winter's night when two people cuddled together in a warm bed. Like a lullaby. It made Brett's heart ache. "From a supporter."

"A supporter?" It was odd, the little things that gave relief to a man whose reason had been stolen.

"Yeah, bro. Wait till you get a gander at the check he gave the foundation. You and Joseph are going to be kissing my feet."

"How about kissing mine first, Brett?" Lorena said. "They hurt like hell."

Ruth wondered at her ability to laugh when she was trembling inside like an orphan who had been told somebody finally wanted her. It had been one thing to be on the other side of the world and tell herself she could make her marriage work, but back in Africa, face-to-face with Brett, Ruth knew better. She knew that no matter what she did, no matter where she went, she could never make her marriage be anything except a sham. Her spirit would never lift with wings at the sound of Malone's voice. Her heart would never race at his glance. She would never wear sunshine on cloudy days simply because he was a part of her life.

"Why don't I get you a chair instead, Lorena?" Brett said.

Ruth wanted to walk away with him, never mind that he was going only a few feet. *Wither thou goest, I will go.*

But she had not pledged those vows to Brett; she'd pledged them to his brother.

What if she divorced Malone? Would two wrongs make a right?

Brett scooped up the chair without even bending over. Strange how the back of a man's head could mesmerize. She couldn't take her eyes off the dark hair that followed the curve of his neck and brushed the top of his collar.

He turned around suddenly, his black eye catching hers, holding, probing, piercing. Desire as fierce as a tiger in the night climbed through her. Riveted, she stared at him.

He knows.

Wrapping her arms around herself, she held back her shiver. It was all there in his black eye—desire, despair, determination. And she knew that no matter what she did, Brett Corday would always be forbidden to her. Because he loved his brother. As she should love his brother.

Unaware, Malone smiled at her. "The day you became my wife was the proudest day of my life. I love you, Ruth."

She had tried so hard to love him. Now she understood that she never would, not in the way a woman should love the man she'd married. Brett was wedged in her mind, and she knew she wasn't going to stop thinking about him or stop wanting him, no matter where she went and no matter how hard she tried.

Like swimmers coming up for air, she and Brett broke eye contact, and he returned with a chair for Lorena.

"Is that better?" he asked.

"You treat me like a princess."

"You *are* a princess, Lorena."

"Speaking of princesses, who in the world is that?"

They all turned in the direction Lorena was looking. The woman standing in the doorway on the arms of Joseph and Eleanor Corday wore a lavender voile dress, a Panama hat with a lavender scarf hanging down her back, and three-inch heels with closed toes and ankle straps.

Ruth reached blindly, and a large hand closed over hers.

"That's my mother." She was surprised that her voice worked. "How in the world . . ."

"I knew she was coming, but I wanted to surprise you. Are you surprised, sweetheart?"

She squeezed the hand she was holding so hard, she felt as if the skin on her knuckles would break. The reassuring warmth pressed her palm.

"I'm stunned," she said.

Margaret Anne saw her and swept toward them like a ship under full steam.

"God, she's a looker," Malone said. "Like mother, like daughter. Right, sweetheart?"

No! Not as long as she had breath in her body.

Malone forged toward Margaret Anne with his arms wide-open.

That's when Ruth discovered whose hand she was clutching. Brett gently rubbed her hand between his.

"Are you all right, Ruth?"

"Yes."

"You look pale. Let me get you a glass of water."

"I'll get it." Lorena hurried toward the kitchen.

"Ruth! Darling!" Her mother was bearing down on her.

"Water won't help," she whispered.

"I'm right here beside you, Ruth. I won't leave you."

Although Brett released her hand, she could still feel his solid presence, his warmth, his reassurance. Somehow he gave her courage to endure the Judas kiss Margaret Anne place on her cheek.

"Just look at you. Marriage agrees with my beautiful daughter. I was just telling your *lovely* in-laws how *different* Africa is from the genteel South, but this party is sure to prove me wrong. My, my, I haven't seen such splendor since the Annual Charity Ball I put together last spring in Oxford."

In a cloud of lilac chiffon and gardenia perfume, Margaret Anne turned her attention to Brett.

"And you must be the Gorilla Man. My, my, I've heard so much about you. Even in the short little distance across this room, my sweet little son-in-law simply *raved* about you."

"I'm pleased to meet you, Mrs. Bellafontaine," Brett said.

"Margaret Anne, please! 'Mrs. Bellafontaine' makes me sound so *old*. I was just telling Malone not to *dare* call me that. Margaret Anne or even Mom, but *never* Mrs."

Everybody laughed, but it was the strained kind of laughter frequently heard at social occasions that brought together people who didn't much like each other.

Eleanor decided that was the main problem with her family now. They didn't like each other. She was merely tolerating Joseph these days, Brett tolerated her, Ruth probably hated her, and the Lord only knew what Malone thought.

When you expected miracles, you were bound to be disappointed. That's what she'd expected when she'd brought Ruth's mother to Africa. And what did she get? A woman who was as phony as her eyelashes. If she emphasized one more word in that exaggerated molasses-and-magnolias accent, Eleanor thought she would scream.

Not that any of that mattered. What mattered was the way Ruth was looking at her mother—like an escaped prisoner who had suddenly been cornered and expected at any minute to be sent to the electric chair—and the way Brett was looking at Ruth—like a man who had discovered the Promised Land, only to be banished forever.

Now that the greetings were over, nobody knew what to say.

"Why don't I get us all some drinks?" Malone said.

As if drinks would save any of them. But at least alcohol would soften the sharp edges of truth for a while and make it bearable. Eleanor guessed that was all she could ask. In the long silence that gripped them, she sought Luke Fisher's eyes. Across the room he solemnly lifted his glass to her.

She wished Malone would hurry with her drink.

Suddenly Margaret Anne Bellafontaine flung her arms wide, and the long chiffon scarf on her hat flew outward, then wrapped twice around her neck.

"I'm so happy," she said. "I'm happy for all of us."

44.

MALONE SLIPPED OUT OF HER BED IN THE wee hours of the morning. She heard him put on his clothes, then the sound of the front door closing.

Ruth rolled over and looked at the clock. Three A.M. Where in the world was he going?

Suddenly she remembered the way her mother had been with the Corday men at the party—vivacious, simpering, predatory. Rage filled her, rage and a terrible dread.

She left the bed and pulled on jeans and a T-shirt. Surely Margaret Anne hadn't lured Malone out at this time of night on some pretext. Even she wouldn't stoop that low. Or would she? Malone was so kindhearted, he'd believe any old story Margaret Anne told.

Ruth had to save her husband.

"Malone!" she called, racing to the window. But she was too late. The taillights of the Jeep disappeared around the bend.

What was she going to do? She could telephone the main compound where her mother was staying, see if Malone had gone there. She was smart. She could think of some pretext for sounding an alarm at three o'clock in the morning.

But suppose Malone hadn't gone there? Suppose he found she'd checked on him. He'd think she didn't have enough faith in him to trust him out of her sight.

Miranda left her basket by the window and rubbed herself against Ruth's legs.

"Sometimes I envy you, Miranda. Feed you and give you a warm, dry place to sleep, and you're happy."

Ruth scooped her up, carried her into the study, and turned on the light. She might as well work. There would be no sleep for her until Malone was safely home.

As she took her dissertation out of the desk, she remembered the way she'd felt when Margaret Anne had kissed her cheek. Cheap. Soiled. She'd wanted to scrub herself with soap. Even then her skin would still burn from the kiss of betrayal.

And the lies Margaret Anne had told—of Ruth's genteel upbringing, of old-family money, of familial love so thick and sweet, it made molasses look like vinegar water.

Ruth forced herself to pick up pen and paper. Work would be her salvation for the next few days, and then Margaret Anne would be gone, taking her lilac-scented dresses and her rose-colored lies with her.

"You don't have to come in tonight."

Brett stood on her front porch the way he had many nights, beautiful in the glow of the naked bulb that made a nimbus around his head. Had it been years? To Lorena it felt like only yesterday.

"Fact is, I don't want you to come in."

Why didn't he argue with her? Foolish question. She'd seen the reason he didn't argue with her.

"I wasn't very attentive at the party tonight, Lorena. I'm sorry."

"That has nothing to do with my not wanting you to come in."

He didn't have to ask why. She wished he had to ask.

She clutched her purse and felt her heart actually shriveling up, just like the rest of her. The best thing she could do for both of them was tell the truth. She could cry when she got into her bed in the dark where nobody could see. The funny thing was, she never thought she'd cry over a man.

"She's more than a beautiful woman, Brett. She has spirit, and that's what counts."

"She's my brother's wife."

"Hearts don't ask who someone belongs to. They have a way of attaching themselves anyway."

"Mine is not attached . . . and it's not going to be."

"It's attached tighter than a tick on a hound dog."

When he made a sound of protest, Lorena put her hand over his lips. Perfect lips that had kissed her in ways that made her feel like a pretty woman. Maybe she was wrong to be so noble. Maybe she'd change her mind and let him come in anyway. Forget pride. No wonder folks said it was foolish. Lorena was living, breathing testimony.

"You don't have to explain anything to me, Brett Corday. I know you better than anybody in the world. I, of all people, understand that you'd never do anything to hurt your brother. But the plain fact is, even if you came in, you wouldn't be here. And I can't stand the idea of three in a bed."

"You're a good woman."

"Sometimes I wish somebody would tell me I'm a gorgeous, sexy, irresistible woman."

Brett cupped her face, and she had to swallow a lump the size of Texas to keep from bawling like a newborn calf and embarrassing the hell out of both of them.

"Lorena, you've been all those things to me—gorgeous, sexy, irresistible—all those things and more. You've been a very good friend."

"Don't say 'have been' like I'm fixing to cut friendship off like a water tap."

"You'll call me if you need me?"

"Yep, but it's liable to be a mighty long haul for you to get to Georgia."

"You're going home?"

"Well, I've been thinking about it lately. It's not a settled fact. But I might head that way come Thanksgiving or Christmas. Holidays are always good times to make folks forget they've been mad because I've neglected them for years."

"You could really leave Africa?"

"I know that's hard for you to understand, but yes, I think I might."

"We'll miss you, Lorena. Terribly."

She wished he'd said, "I'll miss you," but he hadn't. And he never would. Even though she was older than he and much uglier, she realized she'd harbored the hope that Brett would actually fall in love with her.

"I'll miss you, too, but not so terribly that I'll be sitting at home moping."

Lord, Lord, she loved his laugh. She loved the way he smelled, the way he looked, the way he talked. When he held her close, she shut her eyes and tried to memorize everything at once, how his shirt felt against her cheek, how the top of her head barely grazed his chin, how she could feel his thighs flat against hers if she bent her knees slightly and leaned in.

"Don't tell me good-bye," she said.

"I won't."

He didn't hold her long enough. Or maybe he held her too long. She barely made it through the door before the tears started. Blindly she went into the kitchen and reached for the tea kettle. She knew where it was, even in the dark. Without turning on the light she filled the kettle with water and put it on the stove to boil. Then she sat in a straight-backed chair, wrapped her arms around herself, and rocked back and forth, keening the way she'd heard African women do when they mourned the dead.

Lorena Watson. Silly old fool. The only good thing she could say about herself was that she had not told Brett she loved him. At least she'd saved them that embarrassment.

When the kettle whistled, she got her cup and her tea bag, then sat back down at the table. She'd drink her tea in the dark. It was the best way to contemplate the misery of unrequited love. And maybe in the morning when the sun came up over the Virungas, she'd be too busy chasing that ornery old buffalo out of her garden to be miserable.

The deed was done.

Malone sat in his Jeep, hidden by the dense bushes at the side of the road, unable to move. Suddenly he jerked his face upward, toward the mountains. The jungle was full of eyes, and they were all watching him, accusing.

The bile of shame rose in his throat. He bailed out and stood heaving. Sounds seemed louder, more distinct. A Jeep coming around the bend in the road sounded as if it would run right through him.

He jerked his head up, alert as a cornered animal.

The last person he wanted to see was at the wheel, the one person who would look deep into his eyes and know what he had done.

Malone cowered there like a naughty child until his brother had passed by.

45.

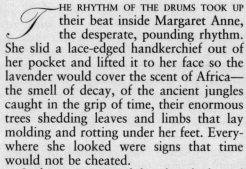

HE RHYTHM OF THE DRUMS TOOK UP their beat inside Margaret Anne, the desperate, pounding rhythm. She slid a lace-edged handkerchief out of her pocket and lifted it to her face so the lavender would cover the scent of Africa— the smell of decay, of the ancient jungles caught in the grip of time, their enormous trees shedding leaves and limbs that lay molding and rotting under her feet. Everywhere she looked were signs that time would not be cheated.

Such terror overtook her that she leaned into her handkerchief, coughing and shivering.

"Are you all right?" Eleanor touched her upper arm, the silver in her hair shining in the moonlight. How could she stand to wear the banner of age?

Margaret Anne wanted to scream at her, to tell her that she hadn't been all right in a very long time. But pride held her back.

They believed the fiction she'd created. Sometimes even she believed it . . . except times like these, times when the sleek young bodies swaying before her reminded her of long-ago dreams, and desires unfulfilled.

"I'm fine," she said. "A little tired, I guess. Africa has been quite an adjustment from Mississippi."

"I'm sure it has."

Eleanor eyed her pink voile dress and her strappy high heels. *Well, let her get her eyes full,* Margaret Anne thought. Anybody who went around in baggy britches and colorless shirts was bound to be jealous that Margaret Anne had managed to spend a week in Africa without sacrificing one iota of her femininity.

"Do you want to call it an early night? I'm sure you'd like to have time to pack and rest up before you start that long journey home."

The long journey home. Back to an empty house where the clock ticked without ceasing. Back to defeat. Back to oblivion.

"You are so thoughtful. But I think I'll stay till the dancing is over. I'd hate to miss a thing. After all, it's *my* going-away party." The native beer she'd drunk made everything around her softer, as if she were seeing through mists. She wondered if she could smuggle some back to Mississippi. "But you go ahead if you're tired."

"Of course not. I'll stay."

"I can't tell you how much this visit has meant to me. Seeing how contented my daughter is with your son has made me a very happy woman."

Eleanor didn't know if the woman was totally dense or merely a damned fine actress. As she glanced at her family gathered round the fire, she swore never again to interfere with any of their lives. Brett hovered on the edge of the gathering like a dark avenging angel. Malone was so drunk, he couldn't even sit up straight.

And Ruth. Her chin was high, her face a study in determination. She hadn't left Malone's side since they'd returned from the States. Every gesture, every word, was carefully solicitous. She was an absolute model of the perfect wife.

But her eyes were tragic.

Eleanor had made all of them miserable. She swore to herself that when this was all over, when Miss Hospitality of 1944 finally went back home, she'd tend to her own business . . . after she'd mended a few fences with her daughter-in-law.

The only one of them who had escaped the consequences of Eleanor's meddling was Joseph. Lord, he didn't even know he was in the world, sitting over there talking gorillas with Matuka's husband, who didn't give a flip about a thing Joseph said, but who loved him so much, he grinned and nodded with every word her husband uttered.

"I'm sorry you didn't get a chance to visit with Cee Cee," she said to Margaret Anne, though why she bothered was beyond her. The woman was obviously interested in nothing except making sure her nail polish matched her dress.

"Maybe next time."

"Certainly."

"Time has a way of flying by when you're having fun, doesn't it?"

"Yes."

It was understandable to Margaret Anne that anybody who spent all her time with monkeys would hardly be able to carry on a conversation except in monosyllables. How anybody would want to hole up in these nasty old mountains was beyond her, though the Dark Continent certainly had its compensations. She glanced over her shoulder. One of the bold young dancers stared back at her.

Where would he go when he left the compound, that fierce young Watusi? And what would he do, that strapping dark man with his dangerous smile?

Ruth saw the look her mother exchanged with the Watusi dancer, and the hair on the back of her neck stood on end.

"Malone?"

"Whash my li'l girl want? Huh?"

Memories that don't hurt. A different life. Brett.

"I want us to say good-bye quietly to Margaret Anne,

then go home and get a good night's rest so we can start fresh tomorrow."

She felt Brett watching them, but she didn't look, wouldn't let herself look.

"Jush one more pombe, honey."

When she'd married Malone, she'd counted so heavily on his kindness that she'd overlooked his weakness. Her heart felt like a stone.

"Come on, Malone. Let's go home." She leaned close and whispered in his ear. "Do it for me, darling."

"Anything for my baby."

He leaned heavily on her. Margaret Anne pretended not to notice, but Eleanor didn't pretend. She met them halfway across the clearing.

Ruth lifted her chin. She'd take her share of the blame for Malone's drunkenness, but not all of it. By George, not *all* of it.

To her astonishment Eleanor, who hardly even touched her own husband in public, put her arms around Ruth.

Ruth knew the difference between real hugs and false ones, had learned the difference many years ago when she'd come back from New Orleans in Max's fine car and her mother had hugged her in the front parlor filled with Oxford's elite. Eleanor's hug was real.

"I only want what's best for my family," Eleanor said.

It was a peace offering and an apology . . . for everything—for the accusations at Brett's camp, for springing Margaret Anne on her, perhaps even for Malone's behavior.

"And Ruth . . . in spite of everything, I think you are good for Malone."

"Thank you." Ruth almost cried.

When she told Margaret Anne good-bye, it wasn't her mother she reached for but her mother-in-law. She felt the warm pressure of Eleanor's hand.

"Malone and I came to say good-bye." She couldn't bring herself to say "Mother."

"Good-bye? Not *good-bye,* darling. Au revoir. Until we meet again."

Ruth vowed that when she got out of everybody's sight, she'd stop smiling and not smile for a week, maybe even a month. And not even then unless she had something damned good to smile about.

Malone saved her the embarrassment of some inane reply.

"Until we meet again, beautiful Mom."

His beer-fogged brain understood the seriousness of the occasion, and he said his farewell without slurring. He even managed to bend over and kiss Margaret Anne's hand without falling into her lap.

Later, lying beside him on the bed with her legs apart from his so she wouldn't have to touch him, and her face turned away so she wouldn't have to breathe his alcoholic fumes, Ruth remembered things she'd tried to forget. She thought of the way Brett had looked at her when he'd removed the torn ribbon from her hat. Such a look. As if they were alone on the planet, as if nothing else mattered except their shared touch.

She left the bed and went to the window. There was nothing to see except darkness, a night so black, it had swallowed every living thing, a giant trap, as dark and scary as the one Ruth was caught in.

She was glad she wasn't pregnant yet. But if she was, would it not make things better? Wouldn't Malone have more reason to stay sober? Each month when her menstrual cycle began, he said they'd have to try that much harder. He really did want a child.

On the bed he snored and mumbled in his alcoholic stupor.

Tomorrow it would be the same. And the next day. And the day after that. Unless Ruth did something about it.

Hands on her hips, she marched to the bed.

"Malone Corday, if you think I'm going to spend the rest of my life watching you kill yourself with alcohol, you're sadly mistaken. In the morning the first thing you're going to get is a pot of strong black coffee. The next thing is a lecture from Ruth Bellafontaine Corday. And if you think that's something to take lightly, you'd better think twice."

Of course, he didn't hear a word she said, but that didn't matter. The important thing was that Ruth was taking charge of her life once more.

She lay down beside her husband, careful this time to take his hand. Lacing their fingers together, she held on as hard as she could.

"We're going to have a real home together, Malone Corday. I mean that."

46.

THE SCREAMS WOKE HIM UP.

Brett bolted from his bed and raced toward his Jeep, pausing only long enough to grab his pants and shoes. They came again out of the night, high-pitched screams of terror.

"Let this not be what I think it is," he prayed as he revved the engine to life and raced down the mountain toward the compound. It was a dark, moonless night, exactly the kind of night for the monstrous deed Brett feared was happening. He hoped and prayed he was wrong.

The screams came once more, closer now as he veered off the road and pressed into the jungle. Progress in the Jeep was nearly impossible through growth so thick, it swallowed up anything that passed through. Abandoning his vehicle, Brett set out on foot, loping in the long, loose gait he'd learned as a child from the natives.

As he passed the nesting place of Doby's

group, he saw the gorilla's huge shape, agitated, swinging from branch to branch checking on his females and their offspring.

"Thank God," he said. If any of the male silverbacks in the Virungas could be trusted to keep his group safe, it was Old Doby.

A small herd of duiker flashed by, and the air was thick with birds frightened from their night perches. One single strangled scream sounded from the distance, and then there was silence, eerie silence more terrifying than sound.

Brett was too late. Still, he kept running, pushing as hard and fast as he could through the tangled limbs and vines that tried to keep him from his purpose.

He came upon them unexpectedly. Two bodies twisted together, grunting and screaming with such an excess of passion that they had not heard anything else. The pink voile dress lay torn on the jungle floor. She still wore her high-heeled shoes. They flailed the air with each vigorous thrust of the strong young Watusi above her.

At first Brett thought she was being raped. He searched the ground for a weapon, anything large and heavy he could wield across the gleaming naked back.

"Pleasepleaseplease," she begged. "Don't stop. Don't ever stop, Lerogi!"

Lerogi, the young stud from the village of Kisoro. The tales of his conquests were known far and wide . . . and now he would have another conquest to add to his list, another tale to tell: how he had seduced Ruth Corday's mother.

"Over my dead body," Brett said. "Lerogi!" he yelled, startling the young buck so that he rolled off Margaret Anne and landed on his backside.

"She asked me to," he said in rapid Swahili. "She followed me from the compound. I told her no, I don't want no old dried-up white woman, but she said she'd pay me."

When he lied, he rolled his eyes back, showing the whites like two large summer moons. Lerogi was renowned for his lack of discrimination. Anything in a skirt would do to appease his randy appetites.

"How much?" Brett carefully averted his eyes from

Margaret Anne Bellafontaine. She made small mewling sounds as she scrambled to find her clothes.

"Ten American dollars. I'd have done it for free."

Brett pulled out his billfold and started counting money into Lerogi's palm. Movement on the ground caught his attention. Margaret Anne, in her slip and high heels and holding her dress against her chest, was scuttling toward the path.

"Stay right where you are. I want you to hear this."

"How dare you tell me what to do!"

"I dare." One look quelled her. He guessed Malone was right. His brother often said that when Brett wanted to, he could look like the very devil himself.

"I'm not paying you for services rendered, Lerogi. I'm buying your silence." Even after the young Watusi's face showed his satisfaction with the deal, Brett continued to count out money. When he'd paid what amounted to a fortune to the young man, Brett pocketed his billfold.

"If I ever hear one word of what happened tonight, I'll deal with you personally. Is that clear?"

The Gorilla Man had a reputation of his own. With nothing more than his bare hands, he'd gone against a giant wielding a knife. The story of his battle with the Bat was a legend that had been enhanced with each retelling. The sight of his eye patch was enough to make most men think twice before they crossed him.

"You can count on me, Gorilla Man. Anything you want, you call Lerogi." Lerogi bowed so low, his forehead nearly touched the ground. "At your service, Gorilla Man."

The young Watusi disappeared quickly into the jungle, moving as silently and as swiftly as the wind.

"My Jeep is nearby," Brett told Margaret Anne.

"What makes you think I'd go anywhere with you?"

"I'm taking you back. You have no choice in the matter."

Margaret Anne considered her options. It had been a long walk in her high-heeled shoes, a walk she'd gladly make twice a day for the pleasure she'd received. No, not mere pleasure. Ecstasy. Something approaching the way Blue had made her feel. She wanted to scratch Brett Corday's eyes out, more for the deprivation than the humiliation.

He didn't look like the kind of man she wanted to argue with. More like the kind of man she'd like to screw. Too bad he'd seen her at her worst. She must look a fright with jungle leaves tangled in her hair and her makeup melted off by Lerogi's vigorous sweating.

"Well, are we going to stand here all night, or are you going to take me back to the compound?"

He didn't even take her elbow but left her to struggle along behind him.

"A gentleman always takes a lady's arm in terrain like this."

"In that case neither of us need be concerned about breach of manners."

She hoped one of the jungle limbs would swing around and put out his other eye.

"I'll be glad to get back to Mississippi, where the only animals I have to deal with are the teenage sackers in the grocery store."

He didn't acknowledge her presence by so much as a grunt.

When she finally got to his Jeep, she didn't even bother asking him to turn his head while she put on her dress.

"You will never again humiliate Ruth in this way," he said.

"I was the one humiliated. By *you.*"

He acted as if he hadn't even heard her. She wondered if the knife had sliced into his ear as well as his eye.

"What you do in Mississippi is of no concern to me, but if you ever return to the Virungas, you will conduct yourself like the lady you pretend to be."

"You wouldn't know a lady if you saw one, living in this godforsaken place with nothing but a woman who dresses like a man for an example. I'll have you know I've earned the right to be called a lady."

Somewhere in the jungle was Brett's worst nightmare come true—poachers—and he was stuck in his Jeep playing his brother's keeper. Only this time his brother wasn't his main concern. Suddenly the softness of Ruth invaded his senses, and he felt a growing kindness, even toward the woman sitting on the seat beside him.

Who was he to judge her, he who coveted his brother's wife?

"Mrs. Bellafontaine, I don't mean to be harsh and judgmental with you . . ."

"You could have fooled me!"

"There is a code of honor we live by in the Virungas, and if that code is violated, someone will pay. In this case, Ruth. I'm sure you don't want to do anything to hurt your daughter or to besmirch her reputation in her new home."

"What she does is her business, and what I do is my business, no matter where I am. Besides, she didn't bother informing me about her wedding. Why should I bother to inform her of my extracurricular activities?"

Brett saw that he was fighting a losing battle. No matter what he said, he would never get through to this woman.

She would fly home in a few hours, and if the fates were kind, she wouldn't come back to the Virungas. Wishful thinking. The fates were seldom kind, especially in Africa. Didn't he know that more than anybody?

Who knew what fate had set in the path of Margaret Anne Bellafontaine? What she needed was not censure but mercy. What they all needed was mercy.

"Mrs. Bellafontaine, I'm sorry that this happened. Let's put it behind us, if not for our sakes, for Ruth's sake."

"That's three times you've mentioned my daughter's name. If you weren't such a puritan, I'd say you had the hots for her. You wouldn't be the first man." Margaret Anne swiveled to study him in the faint glow coming from the lights outside the compound. "You *do* have the hots for her!"

He didn't even bother to deny it. He knew her secret and she knew his. Her language was a crude description of a connection he had considered metaphysical, but Margaret Anne, who had rutted in the jungle like an animal, had seen the animal in him, had seen the desire that burned through him every time he looked at Ruth, thought of Ruth, spoke of Ruth. Perhaps he'd better examine the truth. Perhaps he was the one who needed to fly out of Africa and never return.

Margaret Anne held her torn bodice over her breasts and reached for the door.

"Don't bother helping me out. I think we've already established that I'm no lady . . . and you're no gentleman."

He waited under the dim lights until she was safely inside. There was no need to hurry now. He knew what he would find in the jungle.

47.

THE SKY WAS PALE GRAY WITH AN OPAL-
escence it always took on just before the sun made its appearance.
Ruth had been awake for two hours and
couldn't stand the waiting anymore. She
tiptoed from the bedroom and put the coffee on to perk. The smell braced her for the
task ahead.

She knew it wouldn't be easy. She also
knew it would be best if she sought profes-
sional help. There were intervention
groups, support groups, all sorts of groups
trained to deal with alcoholics. Somehow
the word seemed too harsh for dear, sweet
Malone . . . and the remedies. It would
be best if she could change him with gentle
persuasion.

And what about herself? How was she
going to change the way she felt when she
looked at his brother?

She *must* put Brett out of her mind, out

of her heart. And she *would*. It was the only way her marriage would survive.

She poured herself some coffee and sat at the table, nursing the cup. The kitchen door swung open.

"Ruth! I have to talk to you." Her mother stood poised in the doorway.

The cup tipped over, and the hot brown liquid ran down the side of the table. Ruth jumped out of the way, then grabbed a cloth and began to swab at the stain.

"Are you planning to ignore me, Ruth?"

Was she? If she'd been thirteen, she'd have run to her room and slammed the door. But she was no longer thirteen.

"Why did you come here, Margaret Anne?"

"Do I have to have a reason to come and tell my own daughter good-bye?"

"We said good-bye last night."

"No. *You* said good-bye. I said, 'Until we meet again.' I've decided it's time to meet again. I walked *two miles* to see you." Margaret Anne pulled out a chair and sat at the table. "Are you going to offer me a cup of coffee, or has Africa completely robbed you of every social grace I struggled so hard to teach you?"

Ruth poured the coffee, but she didn't sit down.

"I thought you had a plane to catch."

"I thought marriage would change you, but *no*—you're still the smart-mouthed girl you were back home in Mississippi."

Ruth kept her silence. She didn't intend to get into an argument with her mother. What good would it do? Nothing had changed between them, nor would ever change.

"I should never have allowed you to get out of hand. Look where it's led you—straight into the bosom of a family with no more manners than a pack of jackals."

"The Cordays are a fine family, respected worldwide."

"Pity they don't extend that same respect to their in-laws."

"Malone has treated you with nothing but kindness."

"I'm not talking about Malone. It's Brett I'm talking about. Mr. High-and-Mighty himself."

"Don't you dare make slurs about Brett. He's one of the finest men I've ever known!"

Margaret Anne shoved her coffee aside and stood, gripping the edge of the table.

"Talk about your husband and you barely blink an eyelash, but say anything about that bastard Brett and you get fighting mad. Why is that?"

"Leave. I won't listen to any of your ugly accusations."

Margaret Anne had truly intended only to say good-bye to her daughter one last time. Properly. As a mother should. She'd even harbored the faint hope that a quiet mother-daughter talk that Ruth had so studiously avoided the entire week would set everything right between them. But Ruth knew just how to get under her skin, knew just which buttons to push. By damn, she'd pushed the wrong one now. Margaret Anne was going to give her more than she'd bargained for.

"You want to know about ugly accusations? Well, I'll tell you about ugly accusations. Ask Brett Corday what right he had to come sneaking up behind me in the jungle and preach to me about besmirching the almighty Corday name. Ask him who he was protecting when he ordered me back to the compound. His brother . . . or his brother's wife?"

Ruth's white-knuckled grip on the kitchen counter told Margaret Anne she'd scored.

"What were you doing in the jungle?"

"As if you didn't already know."

"What were you doing, Mother?"

"Fucking."

Margaret Anne didn't even look back when she made her exit. The only way to survive was never to look back.

Ruth thought she was going to be sick. She wrapped her arms around herself and stood in the middle of the kitchen floor heaving.

Suddenly the rage she'd suppressed for years boiled to the surface. She grabbed her mother's coffee cup and threw it against the wall. It shattered with a satisfying smash. Brown liquid stained the wall and spattered onto Ruth's clothes. She threw her own cup, then another and another. There wasn't enough china in the house to satisfy her thirst for destruction, not enough china in the world.

If somebody didn't stop her, she was going to rip the whole house apart.

"Malone," she screamed, racing toward the bedroom.

He lay on his back, so deep in his alcoholic slumber that it would have taken a circus parade with brass band and six elephants to wake him.

Standing in the same room with her husband, Ruth felt totally alone, just as she'd felt alone in the Big House in New Orleans with Max. The terrible emptiness spread through her so that she felt as if she were disappearing, piece by piece. Soon she'd be nothing more than a shadow, someone who could pass unnoticed through a crowd. Unless she got help. Unless she turned to the one person who could help her.

There was carnage everywhere. The giant body of the male silverback lay in the clearing in a pool of his own blood, headless and handless. Two of his wives lay six feet away, slain senselessly. The surviving gorillas in Petey's group wandered between the bodies, pausing occasionally to squat and watch, as if vigilance would bring their leader and his favorite wives back from the dead.

Rage almost obscured Brett's vision, but he pushed it aside. The important thing was to assess the damage, then take steps to ensure that the remaining gorillas were safe.

He counted the survivors, missed two young ones clinging high in the trees, then counted once more. Three gorillas dead. Two missing. Maymay and JoGina. Mere babies.

He searched for the young gorillas, being careful to stay far back from the young males. Already Johnny Jumpup was making noises of dominance. If he could establish himself quickly as leader, the remaining females would stay rather than migrate to another male, and the group would remain intact.

This slaughter was more than a routine poaching mission. Poachers took the heads for trophies, the hands for ashtrays. They didn't steal the babies, for quick profit was their motive, and selling young gorillas on the black market was too complicated, too much trouble.

The first thing he had to do was notify Joseph and Malone. The next thing, bury the bodies.

As he headed back to his own vehicle, a bone-chilling scream ricocheted through him.

"Brett!"

His heart almost stopped. He'd know that voice anywhere.

Ruth called his name once more; then suddenly she burst through the clearing, her clothes ripped and torn by the merciless jungle growth and her face wet with tears.

"Ruth . . ."

She raced blindly toward him, arms wide-open, saying his name over and over.

He didn't stop to think, didn't take time to question; he merely opened his arms and took her in. She cuddled against him like a child, sobbing so hard, her shoulders shook. He wove his hands into her soft hair and cradled her head.

For the moment it didn't matter what had brought her to him, only that she had come. Ruth, whose control was as tight as his own, had come to him for comfort.

He soothed her with his voice and hands.

"I'm here, Ruth," he crooned. "I'm here."

She clung to him, her fingernails digging through his shirt into his skin. He'd have marks. Blessed marks. Evidence that she trusted him enough to cry in his arms, to be completely vulnerable with him.

"It's all broken," she whispered.

"What's broken?"

"All of it. I broke all of it."

She was incoherent, shivering, close to shock.

He wrapped his arms around her and pressed her close. Body heat, he told himself, knowing better—knowing he did it for himself, for the pleasure of feeling her soft feminine curves, of feeling how well the two of them fit together, perfectly, as if fate had always intended them for each other.

"Shhh, it's all right," he said, knowing it wasn't. Knowing that nothing would be all right for them, ever. "It's all right, my love."

"It's broken. All broken."

He could say all the endearments he'd wanted to say, and she wouldn't hear. He could touch her freely and she wouldn't know. Desperate with hunger, he pressed his lips against her cheek.

"Shhh, it's all right. I'll fix it for you. I'll fix it, my darling."

"Yes . . . yes," she whispered. "Only you. Always you."

For one magical moment she was his. He was the man she sought, the man she wanted, the man she trusted. Only him. Always him.

He could kiss her and she wouldn't turn away. The knowledge coursed through him as heady and intoxicating as new wine.

"Ruth," he whispered. "My sweet Ruth."

He cradled her face in his palms, drinking her in with his good eye as if he could never quench his thirst for looking. She didn't pull back, didn't deny the truth. She was *his*, had been his from the moment she'd arrived in the Virungas, had been his from the beginning of time.

His lips brushed her hair, her eyelids, her cheeks. Her lips were close, tempting, heart-shaped at the top and full at the bottom, full and ripe, wet with the tears that had flowed so freely. He knew how they would feel under his lips, knew how they would taste, had known since the moment he saw her step out of the Jeep with his brother. Tender. Sweet. Delicious. He wanted to taste them. Wanted to taste her. All of her.

"Ruth . . ."

Her lips trembled. He was so close that when he inhaled, it was her breath he took into his lungs, her sweetness he absorbed into his body.

She wove her hands through his hair, and with gentle, subtle pressure pulled him closer. One small movement, even one as small as a cat's whisker, and his lips would be touching hers.

Ruth wanted them touching hers, *needed* them touching hers. She longed for his kiss, longed for it with every fiber of her body. Would it be so wrong? A brief, cathartic joining, a temporary respite from pain?

She slid her tongue over her bottom lip, catching tears

. . . and magic. For one fleeting moment her tongue touched his bottom lip. His breath whistled sharply through his lungs.

Don't move, she silently pleaded. *Don't go away.*

As if he could read her mind, he stayed close, holding her . . . merely holding her. She'd waited all her life for a man whose arms were a haven, a man who could give and expect nothing in return, a man who could hear the truth without judging.

Through her mist of tears she saw the eye patch, saw the beloved planes of his face, the dark shadow of his beard, the thick wild hair that defied taming, that always looked as if he'd come down from the top of his mountain in the midst of a windstorm. All those things anchored her, softened the rage, lessened the horror of her mother's latest betrayal so that Ruth knew she could survive. Once more she could pick up the pieces and go on. Because of Brett. Because of who and what he was. Noble. Kind. Solid. Enduring. Someone to run to, someone to lean on, someone to understand.

She let the tears of release pour down her face, unchecked.

"Brett . . . I want so much . . . so much."

"I know. So do I."

They both knew what she wanted. What he wanted.

A miracle.

He circled his fingers on her face, slowly, gently, as if he were memorizing her. With his index finger he caught her tears, then lifted them to his mouth, drinking them in, absorbing that part of her into himself.

For Ruth, the gesture was heart-wrenchingly tender and intensely erotic. She would do anything in the world to have him . . . anything except betray his brother.

She couldn't stop crying. Her tears were not for herself alone, but for them, for the great aching void within them that could never be filled.

"Ruth . . ."

The way he said her name was more fulfilling than any caress Malone had ever given her, any kiss, any lovemaking. Brett pulled back, ever so slightly, and she knew he wouldn't kiss her. Not then. Not ever.

"Do you want to tell me why you're crying?"

"My mother . . . you found her . . ."

"How did you know?"

"She told me." She'd never heard Brett use any language not suitable for Sunday school—until that moment.

"I should have warned her," he said. "I should have made her promise never to tell you."

"I'm so ashamed."

"Hush." He held her hard against his chest. "You have nothing to be ashamed of. *Nothing.* Do you hear?"

"Yes, I hear."

"Do you believe?"

"When you say it, it feels like the truth."

Fragile as the wings of a dragonfly, she held on to trust, the solid tether that anchored her, that kept her from being jerked out of his arms and ripped to shreds by ugly reality. She grasped the front of his shirt and indulged in a crying jag.

"It's all right, Ruth. Cry as many tears as you want. I'm here to wipe them away." He smoothed her hair and caressed her back, slowly, tenderly, and he marveled that she had come to him, marveled and thanked whatever fate had smiled kindly on them that day.

But even as he thanked the fates, he wondered that Malone had let Ruth leave in such a state. What was wrong with his brother? Didn't he know how to deal with anybody's pain except his own?

As if she'd read his thoughts, Ruth lifted her head. With the back of her hand she wiped her tears away.

"I shouldn't have come here . . . to you . . . like this." She swiped at her tears once more, and he pulled out a handkerchief.

"Here. Let me."

It was one last opportunity to touch her without guilt. Holding her chin in one hand, he wiped her tearstained cheeks, absorbing not only her tears but the fragrance that clung to her skin. Long past the time when the sweet chore ended, he held on to her. She lifted her eyes, caught the look in his, the look that said *I don't want this to end.* But she didn't pull away. She held his gaze so that they fed off what they saw in each other, fed off the flames of passion until the fire they created threatened to consume them both.

"I don't want Malone to know," she said, as if to remind them both that she had a husband, that he had a brother. "About Margaret Anne . . . I mean."

"He'll never know. No one will know. I took care of that."

"He was sleeping when I left. It's a miracle the china didn't wake him up."

"The china?"

"I threw it against the wall and broke it . . . I was so upset. I didn't mean to do it. I hope it's not a family heirloom."

Brett rammed the handkerchief into his pocket, furious at his brother. How could he sleep through shattering china unless he was drunk?

"It's discount-store special. Don't you worry about the china."

There were far greater things to worry about. Things she hadn't seen yet. Now that she was coherent, he maneuvered her back toward her Jeep. She glanced over her shoulder, then pressed her hand over her mouth.

"Oh, my God. How could this have happened?"

"Poachers." It was the simplest explanation.

"We can't just leave them here."

"I'll come back and deal with this."

"I can help you."

"No." She got that stubborn look that told him she wasn't about to be treated like a weakling. "I need you to stay at the camp with Cee Cee. I'll go get Joseph and Malone to help me."

"Of course. That makes sense. I'll follow you in the Jeep."

He wasn't about to put her behind the wheel of a Jeep, not after the shocks she'd received.

"Leave it. I'll pick up Malone, and he can drive it back."

Ruth had always taken care of her own problems, took pride in her independence, but it felt so good to let go, just this once—to give all her problems to Brett and let him handle them. She wished she could curl up beside him and stay that way for the next few days, the next few weeks, even years, her head resting on his chest, her leg touching his, her hand curled into his, fingers twined.

But she was a married woman, and there was no longer any excuse for the kind of uninhibited behavior she'd shown. She sat on her side of the Jeep, holding on to the door handle.

The jungle was quiet, not even a breeze stirring the trees, as if the plants as well as the animals knew the tragedy that had befallen them, knew of the slaughter on the mountainside.

As they came closer to Brett's camp, Ruth remembered the last time she'd been there, remembered the ribbon on his bed and the way Malone had defiled it. She had sworn never to go back.

"Brett . . . I have to explain . . . about your bed . . ."

"No!" The word was more than a command; it was a denial. "It's over and done with. Finished. What happened is between you and my brother."

He believed she had lain in his bed deliberately, too anxious to mate with Malone to wait for an appropriate time, an appropriate place. She had to make him understand how it had been, how she hated having Malone touch her, how she shut her eyes and pretended to be somewhere else, *anywhere* except in the arms of her husband.

And yet, how could she say those things without betraying Malone, without making Brett somehow an accomplice in the betrayal of his brother?

Ruth kept her silence.

48.

MALONE CAME RUDELY AWAKE. SOME-one was shaking his shoulder. He opened his eyes, then wished he'd kept them shut. Brett was leaning over him scowling, a look that didn't bode well.

"Time 'zit?" Malone mumbled.

"You smell like a brewery." Brett stalked across the room and tossed Malone's pants to him. "Here. Put these on. I'll have a pot of coffee in the kitchen."

"Don't want coffee." He rolled onto his back and put the pillow over his face. "Want to sleep. Head feels like a watermelon."

Brett jerked the pillow off his face and threw it against the wall—behavior totally out of character for him.

"What the hell . . . ," Malone said.

"Get up under your own steam or under mine. Take your choice."

"All right . . . hold your horses. I can take a hint."

Brett was not amused. Another bad sign.

"Go, already," Malone said, sitting up and waving him off. "I'm halfway up."

"I'll be in the kitchen."

Malone reached for his pants, and Brett stalked out of the bedroom.

Broken china was scattered all over the kitchen floor. It looked as if Ruth had broken every piece of china in the cabinets. Brett studied the destruction. Surely the knowledge of what her mother had done was not enough to cause such rage.

He put on a pot of coffee, then got the broom and dustpan from the pantry and began to clean. As soon as he got back to camp, he was going to find out what had caused Ruth to go on such a rampage.

But first things first. He had the loss of gorillas to deal with. And his brother.

Malone stood in the doorway scratching his head, then slumped into a chair.

"What happened here? Looks like a damned tornado struck."

"Your wife did this."

"My wife?"

"Yes." Brett dumped broken china into the garbage can, then poured two cups of coffee into pottery mugs he'd found deep in the cabinet. "While you were in bed drunk."

"I wasn't drunk."

"Cut the crap. We both know that's a lie."

"Well, maybe I had one too many."

"You've been having one too many for too long now, and I want it stopped."

"Now, just a minute . . ." Malone shoved back his chair.

"No, you wait just a minute." Brett pushed him back into his chair, and none too gently. "There are things happening on this mountain that are going to require a cool head, not the least of which is taking care of a wife who needs you."

"That's the second time you've mentioned my wife. What in the hell gives you the right to tell me what she needs?" Malone swung his head toward the door. "Where is she, anyhow?"

"At my place."

Brett knew he was treading on dangerous ground. It would take a blind man not to see his true feelings. And Malone was far from blind. Fortunately, he was not too sharp at the moment. His senses were dulled by alcohol and at least a residual loyalty to his brother—or so Brett hoped.

"She and her mother had a misunderstanding this morning before Margaret Anne left, and she couldn't wake you up."

"So she came running to you? Is that what you're trying to tell me, big brother?"

"Who do you want her to run to?"

Malone looked down at his coffee cup. Why did he always end up wrong and Brett always right? He must have been born under the wrong sign.

"Me, dammit. I want her to run to me."

"Then I suggest you quit drowning in the bottle whatever sorrows you think you have and be there for her. No . . . not suggest. I insist." Brett slapped both palms onto the table so hard, the coffee mugs jumped, then leaned into his brother's face. "I have no intention of sitting back while my brother destroys himself and his marriage with alcohol."

"What do you plan to do about it?" Malone was half-humbled, half-belligerent.

"I went against a knife-wielding Watusi for you with nothing but my bare fists. I think I'm capable of going against a liquor bottle."

"Are you reminding me that I cost you an eye?"

"No, I'm telling you to straighten yourself up before I have to do it for you."

"Do you get off cleaning up my messes, bro?"

Brett had never wanted to hit his brother. But he did now. He wanted to take Malone by the nape of the neck and beat him to a bloody pulp, beat him until he could act with some sense.

He made himself wait until he was calm before speaking.

"No. I've never enjoyed that role."

They stared at each other. Both of them knew which role Brett meant: favorite son. He would gladly have been his brother's keeper, but the burden of being his parents' favorite had taken its toll.

"Neither have I," Malone said. He got up and dumped his cold coffee into the sink, then poured a fresh cup. His hands shook like somebody's thirty years older than he. Damned alcohol. Brett was right, as usual. He was drinking too much.

"I don't know why I've been drinking too much." Malone knew, but he wasn't telling Brett. Some things were too personal even to tell a brother. "But I swear to you, I'm going to do better."

"Don't just do better. Stop."

"Cold turkey?"

"Cold turkey. Dump it all down the drain."

"Shit. You drive a hard bargain."

Malone gave one of the winning smiles that made him look like an endearing, slightly naughty little boy, the kind of smile that always softened Brett. He realized that he was partially responsible for Malone's weakness. All their lives Brett had intervened when Malone had been in trouble, shouldered the burden, made things easier for his brother.

Not this time. Too much was at stake.

"Here." He refilled Malone's coffee cup. "Drink this. You're going to need it."

"Hey, lighten up. That face of yours is enough to scare little old ladies and make babies cry."

"I have a lot to scowl about."

"The problem is not that serious. I can lick it with one hand tied behind my back."

"This is about more than your problem. . . . Last night someone massacred Petey's group. Severed the heads and hands of Petey and two of his wives, then took two of the infants."

Malone shoved back his chair, rushed into the bathroom, and hung his head over the toilet, retching. God, he'd never thought it would turn out like this. Why couldn't it have been clean and neat? Why couldn't they have used blow darts to tranquilize Petey and the females?

He held his head under the faucets until the thought of all that blood cleared from his mind. When he was reasonably calm, he went back into the kitchen to face his brother. He and Brett had had problems. Didn't all brothers? But they'd never lied to each other. It was the lying as much as the killing that troubled Malone.

Why hadn't he known how hard it would be?

"What are we going to do about these poachers?" he asked Brett.

"These aren't poachers. The Batwas don't steal babies. They're too much trouble to get out of the Virungas, too hard to market."

"Hell, the little pygmy bastards are liable to do anything."

God, it would be just like Brett to have figured the whole thing out. And if he hadn't already, it wouldn't be long before he did—he was just too damned smart.

Why hadn't Malone thought of that? Why hadn't he thought of a lot of things? Like how blood money wasn't half as sweet as money earned the hard way. He'd never again look at Ruth's rubies without seeing the taint of blood.

"Maybe they did the dirty work, but I think there's more to this."

"You're going to investigate?"

"Yes. But first we have to take care of the bodies, then organize patrols to see that this doesn't happen again. Whoever did it is probably not foolish enough to try it again soon."

"Probably not." Of all things, Malone hated being called foolish. Not that he had done the actual killing, but he had been the mastermind. Shit, why hadn't *he* thought of tranquilizers?

"More than likely they'll wait for us to get lax before they try again."

"Yeah. More than likely."

"They can wait till hell freezes over." Brett shoved back his chair and stood up. "They'll take another mountain gorilla out of the Virungas over my dead body."

Malone wanted to crawl under the kitchen table and hide. Chu Ling was not the kind of man he wanted to cross. But, then, neither was his brother.

"Are you coming, Malone?"

Malone felt like an old man. He wished he could crawl in a dark hole somewhere.

"Yeah. I'm coming."

49.

*I*T WAS WORSE THAN MALONE HAD IMAG-
ined. All the blood. Petey, the male
silverback who had once been so
magnificent, mutilated.

Malone leaned against a tree and lost all
the coffee Brett had forced on him. Joseph
put a hand on his shoulder.

"Are you going to be all right?"

"Yeah. I'm going to be all right."

"Brett and I will finish up here if you
want to go back to the compound."

"No. I'll do it. Quit treating me like a
half-wit stepchild."

He'd never spoken to his father like
that. But Joseph didn't seem to notice. He
was too disturbed over the deaths of his
beloved gorillas.

There was so much to do, so much to
take care of. Burying the bodies was only
the beginning. Malone had to check on the
stolen babies. Chu Ling wouldn't pay for
dead gorillas, and their survival depended

on him. He had to set up a schedule of feeding and care, then check periodically to ensure their smooth transition from the wild to their new zoo homes.

How would he explain his sudden travel plans to his brother and his father? He'd meant to tell Ruth he was going on a quick fund-raising trip, but Brett's discovery of the bodies had changed all that.

He took up his shovel and began to dig. It would take a mighty grave for Petey.

"It seems like only yesterday he was a mischievous teen-ager," Joseph said. "I can't believe he's gone."

"He won't be the only one if we don't get these patrols in place quickly. Juma and Bantain can head two groups, but we'll need more." Brett stripped off his shirt and tossed it onto a low-hanging branch of a tree. "One of us should go down to Rumangabo and pay a visit to the conservator of the Park. He needs to know what's hap-pened so he can keep his eyes open."

Malone knew, suddenly, that he had a guardian angel. "I'll go. It'll be quicker to fly."

In all the years since Brett had lost his eye, Malone had never seen him show any emotion about not being able to pilot their twin-engine Cessna. Bitterness flared briefly, then was gone.

"He's right," Joseph said. "Besides, you need to stick close to Cee Cee, and I need to keep a tighter watch on the other groups. They'll be disturbed by these brutal kill-ings."

"That makes sense," Brett said.

"Look, while I'm there, I'll try to find somebody reli-able to head another patrol. Maybe one of the park guards knows somebody. We'll need more than Juma and Bantain."

"Good thinking, Malone."

What would his brother say if he knew the real purpose of the trip?

"It's liable to take a few days."

"Take all the time you need, Malone. Brett and I can carry on here."

The way they always had. Without him. At least now

Malone knew something that they didn't—but the knowl
edge gave him small comfort.

The three of them lowered Petey's headless body int
the grave; then Joseph knelt in the freshly turned earth.

"Good-bye, old friend."

Brett put a hand on his father's shoulder, but Malon
couldn't bring himself to touch him. It would seem too
much like an insult.

He was anxious to be away from the scene, anxious to
get the baby gorillas started on their journey out of Africa

"If I leave now, I can be there by dark," he said.

"What about Ruth?"

Any other time Malone might have been jealous o
Brett's concern for his wife. At the moment, though, h
didn't want to face her. She knew him too well, he feared
not to see that something was bothering him. As soon a
he got things taken care of, got paid for his troubles—then
he would face Ruth.

"Take care of her for me, will you, bro? With all thi
going on, I'll feel better about leaving her if she's with
you."

Actually, he felt pangs of jealousy even in his agitated
state, but it would look suspicious if he left without ex
pressing concern for her safety, though he knew that n
one was going to come after any of the Cordays. They'
damned well better not.

"You want her to stay at my camp?"

"Yeah. For a day or two. I won't be gone long."

Brett didn't look too taken with the idea, and Malon
was immediately ashamed of his suspicious nature. Thi
was the brother who had been looking after him for years
the brother who loved him enough to sacrifice an eye. Th
last thing in the world he had to worry about was Bret
and his wife.

Malone put his arm around his brother's shoulder
"You'll tell her why I had to leave in such a hurry, won'
you?"

"Yes. I'll tell her."

"Make it good." He flashed his smile, not because h
felt like smiling, but because he wanted to see if his charm

was still working with Brett. "Make me sound like some kind of hero."

"You are, Malone. You've always been a hero."

Malone was not a praying man, but right then he prayed that Brett would never discover the truth—or if he did, that Malone would be turning up daisies.

He knew just how Brett would react—with disbelief, then fury and contempt, and finally with disappointment and pity. He could never bear his brother's pity.

5o.

*I*F CEE CEE IGNORED THE STINK FEMALE long enough, maybe she would go away. She kept her back turned and her eyes focused on the television screen. Her favorite tape was on, *Murphy Brown*. If she had some red shoes, she could be like Murphy. And then Brett would notice her instead of the stink female.

"Talk to me, Cee Cee," Ruth signed.

Cee Cee signed *"Dirty stink go away,"* but not so the stink female could see. Then she punched the button to turn the volume up *very* loud and covered her ears with her hands. But she kept her fingers splayed so she could still hear her show.

Ruth sat down on the straight-backed chair outside Cee Cee's enclosure. Brett didn't yet trust her inside with the gorilla, and with good reason. It was obvious to Ruth that Cee Cee hated her, and she didn't know how she would ever get around that.

But she was going to try.

"You don't fool me, Cee Cee. I know you can under-stand me because I see your fingers spread wide. All I want to do is talk to you about food. You like food, don't you?"

Brett had told her that mention of food was one sure way to get Cee Cee's attention. That was before the gorilla discovered the emotions of love and hate, longing and jealousy.

If Ruth weren't so drained by strong emotions herself, she'd be very excited about Cee Cee's behavior. It was clear evidence of her intelligence, of her ability to reason on a higher level than scientists had ever thought possible. Who knew how much more they would discover in their studies of Cee Cee?

"I'm going to prepare your food," Ruth signed. *"When I come back, you'll have to come over here and talk to me if you want to eat."*

"Me hate no eat dirty stink female food." Cee Cee kept her signs hidden from Ruth. She understood the pleasure Brett got when she talked, and she wasn't about to give that pleasure to the woman who was trying to take him away from her.

"Brett won't be back to feed you, Cee Cee. He told me to feed you. While I'm gone, you can make up your mind whether you want to eat or go to bed hungry."

She wanted bananas, and while she watched *Murphy Brown,* she tried to figure out how she could divert the stink female's attention so she could get the food without having to sign.

Preparing the food gave Ruth something to do, something to take her mind off the scene with Margaret Anne and the slaughter in the meadow. High in the mountain camp, she felt far removed from the rest of the world, as if nothing that happened outside could possibly harm her.

Brett's kitchen was shipshape and sparingly furnished. Just like his bedroom. The memory of the bed sent her flinging open the window. Blue shadows lay on the land, and birdsong wafted to her on the breeze that stirred the moss in the trees.

She would hold the present joy, hold it so tight that

when she finally had to go down the mountain to face
Malone, she'd have a storehouse of strength.

As she prepared the food, she kicked off her shoes, then
reached into her pocket and put on the dangling clip earrings she'd donned early that morning in preparation for
her talk with Malone. Why, she couldn't say, except that
perhaps reality seemed so very far away and she was feeling somehow festive.

Ruth arranged the food on a tray, then went barefoot
back to Cee Cee's indoor enclosure. To her delight the
young gorilla was waiting for her at the gate. Only iron
bars separated them.

Ruth set the tray down so she could sign as she talked.

"Hello, Cee Cee. I'm happy you decided to eat."

"Cee Cee good girl," the gorilla signed, then sat back
on her haunches and gave one of her enormous grins.

"Yes. Cee Cee is a good girl. I like Cee Cee."

"Cee Cee like banana want banana gimme banana."

"Because you're such a good girl, you can have one."

Cee Cee watched while Ruth bent over the tray to get a
banana. Soon she would step close to the bars to hand it
through. Cee Cee was mad about having to make signs for
the stink female, but as soon as she'd seen the "moving
stars shine" on her ears, she'd changed her mind about not
signing.

Now she had a new mission in mind. If she was quick
enough, she could get what she wanted and the food too.

The minute Ruth got close enough, Cee Cee plunged
both hands through the bars. She snatched one of the earrings first, and then the banana. Ruth had no time to do
more than jump back and squeak in surprise.

"All right, Cee Cee, have it your way." With her bare
foot she scooted the tray close enough so that the gorilla
could reach through and get the rest of her food. Obviously she had no intention of letting Ruth be a part of her
training—or her mealtime, either. And she knew better
than to argue with Cee Cee over the possession of the
earring.

Outside, dark began to fall on the compound. Ruth was
exhausted, emotionally and physically. In the large ante-
room that opened toward the enclosure, she stretched out

on the sofa so she could keep watch on Cee Cee and the front door at the same time.

Malone would be there to get her soon . . . and Brett.

Ruth was asleep on the sofa. Brett stood in the doorway, riveted by the sight of her. One arm was tucked under her head, a long gold earring dangled against her cheek, and her feet were bare. They were crisscrossed with blue veins on the top, and dusty on the bottom.

She'd gone barefoot in his house. The gesture suggested trust . . . and intimacy. He pictured how it would be to wake up beside her in the morning and watch her walk to the window in her bare feet. She would lift her hair off her neck with one hand and lean with the other against the windowsill. The morning breeze would caress her skin and stir her silky gown, molding it against her long legs.

As he looked at the dusty bottoms of her feet, he almost wept.

Quietly he closed the door, then stood over the sofa watching her. She'd left a lamp burning, and the light spilled over her face. He reached toward her, but stopped himself when his hand was a mere fraction of an inch away from her soft cheek.

He had no right to touch her, even in her sleep—*especially* in her sleep.

"Ruth." He spoke her name softly, but she didn't hear, didn't stir.

It had been a very long day for both of them. He'd meant to explain to her about Malone's sudden departure, then offer to drive her back to the main compound so she could stay with Eleanor and Joseph. But he was exhausted, she was exhausted, and there was no point in taking up what little was left of the night in preserving propriety.

Besides, hadn't Malone asked him to take care of her?

When he lifted her into his arms, she cuddled close, making soft, delicious bed sounds that almost drove him wild.

"Can you hear me, Ruth? I'm taking you to bed."

"Hmmm." She turned her face into his chest, and he could feel her warm breath through the front of his shirt.

How much temptation could he endure in one day?

Resolutely he set his face toward the spare bedroom. Moonlight spilled through the window, and he laid her gently in the center of the bed where the light could touch her. Sighing, she settled into the pillow. The sound of her breathing was soft and even.

He covered her with a light quilt, and as he stood watching her sleep, he saw how it would be possible to lose his mind over her. Not only his mind, but every shred of honor he possessed.

Her hair was disheveled, fanning across the pillow and tumbling across her face. Did he dare brush it out of her eyes? He bent over her softly. Her warm breath stirred against his cheek and her hair clung to his fingertips.

He was perfectly still, enchanted, not even certain that he breathed.

Did he have the willpower to leave her there, to walk down the hall to his own bedroom?

What would it be like to see her hair spread upon the pillow next to his?

51.

RUMANGABO

THEY MET IN A SMALL ROOM OVER A general store in the seedy part of town. Dark and hot, it seemed an appropriate place to Malone. Much the way he imagined hell.

"Did you have to kill Petey and the females?" he asked.

"We had no choice. He would have killed one of us if we hadn't."

The speaker was Shambu, a tall, fierce Watusi who had been bought at great cost. But he was a park guard, and necessary to Malone's scheme. In his position of authority he could not only turn a blind eye to the activities, but coordinate the actual kidnapping so that it coincided with a time when none of the other park guards would be nearby. Not that they ventured much near the Corday compound. For years it had been known among the guards that

Brett kept close watch over all the wildlife in that part of the Virungas, particularly the gorillas. He made their job much easier.

"I'll get some tranquilizer darts for you to use," Malone said.

"Won't that look suspicious? Your brother will know that *somebody* supplied the pygmies. He might even be smart enough to connect the tranquilizers to you."

"You're right." Malone felt like a fool. Furthermore, he felt as if he was losing control to the Watusi. "Next time see if you can distract the group leader and the females so you can snatch the babies without bloodshed."

"The Batwa pygmies are hard to control."

"I'm paying you to control them."

"No. You're paying me to steal gorillas."

"Well, dammit, I'm sure not paying you to *kill* them."

Shambu reached for the panga at his side, then stood staring at Malone. Sweat dripped off the side of Malone's face. Maybe Brett was willing to go after a Watusi with a knife, but Malone was a coward. He preferred to settle differences the easy way.

"Hey, look. I didn't mean to come down on you so hard. It's been a long day."

Shambu gave a contemptuous smile, then started toward the door.

"Wait . . ."

The Watusi kept on walking. Malone jerked his billfold from his pocket and threw some money onto the table.

"Maybe that will ease the pain of dealing with a bad-mannered white man," he said.

"The hurt hasn't gone away."

Malone threw another bill to the pile.

Grinning, Shambu wadded the money in his big fist. Then he jerked his head in the direction of the stairs.

"Come, I'll take you to the gorillas."

The captives were in small cages in the back of a covered truck. JoGina was curled into a ball fast asleep, but Maymay, sitting in a pool of her own waste, looked up at Malone with tragic eyes.

"That one's not going to make it," Shambu said.

"Dammit. She's going to make it." Malone got his bag

of medicines. "Get her out of there so I can take a look at her."

The little gorilla was seriously dehydrated and had an elevated temperature. When Malone picked her up, she laid her weak little head on his chest.

For the second time that day, he felt like a Judas. Not only had he betrayed his family, but he had betrayed the mountain gorillas. Was the money worth the price of his honor?

"What are you going to do, Doc?"

It was the first time anybody had ever called him Doc.

"I'm going to stay here and take care of her until Maymay is well enough to travel."

Malone thought how his life might have been if he were brave. He'd have turned down Chu Ling's rubies and his money; then he'd have gone back to the hotel room where his beautiful wife waited and said, "Ruth, let's go to Alabama and find a little town that needs a veterinarian." They'd have gone there together and built a modest practice and raised four children and six dogs. The two of them would have been the happiest couple in America.

If only he were brave.

As he started an IV in Maymay's arm, he made a promise to himself. If she lived, he was going to do better.

"You're not going to die, little one," he whispered. "I'm not going to let you die."

52.

*S*OMETHING WAS CHASING HER, AND Ruth was running as hard as she could, but she couldn't get away. Hands clutched at her, pulling her back, back toward something so terrible, she couldn't even think about it. The smell of roses was everywhere. White roses.

She was suffocating. She couldn't get away from the roses. There was no place to run. No place to hide.

There was someone she needed, someone she wanted.

Riveted, Brett sat up in bed. What had awakened him? What had caused the hair on the back of his neck to stand on end?

"Brett!"

Ruth was calling his name. He bolted from the bed and raced down the hall. She cowered against the headboard, the quilt pulled high up under her chin, tears streaming down her face.

"Brett! Brett!"

She wasn't even aware that he was in the room. He sat on the bed and cradled her in his arms, rocking her as if she were a child.

"Shhh, shhh. It's all right. I'm here, Ruth. I'm here."

She struggled against him.

"No. I want Brett."

"It's me, Ruth." Taking her face between his hands, he forced her to look at him. "It's Brett." Her eyes were wide and unfocused. She looked at him, but she seemed to be seeing something beyond him. "Touch me, Ruth. Touch my face." Still terrified, she stared through him. He took one of her hands and ran it over his face. "Touch my cheeks, my chin, my lips."

Oh, God. Ruth in his arms. Her hands on his face. Suddenly he knew what heaven was.

Tentatively, her hands began to move. As light as angel wings, they brushed his lips, tracing the bottom, then the top. He wanted to take her long, slender fingers inside his mouth and wrap his tongue around them, sucking until she made soft, kittenish sounds of arousal and surrender.

What kind of depraved animal had he become? She needed him, and all he could think about was his own carnal desires.

"Touch my eye patch, Ruth." He took her hands away from his lips and pressed them against the leather that guarded his blind eye. She traced the edges of the patch, the leather string that held it in place. He had never allowed anyone that familiarity, not even Lorena in all the years they'd been intimate.

"It's me, Ruth. I'm here for you."

The moonlight fell across her face as she stared at him, suddenly comprehending.

"It's really you?"

"Yes. It's really me."

The trembling started in her lips, then spread through her body. She collapsed against his chest, holding him so hard, he could feel his skin tear where her fingernails dug in. Sobs shook her, racking sobs.

"It's all right, sweet baby," he said, smoothing her hair,

caressing her face, her arms, her back. "Cry. Cry all the tears you want. I've got you."

"Don't . . . let . . . go."

"No. I won't let go."

Her face was soft against his chest, her tears hot against his skin. He suffered because she was suffering, mourned because she was mourning. And yet he'd never felt such joy. Ruth had called *his* name. Not Malone's. *His.* She'd cried out in her sleep for him, wanting him, needing him.

In the morning he would take a somber look at what had happened during the night, but for one precious moment she was his, cuddled close in the middle of her bed with the moonlight bathing them in silver and sounds of the jungle drifting through the open windows.

This was the way it should be. Trust between a man and a woman. The most important intimacy of all.

When Ruth spoke, her voice was so soft, he couldn't hear, but something in her tone sent chills through him.

"What?" he asked.

"He raped me," she said, clearly this time.

"Who?"

"He took me to New Orleans and put me in a white room with white silk sheets and white roses, and he raped me. I was only thirteen."

He wanted to roar his rage, to smash furniture and kick down walls, to rip trees up by the roots and tear down buildings.

"Who did that to you?"

"My mother. She sold me like a sack of potatoes. He had me all to himself for two weeks, and she got her future secured for the rest of her life."

"I'm so sorry, Ruth. So sorry."

Who? he wanted to know. *Who?* But he didn't dare interrupt her soul bearing with more questions. The best thing he could do for her was be sympathetic and nonjudgmental.

"I married Malone to escape, but I can't. The past keeps following me around. It's hung around my neck like an albatross, and I can't get rid of it."

Her shoulders shook with fresh sobs, and he gathered her close.

"You're rid of it now, Ruth. You gave it to me. I've got it now, and you don't ever have to think about it again. You don't have to run anymore. You don't have to have bad dreams. You don't have to worry. I'll take care of everything."

Her sobs became sniffles, then hiccups. She sucked in great gulps of air, holding on to him . . . holding on.

She'd married Malone to escape. The knowledge rushed through Brett like high winter winds off the snowcapped peaks of the Virungas—sharp, refreshing, invigorating.

Late at night when he was alone in his bed and Ruth lay with his brother in the cottage down the mountainside, he would remember what she'd said, remember and take selfish comfort.

"I'm sorry," she whispered.

"Don't be."

"I shouldn't have told you those things. They're private."

"Your secrets are safe with me, Ruth. No one will ever know."

Ruth was reluctant to lift her head off his chest. His arms were around her, and she was snuggled into him as if she belonged there. The warmth of his body seeped into her, and for the first time in her life she felt safe, truly safe.

She wanted nothing more than to close her eyes and stay right where she was.

"I feel as if I could sleep for the next three days," she said.

"Rest." His hands smoothed her hair. "Sleep."

She closed her eyes, content. When she startled awake, she was still in his lap, both arms wrapped around his neck, her head in the crook of his shoulder, his cheek resting against hers.

"Brett?"

"I'm here."

She was vaguely aware of having told him things she'd never told another human being . . . and acutely, stunningly aware that he was naked.

She remembered dreaming, calling his name. As she always did. And suddenly he'd been there for her. But how?

"How did I get in this bed?"

"You were asleep when I came home. I put you here."

Her dress was tangled high around her legs, and her bare thigh rested intimately against his. She looked at him, and he at her. It was one of those moments that would later shine in her memory like a beacon. There was hunger between them, a deep, atavistic hunger that went beyond mere passion, beyond reason, beyond propriety. She felt as if she'd just been given the keys to a house she'd always wanted but then told she couldn't go inside.

Tears eased down her cheeks, but they were no longer the tears of fear.

"Where's Malone?"

"In Rumangabo reporting the deaths of the gorillas."

"Oh . . ."

Even talking of mundane things, they didn't shift apart. *Couldn't* shift apart. Not yet. The desire between them was a separate being, a thing with a life entirely its own.

"He left early so he could get there before dark. He asked me to take care of you." Brett shuddered with the tightness of his control. "He'll be back in a few days."

She was free, free from Malone's self-pity, his drinking, his nightly gropings.

Free to be with Brett.

"I see." Every nerve ending in her body was tingling, responsive to the man whose body was pressed next to hers. In the bed. In the dark. On a remote mountaintop where no one would see. No one would know.

"We don't know what's going to happen," he said.

Neither did she. A glow appeared in the east as the first rays of sun pinked the windowsill.

"It will be daylight soon."

"Yes."

She couldn't bring herself to leave his embrace, not because of desire, but because of kindness. Certainly desire was in her, a rich, ripe unfolding that surprised her with its intensity. But the most remarkable thing about being so intimately entwined with Brett was the overwhelming trust she felt—trust in his kindness and loyalty and integrity.

How could such emotions be impure? How could holding him, merely holding him, be wrong? And yet she knew that in the eyes of society what they were doing was wrong.

"I'll go back to the cottage as soon as it's light enough to see," she said.

"No."

The glow that filled the bedroom was faintly tinged with gold, like a promise. He tightened his embrace, and she knew that she would never have the courage to let him go. Daylight could pour into the bedroom, and the entire population of Africa could troop in to watch, but Ruth would not be able to say no to the man holding her now . . . no matter what he wanted.

If wanting to sip briefly of joy made her weak, then she'd have to live with herself. Unexpectedly she thought of her mother, of how circumstances might have shaped her and of how she might not have been strong enough to resist.

At the moment Ruth was not strong enough. Perhaps tomorrow she would be. But not now. Not with Brett's arms around her and the first sweet light of morning making her wish for things she knew she could never have.

She knew before Brett pulled away that he was going to let her go. There was nothing concrete, no big sigh or last-minute crushing her to his chest, only a sudden sense that he had become as solid and unshakable as the hundred-year-old oak tree that grew beside her mother's house in Mississippi.

Hope was sometimes cruel.

When he let her go, she lay very still against the covers, but she didn't avert her eyes when he stood up. He didn't try to cover himself, didn't try to hide his nakedness.

Both of them might have been ashamed if he had, and they had nothing to be ashamed of. Instead he treated his nudity as a natural occurrence, something that happened because he'd been roused from his sleep in the middle of the night by her cries.

"It's best that you stay here until Malone returns."

"I can't leave Miranda by herself."

"We'll go down tomorrow and bring her back."

If he had been anybody except Brett Corday, it might have struck her as funny that he was standing in her doorway naked talking about a cat. But such was his dignity and presence that he could have been on top of the Empire State Building addressing all of Manhattan in the nude, and it would have seemed not only logical but somehow the right thing to do.

"I apologize for waking you up in the middle of the night," she said.

"You can wake me up anytime you need me. The next time I'll grab my pants."

"There won't be a next time." A look passed over his face—rage? resignation?—but it was gone as quickly as it had come. She thought how she must have sounded. Harsh. Ungrateful.

"I didn't mean that the way it sounded," she said. "I'm very grateful to you for letting me cry on your shoulder. I've never done that before . . . cried on anyone's shoulder."

"I'm glad you chose mine."

"So am I."

"Ruth . . ."

She was on the bed and he was still at the door, so close and yet so very far away. If she reached out her hand, would he take it? Could she live with herself if he did?

"I want you to know that you can cry on my shoulder anytime you need to. I care about you, not just because you are my brother's wife, but because you are *you*."

"Thank you, Brett. I value your friendship."

"That pleases me very much, Ruth. More than you'll ever know."

He left suddenly, and she stared at the empty doorway. Somewhere down the hall he would climb into his bed and perhaps be as lonely as she was in hers. Only a short distance separated them, but she knew that neither of them would ever close the gap.

She was his brother's wife.

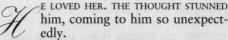

53.

HE LOVED HER. THE THOUGHT STUNNED him, coming to him so unexpectedly.

Brett was standing at the window drinking coffee when Ruth walked into the kitchen, barefoot, no makeup, her hair caught high with a barrette and a few tendrils resting against her slender neck like little invitations.

"Good morning," she said, her voice soft and musical.

"Good morning, Ruth. Coffee?"

"No. I'm a juice person, myself."

"Orange? Pineapple?"

"Whatever you have. I'm not picky."

She leaned against the counter, ankles crossed, head tossed back, eyes closed. He coveted her, coveted his brother's wife.

"Hmmm." She made the small humming sound low in her throat. Something wild climbed through him. "I love music in the morning."

"So do I," he said, holding on to his coffee cup, holding on to his sanity.

"A Brahms intermezzo. Music for the soul."

"And the heart."

She opened her eyes and stared at him, understanding, *knowing*.

Neither of them was capable of moving, neither of them could stop staring; but they got through it somehow, that awkward moment when they might have ruined what they had with admissions that would change the way they viewed each other.

They were not free to give each other love, and so they would give what they could—friendship, kindness, easy camaraderie, and trust. Most of all, trust.

"After we eat, I'll drive down the mountain and we'll pick up your cat."

"Good. Poor old Miranda. I'm sure she feels abandoned."

"I've seen the way you pet that cat. She probably thinks you're off planning some kind of entertainment specifically for her."

"Are you hinting that I spoil my cat?"

The sun was warm on her bare feet, and since the sun was so rare in the early mornings in the Virungas, Ruth took it as a sign that what was happening in the kitchen, this remarkable connection of minds, spirits, and hearts, was right and good—so long as they both understood that it would never lead to the ultimate connection, the splendid oneness that comes with the joining of bodies perfectly attuned to each other.

"No. I'm not subtle enough to hint. Comes from living alone, I guess. I don't have to bother with manners up here. The gorillas don't care."

"Thank goodness." Ruth looked down at her feet. "I'd hate to think I had to put on shoes for the sake of a prickly mountain gorilla."

Their laughter rang through the kitchen like church bells on a clear Sunday morning. Pure and beautiful.

The ease and delight they felt with each other stayed with them all through breakfast and through the trip down the mountain to retrieve Miranda.

And it was with them still, that easy grace, that delight, that contentment. As the three of them approached Cee Cee's enclosure, he held his hand out to Ruth, she took it.

Neither of them expected that Cee Cee would be enchanted by the cat. The minute she saw it, she claimed it as her own.

"Me want," she signed frantically when Ruth put Miranda down and the cat strolled by her enclosure.

"Want what?" Brett asked, signing.

"Fur ball love gimme fur ball."

"The cat?" he asked, signing, then pointing to Miranda, who had settled into a sunny spot on the windowsill.

"What cat?" Cee Cee asked.

"That." Brett pointed. *"Cat."*

"No, no, no. Fur ball. Me want gimme."

"She wants the cat," he told Ruth.

"What will she do with her?"

"Let's ask her. . . . *Cee Cee, why do you want the fur ball?"*

"Cee Cee love fur ball." She made a cradle of her arms and pretended to be stroking the cat. Then she hid her eyes and peered shyly at Brett between her fingers.

"This is astonishing." Brett could hardly contain his excitement. "She either wants to love the cat as a pet or as a substitute child. Either way, it's remarkable behavior for a gorilla."

"Will she hurt Miranda?" Ruth asked.

"No. But I'll be with her to ensure both their safety."

Ruth had a sudden inspiration.

"Tell her the fur ball belongs to the stink female."

"The stink female?" Brett said, grinning.

"That's all she ever calls me. Tell her if she wants to love the fur ball, she has to be nice to me."

"A little bribery, Ruth?"

Brett was in high spirits, though how he could be, under the circumstances, was almost a miracle. He understood what the miracle was and that it would be his for only a few days. Still, he would not look toward the future, but be happy in the moment.

"She's just a gorilla," he added. "Do you think she'll understand?"

"If she understands jealousy, hatred, and deception, she's bound to catch on pretty fast to bribery."

"Let's give her a try . . . if Miranda is willing."

"Miranda will do anything for me."

So will I, he thought, but saying so would have put her in a position of compromise and defense. And he would never do that to her.

"Cee Cee," he said, signing, *"this is Ruth."*

"No. Stink female."

"Not stink female. Ruth. The cat belongs to Ruth. If you are nice to Ruth, you can play with the cat."

Cee Cee poked out her lips in an enormous pout, then turned her back on them. But not for long. Her curiosity got the better of her. She peered over her shoulder to see what the cat was doing. Miranda chose that moment to leave the windowsill and wrap herself around Ruth's legs, purring.

Cee Cee turned around so fast, she fell flat on her bottom. *"What fur ball say?"* she asked, even before she got off the floor.

"Fur ball does not talk like Cee Cee. Fur ball is purring."

"What purring?"

"Happy sounds."

"Me want gimme gimme. Me good girl, fine animal gorilla, love Ruth." Cee Cee wrapped her arms around herself in an exaggerated hug.

"See," Ruth said. "I told you bribery would work."

"You were right. There's no telling what else we'll discover while you're here."

The look that passed between them was temporarily blinding. If they got caught up in it, they would destroy more than themselves: They'd destroy the Corday family and all it stood for.

With every fiber of her being, Ruth wanted this man, wanted to touch and be touched, to kiss and be kissed, to love and be loved, for the first time in her life, *truly* loved.

She wished she didn't have to think about what was best for anybody but herself.

"Careful there, Dr. Corday. You're liable to have to step out of the limelight to make room for the Gorilla Woman."

"It's about time this family had a pretty face in the limelight."

The room filled with their laughter. Better laughter than tears, Ruth thought.

54.

RUMANGABO

CHU LING COUNTED OUT THE MONEY, watching Malone's face. Excitement was there. And greed. Both good signs, indications that Malone was his man. But something else was there, something that disturbed Chu Ling.

"You did an excellent job, Malone."

"That's what you paid me for."

"My man says one of them would have died except for you."

"I'm a veterinarian. I'm trained to save the lives of animals."

Ah, there it was again. That little glimmer of belligerence—and remorse. Chu Ling knew that the kidnapping of the baby gorillas had resulted in a bloodbath.

"When can I expect another delivery?"

"I've been thinking. . . ."

Chu Ling sat quietly, his hands folded in a steeple, while Malone's voice trailed off.

If Malone expected him to ask questions or to speculate, he was doomed to disappointment. It was not Chu Ling's way. Appearing anxious sacrificed face and power.

"I never expected such carnage." Malone waited futilely for a response, then got up and paced the room. "I didn't know I'd feel like such a betrayer when I saw my father and brother and when I saw Petey . . . dead." His voice broke, then he gathered his courage and came back to the chair facing Chu Ling. "I can't do it again."

"We made a bargain."

"I fulfilled my end of it, and you paid me. Fine. Period. End of deal." He leaned forward in his chair, a fine sheen of sweat on his earnest face. "You know, I've been thinking . . . I don't really need your money. Ruth's not the kind of woman who goes for expensive jewels and crap like that. As much as she loves to putter around that cottage, I don't even think a big, fancy house would turn her on."

So now they were at the crux of the matter. Corday's wife was frigid. At least with him. Chu Ling repressed his smile. Amazing what could be learned through silence.

"How 'turned on' will Mrs. Corday be when her husband is in jail?"

"Jail?"

"What you did is illegal."

"But you . . ."

"I was in San Francisco. I know none of the people you hired. They don't know me, but they all know *you*."

"It wouldn't be long before they'd trace the whole scheme back to you."

"Months, perhaps years. African officials don't get too stirred up about these matters, and I hear conditions in the jails are somewhat undesirable."

Hellholes. That's what they were. Malone felt his newfound courage shriveling. He'd finally got himself into a predicament that no one could get him out of. Not even Brett.

"Okay. Let's say that I do continue this . . . project." He crossed his legs to stop the trembling. "There have been developments you should know about."

Chu Ling doubted Malone could tell him something he

didn't already know, but he adopted his usual silent posture.

"Patrols have been organized. I have control over two of them because I hired them, but Brett's men run the other two, and they can't be bought. Furthermore, Brett himself will take to the jungle. I know my brother. He won't sit back and let somebody else do the dirty work."

Malone was sweating in earnest now. If he could have dropped off the face of the earth, he would have. Vanish while he still had the regard of his family. But he couldn't. And he couldn't go back and undo what had been done, either. The only thing he could do was try to salvage whatever possible.

"I won't endanger the lives of the men on patrol for this project, and I for damned sure won't jeopardize my brother." He felt the bile rising in his throat, but he swallowed hard and made himself hold it in. He'd be damned if he'd puke in front of this coldhearted bastard.

And if Chu Ling was a coldhearted bastard, what did that make him?

"I'll get the baby gorillas out for you, but it has to be in my own time."

"Take all the time you need." Chu Ling smiled at him. "Take the rest of your life."

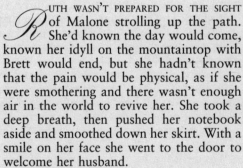

55.

R UTH WASN'T PREPARED FOR THE SIGHT of Malone strolling up the path. She'd known the day would come, known her idyll on the mountaintop with Brett would end, but she hadn't known that the pain would be physical, as if she were smothering and there wasn't enough air in the world to revive her. She took a deep breath, then pushed her notebook aside and smoothed down her skirt. With a smile on her face she went to the door to welcome her husband.

"I'm home," he said, grinning from behind a huge bouquet of yellow roses.

Loss. She felt an overwhelming sense of loss.

"Hi, sweetheart. How was your trip?"

"Physically and emotionally draining. I'm glad to be home."

He leaned around the roses and kissed her on the cheek. A strange restraint for him. And a welcome one.

"I brought flowers." He held them out like a little boy.

"So I see. Thank you."

His grin was infectious. She couldn't help but smile back.

He plopped onto the sofa facing Cee Cee's enclosure and kicked off his shoes.

"Miss me while I was gone?"

Brett appeared in the doorway behind the sofa, his knuckles white on Cee Cee's lunch tray.

"Yes," she said to her husband, her eyes riveted on the man in the doorway. "I missed you," she whispered.

For an instant there was a look of utter devastation on Brett's face. Ruth wanted to cry. Instead she turned her face away from her husband's brother.

"Malone," Brett said, coming forward, his face fixed in a look of welcome. "Tell me everything."

"I got two patrols organized, and I saw when I came up the trail that you already have Bantain and Juma on the job. I guess those bastards will think twice before they come back here and try any more dirty work."

"I hope so. This delays Project Cee Cee, though."

"Why? I thought things were running right on target. Hell, with my beautiful wife helping out, they should be ahead of schedule."

Malone reached for Ruth's hand and pulled her down onto the sofa beside him. She braced herself for a blatant display of desire, but he did no more than hold her hand and smile at her in his endearing way. She could almost believe he was the sweet, rather shy Malone she'd met in Hawaii.

Besides that, he was completely sober. There was not even a hint of alcohol on his breath.

Hope began to stir in her once more—hope for their marriage, hope for their future.

"I won't risk putting Cee Cee in the jungle, even briefly, while the threat of violence to the mountain gorilla is hanging over us," Brett said.

"Hell," Malone answered, "with the patrols puffing through the jungle like dragons, things will be back to normal in no time."

"I hope so."

"They will. You'll see." He squeezed his wife's hand. "Are you ready to go home, Ruth?"

She couldn't look at Brett.

"I'm ready."

"Thanks for taking care of her, bro."

"My pleasure."

Brett had known it would hurt to see her walk out the door; he hadn't known how much. The thing he thought of when she climbed into the Jeep with his brother and disappeared into the mists was not being in her bed, not holding her in his arms but seeing her in the kitchen, wearing no makeup, with the morning sun shining on her bare feet. His entire body hurt, as if it were fighting chills and a high fever. He had to sit down right where he was, just plop into the doorway and lean his head against the doorsill.

He realized suddenly that part of his inertia was anger, and part of his love was hate. For at that moment he hated her, hated her for marrying his brother, hated her for unlocking his heart, then walking away with the only key.

Mists swirled around him, and Brett was glad the sun hadn't burned them away yet, glad he couldn't see clearly. He didn't want to view a world without Ruth. From a distance came the sound of Malone's Jeep, taking her away, and high in the Virungas one of the giant male silverbacks drummed his chest and screamed his intent to mount one of his wives.

Brett could taste loneliness. It was bittersweet, like the stamens of honeysuckle that grew wild in summertime along the side of the road in Alabama. On rare visits to his mother's home when he was a child, he used to pluck the flowers, suck their insides, and toss them away, thoughtlessly, carelessly. He made silent apology to all the flowers that lay crushed along the road, buried in dirt because of him.

He went hollow inside. Her fragrance lingered on the sofa where she'd lain. In the kitchen he picked up the coffee cup she'd used only that morning. With his index finger he traced the rim, as if the sweet moisture from her lips still lingered there and he could collect it and put it in a box for safekeeping.

Slowly he walked to the sink. The day before, she'd stood there with the sun shining on her bare feet. He pulled off his shoes and stood exactly where she had, as if by some miracle he might absorb her through the soles of his feet.

"You're awfully quiet, Ruth," Malone said as he guided the Jeep down the mountain. "Not that I'm complaining."

"Just tired, I guess."

Heartbreak was extremely tiring. What was Brett doing now? Was he bent over his desk, his dark hair falling across his forehead, intent on recording Cee Cee's daily life? Did he glance up to catch her eyes the way he had a habit of doing, hoping that by some miracle she might still be there?

If she thought about her loss too much, she would burst into tears, cry buckets and lakes and rivers. *Then* how would she make her husband believe it was allergies?

"Me too," he said, never guessing. "I'm not much in a talkative mood."

They rode in silence until their house came into view, but it wasn't the easy silence of beloved companions; rather, it was the uneasy silence of two explorers approaching the rim of an active volcano.

"There it is, Ruth. Home sweet home."

The only miracle she dared wish for was that Malone's words would come true. That the cottage really would become a home.

She approached the door with a sense of dread. Now that they were in private, Malone would practically tear her clothes from her body, taking undue liberties now that he didn't have the restraints of birth control. Emotionally, she braced herself for the assault.

Instead she found herself lifted off her feet.

"Malone? What in the world are you doing?"

"Carrying my bride over the threshold. It's something I neglected to do the first time." He kicked open the door, and when they were inside, he set her on her feet. But still he did nothing more than reach for her hand. "There are lots of things I neglected to do, Ruth, and I intend to make up for them."

"You've been a wonderful husband," she said. "Kind, thoughtful . . ."

"Childish, petulant . . . drunk." When she started to protest, he put a finger over her lips. "Don't think that change is going to be easy for me, Ruth. It's not. I know I've been drinking too much. If I hadn't been skunk drunk the night before your mother came to visit you, I'd have been there for you, and you wouldn't have had to go running off to my brother."

"He seemed the natural one to turn to."

"I'm not blaming you. I've gone running to Brett myself. Hell, we all run to Brett with our problems. What I'm saying is that *I* want to be the one you run to, Ruth. Will you let me prove myself worthy of your trust?"

"You don't have to—"

"Don't make excuses for me anymore. I've decided to grow up and take responsibility for my own actions." He cupped her chin and tipped her face up to his. "Will you, Ruth? Will you let me prove myself?"

Quiet pleasure filled her. Compared to the vaulting joy she felt in Brett's presence, it was merely a consolation prize—but it would do. It would do.

"Yes, Malone. I'll let you."

Book Three

56.

*S*TERILE. THE WORD ECHOED LIKE THUN-
der around the walls of the stark
clinic in Ruhengeri. Ruth didn't
dare look at Malone, afraid of what she'd
see in his face. Disappointment. Anger. Accusations. As if somehow their failure to
conceive was all her fault.

"Are you sure?" Malone said. "Labs
make mistakes."

"There's no question about it." Dr.
Tigrett doodled on a notepad on his desk.
"You are sterile. You will never be able to
father a child."

"We could go somewhere else, get more
tests." Malone turned to her, desperate.
"We'll go to Nairobi. They have a bigger
medical complex, more sophisticated
equipment."

Ruth's heart bled for him, bled for them
both. In spite of the uncertainty over the
fate of the gorillas, she'd been at peace
these last few months. True to his word,

Malone hadn't touched a drop of liquor. He'd been kind, thoughtful, attentive. She'd come to love him. Not in a grand, passionate way, but with a quiet sort of contentment.

"You'll be wasting your money," Dr. Tigrett said.

"We'll adopt." Ruth reached for Malone's hand. "There are many children who need a good home, good parents."

Malone didn't answer her.

"Are you disappointed?" he said later that night as they lay in bed side by side.

Was she? When they'd first started trying to conceive, she hadn't viewed the child as real. Rather, it had been something that would fix their marriage, much like a cure for a disease. But since Malone had reformed, since she'd stopped going to the mountaintop to see Brett, the child had taken on a life of his own, as if he had already been born.

"Yes," she said. "Our son would have been beautiful."

She pressed her hands together over her empty womb, mourning her loss, as if her son had lain there for months and had suddenly been ripped away.

"How do you know it would be a son?"

"I made up my mind."

Malone laughed. "Lord knows, when you make up your mind, it's as good as done."

"Are you calling me stubborn, Malone Corday?"

"Well . . . hell, yes, I'm calling you stubborn. Who else but you would have coaxed that coconut-cake recipe out of Matuka?"

"Eleanor helped."

"She didn't have a damned thing to do with it. Matuka's been eating out of your hand ever since you let her play your piano."

Through the open doorway the rosewood cabinet gleamed in the moonlight. It was an old upright with real ivories, yellowed over the years, and a stool that swiveled. Malone had bought it for her shortly after he'd returned from Rumangabo.

She would never forget the day. She'd been bent over

he pots on her front porch watering her flowers when
she'd seen them laboring up the mountain, Malone at the
wheel of an ancient flatbed truck, and four husky natives
stationed at the corners of the piano to keep it from top-
pling off.

She'd shaded her eyes against the setting sun. The old
truck had shuddered to a halt, and Malone had got out
with a flourish, as if he'd dismounted from an Arabian
stallion.

"What in the world . . ."

"A piano. For you."

"For me?"

"Who else would I be bringing it to?"

"You brought a piano all the way up the mountain for
me?"

"Is that a smile I see? Just a little one, maybe?"

"It's . . ." She'd felt her face to be sure. "Yes. It's a
smile."

" 'Bout time. You've been Miss Gloom ever since I got
back from Rumangabo."

Missing Brett. Wondering how she could get through
each day without him.

"The deaths of Petey and his wives . . ." She'd hated
lying to him. Especially since he was trying so hard to be
good.

"Where did you get it?" she'd asked.

"Ruhengeri. I didn't plan to buy a piano, it was just one
of those things that happened, you know? I was sitting at
that run-down café next to the post office trying to cool
off with a piss-warm cola, when this old man pulls up out
front and comes in looking for directions."

Malone was so proud of himself, he was strutting like
an actor on a stage.

"He's leaving this hellhole, he says. Taking his whole
family and all his worldly goods."

"One of which happened to be the piano?"

"How did you know? Are you clairvoyant, in addition
to your many other talents?"

"Maybe."

"He said he had no use for it. He'd never played, himself, and his wife was long dead, but he couldn't see driv-

ing off and leaving a perfectly good piano behind." He'd smiled at her. "Do you like it?"

She'd climbed into the back of the truck and run her hands over the wood. With a bit of polish it would shine like a full moon in Indian summer, she'd thought.

"Do I like it? I *love* it."

Music surged through her in currents as strong as the Pacific. Why had she done without it for so long?

"I figured anybody who could sing like you was bound to be able to play too. Am I right?"

One of the men leaning against the piano had helped her down from the back of the truck, and she'd kissed Malone's cheek.

"Tonight there will be a private concert. Just for you."

"You really do like it?"

"Malone, it's the best gift I've ever had."

The piano had somehow set the tone for their marriage. Things had got better for them, as if the music had lifted them out of their old ways and taught them a new appreciation for each other.

The piano had even brought her closer to Eleanor. It was one of the civilized things she'd missed, she told Ruth, and now, in the evenings sometimes, Eleanor and Joseph walked down from the main house to sit in rocking chairs and listen to Ruth play and sing.

Tonight the moon was full. It gleamed on the ivories. Ruth had imagined herself sitting at the piano with her child, teaching him how to sing.

"Malone?"

"What?"

"I'm disappointed about the baby, but I certainly don't blame you. We can have a baby, we can adopt, and he will be every bit as much our child as if we had conceived him."

Malone had pictured how Ruth would be after she'd borne a child—mellow and passionate for the first time in their marriage—and he wasn't ready to give up on that dream.

"You can have a child," he said, seized by sudden inspiration.

"That's what I was saying. There are plenty of homeless children—"

"Your child," he said. "One you've carried nine months in your womb."

Her heart quickened, but she lay very still, not daring to hope too much.

"Donor sperm," he said. "People do it all the time."

Could Malone handle that? He was doing so well, but seeing her pregnant with another man's child might be just the thing to tip him back into a drinking spree.

"I don't know. There are children already born who need homes."

"Why should you be denied the joy of giving birth just because I'm sterile?"

"Malone . . . I don't look at it that way." She sought his hand, but he got out of bed and pulled on his pants.

"I'm sorry. I didn't mean to upset you," she said.

"I'm not upset. I can't sleep, that's all."

"It's not that I'm *against* artificial insemination. It's just that I don't want you to feel left out of the process."

"Don't coddle me, Ruth. I would never have suggested it if I couldn't handle it."

"I'm sorry. I—"

"Stop being sorry!" Immediately contrite, Malone sat on the edge of the bed and took her hand. "Look, I'm an asshole. We both know that." Smiling, he covered her lips with two fingers. "Shhh. Don't say it."

"Say what?" she mumbled.

"We both know what you're going to say. 'You're a dear, sweet man, Malone Corday, and don't you deny it.' "

"Do I say that?"

"About six million times since you married me."

Laughing, she reached for the bedside lamp, then scooted up against the headboard.

"Malone . . . do you think we can get started right away? I think it would be nice to be pregnant when I go to Hawaii to defend my dissertation."

"Double cause for celebration?"

"Precisely."

"I've always imagined three on a honeymoon."

"You're a dear, sweet . . ."

"I know . . . I know."

They both laughed. Malone reached for his shirt, and Ruth glanced at the bedside clock. Midnight.

"Why are you getting dressed at this time of night?"

"I thought I'd check on the patrols. Juma's not on to night, and the others can always use some support."

"Be careful."

"I will." He leaned over and kissed her cheek. "Go t sleep."

"When will you be back?"

"As soon as I can. Don't worry."

It was the wrong kind of night for what he needed t do, but Malone didn't care. He might be too useless t father a child, but he could prove he wasn't completel powerless.

He knew which side of the rain forest Brett's ma Bantain would be patrolling. Malone headed to the othe side of the mountain. The patrols he'd organized i Rumangabo were mere covers. It was a perfect setup. Un der the guise of protecting the gorillas, they'd know ever move Brett's patrols made. There was no chance of gettin caught. When the time was right, they'd strike again.

And the time was right. Only this time Malone woul be there. He wouldn't risk another fiasco like the one wit Petey.

Shadows hung violet around the peak of Moun Karisimbi. From somewhere in the distance a lone ele phant trumpeted, and the air was heavy with the lament of night birds, as if they were already mourning the loss o their own.

The giant Watusi, Shambu, emerged from the shadows

"Tonight is the night," Malone told him.

"The moon is full. It's not a good time."

"Who will be there to see? I say the time is right."

"Whatever you say. You're the boss."

"That's right. I'm the boss." Malone began to sweat Telling himself he was going to be there when the kidnap ping took place was one thing, but doing it was another He hoped he didn't make a fool of himself.

"Who's on the slopes?"

"Old Doby's group. He's a mean-looking son of a bitch."

"Looks don't deceive. We can't mess with Doby. He'd create too much trouble. There'd be too much killing. Who else have you spotted?"

"There's a little fringe group higher up the mountain. But it's awfully close to Brett's camp."

"Ned's group. He's a pussycat. Still young, unsure of himself. It's perfect. Lead the way."

"What about your brother?"

"He patrolled last night. He won't be out tonight."

Silently they filed through the rain forest. In some places the growth was so thick, it felt as if they were in the center of the earth, totally without light. They came upon Ned's group suddenly. It was a peaceful scene with most of the gorillas nested down, asleep. A couple of teenagers halfheartedly roughhoused on the fringes, but they were too young to create problems.

"Which one's Ned?" Shambu asked.

"That's him." Malone pointed to the male silverback on the slopes of the mountain. "Two of his wives are with him. We'll go well to the east of him. See, over there. Three young females and their babies are separated by that group of trees. Try to cut them off from Ned."

Shambu slid his panga out of his belt. Malone had a sudden vision of his brother, lying on the floor with blood pouring down his face.

"For God's sake, try to take the babies without bloodshed. There's been too much bloodshed."

"Are you coming?"

"No. I'll wait here . . . to keep a watch on Ned."

Moonlight gleamed on the blade of Shambu's knife and on the spears of the Batwa pygmies. There was too much light. If Malone hadn't had so much to prove, he'd have called a halt to the whole thing.

Lucy, the youngest of Ned's wives, was the first to spot the enemy. Clutching her baby to her chest, she sounded the alarm. Suddenly the slope was dark with moving shapes. Gorillas leaped for the safety of trees, snatching babies and screaming at the youngsters.

One of the Batwas hurled a spear. With a sound as

sharp as a hammer striking flint, it buried itself in the trunk of a tree.

Suddenly there was a new sound, a roar of outrage as Brett Corday crashed through the bushes. Malone's bones turned to butter when he saw his brother.

For a moment he was temporarily paralyzed; then his brain kicked in.

"Halt!" Malone yelled. "Don't let the poachers get away, Shambu."

"Which way did they go?" Shambu was nobody's dummy.

"That way." Malone pointed to the direction opposite Brett's camp.

Shambu and the rest of his patrol raced off into the jungle in hot pursuit of the "poachers." Brett would have followed, but Malone grabbed his arm.

"Leave it to them. Anyhow, they have such a head start, you'd never catch up."

"You're right. Still, I'd like to get my hands on the ones who did that to Petey and his group."

"If they can be caught, Shambu is the one who will do it."

"They'll be caught. And when they are, I'll see that justice is done."

The look on his brother's face sent shivers down Malone's spine. Ten minutes more and he'd have been caught red-handed. He didn't even want to think about what would have happened.

"You and me, too, bro. Let's go up to your camp and wait for them," Malone said.

"What are you doing out tonight?" Brett asked as they made their way back through the thick jungle growth to his compound.

"Couldn't sleep. What about you?"

"Same thing. And then I heard the gorillas screaming. Any particular reason for your insomnia?"

Something inside Malone snapped. Everything he'd been holding inside, the dark secrets, the rage, the insecurity, all boiled to the surface in one screaming need.

"Yeah." He was close to tears, and he realized suddenly that he needed his big brother, needed him in ways that he could never need his wife or his father or his mother. Brett was his anchor, always had been and always would be.

There was no need for words between them. Brett understood. He draped his arm around his younger brother's shoulders, and when they were inside his compound, he led Malone to the sofa, then straddled a chair opposite him.

"Now . . . tell me what's bothering you, Malone."

How could he tell his brother that it was all the blood that was bothering him, that he was the one killing the gorillas?

"It's this damned jungle. If I could only get out . . ."

"You really hate it, don't you?"

"I always have."

"I've done you a disservice, keeping you here."

"Don't go blaming yourself, bro."

"I thought if you did something that let your light shine, you'd be all right. You're good at fund-raising, Malone. The best."

"It's more than that, more than this whole mess. . . ."

The burden of deceit weighed so heavily on him that he put his head on the table and shut his eyes. He didn't really care whether he ever opened them again. Brett's hand was on his shoulder.

"There's nothing wrong that can't be fixed. Remember that, Malone."

"Yeah. As long as you do the fixing. If I try, all I do is fuck up."

Malone rammed his fist into his palm, and Cee Cee roused from her sleep. Seeing Brett, she shambled over to the bars, dragging her blanket behind her.

"Don't be too hard on yourself," Brett said.

"Why the hell not? I can't do anything right. I can't even get my wife pregnant."

Brett felt as if a large hole had been blown through his chest. All these weeks he'd tried to put her out of his mind, had even succeeded, to a certain degree. It was only late at night when he was in bed alone that he felt the loss. And now Ruth was with him, as if she'd walked through the door.

"Ruth wants a child?" Not just a child. Malone's child.

"Yeah. But it seems I'm shooting blanks."

Brett hid his selfish exultation behind a carefully blank expression.

"What about adoption?"

"I want her to have the joy of carrying a child, of giving birth . . . and I want you to be the father."

Brett's chair toppled over as he strode to the window. He didn't dare let Malone see his face, even in the moonlight.

"What does Ruth say about this?"

"This is my idea. Not Ruth's."

"She'll never stand for it."

"She'll never know."

The full moon was enormous in the black sky, its light making everything in the jungle seem bigger than life. That's how Brett felt. Bigger than life. He had a vision of Ruth, large with his child. *His.* The wonder of it almost broke his heart.

A child of his own, with his grit and Ruth's spirit. A child who would grow strong and sturdy under the watchful eye of his mother and his father.

Could he sit back and watch Malone rear his child? Could he play the role of uncle? Could he hide the truth from his child? From Ruth?

"I can't," Brett said, turning back to his brother.

"Why not? Just think about it. My child would at least have Corday genes. If we get an anonymous donor, there's no telling whose genes the baby will have."

"It's too complicated, too risky. How would you feel knowing I'm the biological father?"

"Hell, I never would have asked you if I'd expected to feel anything except gratitude." That's what Malone had always felt for his brother. Gratitude. If he lived long enough, maybe the tables would be turned and someday Brett might have occasion to feel gratitude to *him.* Of course, he loved his brother. Still . . .

"It's not right. This discussion should be between you and Ruth. I should not be a part of it."

"She's gung ho for the idea. In fact, she wants to get pregnant as soon as possible."

"Leave me out of it, Malone. I don't want to be the father of Ruth's baby."

"It's my baby too. All I'm asking is that the man I love and admire and respect more than any other man in the world donate a little sperm so that I can have a child who at least stands a chance of inheriting the Corday stubbornness."

The idea of Ruth great with his child grew in Brett until he didn't trust himself to speak. Instead, he let his silence speak for him.

"Fine, then." Malone jumped off the sofa. "Fine and dandy. You keep your damned precious sperm, and I'll fill my wife full of somebody else's. Somebody we don't know from Adam's house cat. Hell, at least the kid will have Ruth's genes."

He stalked toward the door—mad at Brett, mad at Chu Ling, mad at the doctor. But mostly mad at himself.

Malone Corday, *failure*.

"Wait." Brett knew that what he was about to do would forever alter the course of their lives. But the idea of Ruth bearing a stranger's child was more than he could endure. He had sacrificed an eye for his brother. He would give up a child for Ruth.

"I'll do it," he said.

"You mean that?" Malone grabbed his arm, grinning. "You'll part with a bit of the old seed so Ruth and I can have a real, genuine Corday baby?"

"On condition that she never know."

"Hey . . . that's a given. I'd cut out my tongue before I'd tell her. This calls for a celebration."

"Orange juice?"

"Maybe something stronger? Just this once?"

"Not a chance."

Brett went toward the kitchen to get the juice, and Cee Cee rose from her place in the corner. She made "let's play" noises to get Malone's attention.

"Hey, old girl. What are you doing up? Aren't you supposed to be in bed asleep?"

He didn't bother to sign. Cee Cee liked that. Sometimes she got tired of people signing at her all the time as if she couldn't hear.

She didn't bother to sign to Malone, either. She didn't need signs for what she was going to do. She did a few tricks and made a few grunting noises just to keep his attention.

"If Brett comes back and catches you doing that, he's going to skin my hide. Take your blanket and get back in bed like a good girl."

Cee Cee stuck out her tongue at him, then waddled over to her nest. She kept secrets there—a banana Brett didn't know she had, the pants she'd pulled off her doll trying to see what it looked like down there, and the shiny stars move. Her hand closed around the tiny object, and she shambled back toward Malone.

"Hey, I thought you were headed back to bed. Go on, now. Quick, before Brett gets back."

The door opened and Brett came through, bearing two glasses of orange juice.

"Cee Cee, what are you doing up?"

She stuck out her tongue, turned cartwheels, swung on her parallel bars. Brett set the juice on the coffee table and began to sign.

"Stop that, Cee Cee. This is not the time to play."

She doubled her antics, adding sound effects.

"She's unusually agitated. Did anything happen while I was in the kitchen?"

"No. She just started cutting up. I may have to give her something to calm her down."

"I'd rather not resort to that if I can help it."

Brett and Malone went inside her enclosure, and she led them on a merry pursuit that ended in a tussle with them both. She dropped the shiny object at Malone's feet.

"Hey . . ." He picked up the earring. "Where did this come from?"

Brett stared at the earring, remembering how its mate had looked against Ruth's skin . . . and how much he'd wanted her, how much he wanted her still.

In that brief moment when Brett let his guard down, Malone saw naked desire on his brother's face. His jaw tightened and his hands balled into fists.

"No wonder you didn't want to donate sperm."

"What are you talking about?"

"You play the almighty saint, not wanting to get involved in my little *problem,* and all the while you're carrying my wife's earring around in your pocket. You don't want to artificially inseminate her. You want to *fuck* her."

Brett had never been so close to hitting his brother.

"Get out of this cage! But whatever you do, *don't* upset Cee Cee."

Far from being upset, Cee Cee shambled off to her nest and lay among her blankets with a smile on her face.

"Calm down, hell. My wife was here for four days. What other souvenirs did you take besides her earring?"

Brett grabbed Malone by the shoulders and shoved him onto the sofa.

"Don't move!" He whirled back around and fastened Cee Cee's enclosure, then hauled Malone up by the front of his shirt and marched him into his office. "I won't listen to you making filthy accusations about a woman who has been nothing but good to you. No, not just good. She's been a saint. Putting up with your drinking, your childishness." Brett banged his fists on the top of his desk. A can of pencils overturned and rolled to the floor. "How dare you besmirch her honor—and mine!"

Malone had never seen Brett so mad. But he was pretty damned pissed himself.

"Are you telling me you kept a beautiful woman like Ruth up here for four days and didn't *once* give in to your animal instincts?"

"The thing that separates us from the animals is conscience."

"You don't deny it?"

"I won't dignify it with a denial."

Malone tossed the earring onto the desk. "How are you going to explain that?"

"Cee Cee."

"Oh, sure. Blame the ape."

The way Brett looked at him made Malone feel like a worm. Now that he'd had time to think, he knew Brett would never touch Ruth, even if he wanted to. He was too damned noble, too damned honorable.

Silence thundered between them. When it became painfully obvious to him that for once Brett was not going to come to his rescue, Malone rubbed his hand over his tired face.

"I guess I made a mistake, huh?"

"A mistake? I'm not going to let you get by with calling your behavior a *mistake*."

"All right. All right. I apologize. I had no right to jump to conclusions. Ruth would never betray me, and neither would you. I'm sorry. That's all I can say."

"That's all that's necessary." Brett put a hand on his shoulder.

"I guess this means you won't be giving me any seed for a little crop of Cordays?"

Brett knew he should say no. Malone had given him the perfect opportunity to back out of the deal.

A shaft of moonlight glinted on Ruth's earring. He could picture her bending over her notes, golden earrings gleaming against her skin, her chair pushed far enough away from her desk to accommodate the child she carried in her womb.

His child. It could be no other.

"No. I haven't changed my mind. Have you?"

"Hell, no." Feeling foolishly close to tears, Malone hugged Brett. "What would I do without a brother like you?"

"I hope neither of us ever has to find out."

57.

LOS ANGELES

THE REPORT LAY OPEN ON HIS DESK. Max picked it up and read it once more. His man had been thorough. Everything was there: the name of the doctor, the day, even the precise hour when Ruth Corday had walked into a clinic in Nairobi and become impregnated with donor sperm.

If she'd stayed with him, she would never have had reason to use another man's sperm. But no matter. She was young. She could have more.

He folded the report carefully, then filed it along with the rest. Outside his window he could see the florist's van bringing the twice-weekly delivery of white roses. The entire house, even the exercise room, was full of their fragrance.

Max mounted the stationary bike and began to pedal. It took him twenty minutes to work up a sweat. He prided himself on having the body of a man twenty years his junior.

It was easy to stay in shape when he had a purpose.

The rhythm of the wheels hypnotized him. Each rotation whispered her name.

Max pedaled harder and harder. Underneath his sweat suit, his erection was so huge, it was almost painful.

"Soon, Ruth," he said. "Very soon."

58.

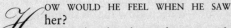

HOW WOULD HE FEEL WHEN HE SAW her?

On his brother's front porch Brett paused in the process of knocking. He could go back to his camp now. No one would ever know he'd been there.

Leave.

He couldn't see her now, not knowing what he knew. She'd look at him and see it in his face.

From inside came the sound of music, a haunting blues tune sung in a low, throaty voice. Ruth singing. The lamplight gleaming on her hair. A tender blue vein pulsing in her throat.

He felt like weeping.

When the song ceased, he heard his brother's voice.

"Play something lively, Ruth. Something to celebrate."

"Let her play what she wants to. Eleanor always told me the only time she ever got *her* way was when she was pregnant."

"I didn't say that. You made that up, Joseph Corday."

The sound of his family's laughter drifted out to him. They were all in high spirits, celebrating.

If he didn't go in, they'd wonder why. Steeling himself for the sight of her, Brett pushed open the door.

"Well, look who's here." Malone left his place beside the piano and clasped Brett's shoulder. "What took you so long, bro?"

"Cee Cee was in one of her moods." He realized suddenly that the secret he kept was already starting to erode the family. Now he was reduced to lying. "Hello, everybody. Ruth . . ."

She lifted her eyes to his, and he caught a fleeting glimpse of something deep inside, something immeasurably sad.

Brett couldn't tear his eyes away from her. She carried his seed. Though she was months away from showing, she already had the look of a woman carrying a child in her womb—a deep glow that transformed her. She had always been a beautiful woman, but now she was radiant.

"Brett . . ." She left the piano and took his hands, her natural Southern charm overcoming whatever obstacles she might have felt. "I'm so glad you could come."

"I wouldn't have missed this celebration."

"We don't even know if there's anything to celebrate yet, but Malone insisted."

"Hell, yes, there's something to celebrate."

Malone put his arm around her waist and dragged her close. Her eyes never left Brett's.

"How can you be so sure?" Joseph asked, teasing.

"Because Ruth made up her mind to get pregnant, and when she makes up her mind to something, it's as good as done."

Although it would be a while before her pregnancy could be officially confirmed, Ruth already *knew,* had known from the moment a stranger's seed entered her body. It was as if she and the son she would have were communicating in some secret way.

With her hand on her womb, a sweet, deep joy flooded

her . . . and the most unutterable sadness she had ever known, as if her unborn son were pushing her toward Brett and away from him at the same time.

"Never underestimate the power of a woman," Eleanor said.

"Especially a Corday woman." Joseph winked at her.

"Especially a Corday," she agreed. "We're so happy about this baby, Ruth. It will give us all something to think about besides gorillas."

"Are you saying I spend too much time in the jungle, Eleanor?"

"No, Joseph, I didn't say that. You did."

"Ha. My kid will have to take a map to find either one of his grandparents. You *both* spend too much time in the wild."

"Are you saying we're getting too old?" Joseph patted his gray hair.

"No, Joseph. Malone didn't say that—*you* did."

Eleanor was glad to see her family together again, laughing. It had been a long time since they'd been together—not since Margaret Anne Bellafontaine's disastrous visit. It was amazing to her that a tiny unborn baby could accomplish what all her planning and scheming could not. Family unity. Family harmony.

Her oldest son was unusually quiet, even for him. It didn't take a genius to know the reason, but Eleanor had long since stopped worrying about that. Not that she ever had any reason in the first place, knowing her son as well as she did—and knowing Ruth as she'd come to. Over and over she had shown her loyalty to her husband.

"You've hardly said a word, Brett," Eleanor said, trying to draw him into the center of the family circle.

"He's still getting used to the idea of being an uncle." Malone clapped his brother on the shoulder. "Right, Brett?"

"Right."

Brett couldn't look at Ruth. In one blinding moment he understood the enormity of what he had done: In giving his brother what he wanted, he had betrayed the woman he loved.

If seeing her now was unbearable, what would it be like

after the baby was born? How would he feel to hear his child calling another man Daddy . . . even if that man was his brother?

"What are you going to name the baby?" Joseph asked.

"Malone," Ruth said, careful to keep her eyes on her husband. "After his father."

Brett sat in his chair as stiff as a jungle animal somebody had stuffed and mounted for display. He had deliberately chosen a chair that turned his blind side to Ruth, but it didn't help. When he'd slipped in the back door of the clinic in Nairobi, he'd emptied himself of more than his seed: He'd emptied himself of his heart. Now there was no hope for them.

There never had been, really.

He wondered that nobody could see his rage. He wondered how it was possible to love a woman . . . and hate her at the same time.

"See, I told you. Not only did she make up her mind to have a child, but she's already made up her mind it's a boy." For the first time in his life Malone was the center of attention, and he took full advantage, moving to the middle of the room like an actor on a stage. "We're going to take a vacation in Hawaii, just the three of us, and when we get back, Ruth's belly will be so big, I'll have to have help getting her through the front door."

"At three months?" Joseph turned to his wife, grinning. "Eleanor, didn't you teach this boy about the birds and the bees?"

"No, Joseph. *You* did."

Joseph laughed. "Let that be a lesson to you, Malone. No matter what you do, everything's always going to be your fault."

"I already know that, but I don't care. The kissing and making up is worth it. . . . As I was saying . . . Hey, it's about time somebody else said something around here. I'm running out of breath."

"What you're running out of is hot air," Joseph said.

"Malone's right. It *is* about time somebody else took the floor," Brett said, standing up.

No matter what else he felt, one thing was certain: He loved his brother. He would *always* love his brother.

Ruth had made punch for the occasion. When Eleanor saw his intent, she helped him pour and pass around the glasses. Brett lifted his high.

"I propose a toast to Malone Corday, the finest brother a man could ever have, and to his wife, Ruth . . ." He almost lost his courage when he looked at her. Unconsciously, she pressed her hand against her womb. ". . . a wonderful sister-in-law, and to their unborn child. May he possess his mother's beauty and intelligence, his father's strength and courage, and his own passion for life that will lift him out of the ordinary and into the realms of angels."

The Cordays intertwined arms and lifted their glasses, and Ruth found herself linked to the man she was married to, and the man she loved. The thought of her baby carried her through.

Though Ruth had conceived her child partially as a means of cementing a shaky marriage, the moment her egg had received the donor sperm, she had loved the baby for himself. He was a separate person, pure and innocent, and she would move heaven and earth to see that Brett's wish for him came true.

Strength poured through her, and she knew that whatever happened, she would endure.

59.

HAWAII

EARING A PANAMA HAT WITH A RED ribbon and a loose smock embroidered with red and yellow birds, Ruth moved among the flower and fruit stalls, her arms loaded with packages. She had officially completed all work on her doctorate that day, and later she and Malone would celebrate. She spotted a large display of lokelani, heavenly rose. The small pink flowers were innocent looking, sweetly scented, perfectly formed. They would make a beautiful centerpiece.

She purchased enough for a bouquet and added that to her growing mound of packages.

He stood behind one of the stalls watching her. She had grown even more beautiful with age, more desirable. It pleased him to know this . . . and to feel the passion that flowed through him hot as lava. She paused to heft a large coconut, and her mountain of packages tilted precariously.

Max moved quickly, coming behind her and wrapping one arm around her waist to catch the bundles before they fell.

"Let me help you with those, Ruth."

Her entire body stiffened. She turned slowly, her eyes as wide and frightened as when she'd first awakened in his bed in New Orleans.

Her fear pleased him. It meant he still had power over her; it meant he could still control her.

"I don't need your help." She jerked away from him so fast, her packages toppled. On her knees, she glared at him. "Leave, Max."

Laughing, he knelt beside her close enough that his leg touched hers. Explosions of pleasure made him actually groan aloud.

"You disgust me," she said.

"Your face gives you away, Ruth. That flush is not disgust, it's desire. I've seen it enough to know."

"Bastard." She struggled to rise with her unwieldy packages, but the slight bulge in her abdomen hampered her.

"A woman in your condition shouldn't get upset."

Ruth went deathly still. She'd chosen the loose smock for comfort rather than need. At three months she was barely showing.

"I don't know what you're talking about," she said.

"Three months ago you received donor sperm at a clinic in Nairobi because Malone Corday can't impregnate you. How does it feel to be carrying the child of somebody you don't even know, Ruth?"

She felt as if her world had turned upside down. There was no need to ask how he knew. "How" didn't matter. *Why* was the important question.

"Don't look so upset, sweetheart." His hand was on her arm, rubbing back and forth, hypnotizing her. She couldn't have moved if a hurricane were threatening to blow the island away. "The child doesn't matter to me. We can still have our own."

"You're insane," she whispered.

"You love me, Ruth, just as I've always loved you." His hands were on her face now, tracing her cheeks, touching her lips. If she moved, she might start screaming. As she had so many years before, she vanished to her private inner world and left behind her shell.

"There's no one else in the world for you, sweetheart. No one else can make you feel the way I do. Soon you'll realize that. And when you do, you'll come to me."

"Never!"

"Your house is waiting for you, the bedroom an exact replica of the one in New Orleans, every room filled with white roses."

She thought she would suffocate from the fragrance of roses. Her stomach heaved, and she threw her bouquet of lokelani as far away as she could.

"Remember how it was with us, sweetheart? Remember how you loved to please me?"

A wave of dizziness washed over her, and she wrapped her arms around herself. Her distended abdomen was a vivid reminder of the child she carried, a helpless unborn baby totally dependent on her. Suddenly strength poured through her, and she rose to face her old adversary.

"I never loved to please you, Max. What you did was rape, not love."

"No. It was always love. Always."

"What I did was make the best of a horrible situation. I don't have to do that anymore, Max. You have no control over me now. None."

Max smiled.

"I'm glad to see that the Virungas haven't changed you. One of the things I always loved best about you was your spunk."

"Go screw yourself, Max."

Two of Ruth's packages were still on the ground, but she didn't care. She walked away from him as fast as she could.

"That's right, Ruth. Walk away. Go back to that weak husband of yours. He's probably in your little cottage on Diamond Head gargling mouthwash so you won't notice the liquor on his breath."

Ruth felt as if all the air had been socked out of her.

Malone was drinking again—had been since six weeks after they'd arrived in Waikiki. Slowly she turned back to
Max.

"That's right, Ruth. I know everything about you. I
know every move you make. I even know that you use
your pregnancy as an excuse not to have sex with your
husband."

"Why are you doing this to me? Why can't you let me
alone?"

"Abandon you to a man who sits in beach bars and
whines about how his wife won't fuck him?"

Moving like a zombie, Ruth went to a bench underneath a banyan tree and sat down. Nothing was more
fatiguing than fear and loss of hope.

"Don't cry, sweetheart. I can't stand to see you cry."

"I'm not crying."

Max sat beside her and offered her his handkerchief.

"I'd rather have snot running down my chin than use
anything you've touched."

He threw back his head and laughed. "I hope that
kid you're carrying is exactly like you. You're full of courage."

"No, I'm not. If I were full of courage, I'd have turned
you in years ago for rape, and you'd be behind bars."

"You could never do that to me. I've been too important in your life."

When she was seven, she'd thought he was the most
wonderful man in the world. She remembered sitting
around the campfire with the other Brownie Scouts and
thinking he was the handsomest daddy there.

"I loved you like a father, Max." She grabbed his handkerchief and wiped her nose. "You could have been a wonderful part of my life. You could have been a grandfather
to my child."

"I'll be a father to him."

"He already has a father."

"Who? Do you know who, Ruth?"

Max had always had the uncanny ability to discern
what she was thinking. How many nights had she lain
awake beside Malone, trying to pretend she didn't smell

the liquor on his breath and wondering about the father of her child?

She wadded up the handkerchief and handed it back to Max. The minute she had conceived, all her choices had been made. There were no options open to her now.

"Malone is his father, Max."

He sat down beside her, close enough so that his leg pressed against hers.

Run. Run.

She was halfway out of her seat before she realized that Max no longer had any power over her. The healing process that had begun when she had told Brett about the rape was now complete. While she'd slept and dreamed and lived her life, the poison of her past had gradually drained away, if not leaving her whole, at least leaving her clean.

She looked at the smirk on Max's face a full two minutes; then she reached into her purse and pulled out a pencil.

"Going to make a shopping list, Ruth? Remember to put down those two packages you dropped in the dirt at the market."

"Not a shopping list, Max. This is a different kind of list."

It was her turn to smile. Watching him, she held the pencil aloft, making him wait, making him squirm. When sweat began to roll down his face, she said softly, "How does it feel, Max?"

"How does what feel?"

"When someone else has the power?"

"You don't have the power, sweetheart. You're pregnant and vulnerable and far away from home. I'm here to take care of you."

"Are you, now?"

She skewered him with her eyes. He wasn't expecting that. He held on as long as he could; then he shifted his gaze downward. Trying not to look beaten, he folded his handkerchief carefully, then stuffed it back into his pocket.

She noticed that his hand trembled. Max was nothing but an old man. A harmless old man.

"I've always taken care of you, Ruth." Remembering how it had been between them, Max felt his confidence returning. "I know how to take care of you like no other man. Remember, sweetheart? Remember how you begged for me to take care of you?"

"I remember a scared, vulnerable little girl that you took advantage of, Max. I remember the pain and the fear and the shame. Well, I'm not that scared little girl anymore."

"You're a beautiful woman." She smiled at him, and his hard-won bravado began to waver. "My woman," he added, though he didn't sound as if he were convinced.

"Guess again, Max."

Ruth lifted the pencil as high as her arm could reach, then swung it down hard, driving the pencil straight toward his groin.

"What the . . . !"

He tried to scramble off the bench, but she was too fast for him. The sharp lead point ripped through his pants, tore a chunk off his hide, then broke with a loud snap against the wooden bench.

"Darn. I missed." Laughing, she threw the pencil away.

"You almost skewered my cock!"

Still laughing, she stood up.

"No, Max. I was merely marking you off my list. If I'd wanted to skewer your cock, I'd have aimed a little more to the right." Her laughter gone, she leaned toward him so there would be no question in his mind as to who held the power. "When I was thirteen, I used to stand on the pitcher's mound and aim for a quarter on home plate. I could hit it every time, Max. Still can. Remember that."

She walked off with that long-legged stride of hers, not hurried but loose and easy. Veering toward the marketplace, she retrieved her lost packages; then, with a toss of her head, she strolled away.

Watching her almost took the sting out of his leg. God, she was a woman worth waiting for.

After she'd vanished, he realized his leg hurt like hell. He sat on the bench until most of the pain and some of the humiliation abated; then he got up slowly and set off toward the beach.

It was almost sunset, his favorite time of day to walk. He would walk three miles, then have a light dinner of fish and fruit.

In time Ruth would get over her little snit. Meanwhile he had to stay in shape. Rearing children took energy.

Ruth would be home soon. Malone pulled the crumpled telegram from his pocket and read it for the hundredth time. "WHERE IS THE MERCHANDISE STOP OUR PATIENCE RUNS THIN." No need for a signature. He knew who had sent it and why.

He stuffed the message back into his pocket and took another long swig of liquor, then stuck the bottle on the top shelf of his closet behind a stack of T-shirts. In the bathroom he gargled mouthwash and was just finishing up when he heard the car door slam.

"Malone?"

She stood sideways in the doorway, balancing a load of packages. At that angle and with the afternoon sun framing her, her belly looked bigger than it was. Big with his brother's child. Every time Malone looked at her, he felt a sense of failure.

He forced himself to smile as he walked toward her and kissed her high on the cheek, his face turned into her hair so she wouldn't smell his breath.

"Hi, darling. How did it go?"

"Great."

She put her packages on the table, then sank onto the sofa and propped up her feet. He took one into his lap and began to massage.

He could do these small things for Ruth if he didn't think too much. He could pretend she was actually growing big with his child.

"Do I have to call you Dr. Corday now?" he asked.

"Only when you want to get on my good side."

"Dr. Corday, I got a couple of rib eyes for the celebration dinner, and, Dr. Corday, I also got your favorite ice cream—coconut with macadamia nuts. And as if that's not all, Dr. Corday—"

"Stop. . . . Enough, already."

Malone could always make her laugh. With her feet in his lap and the sun shining on his obstinate cowlick, she could almost forget about her encounter with Max, almost forget that Malone smelled heavily of mouthwash.

"Where are the flowers?" he asked. "I thought you were getting flowers."

What would happen if she told him the truth? *I ran into the man who raped me when I was thirteen,* she'd say. And then she'd lean on his shoulder and expect him to act like Brett. But he was not Brett, and she wasn't brave enough to add another problem to a marriage already reeling under the weight of them.

"I . . . forgot."

"Another symptom of pregnancy?"

"I suppose."

"Who needs flowers when you're in the room?" He nuzzled her neck. "Hmmm, you smell good." Closing his eyes to shut out the sight of her pregnancy, he slid his hand under her skirt.

She caught his hand and held it still.

"Malone . . ."

He knew what she was going to say. *Not now.* He didn't want to hear her turn him down.

"Why don't I start dinner? You look as if you need an early bedtime tonight." He left the sofa quickly.

"Yes. A good night's sleep is just what I need."

When she started off the sofa, he motioned her back.

"You sit right there, keep your feet up. I'll do all the cooking tonight."

The fact was, as much as he loved her, he didn't want to watch the way she moved with his brother's child inside her. She had a habit of shielding her abdomen with her hands, as if she were protecting the unborn baby even from him. In spite of that, in spite of the thickening in the middle that had nothing to do with him, he couldn't look at her without wanting to throw her onto the floor and make wild love to her.

What would happen if he just came right out and said, "Ruth, I'm tired of your frigidity, and I'm having a hard time because you're pregnant with another man's child, and I feel like a failure most of the time because no matter what I do, I'll never be as good as Brett at anything, but I love you more than I've ever loved another person, so please let's just drop all this pretense and start from scratch?"

What would happen was that his wife might walk out the door. And he couldn't stand that. He'd die if he lost her.

And so he stood in the doorway and smiled . . . and wished for a drink of whiskey.

"Thanks," she said. "You're a . . ."

"I know. I'm just a natural-born sweetheart."

Ruth watched Malone fire up the grill and wished she was anywhere except in a cottage on Diamond Head with her husband. How starry-eyed she'd been when they'd first arrived almost three months earlier. How full of hope and dreams and plans. How naive.

No matter where they were, no matter what they did, no matter how many children she bore, nothing was going to change between them. What would happen if she walked out to the patio and said, "Malone, nothing is ever going to work out between us, even after the baby comes, so I'm going to leave before both of us become completely disillusioned"? She could make her own life, have the baby by herself, learn to stop looking over her shoulder at shadows.

She'd coped with Max today. No, she'd done more than cope. She'd triumphed.

Couldn't she do as well with her life?

She got up off the sofa, and she went to the patio door. "Malone . . ."

He looked up, spatula in one hand and a steak in the other.

"What is it, sweetheart?"

"I was just thinking . . ."

"You're always thinking. That's one of the reasons I love you. And I *do* love you, Dr. Corday. More than life itself."

She leaned against the door, drained of resolve.

"I was just thinking . . . Can we go back to Africa tomorrow instead of next Tuesday?"

"I don't see why not. Anxious to get home?"

"Yes."

If she could get back to Africa, maybe things would be better.

60.

THE VIRUNGAS

THE STORM SWEPT THROUGH THE Virungas with the ruthless intent of a thief, robbing the night of all light and stealing the sleep of the Cordays. Ruth tossed and turned in her bed, fighting the covers as well as her dreams. Something was chasing her, some unknown horror that wanted to suck her into a black void.

On the mountaintop Brett left his bedroom and stood in front of Cee Cee's enclosure for five minutes before he was satisfied that she was all right. Disturbed and not knowing why, he sat at his desk naked and tried to read his latest reports on Cee Cee. After ten minutes he tossed them aside and stared into the darkness, listening to the storm.

Ruth was home. That was his problem. Home with his brother. He hadn't seen her, couldn't bear to see her. In his present foul mood he wished the storm would last forever. Then he'd have an excuse to hole up and never see how she looked carrying his child.

In the main compound Eleanor slept on her side with one arm outflung as if she were holding a camera. Dressed in rain gear, Joseph stood looking down at her. She was still a beautiful woman. She could have had any man in the world, and he marveled at his good fortune that she'd chosen him.

She mumbled something in her sleep, and he bent over and smoothed her hair back from her forehead.

"Joseph?" Groggy, she opened one eye.

"Shh. Go back to sleep."

"What're you doing?"

"Just going out to check on the gorillas."

"In this storm?"

"I heard Old Doby a little while ago. He didn't sound right."

"Can't it wait till morning?"

"Don't worry. I'll be back in a little while."

He kissed her cheek. She snuggled back into her covers and was asleep again by the time he got to the bedroom door.

Outside, he pulled his collar up and his hat down against the rain. It fell in great, hard sheets, slanting from the east, slicing into him like knives. He was getting too old to be trekking the jungles on nights like this. He started to go back inside; then, chiding himself for an old fool, he set out in the storm.

The night was perfect for what Malone had to do. Huddled under a copse of trees on the slopes of Mount Karisimbi, he watched Old Doby herd his group into the shelter of the trees. Six of his females had recently given birth. If they could take four, Malone would more than satisfy Chu Ling's desire for "merchandise," and perhaps he wouldn't have to harvest any more gorillas until next spring.

Shambu glanced at the group, impatient to be on about

his business so he could get out of the storm. The Batwas hunkered on the jungle floor, chattering among themselves, totally unconcerned about either the job they were to do or the weather. As long as they got what was promised them, they were happy.

"Wait until Doby settles in," Malone said, "and then try to take the four babies from the youngest females. They'll be less aggressive than the older ones."

"What about the big guy? He's a fierce-looking son of a bitch." Shambu asked. He was nervous about stealing the young gorillas without first getting rid of the male silverback.

"Let him alone." Malone remembered how many times Old Doby's loud chest drumming had awakened him in the middle of the night, and how he used to rail against the inconvenience. Now, though, the thought of destroying something so magnificent as Doby made him sick at his stomach. He slipped a flask out of his pocket and took a drink to ease his conscience.

"If we kill all the male silverbacks every time we take the babies, there soon won't be any babies to take."

"I don't like it." Shambu pulled his panga from his belt. "Some of us will die if he gets aroused while we're taking the babies."

Malone knew that was true, but he didn't tell Shambu so. He wished he'd brought tranquilizer darts, but the continued success of the scheme depended on perpetuating the myth that poachers were taking the babies, and poachers didn't use tranquilizer darts.

"No one is going to die. Just be calm and patient, and we can do this without any problems."

Shambu looked as if he might challenge Malone, but the moment passed quickly, and they all settled down to wait their chance. By the time it came, they were drenched and dispirited. Shambu had not ceased grumbling, and even the pygmies were looking mutinous.

"Now," Malone said.

The pygmies crept silently toward the fringes of Old Doby's group where two of the females were huddled together with their young. There was a whirring sound as they hurled their spears. With startled grunts two of the females fell in a pool of their own blood. Shambu and one of the pygmies snatched the babies just as they began to scream. Old Doby stirred.

"Cover their mouths," Malone yelled, but it was already too late.

The giant male silverback charged, his scream of outrage echoing through the rain forest like thunder.

"Get him," Shambu yelled, dropping the baby gorilla and reaching for his spear.

"Get into the Jeeps." Malone snatched the baby and ran toward the waiting vehicles as fast as he could go. "We can outdistance him."

Shambu was sick of taking orders from a white man who had no balls, and the pygmies hadn't listened to the orders in the first place. Their reaction was swift and automatic. Three spears hurled through the air, catching Old Doby in the chest and both legs. Still, he continued his charge.

"No! Not Doby! Stop!" Huddled beside the Jeep, Malone watched as Shambu's spear felled the huge gorilla.

With shouts of glee the pygmies were all over him, taking their bloody trophies. The remainder of the gorilla group scattered in fear. Malone leaned his head against the side of the Jeep and retched.

"Stop! In the name of God! Stop!" Joseph Corday emerged through the rain like a wild man, arms flailing, glasses teetering on the edge of his nose, and raincoat flapping behind him.

He charged into the midst of the pygmies, fists flying. Paralyzed by horror, Malone watched as one of the pygmies held Joseph on the ground with a spear. In an instant his entire world had crumbled at his feet. His father hadn't seen him yet. If he left now, he might get away and no one would ever know.

No one except him.

What would they do to Joseph? If they killed him, could Malone live with the guilt?

With a courage he never knew he had, Malone charged into the group of pygmies, the baby gorilla still clinging around his neck.

"Stop, you asshole bastards! That's my father."

The pygmies paid him no attention. It was Shambu who saved Joseph's life.

"Don't kill him," he said. "It's the Old Gorilla Man."

"Malone?" Joseph lifted his head, and in one swift glance he took in the entire scene—the slain females, the orphaned babies, and the cages. He crucified his son with a glance.

"I had to do it," Malone said.

"You *had* to? In the name of God. Why?"

"It would have been done with or without my cooperation. At least with me in charge, the Cordays still had some control over the gorillas."

"How could you participate in this slaughter? How could you kill the animals we've worked all our lives to preserve and protect?"

The baby around his neck felt like a stone. The entire family would see his deeds as his father had, as a betrayal of the most heinous kind. Eleanor had never had a very high opinion of him, but Brett . . . Malone couldn't bear to think what his brother would do and say.

He made a last-ditch effort to convince his father that he wasn't the total failure Joseph's eyes accused him of being.

"Look on it as sacrificing a few for the benefit of the rest. The money . . ."

"You took money for this?"

Money tainted in blood. The rubies he'd been so proud of had been tossed carelessly into a drawer in the bedside table. Ruth had worn them only once, and then at his insistence.

At the thought of his wife Malone sank to his knees. She would leave him now. There was no question about it. He'd as soon be dead. Covering his face with his hands, he began to cry.

"It's not too late, Malone. We'll turn this around. We can go to the authorities. . . ."

Joseph's voice ended in a gurgle. Malone jerked his head up in time to see his father fall backward, his throat slit and his head resting in the lap of his favorite gorilla. Two magnificent creatures, united in death.

"You bastards!"

He had no weapon, but he went into the midst of the murderers anyhow. For a moment he believed he was eighteen again, fighting his own battles. If he'd fought his own battles, maybe Brett wouldn't have lost an eye.

A solid wall of bodies closed in on him. The last thing he heard was the chant in Swahili.

"Kill . . . kill . . . kill."

61.

BRETT FOUND THEM IN THE EARLY HOURS of morning. Except for the blood, Joseph looked as if he might be taking a nap on the great furry lap of Old Doby. Malone lay nearby, crumpled as if he were a set of dirty rags someone had tossed onto the floor of the jungle.

Rage and fear almost blinded him as he raced into the clearing. Blood spattered the legs of his pants and threatened his footing. He knew before he got to Joseph that his father was dead. His eyes stared sightlessly at the sky, and his body was already growing stiff.

"Malone . . ." He bent over his brother. The pulse was faint and thready.

"Brett?" Malone's voice was a hoarse whisper. "I didn't mean . . ."

"Shh. Don't talk. Save your strength."

"Brett . . . I . . . I . . . love . . . you."

Brett cradled Malone fiercely against his

chest, willing his own strength into his brother. How could he have stayed on his mountaintop while this was happening? How could he not have known?

"I'm going to get you to a doctor, Malone. Hang on."

His brother was no burden to him as he carried him through the jungle. Brett had left his Jeep two miles back, preferring, as always, to walk through the rain forest. He always saw more when he was walking.

The vision of his father haunted him as he raced down the mountain, but he didn't dare go back for him. He didn't even dare stop for Eleanor and Ruth. Every minute was crucial for Malone.

Lorena was just arriving for work when Brett pulled up in front of the clinic in Ruhengeri.

"My God," she said when she saw his face.

"Help me, Lorena."

She had never seen Brett Corday defenseless. Now he stood in front of her with all his feelings showing, naked and raw.

"Don't let my brother die."

One look at Malone Corday told her it was already too late.

"We'll do everything we can. He'll probably have to be airlifted to Nairobi." She put her hand over Brett's. "Don't expect miracles."

"Brett . . . ," Malone whispered. "I'm dying."

"No! I'm not going to let you die. Do you hear me, Malone? I'm not going to let you die!"

62.

NAIROBI

"Promise . . . ," Malone whispered. His breath came in labored spurts. Ruth held on to him as hard as she could, willing him to live.

With a mighty effort Malone fixed his brother with a bright-blue stare.

"Take care of Ruth."

"I promise."

She couldn't bear to look at Brett, couldn't bear to think what all this might mean.

Ruth heard the death rattle in Malone's chest, and a fury such as she had never known rose in her. She wanted to shake some sense into her husband, to berate him for dying before they'd had a chance to straighten things out, before their child was even born. Instead she pressed her cheek next to his.

"You're not going to die, Malone. I've got you, I've got you."

"Ruth . . ."

"I'm here."

"Is the sun shining?"

The sun had long since disappeared behind a cloud as if it knew what was happening in the narrow hospital room and wanted to hide its face.

"Yes, my darling, the sun is shining."

"Ruth . . . I want to be . . . buried . . . in sunlight."

"Malone . . ."

"Promise. . . . *Promise.*"

"I promise."

He was so still, so cold. She pressed her upper body flat against his, hoping her warmth, her vitality, would seep into him.

"He's gone," Eleanor said.

"No." Ruth squeezed his hand and felt the slightest answering pressure.

"Ruth . . ." She had to press her ear to his mouth in order to hear him. "I . . . love . . . you."

She closed her eyes. Why was it that love had so many faces?

"I love you, too, Malone." The stillness of death was upon him. Ruth lifted her face and stared at him. Had he heard her? "I love you, Malone. I love you."

"Ruth." Brett put his hands on her shoulders. "It's over."

"No." She shook his hands off. "I want him to hear me. I want him to know."

"He knew you loved him."

The tears she'd held back since early that morning, when Brett had come to her door and whisked her off to the plane that would take them to Nairobi, suddenly found release. She tasted them in her mouth, her throat.

"Did he hear me?" she whispered.

Brett hated his brother for dying, hated him for abandoning Ruth and the baby, hated him for severing the lifelong bond between them. But most of all, he hated himself. He'd always taken care of Malone. And now, when his brother needed him most, Brett had failed.

"Did he hear me say the words?"

Ruth grabbed Brett's lapels, then collapsed against his chest. She clung to him, wetting the front of his shirt with her tears.

"He heard you, Ruth."

A lie seemed kinder than the truth. He put his arms around her, hating the small, secret exultation that rose in him.

Behind them a nurse covered Malone with a sheet.

"I want the bastards who did this," Eleanor said. "I want to see their blood run down the mountain just the way Joseph—" She covered her face with her hands. "Joseph!"

Brett put an arm around his mother, then led the two women from the hospital room. The remnants of the Corday family.

"I'll find them," he promised. "If it takes the rest of my life, I'll find them."

63.

ALABAMA

THEY BURIED JOSEPH NEAR HIS BELOVED gorillas, but because Malone had always hated the Virungas and because he wanted to be buried in sunlight, they carried his body home to Eleanor's people in Alabama. Ruth watched as they lowered him into the grave next to his maternal grandfather.

"He always loved this place," Eleanor said. "When he was a little boy, he'd beg to stay here so he wouldn't have to go back to Africa. Maybe I should have let him stay . . . and then none of this . . ."

Eleanor broke down, crying. She'd aged since the deaths of Malone and Joseph, grown more fragile—smaller, somehow—as if tragedy had shrunk her.

"None of this is your fault." Ruth wrapped her arms around her mother-in-law and led her away from the cemetery.

Watching from the other side of the grave, Brett kept his distance. Grieving alone. He envied the women their ability to share grief. But he had to work out his problems alone.

Sunlight poured across the newly turned grave, and mockingbirds called to each other from the branch of a large oak tree that guarded the old iron gates. Brett knelt on the fresh earth for one last moment with his brother.

"I promise you I'll find the man who did this." The sound of the wind in the leaves might have been Malone's voice, whispering one name. *Ruth. Ruth.*

"I'll honor that promise, too, but I hope you never knew what you asked of me. I hope you never knew."

A bright-red cardinal rose from the oak tree and hovered over the grave, its wings flashing in the sun.

"You're in the sunlight now, Malone. You'll always be in the sun."

He stood over the grave for a long time, silently bidding his brother farewell; then he walked the short distance to the farmhouse. Ruth and Eleanor were seated at the kitchen table, nursing cups of hot tea, his mother's eyes red from weeping. Ruth had not wept since the day Malone had died in the hospital room in Nairobi. Instead she seemed to grow stronger each day. He imagined her at thirteen, reshaping her life after she'd been sexually abused. Adversity robbed some people of will, but for the strong, it renewed their courage.

Malone had not known his wife at all. Ruth Corday didn't need anyone to take care of her. She was perfectly capable of doing it all by herself.

He sat down in the chair opposite Ruth, glad her condition was hidden by the kitchen table.

"I think I'm going to stay here awhile," Eleanor said. "It'll give me a chance to spend some time with Mother in the nursing home, and Aunt Katherine says there's plenty of room here for me."

"That sounds like a good idea to me." The fewer people he had to worry about, the more time he'd have to look for the murderers.

"Ruth, darling, why don't you stay here with me?"

"Thank you, but no, I'm going home."

The sense of loss almost overwhelmed Brett. How could he endure losing them both in one day—the man he loved above all others and the woman he loved more than life itself?

"Well, of course you want to go home." Eleanor squeezed Ruth's hand. "It's only natural that you'd want to be with your mother when the baby is born. Maybe I'll stay in Alabama till then and I can just drive over to Mississippi for the birth."

"I'm a Corday. Home is not Mississippi; it's with my husband's people in the Virungas."

There was a just God, after all. Brett gave silent thanks.

"It's not safe there for you with all that's happened. Brett, tell her it's not safe there."

"Mother, what happened was in the jungle, not in the compound. I think it's perfectly safe there for Ruth . . . and the baby." Did he sound too eager? Was he thinking only of himself? "However, I do agree that it would be best if she stayed either here or in Mississippi."

"It doesn't matter whether you want me there or not; I'm going back to the Virungas."

"I didn't say I didn't want you there, Ruth."

They stared at each other, their eyes reflecting possibilities that neither of them could bear to contemplate.

"This baby will be born in the place his father and grandfather devoted their lives to. He'll know what it means to love the mountain gorilla, what it means to be a Corday."

In that kitchen in Alabama, the sunset poured through the west window and fell across her like a blessing. She stood up and leaned across the table for emphasis, and her belly, enlarged with his child, made him want to weep. He ached to touch the swollen flesh where his seed had found fertile ground, to claim mother and child as his own.

"I will not run away like a frightened rabbit. If I do, then the men who killed my husband have won. They've robbed me of a home, and my child of his rightful heritage. I'm pregnant and widowed, not helpless. I will stay in the Virungas and carry on Malone's work."

Brett couldn't claim her, not now, perhaps not ever. Malone stood between them in death, just as he had in life.

"Can I say anything to change your mind?" he asked, hoping he couldn't.

"No. My mind is made up."

"Stubborn," Eleanor said, not without pride. "Reminds me of myself when I was young."

"You're still young, Eleanor," Ruth said. "And after you've had a time of healing, I expect you back in the Virungas helping me to give your grandchild a sense of how much his father and his grandfather wanted him and loved him."

"I'll be back—you know I will. I wouldn't miss the birth of my grandchild for anything in the world." Eleanor's face softened. "Wouldn't it be lovely to have a little girl—somebody soft and cuddly, dressed in pink ruffles?"

"You, dressing a grandchild in pink ruffles?" Brett said. "That'll be the day."

For the first time in days the three of them laughed. Eleanor always wore tailored slacks—had worn them even to the funeral.

"You don't have to worry about pink ruffles. No son of mine would be caught wearing them."

Ruth set her chin at such a determined angle that neither Eleanor nor Brett doubted for a minute that she'd have a boy.

"What will you name him?" Eleanor asked.

"Malone . . . after his father."

64.

THE VIRUNGAS

*I*T SEEMED NATURAL TO RUTH THAT SHE
be in Brett's compound. He had
been present in one way or another
in all the major events of her life. She
reached for his hand.

"Do you know what enormous respect I
have for you?"

"I'm only doing what any decent man
would do under the circumstances."

"No. You're doing more. You always
have."

Suddenly she was aware that she wasn't
merely holding his hand, she was caressing,
almost clinging. It would be too easy to
cling to Brett, to sit back and let him take
all her burdens.

She let go of him and sat down in a
chair on the other side of the room. She
was tired from the long flight, more tired
than she'd imagined she would be.

"My pregnancy seems to have sapped all my energy."

"You expect too much of yourself, Ruth. Here . . . put your feet up while I get my bedroom ready for you."

"Your bedroom?" The flush that came over her had nothing to do with fatigue.

"It's bigger than the guest bedroom. You'll be more comfortable there."

"I *will not* run you out of your bedroom."

"I insist."

"If you're going to be that stubborn, I'll leave and go back down the mountain to the house I shared with Malone."

Funny how the sound of his name put a pallor on the evening. Both of them became silent.

Sounds of the jungle drifted through the windows—the elephants trumpeting as they staked claim to the watering holes, a faint drumming as the remnants of the male silverbacks vied for dominance of scattered and disorganized gorilla groups, the muted call of the hyrax and the muffled barking of a distant duiker.

There were no other human beings for miles around. Just the two of them. Together on the mountaintop. The knowledge made Ruth guilty, as if she were betraying her husband merely by looking at Brett. She stood up and deliberately moved to his blind side so he wouldn't guess what she was thinking.

"I should go to bed," she said.

"That's a good idea."

"What time do you start work in the morning?"

"Six, but you don't have to be up that early."

"If I'm going to be a part of this research team, I intend to pull my full share of the workload. I'll see you in the morning. At six."

She moved with a slow, easy grace, her dress alternately billowing and clinging as she walked. He watched without shame. And when her bedroom door closed, he still stood looking down the hall, his memory so strong of her that he could describe the exact shape of her thigh, the precise contour of her breast, the specific size of her abdomen.

In his own bedroom he stripped and lay naked upon his bed, flat on his back, hands at his side. The red ribbon from her hat swayed against the bedpost with his slightest movement. He made himself lie perfectly still. In heaven and in hell.

He dreaded for morning to come . . . and longed for it like a child awaiting Christmas.

Cee Cee's fascination with Ruth's belly overcame her dismay at having the stink female in the compound.

"What big?" she signed, pointing to Ruth, standing just outside her cage.

Riveted, Brett stood in the doorway watching them. The day before, he hadn't let Ruth come into the cage with Cee Cee. He hadn't been sure how the gorilla would react —hadn't been sure how he would react.

He hadn't slept at all the previous night, and when he'd got up just before sunrise, he'd felt as if his head had been stuffed full of cotton wool.

He'd put on his pants, no shirt, no shoes, didn't even comb his hair, and tiptoed down the hall to check on Cee Cee—though he'd never done such a thing and knew perfectly well that she would be fast asleep.

As he'd neared Ruth's bedroom door, he'd known that was why he'd decided to check on Cee Cee—so he could walk past Ruth's door, perhaps stand outside for a moment while she slept—so close to her that only a bedroom door separated them. Realizing this, he'd started to turn around and go back. Why torture himself? he'd thought. Why risk turning the doorknob, and going inside, and pulling her so close that he couldn't tell where he left off and she began?

But he hadn't been able to go back. Forces beyond his control had pulled him onward. When he'd come close, he'd known she was not asleep. Her door had been slightly ajar and there had been a sound inside—not weeping or murmuring or any kind of sound she'd make with her mouth, but a sort of charged silence, the kind the mind makes when it's so full of emotion, it can't shut down.

Walk on by. Walk on by.

Good advice from a conscience and a mind overloaded with passion. Advice he knew he wasn't about to take.

He'd stood outside her door, riveted, as if somebody

had nailed his feet to the floor. She'd been at the window, her arms on the windowsill, her forehead pressed against the glass, backlit by the moon. Under her thin gown her legs were long and shapely, worthy of hours, years, of contemplation. In profile her face was a work of art— exquisite eyebrows perfectly arched, soft, smooth skin gleaming as if it had been polished.

But it hadn't been her legs that had held his attention, nor her face. It had been her breasts. They were heavy and ripe, the aureoles of her nipples large and dark. Nature preparing them for his child. The need that had burst through him had almost driven him to his knees.

Scarcely breathing, he'd focused on her nipples, imagined himself kneeling on the smooth bare floor in the moonlight, pulling her down with him. Though he hadn't moved an inch, he was in the room with her . . . slowly, ever so slowly easing her gown over her head, letting it fall like the torn petals of a gardenia to the polished floor. He stared at those breasts that would nourish his child, and her nipples became as hard as the hickory nuts he used to find in the fall on his grandparents' farm in Alabama.

They were so beautiful, he was almost afraid to touch them, almost afraid he had dreamed them. Everyone knew that trying to hold on to a dream only made it vanish.

And yet he couldn't resist. He would climb snowbound mountains, ford raging rivers, and march straight into the eye of a hurricane for one touch. Just one.

He put his right hand on her left breast, and it nestled there like something alive, her hard nipple pushing aggressively against his skin, and the soft, soft flesh surrounding it melting and molding itself to the shape of his palm. Her eyes grew enormous and liquid in the moonlight, and he knew that she wanted him as much as he wanted her.

This one forbidden touch was all he would allow himself, just his hand on her breast. He wanted to put his mouth where his hand was, to circle his wet tongue around her rigid nipple, then draw it deeply into his mouth, to drag softly and steadily on it until they were both moaning, to cup his other hand around the small of her back and hold her slightly bent while he pulled her breast deeply into his mouth and suckled her. As if he were a hungry child. A ravenous beast. An insatiable lover. A gentle protector. A husband.

Standing in the hallway, Brett had clenched his fists. He wanted to be her husband. He wanted to be the one who had found her in Hawaii and brought her to the Virungas. He wanted to be the one who had carried her to the marriage bed and opened her up like a flower. He wanted to be the one who had the right to plant his seed.

He'd never had any right to plant his seed in her—even if it had been done innocently and with the sanction of his brother.

At the window she'd tipped her head to one side, turning slightly as if she'd sensed she was being watched. What would he do if she turned and saw him?

He'd held his breath, waiting, his feet nailed down and his erection pointing straight up. In no condition to greet his sister-in-law. In no condition to pretend.

She hadn't turned. Instead she'd pressed her face into the windowpane, hunched her shoulders forward, and wrapped her arms around herself, hugging herself, holding on to her warmth and her grief.

With the stealth of a lion on the prowl, Brett had eased past her door and down the hall. He would never tempt fate that way again, he had vowed. As long as she stayed with him, he would be nothing more than a protective and caring brother-in-law.

That's what he'd told himself early that morning, but now she was glowing and dewy in spite of the fact that she wore no makeup, and he was having a hard time keeping his hands off her, let alone his mind.

Suppose he didn't keep his hands off her? Suppose he told her that her condition was due to him and not a stranger? What would she do?

He stood in the doorway, waiting, watching.

"I'm big because of the baby inside me, Cee Cee," she said as she signed an answer to the gorilla's question. *"This is Malone's baby."*

A sense of loss stabbed Brett like knives.

"What baby? No see baby." Cee Cee approached the bars and aggressively reached toward Ruth.

"Leave the room, Ruth," Brett said, sharper than he meant, fearful for her, for himself, for all of them.

"Leave?" She couldn't believe what she was hearing. "You're treating me like a curiosity-seeking stranger rather than an anthropologist with a Ph.D. . . . and your sister-in-law, to boot."

"That's what I said. *Leave.*"

She felt like a rag doll that somebody had punched a big hole in and let the stuffing out of. She felt as if she were standing in her cottage on the main compound and listening to Brett tell her all over again that Malone had been cut to pieces with a bush knife and was on his way to Nairobi to die. He hadn't said those words, of course, but she'd known.

Just as she now knew why he was shouting at her. It was the same reason she'd stood at the window the night before with her hand stuffed in her mouth so he wouldn't hear her crying. What she felt when she looked at Brett Corday was a melting in her bones that made everything else fade in significance. Even the baby.

She tried to tell herself such feelings were wrong, with Malone barely cold in the grave. And yet she knew that the feelings had never died, not from the moment she'd stood on this very mountaintop with Brett and felt his hand upon her cheek.

There was magic between them. Was it so wrong to want a little magic after all the terrible years?

"I'll move back from the bars," she said, "but I won't leave." She tilted her chin up at its most stubborn angle. If Brett was going to be implacable, she would be immovable.

"You'll do as I say, Ruth. Leave *now.*"

"Is it because I'm a woman that you're ordering me about, or because I'm pregnant, or because I'm a widow . . ."

Unexpectedly, her situation overwhelmed her. She felt as if the entire Gulf of Mexico had been dumped over her head.

Tears seemed to come from every part of her at once— her eyes, her nose, her mouth.

Brett held her as close and as tenderly as he would have a whimpering, shivering, orphaned puppy.

"I'm so sorry, Ruth. So very sorry."

She put her head on his shoulder and sobbed.

"It's not that . . . I'm a wimp or anything. It's just that . . . everything seems . . . too *much*."

Cradling her in his arms, he rocked back and forth.

"Cry, Ruth." Suddenly his own pain formed a tight ball in his throat. "You need to grieve for him. Both of us need to grieve for him."

She let herself go for the second time in her life. What was there about this man that made it so easy to let go? In the haven of his arms she thought how lovely it would be if she always had his arms to comfort her, his chest to lean on, his voice to reassure her. That was the way it should be. A man and a woman together, sharing the sadness as well as the joy.

"We'll get through this, Ruth. Together."

"Yes," she said. "Together."

65.

ALABAMA

*E*LEANOR WAS ON THE FRONT-PORCH SWING facing the east, staring into the distance. Luke Fisher parked his rental car under the shade of two enormous pecan trees, then stood there watching her. It was typical of Eleanor that she hadn't come to him for help. She'd always handled everything by herself. It was one of the qualities he admired most about her, as well as the one that gave him the most grief.

His feet crunched on the gravel walkway as he started toward her.

"You shouldn't have come," she said.

"You're wrong."

"I didn't ask you to come here." She pushed at her hair. It had grown longer since he'd seen her.

"I'd grow old waiting for you to ask me for help, Eleanor." He propped one foot on the bottom step of the front porch. "I decided not to grow old waiting."

She stared at him, worrying her bottom lip with her teeth.

"I'm empty, Luke. I can't give you anything. Not even encouragement."

"Did I ask for anything?"

"No."

"Eleanor, for once in your life let someone else do the giving."

"I don't know how."

"Sit back and relax. See what happens."

The breeze stirred her hair, and a mockingbird scolded two fat squirrels intent on scaling the pecan tree to get at the nuts hanging heavy on the branches. It was a peaceful setting. No wonder Eleanor had stayed holed up there for the last six weeks.

She watched the squirrels for a while, then stared at him.

"I've forgotten my manners," she said. "Won't you sit down?"

"You're entitled to forget manners, Eleanor. You're entitled to a lot of things."

"You came a long way."

"Yes. It was a long way."

"Why did you come, Luke?"

"I'd be lying if I said just to comfort you."

For the first time since the deaths of her husband and her son, Eleanor felt a stirring of hope, not for any thought of a future with Luke, not for the thought of any personal happiness. That was premature. She simply felt a movement and flow in her blood, a sign that she was still alive.

Sitting on the front porch, Luke was a study in brown —felt hat pulled low over his dark eyes, shoes dusty from traveling the back roads of Alabama, tan slacks wrinkled, his skin as weathered and tan as the bark of a pecan tree. Eleanor wished for a camera.

"At least we never lied to each other," she said. "Let's not start now."

"All right. First of all, I came because I'm your friend, and I was Joseph's friend. Friends help each other in time of need. . . . But you know that's not the only reason, don't you, Eleanor?"

She let the swing die to a stop. Her Alabama relatives had rallied around her, but they had no understanding of what it was like in Africa, of the kind of courage and strength it took to live in virtual isolation at the base of the Virungas with nothing but her family, her camera, and the gorillas. That kind of isolation fostered a deep bond that bordered on total dependency. Joseph's death had severed the bond; she'd been set adrift, a small boat without an anchor in a very large sea.

Luke understood. He'd lived that kind of life. He knew that it was not weakness on her part that held her captive in Alabama, but an attempt to renew that part of herself that was missing.

"I know," she said. "And I'm glad to see you, but . . ."

"Don't say anything, Eleanor. Just sit there." Abruptly Luke left the front porch and went to his car. When he came back, he was carrying a camera—not the cheap drugstore kind but a very expensive model, the kind Eleanor could use to focus on a leaf and capture every vein.

He knelt in front of her and slipped the camera into her hands.

"This is a start," he said. "Without a camera, a part of you is missing."

"I don't know what to say." Tears rolled down her cheeks.

"Don't say anything. Just listen."

"All right."

"You've always viewed the world through a lens. Look through it again and find your way back."

She lifted the camera, focused on his face, and snapped.

"I'm glad I'm the first thing you found, Eleanor. I take that as a good sign."

"Maybe it is, Luke. . . . Maybe it is."

She touched his cheek, and he covered her hand with his. They stayed that way for a very long time, and then they went inside to see if they could find something in the kitchen cabinets for supper.

66.

SAN FRANCISCO

"NOBODY WAS SUPPOSED TO DIE," Max said.

"It was unfortunate," Chu Ling replied. "An accident."

He refilled Max's teacup, then folded his hands across his belly and waited. He didn't know what his future relationship with this man would be, but he wasn't about to ask foolish questions. Nothing good ever came from impatience.

"You were in charge. How could you let it happen?"

"Africa is a long way from San Francisco." Chu Ling refused to make excuses.

"This is true, but I thought your men were reliable."

"Shambu was always our man, but Corday hired the Batwas."

"How did it happen?"

"The old man found them taking the gorillas. There was an argument that got out of control. Once the pygmies got the lust for blood, even Shambu couldn't handle them."

"Even if the authorities find out about Shambu and the Batwas, we're clean," Max said. "There's no way the murders can be laid at our door."

"You know this for a fact?"

"My attorney told me. I pay him a fucking fortune to know. If I can't believe what he says, I might as well throw in the towel."

Max was sweating. Chu Ling took that as a sign of weakness.

"We can still get the gorillas. Shambu wants to continue without Corday."

"No!" Max couldn't sit still. He'd always hated that he'd had to sacrifice the gorillas in order to discredit the Cordays. Now that Corday was dead, he had no interest in that illegal activity . . . nor any idea how he would get Ruth back. Alive, Corday was a sitting duck. Dead, he was a martyred saint. "I won't fund it anymore. And if he tries to take them anyhow, I'll leak it to the press. There'll be bleeding-heart preservationists all over the jungle. He won't be able to take a crap without stepping on one."

"Then our business is done?"

"Yes. Our business is done. In case anybody asks, you don't know me and I don't know you."

"Maxwell Jones? I never heard of the man."

"You ought to be in show business, Chu Ling. You're a hell of an actor."

"All smart people are actors when the need arises. It's a gift."

"Or a curse."

Outside the sun was trying to burn through an early-morning fog. Max had chosen his time and his place carefully. No one was about this hour of the day, no one except him and a few stray cats.

As he walked down the block and around the corner to

he lot where he'd parked his rental car, he thought of a
way his plan might still work.

Ruth was staying in the compound of the only remain-
ng Corday. Bring the dead down, and the one left alive
would come tumbling along with them.

And then she'd have no one to turn to except him.

67.

THE VIRUNGAS

BRETT WOKE TO THE SOUND OF RUTH'S singing. Flat on his back in bed, he let the music flow over him, into him, through him. It was a blues tune she sang in her soft, sultry voice. Something from Gershwin, he thought.

He dressed, then went down the hall to stand quietly in the doorway of Cee Cee's enclosure. Ruth and Cee Cee were totally absorbed in each other. They sat on the floor together inside the gorilla's indoor quarters, Ruth singing and weaving a red ribbon around Cee Cee's head, and Cee Cee leaning against Ruth's knee with a big smile on her face.

In the two months since Malone's death, Ruth had forged a close bond with the gorilla. Brett had tried everything he knew to make Cee Cee cooperate with Ruth: reason, cajolery, punishment, bribes. But nothing had worked . . . until one morning Cee Cee heard Ruth singing.

"What noise?" she'd signed to Brett.

"That's Ruth. She sings."

"Sing how?"

"With her mouth."

"Cee Cee sing mouth." The gorilla had opened her mouth and emitted a terrible series of sounds. Enraged by her efforts, she had pounded her chest and signed furiously. *"What sing, you show Cee Cee sing now."*

"People sing, birds sing. Gorillas don't sing."

"Yes. Cee Cee sing, teach now, me, me, me."

"Do you want Ruth to sing for you?"

"No dirty stink female bad, not sing Cee Cee." She'd poked his chest. *"You sing Cee Cee, now teach now."*

"I can't sing."

She'd given him a look of wounded dignity, then sat in the corner with her back to him, pouting. In the kitchen Ruth had continued to sing. Cee Cee had cocked her head, listening; then, embarrassed that he'd seen her interest, he'd pretended she had a bug in her ear and spent considerable time digging around with her fingers to find it. She'd even pretended she'd found one and made a great commotion of throwing it onto the floor and stomping on it.

"Brett?" Ruth had appeared in the doorway. "I've brought Cee Cee's breakfast."

Cee Cee usually galloped around her cage in delight over food, but that day she'd sat stoically in her corner pretending she had no interest in breakfast.

"What's wrong with her?" Ruth had asked.

"She wants to learn how to sing."

"Hmmm. I think that can be arranged. Do you think he'll let me give her a singing lession?"

"Let's ask her. . . . Cee Cee, Ruth will teach you to sing."

"No. You teach."

"I can't. Only Ruth can teach to sing."

Cee Cee had considered her dilemma for a while; then he'd shambled over to Brett, sat down beside his feet, and gave him a coy smile.

"*Cee Cee learn good get six bananas.*"

"*You know you can have only four.*"

"*Six.*" She'd pounded her chest. "*Me sing good, six six, six.*"

Brett had known this was the breakthrough they ha waited for in Cee Cee's relationship with Ruth, but he' also known that Cee Cee would appreciate her victor more if it was hard-won.

"*How do I know you'll sing good?*" he'd signed.

"*Cee Cee try hard, fine female gorilla sing good.*"

"*Ruth is a fine female woman.*"

"*No. Dirty stink female.*"

"*Dirty stink female won't teach Cee Cee to sing. Fin female woman will teach Cee Cee to sing.*"

Cee Cee had cocked her head to one side, considerin her options. Heaving a big sigh, she'd wrapped her arm around herself.

"*Cee Cee love fine female woman, give six bananas, six six, six.*"

"*Yes. If Cee Cee loves Ruth, Cee Cee will get six ba nanas.*"

Instead of digging into her breakfast as she usually dic Cee Cee had pointed at Ruth.

"*Teach Cee Cee sing now, me want sing now,*" she' signed.

"Shall I come inside?" Ruth had asked Brett.

"Not yet. Stay outside the bars where you and the bab will be safe. Cee Cee has to earn our trust."

Heedless of her skirt, Ruth had sat just outside the bar so she'd be on Cee Cee's level. Cee Cee had sat facing her and the lesson had begun.

Ruth had chosen a simple schoolchildren's song, "Ol MacDonald Had a Farm." She'd sung the song through then shown Cee Cee the appropriate places to supply th animal sounds. The gorilla had been a quick study, an soon the two of them were singing a duet, Ruth supplyin the words and Cee Cee howling with delight as she wa alternately a duck, a pig, a horse, and a cow.

Cee Cee had clapped her hands, grinning.

"*Cee Cee sing good, fine female gorilla, eat six bananas sing more more more.*"

The bond forged between Ruth and Cee Cee during that singing lesson had grown stronger every day. And now Brett had no fear as he watched Ruth sitting beside the gorilla, singing.

Suddenly the song stopped, and Ruth gave Cee Cee a startled look.

"Cee Cee! The baby just moved."

"Baby move where?"

"Here." Ruth put her hands over her enlarged abdomen. "My baby kicked me. Oh . . . there it goes again."

Riveted, Brett watched from the doorway. The baby he'd watched growing inside Ruth was alive and well. Kicking. *His* baby. Joy and pain stabbed him at the same time, and he wondered if it were possible to die from such wounds.

"Cee Cee . . . feel that."

"Where baby?"

"There." Ruth took Cee Cee's hand and placed it on her stomach. The gorilla's touch was gentle. "Oh, there it goes again. Did you feel that, Cee Cee?"

"Baby strong kick good," Cee Cee signed.

"Yes." Ruth's laughter was merry and lighthearted. "He *is* strong, isn't he?"

Brett saw the truth, all in a flash, as if the Virungas had lit up with one of the sudden storms that sometimes swept over them, storms that made even the blackest night sky look like broad daylight, storms so full of thunderbolts that it seemed as if God and all his angels were hurling spears toward the heart of the earth.

The truth was that the period of mourning for his brother had finally come to an end, and he was free to approach the woman whose womb sheltered his baby— approach her not as a brother-in-law on whom she could lean, but as a lover full of intent.

"Ruth," he said, not softly but with a new boldness that she saw the minute she looked at him. Her face changed, taking on a radiance that was temporarily blinding.

"Come and sit by us." She held out her hand, and when he took it, he didn't let go. Both of them knew why. "The baby's kicking," she said.

"I know. I heard."

Slowly she guided his hand to her swollen abdomen, then held it there, her hand resting on top of his, reverent as a prayer. The stillness that fell over them was so deep, it was almost as if they had disappeared into the vast reaches of a night sky where there was nothing except the moon and the stars and God.

Then he felt it. The tiniest flutter, like the moving of butterfly wings.

"There," Ruth whispered. "Feel that."

He couldn't speak. Tears clogged his throat and pressed against the back of his good eye.

"That's the future, Brett. All these weeks on the mountain I've mourned the past, but today when the baby kicked, it was almost like a sign. I knew it was time to go forward."

The baby kicked once more, harder this time, as if he knew his father's hand was covering his temporary hiding place. Something burst inside Brett, a jubilation as pure as the sunlight.

"Yes, it's time, Ruth."

Gently he put his free hand on her cheek, and she leaned her face into his palm, as if that's where it belonged.

"It's time to say the things I've been feeling for a very long time, things I had no right to say . . . until now."

"Say them," she whispered. "I want to hear them. I *need* to hear them."

"What I feel for you is not mere desire, not mere admiration, not mere respect, but all those things together. And more." He kissed her hand, then ran his thumb across her knuckles. "I'm not very good at this . . ."

"You're *very* good at this . . . the best."

"I wish I could be poetic. I wish I could give you the moon and the stars."

"Just give me the truth."

His heart stopped beating for a millisecond; then it went on as if nothing had happened. But in that brief flash he understood that in giving her what she wanted, he could lose everything.

"I think it's called love, Ruth, but saying 'I love you'

doesn't convey everything I feel. It's too simple, too easy
to say just those three words, when in fact what I feel for
you is so complex that it would take two sets of encyclope-
dias to explain it all."

"Only two?" She laughed with her head tilted back and
her long, slender throat exposed. He would always remember her that way, accepting his love with the starry-
eyed joy of a child finding everything she'd always wanted,
or even *dreamed* of wanting, under the Christmas tree.

"Maybe three," he said.

"No, six, because we'll need double the space to express my love for you."

He cupped her face and tipped it up to his, and when he
kissed her, he knew that he'd never truly kissed a woman,
that everything that had gone before was a dress rehearsal
for the real thing.

"I've wanted to do that for a very long time," he said.

"So have I. Since I was fifteen, I think, and first saw you
on television with Cee Cee."

"I'm going to kiss you again, but not sitting on the floor
in Cee Cee's cage." He took her hand and helped her up,
then stepped outside the iron bars, closed the door behind
him, and pulled Ruth back into his arms. Except for the
mound of her womb, she was as lithe and slender as a
willow, bending and shaping herself to fit against him.

They kissed until they were both out of breath; then
Ruth drew back just enough so she could look up and see
his face.

"Don't stop," she said. "Please don't ever stop."

"I won't."

"Promise?"

"I promise."

Love bloomed inside her like spring flowers, but with
the beauty came the old fears, and she shivered.

"You have nothing to fear from me, Ruth."

She squeezed him so hard, the tension made her arms
hurt.

"I love you, Brett. It's very important to me that you
remember that—no matter what happens. Promise?"

"Yes."

Somewhere in the back of her mind lingered the fragrance of white roses, and she hid her face in the crook of his shoulder.

"I'm afraid," she whispered.

"Shh, don't be afraid."

"Not of you. Of me. I'm afraid that I'm damaged beyond redemption."

"You never have to cover up your fears with me, Ruth. Let your true feelings show, and I promise that I'll be there for you. I may not always say or do the right thing, but I'll be there trying."

She nodded, and he could feel the old fears trembling inside her, feel how close she was to tears. As reassuring as words were, sometimes they weren't enough. He picked her up and carried her into his bedroom.

"If I do anything you don't want me to, all you have to do is say no, Ruth."

Her hair spread across the pillow, black silk laced with a scarlet ribbon, and her eyes were luminous. Joy mixed with fear. He prayed that when it was all over, there'd be nothing left but the joy.

"I'm glad you're wearing a red ribbon." He bent over her and gently unwound it, then held it a moment against his cheek before he placed it on the bedpost. Pliant and alive from her body heat, it twined around the ribbon already on the post as if it knew where it belonged.

Ruth lay on the bed smiling up at him.

"You're so beautiful, I'm almost afraid to touch you. . . . Almost."

She caught her breath when he reached for her buttons. What would it be like? His hands on her?

She trembled, waiting.

He unveiled her slowly, like a work of art, then sat on the edge of the bed staring. Merely staring.

The air felt cool against her skin . . . and his gaze felt hot.

"Touch me," she whispered.

He put his right hand on her throat where her pulse beat, and she knew. At last she knew.

She would never be afraid of this man, never fear his touch. On the contrary, his touch loosened something wild

nd hungry in her, something that cried out to be caught
nd tamed and fed.

Slowly his fingers trailed down her throat and across
er left breast, then lingered there kneading, massaging,
fting.

"Yes," she whispered as he bent down and flicked his
ongue around her hardened nipple, then pulled it deep
nside his mouth. "Yes, yes, yes."

She caught his free hand and placed it over her womb,
hen held his head fiercely to her breast while he suckled.
n spite of her past, in spite of her marriage, in spite of her
regnancy, she felt young and fresh and alive in a way
he'd never been. Until this moment no man had ever
ouched her. Until Brett, no man had ever kissed her. With
im, only with him, everything was special, unique, a deli-
ious secret, as if the two of them had invented love and
o one else in the world would ever know what it felt like.

She held on to him, rocking, rocking in her newly found
rotic cradle until she had no awareness of anything ex-
ept his mouth on her breast, his clothes piled hastily on
he floor, and his body, naked and beautiful, flat against
ers, lifting a little to accommodate her belly.

"I don't want to hurt you."

"You won't." She felt him swell, felt the awesome
ower of him pressing hard against her thighs. "I want
ou," she meant to say, though what unintelligible sounds
ame out of her mouth, she would never know. She only
new that her first climax hit her even before he was in-
ide, probably before he'd even *considered* being inside.

She dug her fingernails into his back and held on, her
ody rigid with the contractions that shook her. He mur-
nured words that were both soothing and naughty, and
he turned her face into his neck, nipping at the tender
kin underneath his chin.

"Ruth . . . I can't wait any longer."

"Now," she said. "Now now now."

"I hope I can be gentle with you."

She didn't want gentleness. She wanted wild abandon,
rimitive coupling. The deepest, most basic, most power-
ul emotion filled her, and that was lust. Pure and simple.
Suddenly he was in her, and she couldn't remember

how or when he'd got there, couldn't imagine a time when he'd never been there. His flesh was her flesh, his bone her bone, his blood her blood.

As they rode the powerful primal waves of passion, she abandoned the past and gave herself up to him, gave her heart and soul and mind to him. She was free, free at last to love truly and be loved in return.

"Ruth . . . I never knew . . . I never imagined . . ."

Wordless, his shoulder and neck muscles corded as he held himself aloft, he studied her. She wanted his rhythms, his rigid flesh pushing and pulling and pounding into her, around her, over her, through her.

"Please . . . please . . . please. Don't stop. No now."

His smile was the most beautiful thing she'd ever seen.

"Are you happy, Ruth?" he whispered.

"Enormously. Ridiculously. Terribly." She grinned impishly back at him. "But if you don't continue doing what you were doing a moment ago, I'm going to cry and pout and make your life miserable."

"What? This?" He nibbled her ear.

"No . . ."

"This?" He flicked his tongue over her lips, back and forth, teasing, tantalizing.

She engaged his tongue in playful duel, and for a long while they dallied. Deep inside, where they were joined, he began to thicken and pulse. With a wicked gleam in her eye, she arched upward, strong and sure, impaling herself on him.

"Ruth . . . my God . . . Ruth!"

They loved until sweat slicked their bodies and they could no longer endure the exquisite agony of waiting. Together they exploded, then lay atop the wrinkled covers, arms and legs tangled, lower bodies still joined, her head in the curve of his neck and his hand cupped over her hip.

"I may never move," she said.

"You don't have to."

She leaned back and grinned up at him. "What will I do for food?"

"Do you need food?"

"No. Just you." She ran her fingertips down his back. "Only you."

"I hope you don't ever change your mind." He tightened his arms around her.

"Silly." She closed her eyes, content at last to rest, with nothing to run from, nothing to fear.

At last coming to the Virungas made sense, and she knew that when she'd left Hawaii, it was not to run from Max but to run toward Brett. And now she'd never have to run again. All the years of running, all the lies were behind her.

"Whatever happens, Brett, promise me one thing."

"Anything."

"There will never be any lies between us."

He held on to her with the biggest lie of all separating them.

How was he ever going to tell her? How was he ever going to make her understand?

Instead of answering her, he kissed her, the desperation in him translating into a passion that rekindled with the suddenness and fierceness of a canyon fire. Wordless, they fell through each other once more, losing reason, losing time, and losing themselves.

When it was over, he held her close, propped against the headboard with her feet stacked on top of his.

"That was so beautiful, I think I'm going to cry."

He touched her cheek and found moisture there.

"Shhh. Don't cry. There's nothing for you to cry about now."

"Tears of joy," she whispered. "I have to cry tears of joy."

He kissed the top of her head and sang softly to her, songs he didn't even know he could sing, and when her tears had finally stopped, he was still petting and soothing her.

"Shhh. It's all right. Rest, my love. Just rest."

"I'm not tired." She leaned back to look up at him, smiling.

"Do you ever get tired?"

"No."

"Hmmm. That could present quite a challenge." He fel
like a teenager. "But I think I'm up to it."

"Crazy." She punched his arm, then kissed the side o
his jaw. "I love you, Brett."

The lie between them would spread faster than cancer
and like that dreaded disease, if it weren't cut out, it woulc
be fatal.

"Ruth . . . there's something I have to tell you."

"Oh, my. You make this sound like one of those dra
matic soap operas." With a sweeping gesture she put he
hand over her head; then, rolling her eyes, she said in he
most exaggerated Southern drawl. "My darling, there's ;
deep, dark secret I've been keeping from you. Remembe
your husband who was killed when the car went over th
cliff and plunged into the ocean? Well, he didn't die. I an
him. Or is that he?"

He wished he could keep laughing with her. He wishec
that he and Malone had told her from the beginning anc
that she was delighted that now the three of them could b
a family.

The only way to tell the truth was the hard way.

"This is serious, Ruth."

"How serious?" There was fear in her voice. He hatec
that he'd been the one to put it there. "You're not going tc
tell me something else awful about the poachers, are you?"

"This is not about poaching." A premonition as blacl
as thunderclouds rose in him, and he fell silent.

"What, then?" She put her hand over her heart
"You're scaring me, Brett."

He took both her hands in his and squeezed. Hard.

"I'm the father of your baby, Ruth."

She stared at him, feeling deaf, dumb, and blind all a
the same time. Surely she did not hear or see or fully com
prehend what he had said.

"There must be some mistake," she whispered.

"There's no mistake."

"I . . . we used an anonymous sperm donor."

"I'm the sperm donor."

Comprehension swept through her, then horror. Sh
rammed her hand into her mouth so she wouldn't scream
He put a soothing hand on her shoulder, but she shool

him off, scooting as far away from him as the bed would allow.

"You're the sperm donor," she said, her voice sounding wooden. Suddenly it all made sense to her, Malone's late-night prowling, then the quick trip to the clinic in Nairobi. Naturally he'd rather have had Corday blood in his child than the blood of a stranger.

But why had they kept it a secret?

"Malone knew, of course," she said.

"He asked me to be the father of his child."

"His child!"

"Your child. The child both of you would raise."

She felt sick at her stomach, but she held on, controlled her nausea, controlled her anger. She was going to go away as fast and as far as she could get. But not yet. Not until she had the full truth.

"And so you willingly perpetrated this hoax so that the two of you could gloat over having a genuine Corday. It wasn't enough that the baby would carry my blood. He had to have yours, as well."

"That's not true, Ruth."

"Not true! How will I ever know what the truth is if you're the one telling it?"

He could have told her that he hadn't wanted to be the father of her child, that he'd done it for Malone, but that would be a betrayal of them all—mostly of Ruth. He'd desperately wanted to be the father of her child.

"Ruth, I donated the sperm, you got pregnant, and now you're going to bear our child. Those are the facts, and nothing I can do or say will change them."

"Not *our* child, Brett. *My* child. This baby is mine, and nobody is going to take him away from me."

"My God, is that what you think this is about? You think I told you I love you merely to gain possession of my baby."

"Your baby!"

Brett had never seen her so mad. He thought she was overreacting, but then, what did he know about pregnant women? What did he know about women, for that matter?

"Ruth, please calm down. This can't be good for the baby. Or for you, either."

"Oh, I'll calm down, all right." She stalked toward the hall, naked as the day she was born. Naked and vulnerable.

"Where are you going?"

"Somewhere where you'll never find me."

"Ruth . . . think about this."

"I don't need to think. I've already thought."

"At least stay until you've had time to calm down. You don't need to leave in your condition."

"A condition *you* foisted upon me."

"Having this baby was not *my* idea, Ruth."

"Oh, now you want to take it all back, do you? Well, I have news for you, Brett Corday. It's a little too late for that." She put both hands in the small of her back and pushed her stomach out in an exaggerated manner. "The horse is already out of the gate, so to speak."

Anger had propelled her down the hall, but that's as far as it would carry her. Her legs began to tremble, and she was in great danger of melting into a weeping puddle at his feet. He sensed her weakness.

"I love you, Ruth," he said softly, his hand held out toward her.

How easy it would be to take his hand and forget she'd ever heard the awful truth. But she was through with lies.

"How many other lies have you told me, Brett? How many?"

He stared at her, his black eye so piercing, she felt as if knives were probing her insides.

"None," he said.

He looked like Mount Karisimbi on a cloudy day, huge and immovable, timeless and distant, his mind and heart and soul shrouded by mists that she couldn't penetrate no matter how hard she tried, no matter how hard she wanted to.

She thought how it would have been if Malone hadn't died. The three of them in the cottage with Brett coming to call. *Uncle* Brett. Years and years and years of lies. Her son never knowing his true father.

"How much more sperm would you have donated,

Brett?" she whispered. "How many more children would I have borne for you?"

The long silence between them coiled inside her belly like a snake and lay there, writhing.

"We'll never know if you leave, will we, Ruth?"

His deliberate misinterpretation of her question almost crumbled her resolve. His face, his voice, his eyes, were warm and inviting, reminding her of the bright dreams she'd had only moments before, she and Brett together, rearing the child she now carried as well as the children they would conceive. The old-fashioned way. In a bedroom where nothing but love was spoken.

"No," she said, so softly he had to lean forward to hear her. "We'll never know."

He didn't try to stop her from packing, didn't try to keep her from getting into the Jeep. With her fingers white on the steering wheel she felt the most horrible stab of guilt. She hadn't even said good-bye to Cee Cee.

She thought about getting out of the Jeep and going back inside, but she knew if she did, she'd never leave at all. If she saw Brett, she'd crumble. She'd forgive and forget, brush this monstrous lie under the rug where it would grow and fester until it was so big, it would rise and consume both of them.

Resolute, she set her face down the mountain and never looked back.

68.

HE KNEW EXACTLY WHERE SHE HAD gone. Not one day went by that he didn't get a full report on her. But Brett didn't attempt to see her. Not yet. He would give her a little while to cool off so she could think rationally. When she realized that he'd had no malicious intent, that what he'd done had been out of great love, she'd come back to him.

And if she didn't, then he'd go down the mountain and bring her back. It was that simple.

Meanwhile he concentrated on finding his brother's and his father's killers.

His break came unexpectedly with a call from the *chef des brigades* in Ruhengeri, Michael Fouche, an old and trusted friend.

"We've caught one of the poachers," he said. "We thought you might like to be here for the questioning."

The poacher was one of the Batwas, and he came into the stuffy, windowless room with a bandy-legged trot and a defiant look on his face. The look faded when he saw Brett.

Brett motioned Michael aside.

"You've got the wrong man," he said.

"What do you mean?"

"That man is not a poacher; he's part of one of the antipoaching patrols Malone organized."

"Are you sure?"

"I'm certain. There's no need for you to keep him." Brett turned to leave.

"Brett. You're going to want to stay for this."

Something in his tone made the hair on the back of Brett's neck stand on end, and he stopped cold.

"All right. I'll stay."

He stationed himself so he could see the Batwa's face, then stood silently as Michael began the questioning. The Batwa was confident, even defiant, until Michael started asking about his hunting habits.

"Have you ever killed a duiker?"

"Yes."

"Where?"

"In the mountains. Too many in the Virungas, anyway."

"Are you aware that the land is a national park?"

"The land is the land. Nobody owns the land," he replied.

"Did you take baby gorillas?"

"What do I need with baby gorillas?"

"Did you take them?"

"Where would I put them? With my wife? She hates gorillas. Says they are hairy and ugly."

Michael tossed a spear onto the table.

"Have you seen this before?"

"Everybody has one like it."

"Everybody's fingerprints aren't on it. Only yours." Fear crossed the Batwa's face. Michael pressed his advantage. "Did you help kill male silverbacks in order to take baby gorillas illegally out of the national park?" Silence from the pygmy. "Did you throw the spear that caught Malone Corday in the chest? Did you wield the knife that sliced Joseph Corday's throat?"

Brett smelled the stench of blood, saw the bodies of his father and his brother. He waited, still as the panther he sometimes glimpsed above the waterfall.

"It was not my idea," the Batwa said. "Corday wanted the gorillas. He paid good money."

For a moment Brett's entire world turned upside down. "He's lying," he said, starting toward the Batwa. But Michael motioned him still.

"Joseph Corday started the foundation in order to protect the mountain gorilla. Malone Corday was its major fund-raiser. Are you asking me to believe that either one of them would pay you to kill male silverbacks and take the babies captive?"

"I'm not asking you. I don't care what you believe. I only speak the truth."

"You wouldn't know the truth if it came through that door and bit your skinny ass," Brett said in a tight voice.

"Ask Shambu."

"Shambu is a park guard. What do you expect him to know of your sleazy activities?"

"He was there."

"I'll bet he was. Trying to catch your lying hide and throw it in jail." Brett pounded a fist on the table.

"He was the boss. Corday was the only one who told him what to do."

The words spread through Brett like a sickness. He wanted to shake the Batwa into telling the truth, but somewhere deep inside he knew the pygmy was already telling the truth.

"Which Corday?" Michael asked.

"The young one. He paid the money."

Suddenly it all made sense to Brett—Malone's drinking, his increased trips abroad, the ruby necklace.

Malone, Malone, what have you done?

A terrible silence fell over the room, and Michael looked at Brett, embarrassed and ashamed that he had been the one to discover the truth of this dirty business.

"Go on with the questioning," Brett said. "The truth has to be told."

Michael turned his attention back to the Batwa.

"Why did you kill Malone Corday?"

"The old man came and discovered us."

"Who do you mean by 'us'?"

"Shambu, young Corday . . ."

Brett didn't hear the rest of the names. He was too busy trying to shut out the memories. The storm. The conviction of something afoul. The horrible discovery.

"They argued," the Batwa said.

"Who argued?"

"The old man and the young one."

"Why?"

"I don't know. I didn't understand."

"Then you killed them both?"

In the long, flat silence Brett saw the future—the Corday Foundation discredited, their entire life's work negated by the stunning betrayal of his brother. How would he ever get past that betrayal?

"Yes," the Batwa finally said. "We killed them both."

While Michael escorted the Batwa back to his cell, Brett stood at the window looking out. The rain forest girded the mountains in a solid wall of green, and the mists hovered over the peaks of the volcanoes, shrouding them in mystery. The Virungas looked brooding, almost malevolent, and Brett finally understood how Malone had hated them. They could suck a man up and steal his soul.

Michael came up behind him and put a hand on his shoulder.

"I'm sorry, Brett."

Brett faced his old friend. "Do you think he's telling the truth?"

"Do you want a pretty lie or my honest opinion?"

"I want the truth."

"The truth is that the Batwa's fingerprints are on the spear, so it looks as if we have at least one of our murderers. After I bring in Shambu, I expect we'll have the whole story."

"You're skirting the issue."

"You want me to tell you whether your brother did or did not hire Shambu and his gang to kidnap gorillas?" He studied Brett. "What do you think?"

"It's going to take more than the unsubstantiated story of that little Batwa to make me believe my brother would do such a thing." He wished he really believed what he was saying.

Michael clapped him on the shoulder. "Do you want me to call you when I bring Shambu in?"

Brett already knew what Shambu would say.

"Yes. Call me."

Brett hardly remembered getting into his Jeep and driving back to his compound. He went the long way around to his office so he wouldn't have to pass by Cee Cee's enclosure; then he shut the door, drew all the blinds, and sat in the gloom, staring at the file cabinets. Row upon row of them. Accounts of the Corday Foundation. Research into the habits and the habitat of the mountain gorilla. Details of language studies with the orphan, Cee Cee.

Brett felt as if he were on a desert island viewing the records from afar, a mountain of them, obscured by the mists of uncertainty.

He'd been so certain of his mission, so confident that everything he did was for the good of the mountain gorilla and the good of humankind. What a fool he'd been. How quickly had Malone's betrayal turned the spotlight of truth on the work of the Corday Foundation.

What right did they have to take Cee Cee out of her natural habitat and rear her as if she were human? What right did they have to teach her their ways? Why? For whose good? Certainly not for Cee Cee's. She didn't know whether she was human or gorilla. She wore ribbons in her fur, ate her meals from glass bowls, watched *Murphy Brown* tapes, had even fallen in love with him and acted the role of the spurned, jealous female.

How could he ever face Cee Cee again?

And how would he ever forgive Malone?

69.

THE SMALL COTTAGE OUTSIDE Ruhengeri had split linoleum and peeling paint. Two of the windowpanes were cracked. One hard, pounding rainstorm would probably break them to pieces.

What had she done?

Ruth stood in the middle of the room thinking of the bright, cozy cottage she'd shared with Malone. She could be there now surrounded by the things she'd come to love—her piano, her window box filled with crimson flowers, the mountains.

She still had the mountains, of course. They hadn't gone off in a snit the way she had. But they were so distant now that she seemed to have no connection with them.

Standing at her window, her hand protectively over her womb, she sighed. She knew she was being foolish and irrational. She knew she was being stubborn. But, dammit, she'd been lied to. She wanted nothing more to do with Brett Corday and the Corday Foundation. She bore the name. That was all. And her baby would bear it. But as far as Ruth was concerned, the father of her baby was dead.

She glanced at her watch for the fifteenth time. She wondered what Cee Cee was doing. Was she missing Ruth? Was she badgering Brett because she had no one to sing with?

Ruth hoped so. She hoped Cee Cee was giving him pure hell. The thought made her smile; then she became sober again. Time stretched endlessly before her. How was she going to fill it? She didn't want to think about how she was going to conduct her own research without the necessary funding. She could get the blues if she thought about her future too much. She decided to concentrate on the baby.

"Buck up, Ruth," she told herself.

Women around the world gave birth. She'd do what any sane, normal mother-to-be would do. She'd read up on baby care. She'd make sure she had all the things a new baby would require. She'd learn to knit. There had to be instruction books. Anybody who could read could learn to knit.

Ruth grabbed her purse, climbed into her Jeep, and drove into Ruhengeri to purchase the necessary supplies. When she got back home, she spread everything around her and started reading. What in the heck was "purl"? And how did any person with only two hands ever manage to control all that thread and two enormous knitting needles and read the instructions, besides?

She decided to start with something simple. Bootees. The instructions made no sense to her. She read them again.

"I have a Ph.D. Surely I can figure this out." Determined, she did something the book called "casting on," then proceeded to knit.

"Anybody home?"

Matuka stood in her doorway, her hands full of cookies and her face full of laughter.

"Matuka. Thank God!"

"I knew you'd be happy to see me, but I never expected

such a reception." Matuka hurried inside and set the platter of cookies on the table. "Is it because I bring food that I get such a warm welcome?"

Ruth hugged her. For some silly reason she felt like crying. To cover, she reached for a cookie.

"Hmmm. Chocolate. My favorite."

"I thought so. Eat up. They're all for you."

"I'll be big as a house if I eat all these cookies." Ruth reached for another.

"You already are." Matuka patted Ruth's stomach, then sank into a chair. "That's going to be a *big* boy. Both Eleanor's babies were born big." She squinted her eyes at Ruth. "Brett was the biggest."

Ruth suddenly lost her appetite.

"I'd rather not discuss Brett, if you don't mind."

They hadn't told Matuka much about the baby except that Ruth had received the seed by some artificial method they used on cows. The seed wasn't Malone's.

"I'm not discussing Brett. If I was, I'd be telling how he's out all day looking for whoever killed Malone and Joseph, then up all night watching over the mountain gorillas. I'd be saying he looks like he's lost weight and hardly ever takes time to eat a decent meal and how I'm worried sick about him. That's what I'd be saying."

Brett. Not sleeping and not eating.

"He's not sick, is he?" Whatever else she felt for him, she didn't want him to be sick.

"He's not sick. Just tired and stubborn. When I tell him how good you're looking, he'll perk right up."

Too late, Matuka realized her slip.

"Matuka . . . how did you know where to find me?" Brett, of course. He would make a point of knowing where the mother of his baby was. Underneath Ruth's anger was a sort of secret pleasure. "Did Brett tell you? Is he checking up on me?"

Matuka had always loved the movies she got on her little black-and-white twelve-inch TV. If she had been a young woman, she might have gone off to America and been a star in one of the shows. Now was her chance to show her acting skills.

"Can't a poor old woman find some joy in helping others without being accused of spying?"

"I didn't mean to accuse you of anything."

"You don't want me to come here?"

Ruth felt like a cad. She placed her hand over Matuka's.

"Of course I do."

Matuka worked up a tear in her eye, though she was having a hard time disguising the twinkle.

"If you don't want me coming here, just say so. I'm not going where I'm not welcome."

"You're *always* welcome, Matuka." The old woman stared silently, looking utterly forlorn and rejected. Ruth cast about for ways to bring a smile to her face. Finally she hit on one. She reached into her knitting bag, pulled out her handiwork, and set it on the table beside the cookies.

"I tried to teach myself how to knit, but I couldn't seem to get the hang of it. Maybe you can show me what I did wrong."

Matuka picked up Ruth's first attempt at bootees, then put them back on the table, laughing.

"What's that supposed to be?"

"Would you believe bootees?"

"Looks like a winter condom for a very small cock. I'd advise you to stick with gorilla research."

It felt so good to laugh. Wiping tears of mirth from her eyes, Ruth picked up her pitiful bootees.

"I know I can learn if you'll just show me."

"I don't know a buffalo's ass about knitting. But if you want me to teach you some African lullabies, I will."

"I'd love that," Ruth said, really meaning it.

"I wanted to be a famous singer," Matuka added, studying Ruth through squinted eyes. "But, then, I don't guess a woman always gets everything she wants, does she?"

"No," Ruth said, thinking of all the things she wanted and couldn't have. "A woman never does."

Night came suddenly to Africa, as if God had dropped a blackout curtain over the continent. Ruth was in the last place in the world she wanted to be, alone in a run-down cottage with an uncertain future stretched out before her.

"I don't guess a woman ever gets everything she wants," Matuka had said.

Ruth certainly hadn't planned to raise her baby without a father. The prospect was scary.

Had her mother been scared too? Had she sat in the dark by herself and felt the same heart-wrenching loneliness? The same uncertainty?

Funny. In all those years, Ruth had never known whether her mother was scared.

Once, when she was three years old, a tornado had touched down just outside Oxford. With winds howling like wolves outside her bedroom window and limbs being ripped from trees, Ruth had been too scared to move. She'd huddled in the middle of the bed with the covers over her head.

"There's nothing to be afraid of, darling," her mother had said; then she'd stayed in Ruth's room the rest of the night, making up silly games until Ruth was so sleepy, she couldn't hold her eyes open. And when morning came, her mother was still in the bed beside her, her arms wrapped protectively around Ruth.

Ruth left her chair and rummaged in the battered corner desk for pen and paper. Then she turned on the lamp and began to write.

"Dear Mother . . ."

How many years had it been since she'd addressed Margaret Anne as Mother? she wondered.

"You are special," her mother had told her when Ruth was crying because all the other little girls in the second grade had daddies. "It doesn't take any courage to grow up strong and independent in a home with two loving parents, but it takes somebody special to turn out right when they don't have a daddy. And you're turning out right, Ruth. Always remember that."

She had turned out right in all the ways that mattered. Surely she couldn't have achieved that feat without some help from her mother.

"I'm going to have a baby," Ruth wrote, "and somehow it doesn't seem right to bring a child into a world that already has too much hatred without trying to set things right between us.

"I don't hate you anymore, Mother. Maybe I never did. Maybe I just needed somebody to blame for what Max did to me. I'll never understand your role in it, never understand what circumstances might have driven you to sanction his act . . . but, then, I've never walked in your shoes.

"Lately I've discovered that we are more alike than I ever cared to admit. Though our methods were different, both of us tried to redefine ourselves. For me, running away was an attempt to deny my past. I don't know why you re-created yourself, but someday I'd like to find out.

"I know what it's like to be lonely. I know what it's like to be scared. You must have felt both those emotions over the years, but I never knew. I always thought of you as larger than life, more beautiful than most other mothers, smarter, more talented. I guess that's why I was so devastated by your betrayal. I guess that's why it has taken me so many years to understand that I can no longer judge you, that I can no longer live with hatred in my heart.

"You were my hero, Mother, and losing my hero nearly destroyed me.

"I'm not saying that we can ever go back to the easy camaraderie we had before Max stole my innocence. We can never go back. Only forward.

"Please don't take this letter as a sign that I want you beside my bed when I give birth to my child. I don't think I can handle that. Not yet. Nor do I want you to buy out every baby boutique in Oxford and make up amusing stories to tell all your society friends about being a grandmother.

"There I go again. Trying to control things. I guess you can do whatever you take a notion to do.

"What I'm saying is that I want us to try to be honest with each other. No more lies. No more pretense. Whatever past you've created for yourself with your Oxford friends is your business. But I want only truth between us.

"You can start by telling me about my father. I never knew anything about him except that he was somebody wonderful who had to go away.

"I don't know when I can face you . . . or even *if* I can face you. The thought scares me. And right now I have too much to be scared about to add one more terror.

"For the time being, a letter will have to do. I send you my offering of peace, Mother. Maybe someday I can send you love.

"I hope so. Oh, I *do* hope so."

Ruth signed and sealed the letter, then put her head on the desk and cried. Cleansing tears. When she was cried out, she put on her gown and went to bed.

Covering her womb with her hands, she whispered, "You're special, little one. It doesn't take courage to grow up strong and independent in a home with two loving parents, but it takes somebody special to turn out right in a home without a daddy. And you're going to turn out right. I promise."

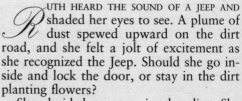

70.

Ruth heard the sound of a jeep and shaded her eyes to see. A plume of dust spewed upward on the dirt road, and she felt a jolt of excitement as she recognized the Jeep. Should she go inside and lock the door, or stay in the dirt planting flowers?

She decided to stay in the dirt. She reached for that inner core of serenity, then pulled off her gardening gloves.

Her heart lurched when he got out of the Jeep. Neither of them spoke. He strode to the flower bed and stood gazing down at her.

Her baby kicked so hard, she saw the movement in the hand laid protectively over his hiding place. Brett saw the movement too. He caught her eye, a volume of unspoken thoughts in his glance.

"I need to talk to you," he said.

"My baby has nothing to do with you."

He touched his eye patch briefly, a gesture she'd seen him use a dozen times, always when he was uncertain—a gesture that broke her heart. She didn't want her heart to be broken, and so she stood and started into her house. She had every intention of locking the door and not coming out, no matter what he said, no matter how long he stood there.

"Ruth . . ."

She stopped in midstride, one foot on the porch, the other on the top step—just stood there pinned to the floor as if she were a mechanical toy and somebody had removed her battery.

"This is not about the baby."

She turned slowly, and seeing him that way—his hair tousled from the wind, the dust from the road settled onto his shoes, his face closed up like one of the masks archaeologists unearthed from forgotten civilizations—she lost all thought of abandoning him in her front yard.

"There's tea inside, and some cookies Matuka brought yesterday. You look as if you could use some."

She issued the invitation as smoothly as if she were a Southern debutante thoroughly schooled in the art of flirtation, who had been just waiting for the perfect man to use it on. Lord, she was flirting with him. What would she stoop to next?

He followed her inside. The room suddenly seemed too small. There was hardly anywhere to go that didn't put her in too close a proximity to him. She escaped to the kitchen. When she got back, he was standing beside the window, looking out, tense as a piano wire that had been stretched too tight.

She wanted him so much, she could feel the desire coiling through her like smoke, warm and dark and dangerous.

With shaking hands she poured tea and knocked a teacup onto the floor. It shattered into a million pieces. Her lower lip trembled, and she thought she was going to make a fool of herself and cry.

They knelt on the floor at the same time. She felt the push of tears against her eyelids.

"Ruth . . ." He touched her hand. Their gazes locked. "Let me."

She could argue with him. But to what purpose?

"All right," she said. He helped her up, handing her gently into a chair as if she were his grandmother's fine china and he was afraid she might break herself. Which she might. Any minute now. If he stayed in her house too long, she'd shatter into bright slivers of glass and embed herself in him.

He was still embedded in her heart. Was she embedded in his?

It was a question she'd never know the answer to.

"I'll get another cup," she said.

"No. I don't really want tea." He threw the pieces into the wastebasket, then sat on the chair opposite her.

"I guess you don't want cookies, either." Why did that make her feel so forlorn? As if she'd lost everything she'd ever had?

"They look and smell delicious."

"But you don't want any?"

"I'm not hungry."

She was hungry. For him. She didn't dare look into his eyes, afraid that he would see. Instead she focused on a spot on the wall just beyond his head. Somebody had squashed a fly against the wallpaper and then never cleaned it up. The former tenant, probably. Why hadn't she seen the mess before? Why was she continuing to live in that rude cottage?

And why hadn't she guessed that Brett was the father of her baby? Oh, Lord, she really was going to cry. She folded her hands tightly together, lacing the fingers the way she had done in elementary school when she didn't want to be the one the teacher called to the chalkboard.

"Are you all right?" he asked.

"If you mean am I eating and sleeping and taking care of myself, the answer is yes, I'm all right. If you mean am I happy about being deceived, the answer is no."

"I understand your—"

"No! You don't understand anything. You don't know what it's like to learn that you and Malone conspired behind my back. Did you gloat when I got pregnant with your baby, Brett?"

It took every ounce of his self-control to sit in his chair without touching her.

"I didn't mean to upset you, Ruth. I merely wanted you to know that I care about your well-being . . . and not because of the baby."

"You don't care about this baby? Your own child?" Ruth knew she was being irrational, but she didn't care. She figured she had a God-given right to irrationality as compensation for being so big that she waddled like a duck.

"Do I care about my own child?"

Brett didn't move from his chair, but his gaze was so intense, she felt as if his hands were all over her. She clutched the sides of her chair to keep from sliding off in a melting puddle at his feet.

"I would die for him . . . and for you." Shivers ran through her. "You want to know if I gloated when you got pregnant with my child? When I knew my seed had taken root in you, I wanted to kneel at your feet and kiss your womb. I wanted to stand on top of my mountain and shout to all the world that I was the father. Call it gloating. Call it whatever you want."

She felt the press of tears behind her eyes, and she realized she wanted to cry not out of anger, but out of joy. This brilliant, courageous, loyal man had loved his brother so deeply that he'd not only given up an eye, he'd given up a child. And she carried that child in her womb.

She would tell her child about his father. She would tell him how he dedicated his life to his family and to the mountain gorilla. She'd tell her son the sacrifices his father had made for all of them. She'd tell him everything except the way Brett had deceived her.

"I shouldn't have said those things to you, Brett. I'm sorry."

"Ruth, I know that what I did is not easy for you to forgive, but I wish you'd at least come back to the compound so I can keep an eye on you."

"I'm a stone's throw from the clinic. I don't need you to keep an eye on me. How's Cee Cee?"

"She misses you. She's making my life hell."

"Good."

"I knew you'd say that." Even though she was near the clinic, Brett had no intention of letting her stay in this run-down cabin indefinitely. His child would be born under his watchful eye—whether or not Ruth Corday agreed.

He studied her in silence; then, satisfied that she was finally relaxed, he got down to the purpose of his visit.

"Ruth, there are some things I have to tell you before you hear any talk from the villagers."

"Talk? About what?"

"About Malone. You know I've been trying to find out what happened on the mountain?"

"Yes."

"I've discovered some truths that aren't pretty."

"You're making me crazy with all this beating around the bush. Quit treating me like a child and get on with the truth. I can take it."

He knew she could. Ruth was strong, had always been strong. The thing he hated was not being able to hold her in his arms while he told her the truth. Any attempt to do so would be upsetting to her, and she had more than enough to handle without emotional complications.

"Malone and Joseph were killed because Malone was involved in the illegal capture and sale of the baby gorillas."

She thought she was going to faint. The room whirled and got dark. Brett squatted beside her chair, put one hand on her knee, the other on her forehead.

"Ruth. Are you all right?"

"No!" She jerked away from him. "Don't touch me. Leave me alone."

"I didn't mean to upset you."

"What did you mean, telling me these awful things? It's just another lie. Just another way to insinuate yourself into my life."

Brett had never felt so helpless in all his life. How would he ever straighten out the tangled web of lies that the Corday family was caught up in?

"I loved my brother more than life itself." He touched his eye patch, remembering the sacrifice. He could almost feel the knife blade slicing down his face. "Do you think

'd say or do anything to harm him, especially now that
ıe's dead?"

Tears stung the back of her eyes, but she blinked them
›ack. She wouldn't cry. Not while Brett was there.

"No," she whispered. "No matter what else you did,
you would never harm your brother."

"He did it, Ruth. He betrayed us all."

She knew he spoke the truth. Her dear, sweet, gentle
Malone would never have done such a thing. But the Ma-
one he'd become—the one who had to prove to himself
:hat he was not a failure, the one who had to prove to his
wife that he was better than his brother—could have.

"How do you know?" she asked.

"Shambu, the park guard who was head of one of the
antipoaching patrols, told us everything."

There was more to the story, much more, but he didn't
want to tell her. Somebody bigger than Malone had been
behind the scheme, somebody Shambu didn't know. Or
wouldn't implicate. In any event, the murder had not been
premeditated. Joseph had happened on the scene. And
now he and Malone were dead, and the truth had died
with them.

"Shambu killed Malone and Joseph?"

"Yes. He and others. They'll be punished, Ruth."

"And then it will all be over," she whispered.

It was far from over, but he didn't tell her that. She had
too much to handle as it was.

"Yes, Ruth. It will all be over."

She stood up. "Thank you for coming by to tell me
this."

He was being dismissed. What else had he expected?

"If you need me for anything . . ."

"I won't need you," she said.

He didn't know how he could leave her there with the
plate of cookies and the cold pot of tea and his baby so big
inside her that she held the small of her back when she
walked.

But she'd given him no choice.

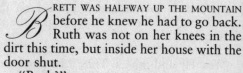

71.

BRETT WAS HALFWAY UP THE MOUNTAIN before he knew he had to go back. Ruth was not on her knees in the dirt this time, but inside her house with the door shut.

"Ruth?"

There was no answer. What if she'd hurt herself after he left? What if she was lying on the floor bleeding?

"Ruth! Open up." He knocked loudly.

There was a long silence, and then he heard her footsteps. The doorknob twisted, and he waited for the door to open. Waited and waited.

Ruth leaned her head against the door. *Ruth Corday*. How proud she'd been to bear the name. It stood for dignity, integrity, compassion, vision. And now all that was gone. Malone had taken it away.

"No," she said through the closed door. "Haven't you already done enough? What more do you want? Blood?"

The minute she said that, she could have bitten off her tongue. There had already been too much bloodshed on these mountains.

She pressed her hand flat against the door, as if she were touching him.

"I'm sorry," she whispered.

Brett leaned his forehead against the door. He was tired. So very tired.

"Don't cry," he said.

"How did you know I was crying?"

"Because I love you, Ruth. I feel your pain. I hear it in your voice." There was silence from inside her house. He put his palm against the door as if he might feel the warmth of her skin through the thick wood that separated them.

"Please leave." Her voice was so soft, he could barely hear.

"I'm leaving now, Ruth, but before I go, I want you to know that my love for you has nothing to do with wanting to take possession of my baby. I would love you no matter whose baby you carried." In the long, terrible silence he waited. "I've always loved you and I always will."

He stood for a long time with his hand on the door, knowing she was just on the other side.

"Ruth," he said.

No answer.

He could stand there till hell froze over, and she'd never answer him. He knew that. Ruth was stubborn. It was one of her qualities he found most endearing . . . and most maddening.

When he left this time, he went straight to Matuka's cabin. She greeted him with a hug and a big bowl of soup.

"You're not eating right," she said. "With all that's happened in these mountains it's not any wonder."

"This smells good, Matuka."

"Eat it all." She bustled around her kitchen, pouring soup into a covered plastic container.

"What are you doing?" he asked, as if he didn't know.

"Sending the rest home with you. All you ever think about is that gorilla . . . and Ruth."

She wiped her hands on her apron and sat down beside him.

"You've seen her, haven't you?"

He didn't ask how she knew. Matuka had always divined his secrets. He'd never sneaked anything past her, not even the lizards he'd hidden in a box at the back of his closet when he was eight.

"I saw her."

He was like a son to Matuka. She knew his heart was torn out. Leaving her chair, she wrapped her arms around him and crooned to him as if he were a baby. She wished he'd cry. Through all the terrible times, even through Joseph's funeral when everybody had been weeping and lamenting, he'd stood like one of the mountains, unchanged and unchangeable.

How many more times would he have his heart torn out?

"Everything is going to be all right," she said.

"Thanks, Matuka." He patted her arm, and she took her chair. This man didn't want coddling—would stand for only so much of it. "How does she seem to you?" he asked her.

"Just like you. Sad, hurting."

"You'll keep visiting her?"

"Every day. Just like you asked. Besides, I like Ruth. She's a brave lady."

"Yes, she's a brave lady. . . . You'll call me and tell me about her?"

"Every day. Just like you asked."

He left with a container of soup to nourish his body and a hug to nourish his spirit.

Ruth was bent over her knitting, the lamplight glowing against the side of her face and shining on her hair. Brett sat in his Jeep, watching. He felt like a thief, stealing these moments with her. Night after night, coming there to check on her.

Never mind that Matuka faithfully reported to him. He had to see for himself, had to know that she was all right.

She stood up and stretched. The huge mound of her

belly was backlit by the lamp. She was ripe with child. *His* child.

Something warm pushed against his eyelids, and he knew it was tears. Unashamed, he let them fall as he watched the woman he loved make her way through the house to her bedroom. Beyond her drawn shades he saw her pull her dress over her head and slowly massage cream onto her rounded belly and full breasts.

A pain such as he'd never known slashed at him. He ached to kneel in front of her and smooth the soothing lotion onto her stretched skin. He longed to place the palm of his hands flat on her belly and feel the fluttering kicks of his child beneath her velvety skin. He yearned to press his mouth against the heavy breasts and gently suckle where his child would feed.

Ruth placed the bottle of lotion back on her nightstand, then turned back the covers. Alert as a duiker she cocked her head, listening, the covers clutched in one hand, the other over her heart.

Brett hated that she was alone. Hated that he wasn't beside her, reassuring her. Hated that he was outside in the dark and might be the cause of her alarm. He was torn between going to her front door and *making* her let him inside, and respecting her desire to be left alone.

Finally she climbed into bed and snapped off the light. Her house was plunged into darkness. There was nothing left to see. Still, he stayed. Seeing was not his purpose, though he fed on those glimpses of her, even if they were from a distance. His purpose in coming night after night was to ensure her safety.

As he sat in the dark keeping watch, he made a mental note to tell Matuka to make some thick curtains for her bedroom, curtains that no one could see through.

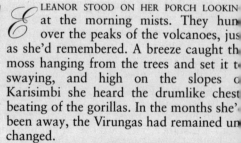

72.

*E*LEANOR STOOD ON HER PORCH LOOKING at the morning mists. They hung over the peaks of the volcanoes, just as she'd remembered. A breeze caught the moss hanging from the trees and set it to swaying, and high on the slopes of Karisimbi she heard the drumlike chest beating of the gorillas. In the months she'd been away, the Virungas had remained unchanged.

Coming home had been the right decision.

She went back inside her house and got her cameras. Work was what she needed. Lots of it. It might help her forget that Joseph was dead. Forget what Malone had done. Forget that Brett had donated sperm for Ruth's baby and that now she was living in a cottage in Ruhengeri.

Tomorrow she'd go down the mountain to see her daughter-in-law. Not to meddle

Not to try to fix things. She was through trying to fix things for everybody else.

An emptiness the size of a cannon ball caught her in the middle of the chest. There was no "everybody" else.

She rammed her hat onto her head, hard, as if she were trying to push the unwelcome thoughts out of her brain. Dew wet her shoes when she stepped off the porch. She'd start small. No photographs of animals today. Only flowers. The ones that grew close to the compound.

Using the lens as her eyes, she focused on the flame flower. Such a brave and beautiful red. Eleanor squatted to get a better angle.

"Eleanor . . ." Ruth stood behind her. "I didn't mean to startle you."

Eleanor thought how selfish she'd been, staying holed up in Alabama licking her wounds while Ruth went through her first pregnancy alone and Brett struggled with the problems of the Corday Foundation and the awful knowledge of what Malone had done.

But she was home now, and she guessed that's all that mattered.

"Darling . . ." Eleanor laid her camera aside and hugged her daughter-in-law. "I'm so glad to see you. Come. Let's go inside."

"I don't want to interrupt your work, but Matuka told me you had come home, and I wanted to see you."

"Work? Ha! I'm just killing time. I'm not good enough yet to work, not focused enough."

Inside they sat together on the sofa, Ruth's right hand tightly squeezing Eleanor's left.

"You know about the baby?"

"Brett told me." Eleanor stopped the flow of advice that bubbled up inside her. Who was she to advise? "Whatever your decision is about Brett, I hope you will let me be a part of the baby's life."

"You're his grandmother. I'll never deny you that privilege, nor that joy."

"I didn't think you would. You look a little pale. Are you taking care of yourself?"

"Yes. Not sleeping as well as I should, but under the

circumstances I guess that's understandable." She patted her big belly, smiling.

"It might help if you moved back into the cottage on the compound. That way you could relax knowing I'd be close by when your time comes. But I won't pretend to tell you what to do."

"Good." Ruth laughed.

"Was I that bad?"

"Getting my mother over here without my knowledge was pretty awful."

"I'm sorry about that. I always did have a knack for either totally ignoring my children or overwhelming them with the wrong kind of attention."

"You're too hard on yourself."

"Maybe I should be. Maybe if I had paid more attention to Malone, none of this would ever have happened." Eleanor felt herself wobble inside like an old woman. She hung on to her daughter-in-law's hand.

"In time everything is going to be all right," Ruth said, hoping it was true. "All this will be behind us."

"It's not myself I worry about, it's Brett. And the foundation. The truth is killing him."

Ruth tried not to think of Brett alone on the mountaintop brooding.

"He's going public with the truth," Eleanor said.

"Going public?"

"He's called a news conference here at noon tomorrow. He thinks it's better that the public hear the truth from him rather than get it in bits and pieces when the trial starts." The authorities were bringing to trial the bastards who'd killed her family. Eleanor picked up a pretzel from the dish on the coffee table and began to nibble. She was going to get fat if she didn't stop this nervous habit of eating.

"Let's don't talk about any of this anymore. Let's just talk about good things."

"Like the baby?"

"Yes." Eleanor smiled. "Like the baby."

They didn't speak of their troubles again, but Malone's betrayal was never far from their minds.

73.

REPORTERS FROM ALL THE MAJOR TELEVI-sion networks were there, as well as from newspapers all over the country. Dr. Brett Corday was not only world renowned, he was somewhat reclusive. A news conference with him was an opportunity not to be missed.

He stood at the window and watched them come up the mountain in a steady stream.

"Like vultures," he said.

"They don't know you're going to talk about the dead."

Eleanor was dressed in a dark-blue suit instead of her usual comfortable khakis, and she wasn't feeling charitable to anybody. Least of all her youngest son, who had caused all this trouble.

"You don't have to face them, Mother."

"The Cordays will present a united front," she said.

Brett thought of Ruth, who didn't even want to see him, let alone present a united front with him.

"Yes," he said. "We need a united front if we're going to convince them that the foundation will continue to carry on the work it started."

They could hear Matuka humming in the kitchen. She didn't care about united fronts; all she cared about was the hoard of people coming up the mountain who were bound to be thirsty and hungry.

As Brett watched out the window, a woman made her way through the crowd. She walked tall and proud, never looking right nor left, ignoring the questions shouted at her, the cameras clicking in her face, the hands reaching toward her.

"Ruth!"

He bolted through the door. When she saw him, she stood perfectly still, her loose blue dress blowing around her ripe body, a carved Madonna in the midst of madness. He moved toward her slowly, as if rushing might cause her to leap away with the grace of a startled gazelle.

"You shouldn't be here." He felt her tremble when he slid one arm around her shoulder. Holding the other outstretched to warn off reporters, he guided her inside.

She moved quickly away from him.

"I don't want you to get the wrong idea about why I'm here." Sitting beside Eleanor on the sofa, she gazed around the familiar room. The tug of this place was strong in her and she wished she hadn't had to come. "If you're going to defend the Corday name, I want to be there."

"It will be rough," he said. "You don't have to subject yourself to this."

"It's my name too . . . and the name of my baby."

She had to turn away from the light that glowed in his piercing black eye.

"You're sure you can handle it?"

"I can handle anything."

Brave words. She hoped she could live up to them. But then, Brett was in the room, and she'd always taken courage from him. Suddenly she was very angry that in keeping secrets from her, he'd denied her access to her greatest source of strength.

"It's time," Eleanor said.

"Yes. It's time."

The three of them went outside to face the reporters, Brett standing tall and proud, flanked by the Corday women.

74.

THE LETTER LAY OPEN ON THE KITCHEN table. Ruth nursed a cup of tea between her palms and sat staring at it. She didn't have to read it to know what it said. The words were emblazoned in her mind.

"I'm glad you made the first overture of peace, because I'd never have had the courage to do it myself. You're like your father, Ruth, full of courage. I don't know whether he's dead or alive. If he's alive, he wouldn't know either one of us. The angel dust took care of that. The doctors said he would never come back from the horrible trip it took him on, and so I packed my bags and left. I had to find some way to support you after you were born, and the members in his band swore they would take care of him—no matter what happened.

"Your father is Blue Janeau, Ruth. One of the jazz greats, they call him. He played the sweetest trumpet this side of heaven. I guess that's where you got all your talent. Your looks too. Blue was a mulatto, and if I hadn't created another past for us, people would have given you a hard time. So I picked the name Bellafontaine to put on your birth certificate. God, how I loved that man, and even though I changed my name, I was never ashamed to bear Blue's child, never ashamed of you. I hope you're not ashamed, Ruth, and I hope you tell your baby about his granddaddy. Maybe someday I'll even get up enough courage to tell folks here in Oxford.

"I hope you can find it in your heart to let me see the baby . . . but please don't teach him to call me Grandma. I prefer Maggie. That's what Blue used to call me. It will be nice to hear somebody call me that again."

Thinking about Blue Janeau almost overwhelmed Ruth. Suddenly, after all these years, to have a father! She went to her bedroom and searched until she found the tapes. The music was in her memory, as clear as if she were still thirteen. She used to shut herself in her room and let the haunting sound of the trumpet take her away from the house in Oxford, Mississippi, and all the things it reminded her of. All those years she'd longed for a father, he'd been right there with her.

Her hands shook as she put her father's tape on. When the sweet strains of blues filled her little cottage, she was thirteen once again—and filled with longing. But her longing was far more complex now. She didn't merely want a home filled with love and a father for her baby; she wanted wholeness.

The music washed over her, and she didn't know she was crying until it ceased and she tasted the tears in her mouth. Wiping them with the back of her hand, she returned to her bedroom and rummaged in the nightstand.

The necklace was at the bottom of the drawer underneath a hodgepodge of stamps and notepads and pencils, tossed there carelessly as if it had no value at all. The tainted rubies. Red as the blood that had run down the mountain—Malone's, Joseph's, the gorillas'. What a terrible price to pay for a necklace.

She would sell the rubies and use the money for the Corday Foundation. It wouldn't bring back the dead, but it would help the survivors.

"It's time," she said. Time to stop running.

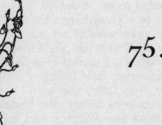

75.

THE COURTROOM WAS PACKED. THE JU-
dicial system moved a lot more
quickly in Africa than in the
States.

"Vultures," Eleanor said. "Here to pick
the bones of the dead."

"Don't look at anybody, don't speak,"
Brett said. "Just hold on to me."

As they made their way through the
crowd, reporters jumped into their path,
shouting questions. Since the press conference the Corday name had been blazoned
across the front page of newspapers all
over the world. Brett had already said everything he intended to say—at least until
the trial was over. Let the fires of innuendo
burn. He had no intention of adding fuel.

"No comment," he said.

"I'm glad I told Ruth not to come," Eleanor said.

"I'm glad she listened to you."

As they moved toward the front of the

courtroom, flashbulbs went off in their faces. Luke Fisher slid into the seat beside Eleanor.

"You didn't have to come," she said.

"I'm not here because I *had* to come; I'm here because I *wanted* to come."

Luke didn't reach for her hand. She would have hated it if he had. The reporters had enough to write about the Cordays without giving them a glimpse of their personal lives.

"I don't know what to say, Luke."

"You don't have to say anything, Eleanor."

Actually, she did know what to say, but the courtroom was not the proper place to say it. She'd invite him to the compound and say what she needed to in the quietness of evening, when no one else could hear.

I'm glad I have you, Luke, she would say. Without warning, desire was reborn in her. She flushed with her thoughts. She, almost a grandmother. And she knew that when Luke Fisher came, she'd take his hand and lead him down the hall to her bedroom.

The judge took the bench, and the trial began. But it was more than the trial of Shambu and the pygmies; it was a trial of the Cordays and their entire life's work. Bit by bit the sordid story of Malone's duplicity unfolded.

Throughout the testimonies Brett and Eleanor held their heads high. By midafternoon she felt as if she'd been flayed alive. Every bone and joint in her body ached, and her skin was on fire from all the stares she'd endured.

"Don't fold," Luke whispered.

"I wouldn't give them that satisfaction."

Suddenly there was a commotion at the back of the courtroom. Onlookers craned their necks, flashbulbs exploded, and reporters rushed the door yelling questions.

"Would you care to make a statement?"

"Tell us about the killing of the gorillas."

"Were you involved in illegal activities with your husband?"

Ruth was trapped against the door like an animal.

"Please . . . ," she said, shielding her belly with her hands. "Let me through."

"Ruth!" Brett tried to push toward her, but the crowd

blocked his way. Over the tops of their heads he could see her still pressed back against the door. But she was not cowering. Far from it. Her chin was up and her color high. Those who didn't know her might not understand the signs, but he did. Ruth Corday would not be intimidated.

Reporters continued to shout questions at her. "No comment," she said until they shouted at her, "What will you tell your child about his father?"

Brett could barely contain his rage. If he had been close enough, he'd have throttled the reporter. He struggled to reach her, but the crowd was too thick. There was no way through.

"What will I tell my child about his father?" A hush fell over the courtroom. Ruth's eyes sought Brett. "I'll tell my child that he can bear his father's name with pride."

Other questions were shouted at her. The judge pounded with his gavel and called for order. Ruth started toward Brett, and miraculously the crowd parted to let her through.

He eased her out into a deserted hallway.

"You shouldn't have come." His gaze swept over her, hungry for every small detail. She had been gorgeous when she'd first come to the Virungas, but now she was astonishing. Her condition enhanced her beauty rather than detracted from it. There was a glow about her that sparkled in her eyes and gave her skin a golden sheen. He'd never wanted her more.

"This is where I belong." Composed and beautiful, she reached for him.

At last he was touching her, hands joined, fingers linked. After all the lonely weeks.

"Ruth, does this mean what I want it to mean?"

"It means I've forgiven you. . . . No, more than that. I'm *glad* you're the father of my child. I'm glad he will have your genes."

"Ruth . . ." He was so full of joy that words almost failed him. "I love you."

"And I love you. I never stopped loving you, Brett, even while I was in that horrible cottage in Ruhengeri."

"I'd kiss you if I thought there were no reporters lurking behind the doors."

"I wouldn't want to stop with a kiss . . . and I don't relish the thought of having my picture—and my life story —plastered all over the newspapers."

The look they exchanged was so bright with passion that it was blinding. Ruth caught her breath, and Brett squeezed her hands.

"As soon as we can leave here," he told her, "I'm going to move you back to the compound." Ruth laughed. "What's so funny?"

"I've already moved."

"Into the cottage on the main compound?" He hoped not. He hoped for more.

"No. Into *your* compound."

He loved the way she smiled at him, a combination of sexiness and sass. Exchanging light banter with her felt so good that for a little while he was content to stand in the hallway and let justice take its own course.

"That was rather brazen of you, wasn't it?"

"That's the kind of woman I am. Brazen and bossy."

"I wouldn't go so far as to call you bossy."

"Matuka and Bantain did."

"Matuka and Bantain?"

"I commandeered them to help me move."

He caressed her knuckles with his thumbs. Touching her was intensely erotic to him, and he wanted more, ever so much more. But for now holding her hand would do.

"Ruth, there's so much I want to say to you, so much I want to do for you and *with* you, but this is neither the time nor the place."

She didn't try to fight the tears that filled her eyes. One of the best things about love was the freedom to express emotions, whatever they happened to be.

"Brett, I want to hear it all. I *need* to hear it all."

"You will. I promise."

Through the open doorway he could hear the stirring of the crowd, the droning of the lawyer's voices. He had to go back inside. The fate of the Cordays depended on him.

"It's time to go back inside, Ruth. Are you sure you can handle it?"

"I can handle it. I can handle anything as long as I have you."

76.

LOS ANGELES

THE TRIAL OF SHAMBU AND THE BATWA pygmies for the murders of Joseph and Malone Corday was headline news around the world. No one kept up with it more closely than Maxwell Jones. He sat in his big chair by the window, reading the latest news report. *"Convicted,"* the headlines screamed.

He read quickly, omitting the gory details of the murders. What he was looking for was more important. The murders were called a "group killing." All the Batwas received sentences, but Shambu took the brunt of the punishment—but not the blame. He'd brought Malone Corday down with him.

"Malone Corday, the major fund-raiser for the Corday Foundation, was the mastermind behind the illegal kidnapping and selling of baby mountain gorillas," the article read.

Max smiled. No matter how much that bastard Brett Corday tried to defend his family, the stench of blood was still on the family name, the taint of betrayal was still marring the work of the foundation.

Max riffled through his stack of newspapers, scanning first one article, then another. Brett Corday was quoted extensively in all of them. They'd all wanted to know what the remaining male member of the Corday family had to say.

"It is with deep regret and sorrow that we acknowledge Malone's part in this tragic scheme," he'd said. "As you know, the Corday family has not tried to hide the truth. In fact, we have rigorously sought it." Here the reporter digressed, lauding Corday for calling the news conference to announce his brother's guilt and to assure the public that the foundation would continue.

"The primary purpose of the foundation has been to preserve the habitat of the mountain gorilla and to ensure that the species continues to thrive," Corday was quoted as saying. "That is still our purpose, and we will work diligently toward that end."

Several of the articles quoted Eleanor Corday and showed photographs of her entering the courthouse. She was a damned fine-looking woman.

But not nearly as magnificent as Ruth Corday.

Max knew she had been at the trial, because the articles mentioned the fact that all the Cordays were in attendance, presenting a united front. Either she hadn't had anything to say, or she had been shielded from the reporters.

His hands shook as he searched for a remnant of her—her name in print, a glimpse of her face in the crowd, a quote. Anything.

At last he found it. Not a small mention but an entire story, complete with picture. A wedding picture.

Max's hands began to shake. Ruth and Brett Corday smiled at him from the front page of the newspaper he was holding. "Wedding of the Century," the headline proclaimed, then, in small print, "Dr. Brett Corday weds his brother's widow." A private wedding, the article said, public not invited; but the enterprising reporter had hidden near the compound and caught them coming out of the house after the ceremony.

Ruth looked as if she'd been given the keys to heaven. A black despair settled over Max, and he started to cast the newspaper from him, but curiosity won over rage. He couldn't make himself stop reading about her. The article went on to compare her to her biblical counterpart, the woman who had given up her people to follow her mother-in-law to a strange land. Ruth and Naomi. Ruth and Eleanor. Even her first husband's name was taken from that famous story. Malone. Same name, different spelling.

Ruth Corday. Rescued by a kinsman. Not a cousin this time, but a brother. A powerful man. Courageous. World renowned. A man who had sacrificed an eye for his brother. Not a man to be tampered with. Certainly not a man who could be manipulated.

Outside Max's window the delivery van pulled up to his front door, bringing the white roses. Max gazed at the photograph of the man who had stolen Ruth from him. Brett Corday would never let her go.

Outside, the delivery man rang the doorbell. Max laid down the paper. All hope was gone. Ruth would never be there to smell the roses.

It was Saturday, and his secretary and all his servants had the day off. Feeling alone and suddenly very old, Max made his way down the stairs.

He missed the bottom step and almost fell over. It wasn't like him to be so clumsy. He caught the railing to steady himself. The front door seemed very far away and was tilting sideways, as if some crazy person had come along and knocked it crooked on its hinges.

Max started forward and fell to his knees. His face twisted downward, and he felt the huge tear that rolled out of his left eye.

The sound of the doorbell echoed through the house.

"I'm coming," he said, but the words were unintelligible, even to himself.

The bell rang once more. Help was still on the other side of the door. If only he could get to it.

He crawled forward, inch by inch, wondering why the

left side of his body felt like lead. When he reached the door, he had to rest before he could get enough energy to lift himself on his knees and twist open the doorknob.

The delivery boy was getting into his truck.

"Help," Max said. Why couldn't the boy hear him?

The boy's hand was already on the door. In a few minutes he'd climb into the truck and drive away, and it would be too late.

Desperate, Max gave one last cry, knowing he wouldn't have energy for another. The boy turned, then started running toward him.

"Get Ruth," Max said over and over, but the boy didn't seem to understand.

77.

THE VIRUNGAS

THEY LAUGHED BECAUSE HE WAS CARRYING two over the threshold. After all they'd been through, it felt very good to laugh.

"We're home, Ruth," Brett said, setting her on her feet.

She knew that at last she was. After all the years of running. After all the years of longing.

"I think I'm going to cry," she said. For happiness. For joy. For relief. For all the lost years.

Brett understood.

"Come here." Holding out his arms, he cradled her close. Then, when her tears had subsided, he tenderly wiped them away.

"Better now?" he asked.

"Yes, thank you. Much. . . . What a way to begin a honeymoon," she said.

"It's the way to begin a life, Ruth. With honesty . . . and with love."

She wrapped her arms around him, and they stood that way for a long while, content for the moment merely to hold each other. The trial was over, the jungle was safe for the gorillas, and they were finally together.

Soon holding was not enough.

They lay naked upon his bed, Ruth's hair spread across the pillow and Brett bending over her. He marveled that at last she was his, that he could watch her openly and touch her freely.

"You are so beautiful." He skimmed his hands over her ripe body, over the heavy breasts and the rounded belly. "When you were in Ruhengeri, I used to stand outside in the dark and watch you rub oil on your body. I wanted to be the one doing it."

"Do it. Rub oil on me."

She had brought sweet almond oil. Brett warmed it with his palms, then slowly began to smooth it over her body. His touch was both tender and erotic. Lost in pleasure, Ruth closed her eyes. Safe at last. And loved. So very loved.

She laced her hands behind his head and pulled him down to her breast. He drew her deep into his mouth, and she wrapped arms and legs around him, moaning with the sensations that rocked her.

"I want more," she whispered. "More."

He lifted himself on his elbows so he could see her face.

"I'll be tender with you," he said.

"I know."

He pressed his lips against her swollen belly, then slowly, ever so slowly he made his way downward. With his face in the triangle of soft hair, he found the little button that triggered her small screams of ecstasy. He loved the taste and the scent of her, the way she reached up to hold on to the bedpost, her hands alternately squeezing and releasing.

"Brett . . . Brett."

She called his name over and over, and he answered her cry. He closed his mouth over hers as he entered her, and with her sweet, hot flesh surrounding him, he made careful, tender love to her.

To Ruth. His wife.

78.

RUTH COULDN'T REMEMBER WHEN SHE'D slept better or longer. When she woke for the second time, it was already past noon. Flushed and content, she stretched languorously, remembering how it had been to wake up in the bed with Brett—the soft kisses, the tender touches, the sweet loving.

"Stay in bed," he'd said when he got up. "You need the rest."

She hadn't realized how much until that moment. Suddenly she felt the weight of everything that had happened in the last few months descend on her shoulders. She snuggled back under the covers, he tucked her in, and she closed her eyes. *Just for a little while,* she'd thought.

And now it was afternoon. The first day of her marriage. The first day of her new life.

She pushed back the covers and stood

naked in the patch of sunlight coming through the window, shivering with happiness.

"I have survived," she said.

It had been a long, hard journey from that white bedroom in New Orleans to the Virungas in Central Africa, from the terrified, broken teenager to the self-confident adult.

An idea formed suddenly in her mind, and the more she thought about it, the more certain she was of what she had to do. Tell about the rape. Not for revenge, but for mercy. By telling her story, she might be able to help hundreds who had suffered the same fate. She might give them courage to speak out against their abusers before it was too late to bring them to justice.

Her baby kicked hard, and she took that as a sign that he approved of her decision. She padded barefoot to her closet and pulled out a gauzy yellow maternity frock. As she dressed, she sang a song made famous by her father.

She hoped that wherever he was, he knew.

Brett sat beside Cee Cee in her outdoor enclosure. She was more subdued than usual, sitting with her doll clutched tightly against her chest and her face turned toward the jungle.

"*What is Cee Cee thinking?*" he asked, signing.

In the distance one of the two young male silverbacks beat his chest and issued a hooting cry of challenge.

"*What that?*" Cee Cee asked.

"*Gorilla.*"

"*What gorilla say?*"

"*I don't know.*"

Scowling, Cee Cee punched his chest with her forefinger.

"*Gorilla talk. Tell Cee Cee what say, tell now.*"

How could he explain to Cee Cee that she was the only gorilla he understood, that while he had a very good idea what the sounds of the wild mountain gorilla meant, he could only guess at the precise meaning? Or even *if* there was a precise meaning.

Still, he had to try. He moved squarely into her line of vision so he could get her full attention.

"I am human, Cee Cee. Humans don't talk animal talk. Humans don't understand animal talk. Humans only understand Cee Cee's talk."

"Brett human?"

"Yes."

"Ruth human?"

"Yes."

"Eleanor human?"

"Yes."

Cee Cee nodded her head sagely, then cocked her head, listening for sounds from the jungle. The wild mountain gorillas had moved higher up the slopes, and their cries were now faint and indistinct.

"Cee Cee human," she signed.

It was not a question. Brett didn't argue with her. Perhaps she was right. Cee Cee ate from a plate and slept with a blanket. She watched TV and painted pictures. She joked and pouted and lied and loved. But she had never killed. Perhaps she understood better than Malone what it was to be human.

He hugged her, complimented her on her hair bow, praised her intelligence, and, at her insistence, her singing ability, then went into his office and sat down at his desk. Putting her with the wild gorillas would be the same as sending his own child into the jungle.

He took down the file marked "Project Cee Cee" and wrote "Closed" across the cover. From the bedroom he heard his wife singing. He leaned his head back and closed his eyes, listening.

In a house where there was singing, there was also joy. Brett caught hold of the joy and held on.

79·

LOS ANGELES

THE HOUSE WAS WHITE STUCCO WITH A red-tile roof. Lush trees and flowers and a spacious, well-manicured lawn, as well as a tennis court and a kidney shaped swimming pool, gave it the look of a home of someone rich and famous, which was exactly the intent of the board of directors. White Sands did in fact house many wealthy and famous people, though none of them would ever use the tennis court or do laps around the swimming pool.

White Sands was a nursing home, and Maxwell Jones was one of its famous residents. He sat in his wheelchair with a lap robe over his legs. One of the nurses, Marilyn Quincy, had crocheted it for him. It hid his atrophied legs, and she told him it made him look dashing, as if he were going to get up out of his chair and start directing movies any minute now.

"Bullshit," he said, but she didn't seem to understand him. Nobody understood a thing he said.

She smiled and patted his hand, then pulled her chair close in case he needed any help with his snack.

At the front of the room, the wide-screen television blared. Television's most famous female talk-show host, Kim Cummings, smiled out at them. She was a great favorite with the residents.

They rolled their wheelchairs closer to the screen, but Marilyn was careful that none of them jostled against Max. He always had the best seat in the house. It was a privilege that went with his status.

"Today we're going to talk about childhood sexual abuse," Kim said. "And with us is someone who will tell her personal story."

The camera panned to the face of a beautiful woman, dark hair, dark eyes, olive skin. The lens widened to show her loose blue dress and the dark, exotic foliage beyond the window. At the time the show was being taped, Ruth Corday was pregnant, Kim explained. She and her crew had traveled to Africa to interview Ruth at her request.

Max leaned forward in his wheelchair.

"Turn it up," he yelled.

"I'm sorry," Marilyn said. "This is not turnips. It's cheese and crackers. It's good for you. Eat up like a good boy."

She crammed his mouth full of cheese, and he spit it at her. Damned bitch. Didn't she understand anything? Didn't she see Brett Corday sitting beside Ruth, holding on to her hand as if she belonged to him?

The host of the show carried on about the horrors of sexual abuse, but Max was only half listening. All his attention was focused on the woman in blue.

"And now," Kim said, "Ruth Corday will tell her own story."

Ruth told about being thirteen and going with the man she called Uncle to New Orleans. She told about the remote mansion, about the privacy afforded by wealth, the privilege.

Leaning forward in his wheelchair, Max remembered it all, remembered how her young, lithe body had felt, remembered the power he'd felt when he'd made her his.

"At the age of thirteen I was raped . . . ," Ruth Corday said. There were murmurs of outrage among the residents, and Marilyn remarked that the man ought to be castrated.

". . . raped by the movie director, Maxwell Jones."

Marilyn Quincy dropped the platter of cheese and crackers. It clattered to the floor, pulverizing the crackers and sending the cheese in six different directions. One by one the residents turned to stare at Maxwell Jones . . . and one by one they rolled their wheelchairs away, mashing the cheese into greasy yellow puddles.

Marilyn Quincy stared at him as if she were looking into the face of Satan himself; then she picked up her chair and walked off, snagging his lap robe on a chair leg as she did.

"Wait!" he called, but she ignored him and kept on walking, dragging the lap robe behind her.

Ruth's beautiful face beamed at him from the television. Kim Cummings was asking her questions, and she was talking and talking.

"Shut up, shut up, shut up," Max yelled.

The effort took all his breath. He swung his head and looked around him. He was alone. In the far corner Marilyn Quincy saw him looking and turned her back.

"Who's going to feed me?" he asked.

No one answered him.

80.

THE VIRUNGAS

BRETT HELD ON TO THE RED SQUALLING baby. Filled with awe, he placed the child tenderly on Ruth's breast.

"Ruth, we have a son."

"I know." She lifted her head off the pillow to look at her baby and smile at her husband.

The first rays of the rising sun touched the windowpanes in the clinic at Ruhengeri and turned them to gold. Rays fell across the bed like a benediction.

It was unusual for such light to shine so early in the morning. Generally, the mists shrouded the sun, diffusing the light so you could hardly know the sun was rising.

Ruth took the morning light as a promise.

She touched the tiny damp head of her son. Love swelled in her so big, she thought she would burst. And in her heart she made him a promise that he would have everything she'd never had—stability, normalcy, guidance, and a home with two parents who loved him.

"He will be named for his father." She reached for Brett's hand and pulled him down to her side. With one hand on his cheek and the other on her son's head, she said, "He will be called Brett Corday."

Brett linked his fingers with hers, joining them, and she held on, knowing that he was someone she could hold on to forever.

ABOUT THE AUTHOR

PEGGY WEBB, who holds an M.A. in English from the University of Mississippi, is the author of over twenty-five romance novels and over two hundred magazine humor columns for trade journals. She is very active in church and civic activities in her hometown of Tupelo, Mississippi, and often graces the stage of the community theater.

DON'T MISS THESE FABULOUS BANTAM WOMEN'S FICTION TITLES

On Sale in September

THE PERFECT MISTRESS
by BETINA KRAHN
National bestselling author of *The Last Bachelor*
"Krahn has a delightful, smart touch." —*Publishers Weekly*

The Perfect Mistress is the perfect new romance from the author of *The Last Bachelor*. The daughter of an exquisite London courtesan, beautiful and candid Gabrielle Le Coeur is determined to make a different life for herself—scaid, respectable . . . *married*. Pierce St. James is a libertine viscount who intends to stay single and free of the hypocrisy of Victorian society. For Gabrielle, there is only one way out of the life her mother has planned for her—she must become the virginal "mistress" of London's most notorious rake. ____ 56523-0 $5.99/$7.99

CHASE THE SUN
by ROSANNE BITTNER
Award-winning author of *The Forever Tree*
"Power, passion, tragedy, and triumph are Rosanne Bittner's hallmarks. Again and again, she brings readers to tears." —*Romantic Times*

Rosanne Bittner has captured our hearts with her novels of the American frontier. Passionate and poignant, this captivating epic resonates with the heartbreak and courage of two cultures whose destinies would bring them into conflict again and again as a new nation was formed. ____ 56995-3 $5.99/$7.99

FROM A DISTANCE
by PEGGY WEBB
"Ms. Webb plays on all our heartstrings." —*Romantic Times*

In the tradition of Karen Robards, Peggy Webb offers her most compelling love story yet. From small-town Mississippi to exotic Hawaii to the verdant jungles of Africa, here is the enthralling tale of one remarkable woman's struggle with forbidden passion and heartbreaking betrayal. ____ 56974-0 $5.50/$6.99

DON'T MISS THESE FABULOUS
BANTAM WOMEN'S FICTION TITLES

On Sale in October

BRAZEN
by bestselling author SUSAN JOHNSON
"No one [but Susan Johnson] can write such
rousing love stories." —*Rendezvous*

Susan Johnson "is one of the best!" declares *Romantic Times*. And in
this sizzling new novel, the award-winning, bestselling author of *Pure
Sin* and *Outlaw* entices us once more into a world of sensual fantasy.

____ 57213-X $5.99/$7.99

THE REDHEAD AND THE PREACHER
by award-winning author SANDRA CHASTAIN
"This delightful author has a tremendous talent that
places her on a pinnacle reserved for special
romance writers." —*Affaire de Coeur*

A lighthearted, fast-paced western romance from bestselling Sandra
Chastain, who is making this kind of romance her own.

____ 56863-9 $5.50/$6.99

THE QUEST
by dazzling new talent JULIANA GARNETT
"An opulent and sensuous tale of unbridled passions. I couldn't
stop reading." —Bertrice Small, author of *The Love Slave*

A spellbinding tale of treachery, chivalry, and dangerous temptation in
the medieval tradition of Bertrice Small, Virginia Henley, and Arnette
Lamb.
____ 56861-2 $5.50/$6.99

THE VERY BEST IN CONTEMPORARY
WOMEN'S FICTION

SANDRA BROWN

____28951-9 Texas! Lucky $5.99/$6.99 in Canada

____28990-X Texas! Chase $5.99/$6.99

____29500-4 Texas! Sage $5.99/$6.99

____29085-1 22 Indigo Place $5.99/$6.99

____29783-X A Whole New Light $5.99/$6.99

____56768-3 Adam's Fall $4.99/$5.99

____56045-X Temperatures Rising $5.99/$6.99

____56274-6 Fanta C $4.99/$5.99

____56278-9 Long Time Coming $4.99/$5.99

____09672-9 Heaven's Price $16.95/$22.95

TAMI HOAG

____29534-9 Lucky's Lady $5.99/$7.50

____29053-3 Magic $5.99/$7.50

____56050-6 Sarah's Sin $4.99/$5.99

____29272-2 Still Waters $5.99/$7.50

____56160-X Cry Wolf $5.50/$6.50

____56161-8 Dark Paradise $5.99/$7.50

____09961-2 Night Sins $19.95/$23.95

NORA ROBERTS

____29078-9 Genuine Lies $5.99/$6.99

____28578-5 Public Secrets $5.99/$6.99

____26461-3 Hot Ice $5.99/$6.99

____26574-1 Sacred Sins $5.99/$6.99

____27859-2 Sweet Revenge $5.99/$6.99

____27283-7 Brazen Virtue $5.99/$6.99

____29597-7 Carnal Innocence $5.99/$6.99

____29490-3 Divine Evil $5.99/$6.99

DEBORAH SMITH

____29107-6 Miracle $5.50/$6.50

____29092-4 Follow the Sun $4.99/$5.99

____29690-6 Blue Willow $5.99/$7.99

____29689-2 Silk and Stone $5.99/$6.99

____28759-1 The Beloved Woman $4.50/$5.50

- -

Ask for these books at your local bookstore or use this page to order.

Please send me the books I have checked above. I am enclosing $_____ (add $2.50 to cover postage and handling). Send check or money order, no cash or C.O.D.'s, please.

Name _____

Address _____

City/State/Zip _____

Send order to: Bantam Books, Dept. FN 24, 2451 S. Wolf Rd., Des Plaines, IL 60018

Allow four to six weeks for delivery.

Prices and availability subject to change without notice.

FN 24 10/95